THREE RING CIRCUS

Edward Arno

The Victory Rose Press
LOS ANGELES CA

Edward Arno/The Victory Rose Press
Victory Boulevard
Burbank, CA
www.edwardarno.com

Book Layout ©2018 BookDesignTemplates.com

Library of Congress Cataloguing in Publication Data:
TXu1-581-482
Three Ring Circus/ Edward Arno -- 1st ed.

ISBN No. 978-0-9996465-1-9

For Felix Lagumen
with thanks

CHAPTER ONE

Protest

J ames Pidgley turned the key in the lock and checked to see if the caravan was secure. He watched as his parents' car drove away. Standing outside the contemporary chrome caravan looking up at the edge of the North Hill of Great Malvern, James felt he had found paradise. Behind him was the wasteland he and his brothers had purchased from a very strange woman. She said it had belonged to her late husband's family and she didn't want it. Not wanting her husband's greed siblings to get their hands on the land or the money she had received for it. What was peculiar about the woman was she accepted a much lower price without bargaining. For James's father had been a red flag and he made sure James went through the proper channels and legal procedures to purchase it.

With the site already cleared of debris and greenery, James tried to visualize the houses on the land. A small Port-a-cabin next to his caravan was going to be used as a site office. They were in fact on the common land north of the site. The town planning people had recommended they use this public land. So they didn't have to keep moving the office around the building site. His father had warned him to expect trouble from the locals thinking the gypsies had encamped on the common land. His reply to his father was, "We have, Dad."

The Morris Brothers Circus had made the biggest objection to the building of the houses. Their winter quarters for the circus stood on the land south of the building plot. They claimed the construction would upset the circus animals. The Pidgley family barrister, had during a council planning meeting, caught the owner's daughter Miss Tonya Morris in a lie. The Morris Brothers Circus didn't have animals. They were advertised as a human performing circus. The bad feeling between the Pidgley family and the Morris family had continued with every complaint possible. James had joked it was like the war between the Montagues and the Capulets. Maybe he would end up marrying the daughter rather than ending up like Romeo and Juliet. He knew he would have to find some way to bridge the animosity between the two families before the building of the houses began.

Looking down the driveway at the main gate of the circus winter quarters, he found two groups of people shouting at each other and at the circus employees. The winter quarters' cast iron gates were closed and the circus employees stood guard on the other side. Several cameras had been set up. The crews were running around trying to look important. Several suited ladies and gentlemen were behind the cameras talking on the mobile phones. James thought they were making a film. He remembered seeing a film set at Aston Hall in Birmingham. It was docudrama being made by the BBC. He had taken a girlfriend to show her the beauty of Aston Hall. She didn't like the Jacobean house or standing around watching the filming. The relationship ended the very next day. She announced to the world and her friends that if she had wanted to see old furniture and paintings she would have stayed at home with her parents. It wouldn't have been the problem with his friends if she hadn't added a codicil. James, she said was too boring to have any fun. This had ruined his self-esteem to an all-time low. Maybe looking for an intelligent romantic girlfriend in the Starlight nightclub had been the wrong place. He needed the type of girl who frequented the local library and art galleries.

He stood looking at the camera crews and realized they were from the local television stations. The cameras and microphone all had news channel identity visible. This wasn't a film but a gathering of angry protestors.

One group consisted of long hair, rainbow colored clothing and placards denouncing cruelty to animals. The other group of about ten where skinheads whose age ranged from ten to forty. Dressed in the uniform of a British skinhead with the usually highly polished Dr. Martin Boots. As a group, they acted like an army operating attack and retreat maneuvers.

Neither side was actually causing any trouble, but the mere presence of the protesters provoked the circus staff to carry baseball bats and sticks. The arrival of a nineteen sixty's Silver Cloud Rolls Royce inflamed the crowd. The timing of its arrival seemed to be orchestrated because the camera crews were in position and filming. A young woman was driving it, and she didn't stop when two of the animal rights people tried to stand in her way. She gently pushed them to the side with the nose of the car. Once the car was inside the winter quarters, the cast-iron gates were closed. The right-hand section of the gate was opened a few feet to let the woman out to give an interview. She moved to the stack of news crew microphones ignoring the protesters. James recognized her as Tonya Morris, from the many council meeting altercations. He had only ever seen Tonya in a pinstriped business two-piece suit before, so he was surprised to see her in riding jodhpurs and knee-length riding boots. Her chestnut red hair was pulled back from her face and tied in a ponytail. At first, her speech about the Morris Brothers Circus not having animals seemed to quell the Animal Rights group.

The calm, however, was quickly dispelled. Who threw the house brick would never really be known. The effect it had was instant and explosive. At first, it looked like the two groups were going to fight each other, then they turned on Tonya. She was punched in the stomach then slapped across the face. James ran through the rioting mob and stood over her, helping her to stand up.

A woman charged, waving her placard above her head. To those who described it later to James and the police, it was as though the woman had become Joan of Arc. James didn't see the placard crashing down on him. The effect was as though he was a pack of playing cards crumbling to the floor.

He sat on the brown leather sofa inside Tonya's house. She was talking to a policewoman while the paramedics were checking him out. Apart from a very sore and bruised shoulder, he didn't seem to have any other injuries. He felt a little groggy and had accepted a glass of brandy from Tonya just before the paramedics arrived. The policewoman and Tonya stopped talking and approached him. Tonya gave him a congenial smile and stood behind the policewoman who perched herself on the corner of the sofa.

"Do you think you could answer a few questions?"
"Sure."
"You were hit by a woman brandishing a placard. Do you know who she was?"
"No, I had my back to the crowd, the first thing I knew I had been hit was when I woke up and Miss Morris was standing over me."
"What were you doing outside Miss Morris's property?"
"Actually, I had come to see Miss Morris. When I arrived the two groups were already outside the gates."
"So, you weren't part of the groups?"
"No, I don't think I look like a skinhead and I have always loved circus animals. So, I don't think I could belong to either of the groups."
"Thank you Mister…?"

"Pidgley, James Pidgley."

"He is the man who is building the houses on the land next to us," said Tonya in a tone that could have been taken either way. From her facial expression, James had difficulty working out if the ice had thawed.

"So where are you staying then?" asked the policewoman.

"In the caravan on the common land just North of the development site."

"You have permission to be there?"

"Yes, the council graciously allowed me to put the caravan and site office on the common land."

"Why would they do that?"

"Not sure, but after all the problems we had getting planning permission, my father thinks it was a token of goodwill."

"Thank you, Mr. Pidgley. If we need to ask you any more questions, we will be in touch."

The policewoman left shown out by Tonya. James sat alone looking around the living room. It had been decorated and furnished in a style of an older person. The pictures around the room were of Tonya's family; the similarity in the faces was obvious. One picture caught James eye, it was a family portrait of the grandparents, parents, and children sitting in the circus tent. Tonya returned carrying a tray containing a bone china tea service and a plate of pastries. She poured the tea and handed James a cup of tea, and then a plate for the pastry. As she did this she didn't look at him; her expression was blank and very controlled.

She took her own cup and sat down on a chair opposite him. It was only then she made eye contact. A very thin smile parted her lips showing yellow stained teeth.

"Are you feeling any better?"
"Yes, thanks."
"According to the ambulance driver you may have saved my life. If the placard had hit me on the head, it would have exposed my brain. The wooden post was very thick and made of oak"
James grimaced, and lightly touched his scalp. "Not a soft wood," he added with the hint of a smile. "Why would anyone want to hurt you?"
"Some might say you would, when you consider the games my family played against yours in the courts. As my father would say, 'it's just business'. That woman, whomever she was, wanted to kill you."
"That's what one of the boys said."
"Boys?"
"Sorry, I call all the men who work for the circus 'boys'. I get that from my mother."
"I still don't know what they were protesting about."
"Oh, the animal rights people will protest about anything. I think it's just a hobby for most of them, not a real cause."
"The ones I met at college were very concerned about the rights of animals. They once released forty beagles that had been injected with rabies to see if the medicine which had been developed killed the virus."
"They can't do that sort of testing anymore, not since the EU took control."

Living room door opened and a tall skinhead entered. He hesitated when he saw James. He looked to be in

his mid-thirties. His head was close-shaved and he
wore a blue checked Ben Sherman shirt, and blue jeans
with white patches that looked as if someone had
dribbled bleach on the denim fabric. He wore Doc
Marten boots, high-laced tops in the regulation cherry
red that all the skinheads favored. His entire outfit,
along the shaved head, gave him a menacing look.
James had seen the man before; he was one of the
protestors. Tonya put down her teacup and without
getting up, waved her hand in a 'shooing' gesture to
dismiss him.

Surprisingly, he obeyed her without a word and left,
closing the door behind him. Tonya poured herself tea
and offered to add more to James cup. He accepted
and, placing the cup on the tray while she poured, took
the opportunity to eat a pastry.

"I can see you have guessed, Mr. Pidgley. I hope we
can count on your discretion."
"Sorry, but I'm not following you."
"Oh, nicely put. Well, let's put it this way. Business
hasn't been too good for Morris Brothers Circus lately
and so we dreamt up an idea for publicity. The protest.
In getting hit by that woman, of course, you gave us
more publicity than we could ever have created
ourselves She wasn't one of the paid protestors, I can
assure you of that."
 "Then who was she?"
"We don't know. Dougie — that was him who just
came in, he organized the protest. He's told me he will
do his best to find out."
"I would like to know if he comes up with an answer."
"Know thy enemy? Of course."

"Next you will say 'keep your friends close and ..."
"...your enemies closer."
"It seems we had parents who used the same awful old platitudes.
"Looks like it."
"So, it's your caravan on the common?"
"Yes, and before you ask, I do have permission."
"You'll get a lot of flak from the locals. We have been here forty-eight years and they still complain."
"When do you start traveling again?"
"Not for a few weeks. We spend this time redefining the show and putting new acts in."
"You have a place to rehearse?"
"We have a Big Top behind here. Would you like to see?"
"Yes, please." James' eagerness was obvious. "Sorry, I have always loved the circus."
"Don't tell me. As a little boy you wanted to run away and join one."
"No, I just liked to watch."
Tonya stood up and indicated for him to follow. The scrum of television cameras and press had grown. As they left the house James suddenly knew how celebrities must feel. The constant flash of cameras was distracting and blinding. They both had to look where their feet were treading. Behind the house, where the landscape dipped into a bowl-shaped hollow, a circus tent had been erected. It's bright yellow and green canvas looked a little weather-beaten.

The thrill of entering the circus brought back very enjoyable memories for James. Years ago, his father would take him and the rest of the family on an annual visit to Bingley Hall in Birmingham to see the Christmas circus. Then, in summer time, they would go to Cannon Hill Park to see one of the many traveling circus shows that came through.

So, when Tonya pulled back the tent flap at the entrance, and the smell of the animals hit James' nostrils forcefully, he was taken back at once to his childhood. James loved that smell, and although he soon learned that the Morris Brothers Circus hadn't had animal acts for several years, the aroma of the tamed beasts lingered. As Tonya led him down towards the ring, he could hear cries and shouted comments and, looking up, he saw that acrobats were practicing high above their heads. As they stopped to watch, Tonya explained that the acrobats were the Flying Innocenti, a celebrated Italian acrobatic troupe of father, four sons, two daughters and a daughter-in-law. James' watched in fascination and awe as the Innocenti troupe displayed their astonishing skills with incredible precision, calling out to each other as they flew through the air. There was no way James could hide how he felt. It made him feel like a child again.

James became aware that others, circus workers, he assumed, were also watching the Innocenti family. All except one man. He was staring at Tonya and James, with an angry, frustrated expression. It appeared to James that he wanted to speak to Tonya but couldn't because of James' presence. Abruptly, the man turned and left the tent.

On the far side, a group of men were huddled together in deep discussion, gesturing with their hands. Those rapid, almost violent gestures made James recall seeing a choreographer on a television documentary describing the steps of a ballet with similar gestures. He wondered if these men were dancers or, more likely given the age of some of them, the Morris Brothers clowns without their costumes and make-up.

James began to notice a tension all around. Not coming, as one might suppose, from those watching the daredevil antics of the trapeze artists high above their heads, but from Tonya herself. She seemed either not to notice how her presence affected everyone or, if she did, was deliberately ignoring it. James had long ago learned that women in powerful positions always had the ability to not see or hear things they didn't want or need to.

"Would you like to meet the clowns?" she asked, turning to James and seeing him looking over at the gesticulating men.
"If I'm not intruding."
They started to walk around the perimeter of the ring towards the clowns. As they passed one of the entrance alleys, a woman in a black and white leotard appeared. As she passed by, she nodded at Tonya and said, "Chooryalò."
James instinctively replied, "Na pral."
Both women stopped dead and turned to look at him.
Tonya's mouth had dropped open.
"You speak Romani?" she asked.
"Only a little," James replied, " I understand most things, but my father wouldn't let us speak it at home because he wanted us to speak English first."

Tonya nodded, then realized the other woman was still standing close by. "Sorry," she said, hurriedly, "this is Marie Rose. Part of the Cavolli juggling family."

James smiled at the woman and nodded a greeting. She returned the smile. Tonya was looking at James in a completely new light.

"So, you're Romany?" she asked.

"Yes, with a name like Pidgley, what else could we be?"

It took a moment longer for Tonya to compose herself. "I am so sorry," she said. " If I had realized, we wouldn't have given your family such a bad time."

"Hey, no problem," James replied. "But, now that we're talking about it, why did you think I was a policeman?"

"Oh, that! It was the way you were looking around the Big Top. You reminded me of a policeman I once dated."

Did you say your family name was Pidgley?" Marie Rose asked, stepping a little closer to them.

"Yes, why?"

"From Birmingham?"

"Yes."

"Then you must be one of Matthew and Sarah's children."

"You know my parents?"

"I remember your Dad. We were children together. He was older than me. Ten or eleven probably. His father, your grandfather, often did business with my father."

"My father doesn't talk about his childhood," James replied, "He never really spoke about his own father. My Grand father."

"I'm not surprised. Your grandfather was a right bastard to your father."

"Marie Rose!"

"It's true, Tonya, I will tell it as it was. What Old Man Pidgley made that boy do was unspeakable." Marie Rose turned to James, a sadness about her. "How your father survived, " she said quietly, "is a mystery to me."

An awkward silence followed. Tonya made a hand gesture to dismiss Marie Rose, who merely shrugged and moved away.

"Sorry about that."

"Don't be," James said. " I know my father had a dreadful time as a child. So please, you don't have to apologize."

They continued to walk around the circus ring and joined the clowns who, seeing their approach, had formed row in the second tier of seats. It was odd, James thought, to see clowns without their make-up. It had never occurred to him that they didn't wear it all the time. They sat nervously looking at Tonya, and James noticed that when she spoke, they cringed a little.

"Where is Bryan?"

The clowns shrugged and glanced warily at each other. Several of the older clowns had red stain marks on their faces shaped in the pattern of their clown faces. James thought this was the same as a garage mechanic having grease under his fingernails. The clowns had not responded to Tonya's question. She was irritated, but covered it with a forced smile. They didn't smile back. Sitting with sour unhappy faces as though the happiness had been sucked out of them and all that was left was misery. Their odd clothes, the oversized suits, the green trousers, their blue and red suspenders, all of it made them very noticeable. A tall thin clown, who looked in his mid-thirties, stood out from the rest. His shoes were completely ridiculous, and the wild colors of his clothing would have made him an exhibit in a modern Art Gallery. A strange awkwardness grew as they just stared at Tonya. It was as if they were trying to look into her mind to see what she was thinking, while she stood foursquare like a boxer waiting for an opponent to swing a punch.

Then, almost as one, the clowns turned their gaze onto James. One, a rotund fellow of indeterminate age, gave a shrug and, speaking directly to James, said, "I'm Antonioni. This next to me is Bolt. He's new to Clown Alley. Next to him we've got Cuckoo, and he is, of course. Cuckoo, that is."

The clowns chuckled at this little joke, and James smiled. Cuckoo was the tall, thin clown with the ridiculous shoes. His clown name seemed appropriate. Antonioni pointed further down the row to a fit-looking younger man, still in his early twenties "That there is Bublay. He's an acrobatic clown. Well, he would be, wouldn't he? Still young, so he can do all the gags we used to do, only without hurting himself. Next to him? That's Fiddles. He's our Clown Daddy. Not because he's older than the rest of us. It is because he is like the dad we all wanted and never had. Not one of us. Last, but not least, Professor Brick. He invents things."
"What kind of things?" James couldn't help asking.
"Like the exploding car. Only it doesn't explode."
"I tried but something went wrong," said Professor Brick." I think I just didn't use enough dynamite."

"Dynamite!" said James.

"He is just kidding," Antonioni said. " We don't really use it. Just gunpowder. A lot of smoke and loud bangs. "The battery was flat so the electrical breakers didn't work and the car didn't fall apart," Professor Brick said, apologetically, and the other clowns shook their heads and chuckled.

"I'm a kid when it comes to the circus," James said," even more, when it comes to clowns, if I'm honest. If I had run away to the circus, I would have wanted to become a clown."

"I wouldn't," said Fiddles. "It's hard work."

"And for not much dinari." Cuckoo said, with a sad smile.

Tonya shot Cuckoo a severe look, as if his mention of money, or the lack of it, was not a subject to be aired with an outsider present. Cuckoo returned her look with an insolent stare of his own.

James, sensing the tension, sought a distraction.

"So, the six of you work together on each routine?"

"There are actually seven of us," Antonioni replied. "Brinarno is not here. He's our Head Clown. His real name is Bryan. He has been called away on personal business. Leastways, that's what we think."

Somehow, this statement only increased the tension in the group. A moment of silence fell between them. James shot a glance at Tonya. She was looking down at her feet, deep in thought.

The flap on the other side of the tent opened and the skinhead, Dougie, appeared. The intakes of breath and shuffling of feet told James that the clowns didn't like this man very much. Tonya saw Dougie. "I must have a word with Dougie," she said, excusing herself. "Would you gentlemen look after James for me, please?"

"A pleasure, Tonya," said Fiddles, and his face filled with a grin for the first time.
James watched as she crossed the ring. She took Dougie to the side of the tiered seating, to a spot where the pair were almost out of view. When he turned back, he noticed that the Clowns were watching too. Silent. The tension had returned. James coughed, and attempted to lighten the mood, I saw a TV documentary about circus life once," he said, "and they mentioned Clown Alley. What is that?" he asked.
"It's an area just by the entrance to the circus ring where we change and have our props," replied Antonioni. "In some circuses, it's where the clowns' makeup and put on their clothes." Fiddles added.
"It's our place where we can tell jokes and have a laugh before the show." said Cuckoo.
"Where you tell your silly jokes, you mean." Bolt grunted.
"Is it difficult not to laugh at some of the things you do or see the others do?" James asked.
"A serious question!" Fiddles said, " That one is for you, Professor."
"Me? What have I done to deserve such a question?" Professor Brick protested.
"Nothing. That is why we gave it to you," said Bolt
"I see. If I do nothing, I get all the work."
"Exactly," Fiddles said.
"Then I shall have to answer. What was the question again?"

James had watched them as they went through this unrehearsed banter. Their expressions and body movements were funny and he laughed out loud. He realized the routine was for his benefit and he loved it. Bublay didn't join in. He stayed silent, and watched Tonya and Dougie talking. The routine continued.

"The question was, who is the funniest of us?" said Fiddles
"Are you sure?" said the Professor. "I don't recall it that way?"
"What way?"
"The way it was said, by our friend James here."
"The way what was said?
"The question."
"What question?"
"The one this gentleman asked."
"Ah, that question."
"Yes."
"Could you repeat it, please, James?"
"Sorry?" said James.

But the Clowns didn't answer. The routine had come to an end. Their attention was entirely on what was happening across the ring. Dougie had raised his voice in anger. Tonya was gesticulating at him. Dougie was becoming even angrier and it looked as though he might hit her. Dougie's left hand suddenly raised above his head. Fiddles was the first to stand, but they all came to their feet, prepared to rush across the ring to help. But Tonya stood her ground and, with complete control of the situation, dismissed Dougie with the wave of her hand. He stood looking at her for a few moments before saying something, which resulted in her giving him a hug. The Clowns sat back down and smiled at James. But the tension was still there. James knew it could only be a few days before something exploded.

"Now. Where were we," asked Professor Brick. "Sometimes when something happens which is not supposed to, it's hard not to laugh," said Fiddles regaining his composure.

"Like the time the water cannon wouldn't fire, and when it did we got a little dribble of water out of the end," said Bolt.
"Oh yeah, and Cuckcoo went and picked up a bucket of water and threw it over Bublay."
"It was cold water," said Bublay
 "The audience laughed so much," Professor Brick said, smiling at the memory. Bublay's reaction was priceless!
Tonya rejoined them. "Sorry about that," she said, then glanced at James. "Dougie was trying to find out about the woman who hit you."
"No problem," James replied. "These gentlemen have entertained me."
"They are the best clowns in the world," said Tonya with a smile, all trace of the annoyance she'd had speaking to Dougie gone.

This comment seemed to be a hint that the clowns should get back to whatever they were doing. Fiddles nodded his head to the others to follow him.

"Sir," he said, "I hope you will excuse us, but we have to rehearse a new routine."

"Sure. But please, my name is James. And thank you, it's been fun to meet you all."

The clowns walked away in a single file and reminded James of the seven dwarfs he had seen in a pantomime several years earlier. The dwarfs in that production of Snow White hadn't been small. Two of them had been over six foot tall. It hadn't diminished the production, but it had made the theatre audience snicker every time Snow White mentioned her dwarfs.

Tonya took hold of James's elbow and guided him to a row of seats. They sat on hard plastic chairs. She sat stiffly, looking straight ahead.

"James," she began, " as a Romany you will understand that we circus folk tend to stick together in a crisis." She paused a moment, then looked at him directly. "Someone is trying to ruin this circus. I have my own thoughts as to who it is. But there's a definite plan underway. Dougie just told me the woman who hit you arrived in an expensive BMW with a male driver. She arrived only moments before she hit you with the placard. The placard was taken by force off one of our protestors by her driver."

"Why would anyone want to ruin the circus?" James asked. "And who?"

"I don't own the circus, James. It may look like I do, but the circus is owned by my mother. There are no Morris Brothers, only sisters." Tonya smiled ruefully. "My Dad didn't think Morris Sisters Circus would sell. He was right, of course. So he invented the 'brothers'."

Her head dropped and she looked at the floor. James knew that what she was telling him was hard for her to tell you anyone. Especially, perhaps, an outsider..

" Dad died ten years ago. My sister and I never imagined our Mom would find someone else. But along came Ryan and suddenly my mother had a boyfriend. He seemed like a nice guy at first. The thing is, he's twenty years younger than Mom. He said he wasn't interested in the circus, so I didn't feel threatened."

"What changed that?"

"A year ago he suddenly started to take an interest. At first, it was a lot of questions as to how the shows worked. Then he began to give orders. He said Mom had given him permission and as it was her circus, she had the final word. I confronted Mom and she denied she'd ever said such a thing. It soon became obvious he was trying to take over. I fought back and he stopped bossing everyone around, so I assumed I'd won and we were back to normal. Then three months ago we had our first little problem. A fire in a dumpster next to my caravan."

"Much damage?"

"No. At first we all dismissed it as nothing but an accident. Then other little problems started to happen; a cut rope, missing equipment. Dougie said he saw Ryan cutting the rope, but with Dougie' looking the way he does it was hard for us to take any action without it being dismissed out of hand. In any case, the clowns and some of the others think Dougie is the one causing all the trouble, so he can move in and take over."

"That's because of your involvement with him," James said, evenly. "They're jealous."

"It's that obvious?"

"Yes. It's obvious. I see what you mean, though. Dougie isn't the most innocent-looking person to have around."

"True." Tonya let out a long sigh, "Listen to me," she said, with a shake of her head. "I've only just met you, James, and already I'm telling you all my problems."

"That's because we already have a history, Tonya, even if it was on different sides of a court room. Or the planning permission office

"Sorry about that," Tonya, gave an embarrassed smile. "It was only because we thought we would have problems with the new tenants when the houses are built and not be allowed to use this ground any longer."

"I'll do my best to make sure that doesn't happen," James said. "That's a promise."

"Thanks. But first I have to save this circus from unscrupulous men. Well, one man."

"What about saving your mother?"

"She's old enough to look after herself. I think she knows what's going on. She'll only step in if it gets out of hand."

"What does your sister say about this man? Ryan?"

"Clarissa doesn't want to have much to do with the circus. She had enough growing up. She married and had three children before her husband upped and left her."

"Sorry to hear that."

"Don't be. It was the best thing that could have happened to her. Have you heard of Morris Fabrics?"

"Sure, they must have at least a hundred stores in the Midlands."

"She owns it, started from her living room and it just grew and grew. I'm proud of my sister."

"You should be. But she must have an opinion about your mother?"

"She does. Live and let live."

"That sounds familiar."

"Your family too?"

James nodded, then looked up as Dougie appeared at the tent flap and waved to Tonya.

"Sorry," she said, "Can you wait here? I won't be long."

"Of course. No problem."

James gazed up at the trapeze artists enjoying, as he always had, the grace and skill of the flying performers. The Innocenti Family were trying out new routines, but the father was getting a irritable with one of his sons. The young man kept missing the catch. James realized that from up there, the reason would be hard to spot, but from his perspective on the ground it was clear that one of the young women, was releasing the swing bar seconds early. He James wanted to tell someone, but knew that if Mr. Innocenti were like his own father, outsiders should be seen and not heard.

In total frustration, the father called a halt to the rehearsal. He yelled angrily at his son, and the young man dropped his head, Ashamed. Some of the Innocenti Flyers climbed down a rope ladder to the ring floor. Others dropped onto the safety net. Once they'd landed, they all trooped out of the ring. James could see that the son who'd missed the catch was upset. Mr. Innocenti, the father, was the last to land on the ground. He looked around and saw James wandered towards him. "Hello," he said, with his slight Italian accent, "Is someone helping you?"

"Yes, thank you. I was with Tonya, but she was called away."

"Nothing serious, I hope."

"I don't think so, "James replied. He indicated the trapeze equipment. "It looks like hard work,"

"If you don't want to get hurt, it is," said the older man. "You might have noticed one of my sons having some problems getting a catch right."

"Actually, the way I saw it from here, it looked like the girl was releasing the swing bar too soon."

Mr. Innocenti looked sharply at him.

"Are you sure?" he said.

"Sorry," said James, "I shouldn't interfere."

"No, no," said the father, and rubbed his chin as he looked up at the swing. " You say that's what it looked like from down here?"

"Yes, she was a beat too soon each time."

"Maybe I need their mother to sit down here and watch. Thank you."

The father left. James hoped it was to apologize to his son, but knew from his own experience that it was unlikely that would happen.

It was strange to sit in a circus tent by yourself as though you were waiting for a private show to start. He had never known the feeling performers get when the audience applauds and cheers. He had only once been in a school play. That had been an awful experience. One that he vowed never to repeat. He'd been seven years old playing a wood elf and had had to stand next to Mary Fox. She'd spent the whole play picking her nose and eating what she found. When he was supposed to hold her hands to dance around in a circle, he couldn't do it. The teacher was cross and wouldn't let him explain.

Feeling lost in the strange world of the circus he started to wander around. It wasn't long before the urge to step backstage took over. The scene behind those curtains was just as he had expected. To the left was the area the Clowns had described as Clown Alley. To the right, the area had been marked off in large squares and a nameplate on a wooden stick was set in each square. Most of the squares were empty, waiting for the props of each performer.

The flap leading to the outside moved in the breeze. He went through, finding himself in the living quarters of the various artists and workers. Looking more like a caravan park, there were caravans of various shapes and sizes. Each one had been parked in an orderly fashion. Daylight had begun to fade and several of the caravans had their lights on, the windows glowing with yellows and orange. Silhouettes of the people inside danced on curtains or blinds. Like all families, or lonely souls, it was a time to prepare an evening meal. James suddenly knew what his father must have felt, traveling the country roads and lanes all those years ago. He envied that life and often wished he could have the opportunity to try it. It was for this reason he had agreed to oversee the building project. He would be living in a caravan.

From the other end of the caravan site, a tall thin man with hunched shoulders appeared. He was in his sixties but still had a youthfulness about his movements. His head was down, and he didn't look up as he crossed the concrete area. Arriving at a large chrome caravan he opened the door and entered.

Seeing this man made James wonder why so many people around the circus seemed to have problems. He asked himself if it was just the owner's boyfriend causing it, or if there was something deeper. Whatever it was sunk deep into the life of the Morris Brothers community. Something so deep it was unable to come to the surface and dissipate.

James looked at his watch. He should get to his new home, and realized he was hungry. His mother had left one of her Shepherd's Pies for him. If he were sensible it would last a few days although, from the number of boxes she had brought, he knew his refrigerator and freezer were packed with food.

Looking he checked back inside the circus tent to see if Tonya had returned, but there was nobody around. As he approached the main gate he could see the media. He retreated back into the circus tent and out the back to the caravan area.

There he saw a boy was about thirteen years old. He was a mini version of Dougie. A closer look at the boy and James could see the family resemblance. Either he was Dougie's brother, or his son.

The boy didn't speak, just indicated for James to follow him. They walked through the caravans until they reached a wooden fence. The boy pointed to a hole in the fence behind one of the caravans. James climbed through and found himself in his own field. All he had to do was walk around the edge to the road and he could get home to his caravan without being seen the media herd. At the roadway, he looked back at the fence and saw the boy looking through the hole. James waved. The boy just stared for a moment, then disappeared.

Once back in his caravan, he scooped some Shepherd's Pie onto a plate and placed it in the microwave. Emptying his pockets, he found the check his mother had given him. He'd promised her he would deposit it into his account as soon as he could. But he had a habit of forgetting to put his salary into his account. Then, days later, would wonder why he never had any money in the bank. The microwave bell dinged and he went to take out his meal. Passing by a window, he glanced out and saw the boy and Dougie appear at the hole in the fence. The boy pointed towards James's caravan then looked up at the skinhead as if for approval. Dougie ruffled his hair, and smiled.

CHAPTER TWO

Pronounced Dead

Iirritated by his own lateness to get to the bank, James stood in the line with the other customers. At his old apartment, he had been able to get up, take a shower, eat breakfast and get out of the house in forty minutes. Living in the caravan was completely different. Things were not always at hand and the shower wasn't as good as the one he was used to. He would need to make some adjustments in his thinking if his life wasn't going to become stressful. Connecting the electricity and water hadn't been too difficult. What he hadn't realized was how slow the water heated up. The next time he would take a shower before washing the breakfast dishes. Maybe he could ask one of the clowns how they coped and if they had any tricks to make life easier. He had slept very well but had always been able to do that. The problem was how to put the thing in a way they would be easy to use and find. It had taken him ten minutes to find a pair of shoes he knew he had placed next to his bed only to find them in a cupboard in the living room. He could only speculate his mother had moved them, or could it have been his father? As a child James's father Matthew had shown his children how to live in a very small space in comfort. James was ten and had taken it to heart, packing his entire belongings away. For several weeks his part of the bedroom he shared with one of his brothers was so clean his mother wondered if he had thrown things out. As usual, his brothers made fun of him and he soon lost interest in being tidy. He had retained the desire to be neat.

The line in the bank had grown, eight people now waited for the three tellers. A man at the left tellers' window concluded his transaction, the teller closed her window and left. The male teller on the right closed his window as his last customer finished their banking business. James was surprised no one made a comment; it was lunchtime and the bank staff had gone to lunch. For him, this was no way to run a business. At your busiest time, you increase the telling staff not decrease to one. The old round-shouldered man in front of him gave a deep sigh of resignation. This is how it was and any complaints would only slow the process.

James expected the only teller remaining to close her window when the customer left. She didn't and gave the old man a broad smile as he approached the window. The white line on the floor was there to give a mark of respect for privacy. James was a little too far from the tellers' window to hear what the old man was saying. The girl laughed several times as she checked the old man's account. The atmosphere between them suddenly changed and the raised voice of the old man indicated to everyone in line that something wasn't going according to his liking. His agitation grew to a high pitch, and from that moment on everyone could hear his comments.

"What do you mean my accounts closed? Who closed it and why?"

The line of customers couldn't hear her response. The customers moved forward as they all tried to listen in on the conversation. The next comment stopped everyone in the line from contemplating doing something else. The attention of the whole bank was now on the old man.

"What do you mean it's closed because I am dead?"

The teller became agitated behind the glass screen and looked around to see if a more senior person was available.

"Do I look dead to you?" shouted the old man.

The teller left her station and picked up a phone on the desk behind her. She was obviously having a hard time explaining what the problem was to whoever was on the other end of the phone.

The old man turned and looked at the waiting line; he was angry and needed to vent his frustration out.

"Do I look dead to you?" he asked no one in particular. No one answered, but several had expressions of sympathy.

A man's voice from behind James said, "After all this time and you're still as obnoxious as ever." James slowly turned to see who had said it. More customers had entered the bank so it was hard to see who had spoken.

The girl returned to the window and said something, which sent the old man into a rage.

"My name is Bryan DeWitt. I have had an account at this bank for thirty-one years. I have seen the bank managers here go from teller to manager. Now you are telling me someone came in here and closed my account and you accepted it."

The girl was trying to keep calm, but her facial expression showed she was on the brink of tears.

"You said they had a death certificate, how? I'm still breathing; do you have a copy of it you could show me?"

A tall man with greasy grey hair appeared behind the teller. He approached cautiously and stood to listen for a few minutes before entering the conversation.

The old man repeated what the greasy grey hair man had just said, "You're an associate manager. What's that when it's at home?"

The associate manager indicated to the old man to move over to another window and spoke to the old man from the new teller's position.

"Sorry I can't hear you, maybe it's because I'm dead." The other customers in the bank gave various snorts and giggles at the old man joke.

The associate manager behind the counter stopped speaking through the glass partition. He came into the customer area through a security door to confront the old man face to face. Although James was next in line, he didn't move to the girl's window. Like everyone else in the line, he watched as the associate manager showed some authority in his demeanor by taking the old man by the elbow and guided him into an office. The buzzer broke the tension and James walked up to the window and handed his check to be deposited. He kept glancing back at the glass-fronted office and like everyone else could see the old man becoming more and more angry with the associate manager. James requested some cash and counted it out in front of the teller before leaving the window. He took one more look into the glass-fronted office. The way the old man stood suddenly reminded James of the man he had seen in the area of the caravan in the circus winter quarters the night before.

He left the bank and walked up Church Street; he had a few errands that needed to be done before he met with the builder at two o'clock. After completing his errands he made his way back to the bank where he had parked his car. The old man Bryan DeWitt was standing outside the bank talking to a tall man in his fifties. The man, dressed in a paramilitary grey camouflage outfit, seemed to have a very muscular body for someone his age. James had seen the man inside the bank during Bryan's altercation. Their quiet chat changed to a pushing match. The other man pushed Bryan hard and the old man fell backward onto the ground. Several shoppers rushed to Bryan's aid while the other man took the opportunity to disappear. James stood by feeling helpless as there were so many who had arrived to help. He left and drove to the supermarket. His mother may have supplied him with enough food for several weeks, but she had forgotten some of his favorite items he claimed he could never live without. Coxes' orange pippin apples, dry figs, and raisins were essential according to him.

He arrived back at the building site at five minutes to one and was surprised to see the old man Bryan DeWitt from the bank sitting at the entrance to the winter quarters. He was still in an angry mood and scowled at James as he approached. James for the first time studied the man. Bryan was looking down at his black scruffy shoes and playing with the laces. His charcoal grey trousers looked as though they had been tailored for him. The Norfolk style jacket, out of fashion for such a long time, fitted tightly to the man's

body. The brown leather patches on the elbows had
worn thin.

"Sorry, you had a problem in the bank."

"What's that to you?" said the old man.

James didn't give an answer but continued along the
road to the caravan. Two teenage skinheads were
leaning against a lamppost near the caravan. The look
they gave him was a mixture of hate and disgust.
James had always since he could remember, never run
from such aggression. He opened the door of the
caravan when a stone hit the side of the caravan. He
turned when another hit him. He placed his shopping
inside, locked the door and ran after the boys. They
raced down the road but James was a little too quick
for the taller of the two. Grabbing him by his
suspenders he pulled the boy back and he, grazing his
hands on the roadway. The boy sat looking at the
blood spots on the cut palms of his hands.

The other boy stopped and looked back at his mate.
James anticipated the other boy would return slowly.

"Why did you throw the stones at me?"

"Fucking dirty gypo."

"What? Who told you?"

The boy sat silently and looked up at him.

"Not going to tell me? Then I shall have to call the
police."

"Go ahead, see if I care," said the boy. His face
obviously showing he did care and was worried James
would carry out his threat. The other boy had
approached close enough to shout at James.

"Let him go."

"No way, I'm calling the police."

"Why?" said the boy sitting on the floor.

"Because you won't tell why you threw the stones."

"Because..." he replied looking at the other boy for help.

The other boy approached even closer; he was also worried. James knew if the police got involved they would be taken into care and possibly the local detentions center for young offenders.

"If we tell you, what will you do."

"That depends on why you did it."

The boy sitting on the floor gave a nod and the other boy came up to James.

"Look we are sorry, but Marty told us to."

"Who is Marty?"

"He's the sort of leader of the skins around here."

"What's his real name?"

Again the boy on the floor nodded his head and the other boy, who was now very nervous, answered.

"Martin, he is older than the rest of us."

"He's a copper."

"A policeman. What's his last name?"

"Don't know. We're not really part of his group."

"You want to be, and he said if you hassled me he would let you in?"

"Something like that."

"So why did he tell you to throw the stones."

"He said only gypsies live on the common in caravans. And he hates gypsies."

"I'm building the houses on this site and that's why my caravan is on the common. With permission from the council tell him."

The boys looked at each other.

"Sorry, we didn't know."

"What are your names?"

The boy on the floor stood up and held out a hand for James to shake it.

"I'm Terry and this is Nicky. We are sorry. We just want to be in his gang."

"Fascist groups are what your parents and grandparents fought against in the Second World War."

"Yeah, my grandpa talks about the war all the time."

"Marty says Adolf Hitler was the greatest leader ever. When I said this to my father, he punched me in the face."

"Marty is making you patsies and you're the ones who will get in trouble, not him. There is nothing wrong belonging to a gang of friends but when one of them tries to make you do things they won't do themselves you shouldn't trust them."

"You don't know what it's like."

"I do. I was a kid once. I grew up in Birmingham and there it's all about keeping in with your mates."

Terry looked at his hands. Obviously they were becoming painful.

"You'd better come over to my caravan. Let's clean that up before it becomes infected and Nicky has to cut your hands off."

"What!"

"Just kidding."

They sat on the sofa inside the caravan. Both were amazed at how big the place was and the fact it had a bedroom and bathroom seemed to shock them.

After James had cleaned the wounds and put some antiseptic cream and a light bandage on the hand, he offered them a soft drink.

"Mister, we're sorry. If we had known you're a cool guy we wouldn't have done it."

"So if I were an un-cool guy you'd have still done it?"

"Maybe not," said Terry looking at his bandaged hands.

"Tell me about Marty."

"Why do you want to know?"

"For the second time in two days, I have said this; 'keep your friends close and your enemies closer'."

"What's that mean?"

"Find out all you can about the people who want to do you harm, that way you can understand why they do it."

"Marty wants to be the leader of all the skinheads in Worcestershire."

"In his case, it's all about power. He has a gang and they all do as he says which gives him power. Just another bully."

"Yeah, I can see that he never does anything. He always makes others do it for him."

"It won't be long before one of you or your mates gets in trouble with the police because of him. If he is a policeman then he can plant evidence on you, if you tried to name him as the leader"

"That's happened. To Ben. One of our mates. He's in court this week for breakin' and entering. He says Marty told him to break into the conservative club and steal its membership books," said Terry.

"He'll get sent away," said Nicky.

"Yeah and not to a summer camp," said Terry laughing.

The boys left the caravan; James stood on the top step and watched as they walked down the street. A car parked at the end of the street started its engine. The two skinheads turned and gave James the two-finger salute and shouted "Wanker gypo." They climbed into the car and it accelerated away. James felt sick. Why

was he such a sucker? He had been taken in
completely. 'I've been off the streets too long,' he said
to himself.

He hadn't noticed the time and saw it was past his
appointment time for the builder. Arthur Cox was in
his late fifties. Short and stocky, he was standing next
to a brand-new black Jaguar. The smile on his face had
unnerved James the first time he saw him, and today it
seemed to look like the smile of evil. His father had
checked Arthur out and said he may look like a thief, a
'chor' in Romani, but his track record was he always
did a proper job.

The meeting went well and James was surprised at
how helpful the man was being. He even admitted he
was a cheapskate, but having checked out the Pidgley
family he would only do his best work. He said it was
so easy to cut corners and no one would know. He
promised there would be no substandard work on this
site. For James this was like someone saying
'honestly'; he never trusted them. He would keep a
sharp eye out to make sure Arthur was true to his
word.

They planned to start the groundwork in two days; this
allowed the man time to gather a crew together. Arthur
would find a site foreman and introduce him to James.
After Arthur left, James looked up at the sky and saw
the dark rain clouds gathering for a storm. He hoped
this wasn't an omen of things to come.

James sat in the caravan drinking a cup of tea. He had
seen enough excitement for one day and would spend
time getting used to living him his new home. There
was knock at the door had that official sound to it. He
had noticed that whenever someone from the police or
the council came to a door, the way they knocked

seemed different from the way his friends or other strangers knocked. He had concluded it was because they were on official business and therefore had a confidence as a precursor to their position. Whereas, friends and other strangers hoped you would answer the door if they knocked gently.

James opened the door to the policeman who stood looking up at him was one of the old school types of British policemen. Nearing his retirement, he was given the tasks the younger officers would have found menial.

"I'm sorry sir but you can't park your caravan here."

"Officer, please step inside and I will show you my letter of permission from the Malvern District Council."

The officer entered; James handed him a copy of the letter. He read it and handed it back.

"Why don't you keep it and take it down to the police station. Then when you get other concerned citizens, you have the proof that I have permission."

"Not a bad idea Mister…" He looked at the letter again, "Pidgley. It is strange for the council to give permission. You must know some very influential people."

James didn't reply. He knew leaving that sort of inquiry unanswered would be taken he did have some high-powered friends. The officer took his no response as James had intended and awkwardly move back to the door.

"Sorry to bother you, sir, and good luck with your building plans."

"Thank you, officer," James said it in such a way the officer felt he needed to introduce himself properly.

"Officer Kipler, Mister Pidgley."

"Call me James."

"Then I am Peter. I will check on you each time I pass around here. I know that some building sites recently have had materials taken. The 'do it yourself' brigade unable to afford the materials costs, assume you have insurance."

"Peter, why don't you stop by for a cup of tea if you're in the area."

"Wow, thank you I wasn't expecting that."

"I've already had one problem, Peter, this morning. I solved it myself but having a police car parked outside the caravan by the site will deter those who want to cause trouble."

Officer Kipler left and James watched as he drove away. A little up the road he could see a car parked and its driver and passenger stood by the trunk. The police car stopped by the couple and he showed them the paper James had given him. The man seemed very angry and thumped the roof of his car. The woman tried to calm the man down whom then jumped into their car and started to drive away leaving the woman standing in the street. He stopped as she ran and climbed into the car. The police car followed them slowly as they raced down the road.

Looking the other way the road seemed empty at first then a tall solid built teenage skinhead stepped out from behind a bush. James knew the problem with local terrorists had only just begun.

James sat by the window and peeked out into the road; the skinhead was still standing looking at the caravan. He wasn't doing anything, just watching and waiting. A car drove at speed down the road and stopped just beyond the skinhead who ambled over to it and climbed in gave the two-finger salute.

James had never been more than a few miles from other members of his large family. Consequently, he always expected one or more of them to drop by. Living so far away it was very unlikely they would travel to see him except on weekends.

The caravan was equipped with the latest satellite dish, a television, a radio, and his video game console. James just didn't want to of them. He was restless and he hated himself when he fell into this kind of mood.

It was a relief when a knock came at the door. Either the police had returned or some do-goody was going to lecture him on setting up home on common land. He picked up the heavy flashlight before he opened the door; past experience had warned him of the dangers of opening doors and not knowing who was on the other side. The streetlights didn't stretch this far up the road. He could just make out the shape of a man standing by the door when he peered out of the window.

The person knocked again. James opened the door and was surprised to see the old man Bryan Dewitt standing looking up at him.

He looked drawn as though he had been crying; his eyes were puffy and red.

"I'm sorry to bother you. I just want to apologize for the way I acted toward you earlier today."

"Come in please, and there is no need to apologize. I totally understand what it's like to have the bank make a mistake."

The old man entered. He was bent over more than usual and his clothes were crumpled.

James pointed to the sofa so he could sit down. In the kitchen part of the caravan, he picked up a mug to offer him tea.

"Oh yes, please, that would be nice. I haven't really had much to drink today."

"You've been through a stressful time. Food and tea is the last thing you need to think about."

James poured the tea and handed the old man the mug. He took it and sipped staring at the floor.

"So you didn't sort out the bank?"

"No, the bloody fools say I'm dead. They even have a death certificate."

"Is that right? Remember to tell your employer."

"Why?"

"Because if you're dead you don't need to pay any income tax."

"So there is an upside to being declared dead."

"Why would someone go to all this trouble to get a death certificate?"

"I don't know. It is easier to prove you're dead than it is to prove you're alive once you have been declared dead."

"It's not just the bank, my pensions been stopped. My doctor won't see me because I am no longer a patient being dead."

"Are you serious?" said James beginning to laugh.

"I know it very funny if you think about it. Only it's not; I can't get any money or see my doctor."

"I don't know your name," said James politely even though he had heard his name in the bank.

"Bryan DeWitt, but everyone knows me as Brinarno the Clown."

"You're the one who was missing last night."

"Sorry?"

"I'm James Pidgley. Tonya Morris introduced me last night to the other clowns and she said one was missing."

"I was at the library."

They sat and drank the tea. James finished and offered to replenish Brinarno's mug.

"Oh yes, do you have any biscuits?"

"I can do better than that. Would you like some homemade apple and blackberry pie?"

"You made it?"

"No, my mother."

"Yes, that would be nice."

As James cut two large slices out of the pie he felt the anxiety Brinarno was feeling. He needed to do something to cheer this very funny man up.

"I saw you years ago when you performed at Bingley Hall in Birmingham."

"Looking at you, I'd say fifteen years ago. My wife was alive then."

"You did this routine about wanting to play in the band and the ringmaster wouldn't let you."

"Old Charlie Bisket, a brilliant straight man. He knew how to set up a gag that could run for twenty minutes when it really should have been about five."

"There was this white face clown in a sequin costume who also tried to stop you putting a custard pie in the face of a man from the audience."

"That was a good routine especially if you picked the right guy from the crowd. Get a dummy and he could ruin it. We had a man last season who turned out to be drunk. Bolt picked him and the next thing we know he is trying to climb the ladder to the trapeze. It took the six clowns and two tentmen to get him down and back into his seat. Made the audience laugh."

"It must a be a great life making people laugh."

"It can be if you're not dead."

The comment had killed the reminiscing, and Brinarno looked deep into the empty cup.

"I want some more tea," declared James standing up and switching on the electric kettle.

"James I'm sorry I know you were trying to cheer me up and it's not that I'm sad but so much seems to be going wrong at the moment in my life."

"Like what, if I may ask?"

"Well, you know I'm dead." Bryan gave a little laugh. "Then we had a fire and equipment disappear. It's as though someone is trying to close the circus down."

"That may be my family's fault. The land the winter quarters is on is worth a lot of money. If the circus closed, then the winter quarters wouldn't be needed, and the land could be sold," said, James.

"Mabel wouldn't sell. She couldn't"

"Who is Mabel?"

"Mabel Morris. She really owns the circus, but her no good new boyfriend would like to see the circus closed."

"Tonya told me about him, well not much, only she doesn't like him."

"None of us do. I can't see what Mabel sees in him."

"Women of a certain age can do stupid things."

"That's true. Are you the guy who got hit on the head during the publicity stunt?"

"Yes."

"Dougie seems very jealous of you. I told him Tonya loves him."

"The skinhead. Seems to be a lot of skinheads in Malvern."

" He looks worse than he is. He has a younger brother Cooper whom he protects and cares for as though it were his own child."

"What about the parents?"

"No one knows, and Dougie won't talk about his parents or what happened to them. I tried several times but he just clams up."

"Tell him I'm not interested in Tonya. She looks too tough for me. I like my girlfriends to be a little soft and less commanding."

"She can be if you let her, but she is good at running the circus."

"There seems to be a lot of tension."

"I think Ryan, that's Mabel's boyfriend, started a rumor that the circus was closing and several of the performers are worried. We all put a lot into this year's show and if it's for nothing, well."

"So now we have to find out why you're dead."

"We? What have you got to do with it?"

"Well, I was there when you found out you were dead. That makes me accessory to the knowledge of your demise."

"Which is overstated. I can't remember the actual quote."

"Oscar Wilde I think."

They sat looking at each other; the realization that Brinarno the clown was dead by someone was a serious thing.

"Do you have a passport?"

"Disappeared along with a whole lot of other papers which could prove I was alive."

"Someone wants you out of the way."

"It's got to be Ryan. he must know."

"What?"

"I don't know why I'm telling you but, please, very few people know this. Years ago when the circus hit hard

times, I lent Mabel's husband money to keep the show going. He gave me a forty percent share in the circus."
"Who knows this?"
"Mabel, and I think Tonya."
"So by default, Ryan and Dougie."
"I don't think anyone else unless they check it out at company house. It's all official. Mabel had insisted."
"So anyone poking around could find out. Have you always been a clown?"
"Good heavens no. I trained as an electronic engineer with government years ago here in Malvern. That's how I joined the circus. I wanted to do something different and ended up working as a tentman. Then next season the head clown Buckingham, a white face, asked me to fill in while one of the clowns had an operation. And the rest, as they say, is history."
"So, first we have to find out how we correct your untimely demise. Then find out who is playing these dangerous games."
"There you go again. We, why are you getting involved?"
"Because for years you gave me and millions of other kids laughter. It is time for one of us to pay you back."
"Hundred pounds would help."
"If you need money, I can lend you some."
"Now that is sporting of you, and we have only just met. What if I run away and not pay you back?"
"Just don't play dead."
"Are we going to have that tea or was it just a promise?"
"Do you like to be called Brinarno or Bryan?"
"When I'm in my make-up I like Brinarno, but when I am out of it Bryan works."
"Bryan, do you have any known enemies?"

"Oh yes, but that was a long time ago, and she is married and has grown kids."

"She?"

"This town girl I courted when I was at college here in Malvern. She wanted to marry me and at the time it was the last thing I wanted. She even faked being pregnant."

"Have you seen her since?"

"Every winter. She still lives here locally and married a local guy who works at Morgan Car Company. I think she had several kids."

"But you don't see her anymore?"

"Every time I go for a pint at the Nags Head on Bank Street, Alison Noble is always holding up the bar. And sometimes it's holding her up."

"Do you think she could be the one causing your problems?"

"No. All mouth, her husband is always working, so he says, but I've seen him visiting a house in Barnard's Green Road."

"Do you still love her?"

"No! James, she made me feel good about myself. My wife never did that. She was always nagging me to make more money so she could spend it."

"Okay, I'll go online later and see if I can find out how you become undead."

"That's the internet, I have a computer I was going to write my life story only it seems so boring to me."

"Maybe to you but to people like me who saw you and enjoyed what you did. To know the man behind the mask is worth knowing."

"It's a broken mask at the moment."

"Not for long Bryan."

"I bet my egg is cracked."

"Your egg?"

"Every clown has his face painted on an egg; it's like a trademark registration. The painted egg collection was kept in London by Clown Cavalcade, not sure it still is."

"I would like to see that."

"A broken mask and cracked egg, that's me."

Bryan sat looking at the floor; despondency washed over him.

"Do you want something else to eat?"

"No, I've taken too much of your time."

James took out his wallet and gave Bryan the hundred pounds. The old man looked at him. Tears formed in the old man's eyes. He wasn't used to such kindness from a stranger.

"I'll come over to the circus tomorrow morning with what I find out."

"Thanks, I think I need to go home and gets some sleep. Tomorrow it may not seem so bad."

"Who was the man outside the bank who pushed you?"

"You saw that too? Now I see why you are so concerned. Someone from my past who has dogged me all my life and will until I really am dead."

Bryan left and James cleared away the dishes. The sink had become full, and if his mother saw it she would have a fit. He washed and dried the items before putting them away. He felt quite emotional about what had happened. A change in the atmosphere might help before he opened the computer to look how to undead someone.

He wasn't really sure why he chose the Nags Head except it was what Bryan had said about his former girlfriend. He knew he was heading for trouble before he stepped inside the pub, but he had always run into a storm rather than wait for it to come to him.

There were about six people in the bar when he entered. The young barman in his twenties smiled and nodded at him. In a corner at a round wooden table, sat a party of four. From the way, the older couple was dressed; it was either a special occasion for them or one of their children. Had the young man proposed to his girlfriend and taken his parents out to meet her? Or was it the parents' silver wedding anniversary? He would never really know unless someone in the bar said something. The other person in the bar was a man who sat at the far end looking sourly into a pint of beer.

"Good evening sir. What can I get you?" said the barman.

James wanted to try some locally brewed beer but not being an expert he would wait for someone who knew about local beers to advise him.

"A pint of pedigree please."

"Tall glass or pint mug?"

"Mug please."

The barman drew the pint and handed it over to James. He paid and found a seat against the wall so he could watch the people who came into the bar. He didn't have to wait long; two women entered. They were in their fifties; both had let the body fat accumulate. The taller of them was a dyed blonde, and her make up looked as it had been applied in a hurry. It was obvious from the moment she opened her mouth. She was a loud woman who always liked the attention.

"Evening, Everett, the usual for us please."

"Coming up Alison."

James wondered if this was the Alison, Bryan had talked about. The other lady was just as common, as his sister Anne would say. She had on a black lace top, which only just covered her ample breasts. Her jeans were large, and from the back, because her knees never seemed to part the material puckered up between the cheeks of her backside. Her arms would look good on any building site worker, and she would win every arm wrestling match she entered. James didn't know her name but from the way she cursed, he didn't want to. She couldn't say a sentence without 'fuck' being every third word. Her hair was short and spiky, and then James realized she was wearing a wig. Her make-up had been applied with a little more care than Alison's, but it was still too heavy, covering up the cracks.

After they received their drinks, James noted they didn't hand over any money. They both turned and leaned against the bar looking at the other people in the pub. At first, they watched with interest the group at the corner table. Then Alison noticed James and the two became almost school girlish in their behavior. Alison pushed the other woman toward him. He drank his beer and looked straight at her as she approached his table.

He wanted to laugh because she was acting like a thirteen-year-old at a school dance having been dared to approach an older boy.

"Hello, you're new."

"No, I've been around for twenty-five years."

"You're new here. Hey, Alison, he got ever so nice manners. You should hear him talk. Not posh but very polite."

Alison stayed at the bar watching her friend. James wondered if she was sizing him up to see if he would play with an older woman.

"Hey, Pauline, what's his name?"

"So mister macho man, what's your name?"

"James."

"It's Jimmy, Ali."

Pauline walked back to the bar. Her hip movement had become more pronounced. She must have thought it was a sexy move. For James it just made him want to laugh.

He watched as she drank a pint of beer in one swallow. She wiped her mouth on the back of her hand.

The door opened and two men entered. They were, judging by their clothes, American tourists. They both had bright yellow and red-checkered pants with Hawaiian shirts in the same colors. One of the men held the door open so two ladies could enter. They looked like Nancy Reagan at the height of Ronald's Presidency. The barman said something to Alison and Pauline as the tourists went up to the bar. Alison obviously wanted to say something but she didn't. Whatever the barman had said, she obeyed and sat quietly drinking her beer.

James thought of Bryan. He would have asked if he could buy the trousers from the men for his circus act. One of James's sisters Elizabeth had gone to America to work. He had promised he would visit. If this couple were what he could expect to see, he would be laughing from the moment he arrived. He would dine out for several months after his return telling everyone how Americans dress.

The pub door opened and the skinhead James had seen watching his caravan entered.

"Hi Mike," said Alison.

"Evening Mister Noble," said the barman

Mike Noble wore a union jack tee shirt and the skinhead regulation jeans. On the left knee, he had a small union jack patch sewn on. Possibly to cover up a rip in the jeans or make a further statement to his patriotic beliefs. The black Dr. Martin boots were fully visible showing all ten-lace holes. He had turned up the bottom of his jeans to expose the boots. The white suspenders normally used to pull the jeans up high hung loosely from the waistband. He walked up to Alison and spoke to her. She opened her purse and gave him some money. He stood at the bar and ordered a drink. Like Alison, he turned and looked around the bar. At first, he made a few comments about the Americans until Alison thumped on the arm.

He looked towards James and turned back to the bar speaking to Alison and Pauline in a low voice.

Alison drained her glass and then crossed towards James.

"My son Mike just told me you have parked your bloody caravan on our common."

James didn't respond. He just looked at the woman who became belligerent and loud.

"Well, what the fuck have you got to say for yourself?"

James picked up his glass and drank the remaining beer. The barman had called for reinforcements and two men appeared beside Alison. James placed his glass on the table stood up and attempted to cross to the door.

Their attention was suddenly diverted to the door as Police Officer Peter Kipler entered. He saw the group around James and quickly crossed to the bar.

"Problem Everett?"

"No not really Peter, only Alison accusing this young man of setting up home on the common."

"That's right he has."

"Well, I hope you bloody well tell him to move."

"Can't Pauline. He has Council permission."

"The Council gave him permission. I knew they were a bunch of tossers."

"Alison it is only for a few weeks while he builds some new homes."

She looked at Peter then at James before returning to her son and Pauline.

"Sorry about that James. I think you may find a lot of people will make comments. And the Nobles think they own the common."

"Thanks, Peter. I'm used to these problems. I saw her son watching me earlier."

"Nobby, that's Mike's nickname. He is a very dangerous young man, and one of these days I will get him. He knows it and he keeps just inside the law."

"What about his father?"

"Works day and night, so the boy doesn't really get any discipline."

"I think if I have any problem he will be behind it."

"I can guarantee it."

"I'd better get back, see you later Peter. If you see a light on stop for a cuppa."

"Thanks, I will."

      The American had suddenly become noisy and the attention of those in the pub had shifted over to their table. James took this opportunity to slip out and head for his caravan.

CHAPTER THREE

Hidden Treasure

If James had known how the day was going to turn out, he wouldn't have stepped out of bed. The drab daylight seeped through the closed blinds in the caravan. He opened his eyes, looked at the alarm clock and rolled over. He jumped out of bed realizing it was already eight thirty and he said he would meet the builder at eight. Stepping under the shower was his second shock of the day. The water dripped out and was cold. He checked in the kitchen area, and the water just trickled out and stopped. He dried his face dressed quickly, and went to the back of the caravan to check that the water pipe the town council had connected was intact. Someone had taken a saw and cut the pipe. The odd thing was they had turned off the water first. He called the district council office and explained to a very helpful lady what had happened. She said she would send out an engineer to fix the problem in a week or so. Frustrated, James walked over to the site. The builder had arrived and equipment was being unloaded from a flatbed truck.

He watched as a foreman gave orders and the men obeyed.

"You look rough," said Arthur Cox, "I'll introduce you to Big John later. He is a reliable man. Knows how to crack the whip when the men get lazy."

For James, from years of being with his father, he shuddered at the word reliable. To him, this was another man to watch. Most conmen say they are reliable and they are not. They say they are honest and then steal. At this moment in time, it wasn't the problem on his mind.

"Someone cut the water pipe to the caravan."

"Kids. I'll get one of the boys to put a metal pipe connection instead of the plastic ones the town council always use."

"Thanks," said James in a dispirited way.

"I think I need to do that as soon as possible, or you're going to have a bad day."

"I already am."

Arthur disappeared behind the flatbed. James watched as the building crew worked as a team. Several were marking the ground with white chalk lines while others hammered wooden steaks into the ground. From behind the flatbed truck, Arthur and two men appeared, carrying several lengths of copper piping and toolboxes.

"Give us about an hour and we will have water restored. In the meantime, the food wagon has just arrived so you can get a mug of tea and a bacon sandwich."

James returned to the caravan and put on a jacket. The morning was cold and he felt dirty from not having a shower. Most of the houses in the street he grew up on didn't have showers in the bathrooms. Some had only installed bathtubs as late as nineteen sixty-four. His father, when he bought the house, installed two bathrooms with showers. He made each member of the family take a shower in the morning. To James, it was how he started his day and without it, he felt everything would go wrong.

He joined the line of men at the food wagon. The building crew was a mixture of races but they knew one another. They joked and teased each other as they stood in line.

James stood by the flatbed truck and enjoyed the greasy bacon sandwich which he knew would appall his mother, but she wasn't around. He was no longer her little boy. After marking of the site had been completed, a small digger rolled over to the far right-hand corner. It began to dig out a trench for the foundation of the first house being built.

James wandered behind his caravan to see how the builders were doing with the pipework. Arthur was inspecting the work when he arrived. The two men looked on with happy expressions on their faces.

"Very good boys. James, you have water and it will be very difficult for someone to cut the pipes again. They encased the copper pipe inside a cast iron pipe."

Suddenly shouting from the building site could be heard. James and Arthur peered around the side of the caravan. One of the men came running toward them. He was speaking so fast it was hard at first for anyone to understand. Arthur ran back to the site. One of the men spoke to him and he indicated for the men to move away. James approached. He knew something bad had been found and hoped it wouldn't hold up the work.

"Sorry James, but the boys think they may have found a World War Two bomb in the far corner."

"Call the police, and let's have a look."

"Charlie called the cops. Do you think we should look just in case it explodes?"

"If it was going to explode, it would have done that when the digger hit it."

James walked over the rough ground to the digger, a little apprehensive. The workmen gathered behind the flatbed truck and peered over the top of it. He looked down into the hole, which the digger had made. He could see two or three cylindrical metal objects hidden by mud. He had never seen a World War Two bomb so it could be one, or something else. He heard the sirens of the police cars approach.

A tall very officious policeman joined him and looked down into the hole. James suddenly had visions of an old Quatermass film and gave a little laugh at the thought. The policeman thought he was going into some kind of shock and led him back to the roadway. The police produced their blue tape and started to rope off the area.

"Are you feeling better now sir?" asked the policeman holding James by the elbow.

"Sorry, I'm fine."

"Then I think we need everyone to move away from this area. If they are bombs then it would be better to evacuate this area for at least a mile square."

James locked the caravan and joined the other men as they walked up the street and onto the slopes of North Hill. The food wagon had followed and set up a little dining area on the road below. James found a rock to sit on and look down on the site. Several more police cars arrived, and he could see the circus people were evacuated from the winter quarters. He watched as they reluctantly strolled up the road to where the workers had stopped. The clowns crowded around the food wagon and then joined James on his rock.

Fiddles offered him a tea, which he took.

"James, I think you're nothing but trouble."

"It looks that way," he replied laughing.

They sat and watched. It took several hours before the Army Bomb Disposal Unit arrived. A group of policemen and women had joined the circus folk and the light-hearted banter between them entertained the workmen.

Fiddles the clown was born at the end of the Second World War but he still decided to reminisce about it as though he had been a teenager at the time. He was a good storyteller and all those around him listened with interest to his tale of the bombing of Birmingham.

He sat on the rock and told the story of how his house was blown up and his mother had just hung the washing on the line to dry when the bomb hit the house. His mother was so mad she screamed at the planes 'I don't have time to wash the clothes again'.

His face became animated and the deep lines, which he used as a guide to applying his clown make up intensified.

"My mother could get so angry. If Herr Hitler had come over here, she would have given him a mouth full."

The crowd laughed. It wasn't that funny. It was just the way he said it, and his body actions, that made it so. James could see why he was a clown. He liked to entertain and this was a perfect opportunity to defuse the situation.

He looked down the hill at the bomb disposal team and hoped it wasn't a bomb, just old metal cans.

James had decided not to inform his family until he knew if it was going to delay the building of the houses. A sudden burst of activity where the bombs were located stopped Fiddles in his stories and the crowd looked down at the site. One of the policemen standing close by spoke into his communicator and then smiled.

"All clear, it's not bombs but a load of water tanks someone buried. You can all go back down."

James and the rest of the crowd walked down the hill. The police kept the crowd of onlookers on the roadway but James and the builders were allowed to approach the water tanks. A senior army officer looked at James and in a very upper crust voice said, "Thank God it wasn't a set of bombs. Something that size would have blown up most of West Malvern."

Arthur Cox put a hand on James' shoulder, "I'll get the boys to move them over to the side by your Caravan. You can decide what you want to do with them later. Might get something for them as scrap."

James nodded. He needed a drink. He wandered back to the caravan. Alison's son had arrived and was standing a little up the roadway. It was then that James saw the graffiti on the caravan. Someone had written in black spray paint the words 'Move on Gypos'.

James felt anger build inside him. He was a Romani, a gypsy to the uneducated, and this kind of racist act really made him angry. He didn't hear Peter Kipler, the policeman, approach and gave a little jump when he spoke.

"Who did that?"

"I don't know but it happened while we were up on the hill, so maybe one of the bomb people saw who did it." "I'll ask them."
Fiddles and Bryan joined James. They looked at the graffiti then up the road to where Alison's skinhead son was standing.
"I can guess who did this," said Fiddles.
James looked in the skinhead's direction who quickly turned and ran off onto the common.
"You may be right. Now I've got to clean this off."
"I'll get one of the boys to do that, the caravan side being chrome-plated metal and the paint still wet we will remove it in no time," said, Arthur.
"What will you do? Put it on my bill?"
"No, we are used to this kind of thing. I suggest you move off the common somewhere. Then we put the site office on that patch of ground, which will become the garden of one of the houses. Down by that wooden fence next to the circus land. The problem may get a little better. This is just a red flag to a bull and soon all the Malvern cranks will be out causing trouble."
Bryan saw Tonya walking toward them and quickly raced over to her. She joined Fiddles and James looking at the graffiti. Dougie and Cooper, his brother, stood a little down the road.
"Bryan has suggested you move into the winter have space for another caravan next to the fence.
Bryan nodded; from his facial expression, he looked angry.
"No, I'm not moving just yet. I will if it is okay with you move later this week, but I just want to teach whomever it was that I can't be frightened by their stupid games.

"When you're ready let me know. I'll bringing one of the trailers and tow you," said Dougie. His brother Cooper tugged at his jeans and Dougie bent down and listened to the boy.

"Cooper said he saw one of the town skinheads here earlier."

"Yes, I saw him a few minutes ago in the street. I think he and I need a little chat," said James.

Arthur's men arrived and very quickly removed the spray paint. They then washed the outside of the caravan and made it look as though it were still inside a showroom.

The workmen removed the five water tanks and placed them close to James's caravan. One of the men made a comment that they were heavy and were still possibly full of water.

James sat inside his caravan. This was how it must have been for his grandfather all those years ago when they traveled. He wasn't going to be intimidated by anyone, least of all by a racist policeman and his skinhead mob.

The rest of the day went without a hitch, and he was surprised how much work the men had been able to complete. They would normally clock off at three-thirty each day, but as they had lost two hours due to the bomb scare, Arthur kept them working until four thirty. James stood looking at the water tanks. If they were full of water he would need to empty them out before selling them as scrap metal. He picked up a stick and hit one of the tanks; if it had been full of water, it would have sounded with a dull thud. This and the other tanks that he hit with the wooden stick sounded with a hollow ring. Four nuts held the top of the tanks in place; using a spanner he removed the nuts and opened the lid.

The contents fell out on the muddy ground. Someone had stored what looked like two gold colored plates and several jewelry boxes inside the tanks. He replaced the lid; this wasn't the time to expose it. Whoever had placed the items inside would come back and recover them.

He wouldn't stop them from removing the items. He didn't know whom they belonged to, so if they claimed it to be their property then it was okay for it to be taken.

As evening came he sat by the window looking out at the tanks. Surely someone would arrive and remove the contents.

He fell asleep at his post and was woken when he heard the noise of someone knocking the tanks with a metal object. His lights were out so he looked out into the darkness. There was just enough light to see Alison's son, Nobby, trying to open the tanks. James grabbed his flashlight and slipped out of the caravan. The skinhead froze like a deer caught in the headlights. James positioned himself so it was impossible for the boy to make a run for it.

"Caught red-handed."

"Just looking."

"Why? Did you know there was something inside the tanks?"

"Maybe."

"Why did you spray paint my caravan."

"I didn't."

"You know who did though."

"Maybe."

"So, if I let you remove the items from the water tanks no questions asked, you'll tell me."

"Maybe."

"Is that your favorite word?"

"Maybe."

"Okay, let's put it another way. If you don't tell me, I'll call the cops and even if you get away, the stolen items it will go to them. If you tell me what I want to know and stop harassing me, you can take the lot no questions asked."

The skinhead thought for a few minutes then smiled. "I could tell you a lie and take them and then you would have nothing."

"Except I am videoing this meeting and I have a microphone here in my shirt pocket."

"No bull."

"No bull shit. I just want to know who did it."

The lights of the car surprised them both; Peter Kipler climbed out of the car and approached them.

"Problem James?"

"No problem Peter, this young man came to see if I was okay. He just said he wanted everyone to live in peace and harmony."

"No shit, and all that from this no good layabout yob."

"I can be reasonable if I want to be," said Nobby.

"Okay, nice to see you doing your civic duty to a stranger. You going to sell those tanks, James?"

"Yes, they'll be gone by tomorrow."

James realized that one of the lids was off and if Peter looked inside, he would see stolen items.

"You want a cup of tea, Peter?"

"Sure, if it's not too much trouble."

"I'll be seeing you, Nobby. If you're interested in moving the tanks, you know my price."

James took the policeman inside the caravan and made some tea. They talked for about an hour. James learned that Peter was born and grew up in Malvern. His older brother, who he idolized, was dead. James didn't learn how the brother had died as Peter quickly changed the subject.

After Peter had left James stood by the tanks. Nobby had replaced the lid but didn't seem to be around. He returned to the caravan and prepared to sleep. At four thirty-five in the morning, he was woken again by a knocking at his door. Nobby stood looking at him. His face was pale and withdrawn. James allowed him inside.

"Problem?"

"Not with you. I've come for the stuff if the deal stands."

"Yes, as long as you tell me who did the graffiti."

"You won't tell anyone if I tell you?"

"I promise, no one will know from me."

"One of the cops."

"Name?"

"Martin Dugdale. Everyone calls him Marty. He belongs to the National Front and is trying to get all the local skins to join."

"You haven't?"

"No. Live and let live that's my motto."

"What about your mates?"

"I think only Robbo has joined but he is usually so stoned he would join the Women's Institute if he was told to. What's your name?"

"James."

"Mike Noble, but everyone calls me Nobby."

James nodded. "What did you tell your Mom in the pub?"

"She knows about the stuff. It's my uncle's and he is inside again, so I tried to get her angry with you so you would move. But I can see you're cool."

"Live and let live."

"Sure."

Suddenly there was banging on the door. It was so loud that James wondered if the caravan was built to stand such an attack. When he opened the door, Alison Noble stood looking up at him.

"You got my son in there?"

"Come on in, Mrs. Noble."

She climbed into the caravan. From the expression, she too was surprised to see how luxurious the place was.

"What do you want, Mom?"

"Just checking son to see if you were having a problem."

"No mom. Me and James have an agreement."

"Would you like some tea?" asked James.

"Any beer?"

"Sure, if that's what you would like."

"I have a little job to do so if you two would like to chat while I load the van," said Nobby.

James and Alison Noble sat and talked about her childhood and early days of marriage before she caught her husband cheating. Life went downhill and she had to bring Nobby up on her own even though her husband was around.

"He is not a bad kid. Didn't do drugs which is a blessing these days."

After an hour Nobby had removed all the stolen items and replaced the lids. He knocked on the door. He and his mother left. James went back to sleep only to be woken again an hour later when the workmen arrived.

The morning dragged. James was still very sleepy and just didn't want to talk to anyone. While getting his bacon sandwich from the food truck, he was informed by one of the workmen that the water tanks were now very light. James told the man he had drained them the night before.

After speaking with his father, he decided it would be better to move into the circus compound if only to have a little protection from the hate mongers. Dougie seemed pleased that James had decided to take up the offer and said they could do it at five that night, giving James time to pack his gear safely for the move. Even Arthur thought it was a good idea after the graffiti. 'Who knows?' he'd said, 'what they would do next. It was sensible to move'. For James, it seemed as though a group of people had invaded his world and were now dictating what he should do. He had always been independent, and he was only doing it because his father and mother had said it was the best thing for his safety. It reeked of parental control and he hated it as much as he hated the fact that whoever was behind the racism had won.

It was obvious that Dougie and other tentmen knew what they were doing. The speed and efficiency they applied to his move were incredible. James had asked Tonya what he could give as a thank you. She had replied, 'Buy some beer'. He produced a five-gallon keg for the men, who seemed very pleased with it. Dougie had been a little reticent and said he didn't have to give them anything. James replied that he did. Within two hours he already made himself at home and cooked something to eat. They placed him against the fence on the other side of the building site.

Through the end window of the caravan, he could see onto the site.

At six thirty Tonya and Dougie knocked on his door.

"James do you want to come and see one of the new acts for next season? They are a group of Chinese acrobats who tightrope-walk and juggle."

"Sure, a new home and a sideshow as well."

"Well, you're one of us, gypsy boy."

Most of the circus people had already arrived and were seated around the ring. The clowns were, as always, together and Bryan was with them. The ten male Chinese acrobats went through their routine to the applause of the other performers.

After the show, there were several groups, each with a Chinese performer talking to them. James liked how the people here made it a family affair. Each person was accepted and welcomed.

Tonya seemed agitated and annoyed.

"Anything wrong?" asked James.

"My mother said she'd come and see the new act, but as always she obviously has more important things to do."

"I think all parents are like that. I know mine was no different."

"It's only since Ryan came into her life that things have become so bad."

"You really don't like him."

"No, not at all. He is a sponger and parasite. I'd better find out why she didn't appear."

Slowly, everyone drifted back to their living quarters. James wandered back to his caravan. He flipped through the satellite programs on the television.

Nothing really interested him. He needed a good book to read. A western that was his favorite at this moment.

He would find the local library in the morning and get
a few books to read. Then he remembered he had to
look up, if he could, why Bryan was made dead. And
once declared dead how do you become undead? He
opened the computer and began to search the Internet.
He did feel a little safer inside the circus compound.
He was always expecting someone to attack him
verbally or even physically when he was on the
common.

He was deep in thought when Tonya knocked at his
door. He opened the door and stepped outside.

"Sorry to bother you but I thought you would like to
meet my mother. She just rang and said she and Ryan
will be over later. They had gone out to dinner and the
restaurant had taken forever to serve them."

"Great, I look forward to meeting her and Ryan."

"You can judge for yourself then."

Bryan's door to his caravan opened and he fell down
the few steps onto the concrete ground.

James and Tonya rushed over to him. He has been
very badly beaten; his face already beginning to swell.
They helped him back into his caravan. The place was
a mess. Someone had opened every cupboard and
drawer and thrown everything out onto the floor. He
seemed very dazed.   James checked his pulse and
looked into his eyes.

"Bryan, what happened?"

"Someone attacked me."

"Who?"

"I don't know. I came home and found the place like
this, and then something hit me, and all I remember
was being beaten."

James didn't believe him; something about the way he
told the story didn't ring true. Now wasn't the time to

challenge him. He would do it later when it was just the two of them. Tonya wrapped some ice in a towel and applied it to Bryan's face. James started to pick up things off the floor. He placed most of the items on the table and sofa. On a pile of clothes by the door, he found a piece of paper and read it.

It was a leaflet telling the local residents that James and his family worshipped the devil and was building the houses for their black magic followers. James handed it to Tonya, she read it and then passed it to Bryan. He looked at it then flipped it to the floor.

"Is that yours?" asked Tonya.

"No." replied Bryan, a belligerence entering his voice. "Sorry James I think I should handle this I'll let you know what I find out."

James was then pushed out of the door and had to grab the handrail on the steps to steady himself. He could hear Tonya raise her voice and Bryan shouted something back. Cooper, Dougie's little brother, stood on the steps of their caravan and watched, as James walked back to his caravan. The boy didn't change expression, just watched. When James entered his caravan, the boy raced towards the Big Top obviously in search of his brother. James realized why he had always lived near his family; it can be very lonely on your own. He needed to find things to do while he oversaw the building of the houses or he would go crazy out of boredom.

He took the leaflet out of his pocket. Was Bryan one of the people behind the problems the Pidgley family had encountered while getting planning permission? He read the wording. Someone who either was trying to sound illiterate or was poor with grammar and spelling had written it. His name had been spelled wrong, so had the road the site was on. The tone was racist and vicious. He couldn't imagine that Bryan would have had anything to do with it. Then there was the way he said no when asked if it was his. And why had Tonya said she would deal with it? Too many questions and he wasn't asking them. He hated not having any answers and not being able to find out the answer.

A knock at the door irritated him.

Dougie stood looking up at him, a worried expression on his face.

"Hi, Dougie, something wrong?"

"You tell me what's happened with Bryan. Tonya said he had a problem."

"We found him, Tonya and I. After someone had beaten him up."

"Who?"

"He didn't say, said he didn't know."

"Tonya said she asked you to leave because you found something."

"I found a leaflet. This one; Bryan said it wasn't his."

Dougie read the leaflet; he was reading slowly, taking each word as though checking for something.

"He didn't write this."

"How can you be so sure?"

"Bryan's, what's the word? Dyslexia."

"There are some spelling mistakes in that leaflet."

"No, I mean really dyslexic. He sometimes can't spell his own name. If he writes anything down it's impossible for anyone to understand, even he can't sometimes."

"Okay, so he didn't write it, but he may have been distributing it."

"Sure, but why would he, when his own family are Romani."

"So if he didn't write it, or distributed it, then someone must have planted it to throw suspicion."

"You mean whoever beat him up just left it?"

"Yes, I found it on top of a pile of clothes, which had been pulled out of a drawer. It was as though someone had just dropped it for me to find."

"You or someone else. He must have been beaten just after the Chinese acrobats had finished the show. He left the Big Top when we were all talking to them. Anyone could have slipped inside the compound and attacked him."

"Maybe Cooper saw something."

"I'll ask but I think he was inside the Big Top near me."

"I used to be like that with one of my brothers. Like Cooper, I idolized my older brother Peter. He was my hero still is I think."

"Cooper has only been clingy since our parents have gone."

"Is that why you are bringing him up?"

"Yes, he had no one else. My father, the bastard, told me that Cooper was a mistake after a drinking binge. Then he said he and our mother didn't want him so they were going to just dump him and the council could look after him. I became his legal guardian when I reached eighteen."

"That explains why he doesn't talk much."

"I've never really understood why. He can talk. Sometime when we are alone I can't shut him up."

"He knows what your parents did. He may not know the details but Cooper knows, so he doesn't trust adults. By not speaking to them he doesn't have to deal with them."

"Funny you should say that at school he talks to the other kids. Makes them laugh as though he was a clown. As soon as an adult appears he goes very quiet."

"He needs to find people he can trust."

"He talks to Bryan and the other clowns but only when they are in makeup. I just don't know how to get him to speak to others adults."

"By example, Dougie. You come across as a hard man, not just the skinhead attire but also your manner. He copies you, you need to lighten up on others and he will do the same. When you and Tonya talk, he has almost a smile on his face. He knows you love her so he can relax."

"How do you know I love her?"

"Overprotective and jealous."

"You psychic?"

"No, just read people."

"You should join the circus and do the dukkering."

"My mother is good at fortune telling but only for fun. She's the one who taught me how to read people. What happened to your parents?"

"Went to Wales and started this hippy commune. Still running it, as far as I know, I watch very carefully when we go near the place. I don't want Cooper to see them, it may open too many wounds."

The door to Dougie's caravan opened and Cooper stood pointing towards Bryan caravan. James wondered if the boy had heard their conversation.

"What's wrong Cooper?"

The boy came closer; Dougie leaned down and listened as the boy whispered into his ear.

"He thinks there may be a problem. He heard Tonya crying in Bryan caravan."

"Let's go and see."

For a second, Dougie hesitated, looked at Cooper and then at James.

"James thanks for your help. We'll even get you into a clown costume before we go on the road."

"It's not every day that someone comes to your rescue and saves you from the gadjo."

"True, we tend to call them the Wood family."

"Why?"

"When we have empty seats we say the Wood family is in because the wooden seats are not filled. We have, over the years, called all none circus folk the wood family."

Cooper was walking beside them and nodded his head in agreement.

As they arrived at Bryan's caravan they could hear what could be laughing or crying. The sound was so difficult to distinguish.

"Thanks, Cooper. Your brother and I are worried about Bryan and Tonya."

The boy looked up at Dougie who nodded his head. The words were very quiet almost as a whisper on the wind, just audible for James to hear. Cooper said, "No problem."

At Bryan's caravan, Dougie knocked on the door. Tonya opened it her face smiling. Behind her Bryan was laughing, a funny almost insane laugh. She stepped outside on the concrete looking from Dougie to James.

"Problem?"

"We were wondering if you and Bryan had a problem. Cooper said he thought he heard you crying."

She put her hand on Coopers' head and stroked his hair. He responded like a cat or dog enjoying the affection.

"We were going over old times. He reminded me of the time I walked into the circus ring during a show naked."

"What!" said Dougie and James together.

"I was three years old."

Dougie and Tonya moved a little away. Cooper hovered and then moved over to the steps of his and Dougie's caravan.

Bryan closed his caravan door and came down the steps. He looked at James searching his face for some clue as to how James was thinking.

"It wasn't my leaflet."

"I know someone planted it on you for some reason."

"It reminded me of when I was in college and a guy called Kippers, that was his nickname, got a petition together. The college was angry about it and he somehow got someone else take the blame."

"Why did it remind you?" asked James.

"Just the wording was the same."

"Was it the man from the bank who beat you up?"

"No. He's just a diseased mind from my past. Did you find anything out on the internet?"

"You're dead and you need to get a doctor and a high ranking police officer to say you're not to be reinstated to the living."

"I don't know any high ranking police officers, only low ranking criminals."

"Me too."

"So James, what happens now?"

Before James could answer their attention was diverted to the circus Big Top. The scream sounded as though an animal had been hurt. One of the Chinese performers ran out of the tent looking for someone to speak to.

His English was limited but from what they could understand the words 'man' and 'death' seemed to be what he was trying to say. Tonya walked into the tent. The others followed and once inside they spread about looking for what the young performer had seen.

James and Tonya were the first to enter the ring; the Chinese performers' tightrope equipment was still erected. A single light shone on the figure that was hanging from the wire twelve feet off the ground.

They stood staring at the man's body. Someone had forced a butcher's 'S' shaped hook into the back of the neck, then hung the man in the center of the tightrope wire by it. The man's arms had been stretched out and dolly clothes pegs had been used to attach his coat sleeve to the wire. James walked around the back of the body and saw that the sleeves were actually held in place by car battery charging clamps.

Dougie and Cooper joined them. The man's head was hanging down and with a top light on him; it was hard to see who it was. Bryan appeared on the other side of the ring and walked up to the body. He felt for a pulse in his foot and shook his head. Joining the others it was James who spoke first.

"Not again."

Tonya looked at him then at Dougie. James regained his thoughts and suddenly took command of the situation.

"Tonya, could you call the police? Dougie, could you and Cooper stop others from entering the tent?"

Dougie nodded. Cooper ran to the entrance.

"Tonya you call the police. I'll call your Mother."

"She needn't know yet."

"Yes, she should."

"Why?"

"Because that's Ryan," said Dougie.

"What!"

"It's Ryan?" asked James.

"They were out to dinner, how could it be Ryan?"

Tonya and Bryan left the ring, leaving James looking at the body. He sat on one of the seats and stared. It wasn't that long ago he had been involved in another murder that almost cost one of his sisters her life. It was one of the reasons he had left Birmingham to forget. And now he was involved in another murder. Bryan returned. He didn't look too happy.

"Mabel's on her way here."

"He doesn't look real does he?"

"No, I've never seen a dead body before, well not one from murder."

"I have."

"I wonder why they pegged his arms like that?"

"Making fun of him."

"No one is laughing."

"The killer was."

"What did you mean when you said not again?"

"Before I came to Malvern I was involved in a murder in Birmingham."

"Involved?"

"Yes, my father was accused of it and I proved with a friend he didn't do it."

"That's why I know your name. It's been bugging me since we first met. I thought it was the Romani connection, but I read about the murder in Longbridge. Wasn't there a Coronation of the Queen connection too?"

"Yes, and here I am finding another body."
"Look I won't mention it to the others about the Longbridge business but I would like to talk to you later. I think I may know who did this and what the connection with the leaflet is."
"I think we should go outside with the others and wait for the police."
As they left, they didn't see Cooper approach the body and remove something from the left pocket.

CHAPTER FOUR

James P.I.

The police arrived and took control of the circus winter quarters compound. Everyone was told they were not to leave until the police had spoken to them. James returned to his caravan and made something to eat. He looked out of the window and saw the police visiting the other caravans taking its occupant to the Big Top for questioning. Tonya seemed to spend the longest time with the police; she left the Big Top with an older, white-haired woman whom he assumed was her mother Mabel.

Bryan was escorted across the compound; he looked like a condemned man on the way to the gallows. His shoulder more hunched over more than normal. Something was bothering that man thought James. Why would someone beat him up and Bryan not want the police told? James laughed, and said out loud, "Here I go again, and next I will want to solve the murder." He wasn't sure where he obtained his curiosity from but he knew he would want the answer to his satisfaction before he would leave it alone. The police, in his opinion, often made the wrong assumptions and arrested the wrong people. They, like so many government officials found, it hard to accept they had made a mistake and many innocent people suffered. The circus, because of its traveling status and therefore in the eyes of the general public, had very loose morals. He knew all about that. He had grown up knowing differently. It was what went on behind closed doors in people's houses, which should worry the general public. Crimes of the family were one of the most well kept secrets in society today. Incest, rape and other abuses, such as mental and physical abuse, were the secrets of the modern British family. No longer regarded as a lower class problem, too many secrets revealed in the tabloids exposed the truth that abuse had no class boundaries. He sat pontificating over his bacon sandwich and third cup of tea when someone knocked on the door. He assumed it was the police until he opened the door and saw Tonya with a white-haired lady looking up at him.

"James can we have a word with you."

He stepped aside and allowed them to enter. Mabel looked around as though she was looking for something. She spotted the cut glass bowl his mother had placed on a side broad. The smile was small and thin but he knew she had recognized a fellow traveler.

"This is my mother Mabel Morris."

James shook Mabel's hand; it was the hand of a strong determined woman. She gripped him so tightly he felt the pain instantly. He understood from this she was in control even though she wasn't always around.

"Can I get you some tea."

"Now that would be very nice," said Mabel sitting herself down on the sofa.

As he made the tea he looked at them, the awkwardness Tonya displayed was not there with her mother.

"Your interview with the police took a long time Tonya."

"A real grilling, not as bad as the one Dougie got but bad enough."

"Did they give any clue as to what they are thinking?" Mabel coughed, he wasn't sure if that was a signal for Tonya not to speak or she was clearing her throat to talk.

The latter was the case. "I got the impression they think one of us committed the murder. And they told us it was murder," said Mabel.

"Do you think it was one of the circus employees?"

"No, Ryan was a stupid boy who liked to play around. He was cheating on me all the time and I caught him the other day stealing out of my purse. The money that went missing last season I think it may have been him."

"Do you think he spent it on drugs?" asked Tonya.

"No he wasn't into that. I think he may have had a wife somewhere. I found a picture of this woman with kids. He said it was his sister but when we met he said he was an only child."

James handed them tea, Mabel took it looking at the china teacup. Again she gave that thin small smile.

"You asked if you can have a word with me?"

Tonya looked at her mother.

It was Mabel who wanted the word. "James. I know all about you. We have mutual friends up in Birmingham and I spoke to your father earlier. I need someone, not the police, to investigate this murder. If anyone in the circus is involved, we need to know as soon as possible. It could affect the new season's shows," said Mabel.

"Why me?"

"Our mutual friend said you have solved a murder before, even when the police got it wrong you found out the truth."

"That was different my father was accused."

"And I hope you regard us as your family now."

It was James' turn to give that small, thin smile. He looked at the old lady. She must be in her late seventies — even if she boasted of being in her late sixties. She had a youthfulness about her which James found comforting. She dressed not like an old lady but a businesswoman on a mission to conquer the world. Her power of manipulation was very good. She also knew how to listen. Her reply just then had been quick and clever. She began playing with the single string of pearls around her neck.

"I must admit that I'm interested."

"Your father said nothing would stop you from poking your nose in. His words, not mine."

"Thanks, Dad."

"So will you try and find out what's really happening?"

"Tonya said you and Ryan had been out for dinner."

"We had and I wanted to change my shoes and freshen up my make-up before meeting you. Ryan's mobile rang. After answering it, he said he would meet me at your caravan."

"So, whoever called arranged to meet him in the Big Top. Can you tell me more about Ryan?"

"He was one sandwich short of a picnic," said Tonya, before her mother could speak.

"Maybe, but he knew how to please a woman in bed."

"Mother."

"Nothing wrong in being honest, is there? James wants to know why Ryan was in my life."

"Whoever murdered him hated him. The way he was left it is obvious they were showing the world their hatred of the man," said James,

"I didn't see him but from what Tonya said it wasn't very nice."

"When did you meet him and how?"

"He came for a job. It didn't work out so he left sometime last year. Then he reappeared and started chatting me up. I was flattered. Not every day you get a younger man interested in someone my age. He was fifty-one I think."

"Then he moved in with Mom, and started to try and take over the circus."

"He may have tried, but I made it quite clear the circus was mine and no one is going to get their hands on it."

"Some men are good for one thing only and that was what Ryan was good for and nothing else."

"So who would want him dead?"

"Plenty of people"

"Mom do you remember Preston? A group of men came looking for him, and we had to hide him as a clown until they had gone."

"Did they say why they were looking for him?"

"They had two stories depending on which of the men you spoke to. Some said money and another said he had got one of his sisters pregnant."

"I was told different from Mom. One of the older men told me Ryan had raped a girl."

"Three different stories, so we will never really know the truth."

"Ask Bryan, he might know. He talked the men into leaving."

The knock at the door startled Tonya; James had noticed she was very nervous at the moment. He opened the door. A tall policeman was looking up at him. The man expected to be invited in, but James had learned never to invite a member of the police force into your house unless you knew them.
"Yes?"
"Is Mrs. Morris in there?"
"Yes."
"Would you ask her to come back to the tent?"
"You mean the Big Top? I will ask her," said James, closing the door on the policeman.
Mabel stood and picked up the china teacup. James took it from her and placed it into the stainless steel sink.
"We will see you later, James, and please see what you can find out, I have a feeling someone here is going to get arrested when they had nothing to do with it."
James cleared away the tea things and sat looking out of the window. If it were someone inside the circus then only a few would have the strength to hang the guy with the butcher's hook. Most of the men were casual workers brought in only when they were starting to travel. So he could rule out any of them. Who was left were the performers and Dougie. The performers were all very strong they needed to be. Even the clowns, and some of their routines needed a lot of strength to perform.
He needed to talk to all those in the compound; he would get Tonya to let slip he was helping save the reputation of the circus by digging out the truth. This would make them spill a few beans and maybe even other secrets as well. He wanted to find out more about Dougie. Something just didn't add up with that guy.

Yes, he was doing the right thing by his brother but he was hiding a whole lot more.

Sitting by the window reminded James of when he was ten years old and sick. He had just watched an old James Stewart movie, 'Rear Window', and Jimmy Stewart was his hero. In this movie, Jimmy had broken his legs and was confined to his apartment. He was a photographer and watched his neighbor's activities. Jimmy solves a murder by watching from the window. James was so sick he couldn't go out and play so he sat by his bedroom window at the front of the house and watched his neighbors. He became convinced that Mrs. McGill across the street had murdered her husband and was planning to ship him to Australia in large wooden boxes he had seen her packing.

Everyone knew she had a sister living in Australia. His father at first thought maybe his son had stumbled on something, as Mr. McGill hadn't been seen for several weeks. It was only when his brother made fun of James and told their father that James was trying to act like Jimmy Stewart in Rear Window did his father understand the truth. His father brought Mr. McGill to see James a day later and they all laughed at him. Mr. McGill had been traveling on business and his wife wasn't packing wooden boxes, she was unpacking them as she had just received a gift from her sister. Two years later Mr. McGill was arrested and tried for the murder of his wife. Her body was never found. James had the last laugh on his brothers because he claimed he foretold the crime and his interest in solving mysteries began.

The flap of the Big Top opened and Bryan emerged, crossing to his caravan. James needed to talk to the old man, but ever since the problem with the bank and his credit cards Bryan had been reticent. A cold wind blew through the compound. Winter wasn't quite over.

Bryan seemed pleased to see James. When he opened the door, a blast of warm air rushed to meet him as he climbed up the three steps into the caravan.

"James, I was going to come and see you. Tonya told me her mother Mabel had asked you to investigate Ryan's death."

"I wish it was that simple, I know the police won't help me so it's not going to be easy."

"Would you like a cup of tea? It's loose tea, not that tea bag rubbish. I only drink Broken Orange Pekoe, the finest tea in the world."

"Sounds good to me."

"I expect you didn't think a clown could have such sophisticated tastes."

"Nothing surprises me when it comes to clowns."

"What if I told you I haven't always been a clown? I once worked for the British government at a top-secret establishment here in Malvern."

"Really? Doing what?" James remembered that Bryan had told him this once before. Funny how older people forget what they have told others yesterday but could remember things from forty years ago very clearly.

"It was top-secret. I can't tell you. If I did I would have to kill you. Sorry that was in bad taste."

"Really? What were you doing?"

"I was an apprentice electronic engineer at the Royal Radar Establishment."

"Now, that's what I call a surprise. Tell me more."

"Not a lot to tell really, except that most of my college mates are dead."

"What of?"

"Who knows? Old age maybe, although some did
seem too young when they died."

"How did you know they had died?"

"I read the obituaries every day. Sick I know, but I
wouldn't have known about them dying if I hadn't."

"Did you work on anything interesting?"

"Crystal growing. Strange really. The technology for
liquid crystal screens comes from that work. Funny to
think that what I was doing in the sixties is now part of
everyone's life."

"Pity you don't get royalties."

"Yes, could you imagine how much I would be worth
if I had?"

"What made you become a clown?"

"Loneliness. All my childhood I was alone and I just
couldn't take it anymore so I became a clown and
made people laugh and had a big extended family to
go with it."

"What about your own family."

"No idea. Left home at sixteen and never went back
and they didn't come looking for me."

"You didn't have children?"

"No, my wife didn't want any, I think she may have
been a little selfish."

They sat and drank the tea in silence, both lost in
thought. Bryan automatically replenished the teacups
with more tea.

"So, what about Ryan's murder? Any clues yet
Sherlock?"

"Funny how everyone thinks of Sherlock Holmes
when they think of murder."

"Personally, I never believed he solved those murders.
For me, Doctor Watson was much better at solving
crime than druggy Holmes."

"Bryan, I don't know. Whoever did it was leaving a message; the clothes pegs, the butcher's hook. You don't use them unless you are sending a message to someone."

"Well, I may have hated the man and would have loved to hurt him in some way. I would never have murdered him."

They didn't see the shadow cross the door window as they spoke. Someone was standing just outside the door listening.

"What was he really trying to accomplish?"

"He wanted to sell the circus so he could sell this land, it must be worth a great deal of money by now."

"That would mean you are out of a job."

"Not just that, as I have already told you I own part of this circus. Years ago, Mabel's husband was in financial trouble. I lent him some money. In return he gave me a forty percent of the circus. Only Ryan told me he had spoken to a solicitor and the paper I had saying I owned part of the circus wasn't worth anything."

The knock stopped them both; Bryan opened the door and police office Martin Dougdale entered. This was the officer Nobby had said scrawled the graffiti on the caravan. He was also the policeman who was organizing the local skinheads into a right-wing terror group.

"Sorry to bother you, gentlemen, but Inspector Bryce would like another word with Mister DeWitt."

"Again? I've told him all I know. Sorry, James, we should continue this later."

James watched as the officer took Bryan into the Big Top. How much had the officer heard? If he had been listening from the moment James arrived, then he could have heard Bryan say he wanted to hurt Ryan. He returned to his seat at the window in his caravan. The night was closing in and soon it would be difficult to see who was moving about in the compound. The Chinese performers seemed to be very active, going from one caravan to another. The one who had found the body still looked pale and worried. The others seemed to comfort him. James wondered if he should try and speak to the man. He would need an interpreter and how could he know if what the man was saying was being translated back correctly. Maybe he could call his old school friend Tsun-Chung Han to come and help? Then again did TC speak Chinese? He had been born and grew up in Birmingham. He even spoke with a Brummie accent, and never in the ten years James had known him did he speak in Chinese Mandarin or Cantonese.

A figure appeared from the main entrance, it wasn't until he was in the middle of the compound that James was able to see that it was Nobby. The skinhead stood arrogantly looking at the caravan. Once he spotted James', he marched towards it. The Chinese performers looked at him. They were intimidated by his appearance.

James didn't wait for the knock. He opened the door and Nobby entered.

"You moved I see."

"Better to be safe."

"True too many crooks around these parts."

"What can I do for you?"

"Just came to say thanks for not spilling the beans to the cops."

"No problem, what I don't know can't harm me."

"So what happening here, I had to dodge a line of police to get in here."

"I'm surprised you could."

"There is always a way."

"Someone was murdered."

"Really who?"

"Owner's boyfriend."

"What, Dougie?"

"No. Mabel's boyfriend Ryan."

"Oh, poofta Ryan from Solihull."

"You know him?"

"Mate, I know everyone around here this is my manor so I need to know who's on it. Ryan was a conman from Birmingham, did time with my uncle some years ago. "

"Interesting."

"Not really. A small timer who likes old women because they wanted only one thing and he could get at their money."

"Did you ever speak to him."

"Only once. When he first came, I told him 'hi' from my uncle and he flipped. Said if I ever told anyone he'd been in jail he'd kill me."

"So, you didn't."

"No, just kept my eye on the stupid sod."

"Did you see him with anyone?"

"Besides the circus folk?"

"Yes."

"A couple of blokes from Birmingham who I'd seen with my uncle years ago."

"Crooks."

"Not really just a couple tricky dickies."

"Crooks."

"That's such a hard word."

Nobby sat on the sofa and leaned back relaxing, he was one of those people who could be comfortable where ever they were. When standing as a skinhead he looked menacing but slouching back on the sofa he lost the threatening attitude. James was amazed at how well polished his Doc Martins were.

"You like my boots?"

"Sorry."

"You were looking at my boots, I was wondering why."

"You keep them clean."

"Have to. Sign of a clean mind."

"Sorry?"

"If you have clean clothes, look smart, and are washed, then your mind is clean too. Goes without saying really."

"You noticed me looking at them?"

"Yes, I see things."

"So what have you seen which shouldn't have been happening?"

"Look I'm only telling you because you did me a favor. I don't want it to get out I talked."

"It's only you and me and I don't tell."

"Okay, the word on the street was that poofta Ryan was going to do the big one and would be loaded and off to France in the next week or so. He had sold the circus to some wankers from Germany."

"Interesting."

"He owed those blokes from Birmingham who my uncle knew a lot of money."

"So who killed him?"

"That's the big one. It wouldn't be those blokes because they wouldn't get their money until he had done the deal."

"I would imagine they would just kill him and dump his body somewhere. This was a ritualistic type of murder."

"Really? You saw the body. What did it look like?"

"Hanging from the tightrope by a butcher's hook in his neck, and his sleeves pegged to the wire."

"Kinky."

"Not your style."

"I like everything straight, no funny stuff. I tell my birds that."

"So, you have a girlfriend?"

"Not at the moment, the last one ditched me to go to some punk festival in Poland."

"You could start up again when she returned."

"Nope, I never go back."

"Never?"

"You had trouble with Nicky and Terry."

"Sort of, I thought I had helped."

"You can't help wankers like those two. I gave them a good thrashing and told them to leave you alone."

"Why?"

"I don't like people interfering with my friends business if you get my drift."

"Thanks, friend."

Nobby gave a smile, "I've wanted to do that to them for a very long time. They are part of the MMA, Martin's Malvern Aryans."

"I realized I had wasted my time when they gave me the finger. I need to get back to the street again."

"Not really the youngsters of today have no respect. Officer Martin stopped by our house later and told me to back off. I said, if I don't what will you do? plant evidence on me? He left because our nosy neighbor Sharon Church was listening."

He suddenly stood up and opened the door. "Got to go. Thanks."

James watched as he disappeared between the caravans. Cooper and Dougie stood by the Big Top flap and watched him. From the expression on Dougie's face, he wasn't very happy at seeing Nobby inside the compound. James expected a visit from him but he turned and walked towards the house. The policeman who Nobby had said was National Front appeared from behind one of the caravans. He looked to where Nobby had exited and then followed Dougie. James could see why Nobby didn't like the man; he looked like he was a weasel from the children's book 'Wind in the Willows'. Even the way he peered about. His eyes narrowed and his nose wrinkled up as he scrutinized what he was looking at.

James smiled to himself. Funny, ever since he had befriended Bryan he had become aware of how he saw people in a different way. They were either birds or animals, mostly animals.

It wasn't something Bryan had said just the way he and the other clowns observed those around them. It must be because they were looking for characters to imitate. He returned to looking out of the window again. The compound had emptied and the overhead lights illuminate the area. He knew there would be a great many places with shadows for someone to hide and he needed to be cautious.

Mabel appeared followed by Tonya and Dougie; she stormed into the Big Top only to reappear a few seconds later as Police officer Dougdale physically escorted her out. She was obviously angry and was shouting at the policeman. James left his caravan and walked quickly to join her and Tonya. Dougie had disappeared by the time he arrived. Mabel was still arguing with the policeman who had been stationed on the other side of the Big Top flap. Tonya was looking worried and seeing James approach she gave a placating smile. James listened as Mabel berated the police officer about being the owner and not being told when she could have her circus back so they could get ready for the next season. The officer stood motionless and stared at her. James was sure he would love to have shouted back at Mabel. He knew the police officer had been given orders that he was to say nothing and just take the abuse.

Mabel stamped her foot like an angry little girl and turned towards Tonya and James. Her facial expression of gritted teeth and bulging eyes quickly softened. She had been acting out her anger and she didn't really mean all the things she had just shouted. Mabel was play-acting to get what she wanted. James knew most people would give in to her if only to stop her from continuing the rage.

"James, sorry you had to see that, but these men are being so unreasonable not telling me of all people what is happening in my circus."

"Mother they are just doing their jobs."

"Well, that may be okay with you Tonya but I need to know who killed my Ryan."

The tone in which she said 'my Ryan' was obviously meant for the policeman who was listening to what was being said. James knew she didn't care anymore what had happened to Ryan. When he told her what he had learned about Ryan, he was sure she would care even less.

"James, have you found out anything?"

"Yes but this is not the place."

Dougie reappeared. He glared at James and then stood like a naughty little boy next to Tonya.

The police beckoned Mabel over to him.

"What was that idiot, Nobby, doing here?" asked Dougie.

"Thanking me for not shopping him to the police for the graffiti. He gave me some information on Ryan in exchange. Dougie, he may be an idiot but he knows what happens out on the street. It is always good to have something on someone so you can get information."

"How do you know he told you the truth?"

"I don't, but if he lies he know I will tell the police and I don't think he wants trouble with them."

Mabel returned. She seemed a little more relaxed, "They are going to brief us in about an hour they said they will make an arrest shortly."

"Who are they going to arrest?"

"I think it is someone in the circus?" said Dougie.

"Why?" snapped Mabel

"I heard one of the coppers at the front gate saying to the press that the Inspector thinks one of us did it."

"He could be right. Ryan wasn't very popular.

"Wasn't he?"

"Mother, don't play dumb. You knew as well as everyone he was after one thing only."

"Yes, my beautiful body."

"Mother, please! Not in front of James."

"Oh, James knows I'm joking. He knows the real reason, don't you?" She slipped beside James and placed her arm around his waist.

"Nobby said Ryan had been in prison."

"I knew it," said Dougie.

James didn't pass on any of the other information he had received he still didn't trust Dougie.

"Let's meet at the house in an hour and maybe we will get some answers from the police."

James returned to his caravan, he felt the anxiety of the people around him. Sitting on the sofa he looked out of the window on to the hills beyond. They looked mysterious in the darkness. He sipped at his freshly made tea and listened to an original recording of the final part of Edward Elgar's Enigma Variation. The music seemed to somehow set the tone of his thinking. The dark hills, a murderer somewhere close by, and secrets on everyone lips.

He saw Cooper darting between the caravans until he reached James. The knock was light and had he not seen Cooper approaching he wouldn't have heard him. He opened the door and the boy looked up surprised to see James. He handed over a piece of paper and then raced off towards his and Dougie's caravan.

That boy knew more than he was letting on. He had seen things. It may not have been anything to do with the murder, but he had seen something, which might help solve it.

James read the note. It was from Dougie. In a childish handwriting, he asked if James could meet him at the mechanic's workshop as soon as possible.

James closed the music and left the caravan. He stopped a little way from it and returned and locked the door. He hadn't felt the need to before, but suddenly it was as though he had to do it.

The mechanic's workshop was on the other side of the Big Top, and James had to walk around it to get to the other side. He was tempted to see if he could find out what was going on inside, but most of the flaps had been closed, and those which hadn't had a policeman standing by them.

The small door in the mechanic's workshop large doors was open and a light spilled out on to the concrete floor. He saw the policeman by the flap entrance to the Big Top look at him as he stepped into the workshop. The place was big and seemed to have every kind of equipment you could think of. The place was empty of people and for a few seconds, James wondered if it was a trap. As he turned to leave, Dougie stepped inside. He looked pale and, for the first time, a little frightened. He closed the small metal door.

"Sorry for the drama, James, but I think the problems here are about to get worse."

"Why what have you heard?"

"From the police nothing, Fiddles just told me that Bryan had gone missing. No one knows where he is."

"He could have just gone for a walk or something."

"Unlikely. The police aren't letting any of us off the compound."

"So, what do you think happened?"

"Not sure, but I just think things are going to get worse."

"Why are you telling me?"

"I think you can help, I talked to Bryan and he said you stopped two drug dealers from being convicted of murder when they didn't do it. Most people would have let them rot."

"I just want the truth to be known."

"Easier said than done in this world."

"Dougie, what aren't you telling me?"

"I don't know what you mean."

"Sorry, but I think you do. You have a secret and you're scared it will come out. Maybe something Nobby knows which scares you."

"Shit."

"I don't break confidences, I hear. If that's what you're worried about."

"Promise, I don't care for me but Cooper needs a better chance than me."

"If it's has nothing to do with the murder then no one needs ever to know."

"Nobby knows, he keeps taunting me with it."

"I can handle that kid."

"Telling the police about the graffiti won't scare him."

"As I said, I don't tell everything." James smiled. It was a willful smile but the effect which he created served the purpose.

"I've been in jail. No one here knows, not even Tonya. I was scared, if they did, they wouldn't let me stay."

"No need for them to know. Can I ask what for?"

"Petty theft and car stealing. It was a long time ago but it is always held against you."

"Not by me. Thanks for telling me. Now, to solve our problem here. I think the police will arrest Bryan. He didn't do it but they need to arrest someone and he seems the likely candidate."

"Why?"

"In the wrong place at the wrong time. He also thought they suspected him. That is why he may have disappeared."

"I'll see if we can find him."

"I wouldn't. Not yet. And Dougie tells Tonya before the police do."

"She will dump me."

"I don't think so, from what I've seen she is very much in love with you and is waiting for you to ask her to marry you."

"You're joking!"

"I never joke about love."

The door to the workshop opened, and Police Officer Dougdale stepped inside. Dougie gave a shudder. It was obvious that he and Martin Dougdale had known each other for some time. They looked at each other and a sort of unspoken language seemed to pass between them. James had never liked the police. He grew up distrusting them. Nothing would ever change that opinion and this officer would never become a confidant.

"Cozy chat, gentlemen?"

"I was having problems with my car and Dougie said I could bring it in here and fix it. He was showing me where everything is."

"Funny how you traveling people stick together."

You're a gypsy, Pidgley. Right?"

"Mr. Pidgley to you, and I am a Romani if that's what you mean."

"But you don't travel anymore?"

"What do you want Martin?" asked Dougie.

"Nothing from you. Just wondered why you two should get together."

"As James said, he needed help with his car and I offered to show him where things where."

Martin took a piece of paper out of his pocket and handed it to Dougie.

"Hope to see back at the next meeting, Dougie. The boys have missed you."

"Not anymore. I've too much to do here to go to any boys meeting."

"Oh, you'll be back."
Martin Dugdale left leaving the door open. Dougie
looked at the paper then crunched it into a ball and
threw it into a rubbish bin.
"Go and tell Tonya before he does. I'll make sure
Nobby keeps his mouth shut."
"Look, I was a part of his crowd once but, since I've
been with the circus, I realize they were wrong."
"We all make mistakes. As long as we change that's all
that matters."
"I need to find Tonya, see you later."
Dougie left, James waited a few minutes before
retrieving the paper he had thrown in the bin. He
placed it into his pocket without looking at it. Looking
at his watch, the hour was nearly up so he switched off
the light and closed the door behind him as he left the
workshop.

The figures, which had been hiding behind the oil
drums stood up. Bryan looked scared his face drained
of color. The young Chinese acrobat who had found
Ryan's body looked at the clown. He placed a hand on
the old man's shoulder and squeezed it.

James arrived at the house and knocked on the door
Fiddles opened it. He had a worried expression on his
face, which accentuated the deep lines. He took James
into a large dining room. Most of the performers were
there. James looked around to see if Bryan had
surfaced but he hadn't. Mabel crossed the room and
gave James a friendly hug. He felt the eyes of
everyone in the room on him; Tonya and Dougie
appeared from another door. Dougie smiled and

nodded to James. He mouthed something but he was too far away for James to understand.

The Chinese acrobats had grouped in a corner. Their translator stood next to them.

"The police have summoned everyone to be here. I don't see Bryan but the other clowns are all here and they say they haven't seen him for several hours."

"Mabel, if anything has happened to Bryan we will soon find out."

"Oh I do hope so, the stress is getting to me, and I'll hit the bottle again if this continues."

"Mother, will you stop lying! You have never hit the bottle you don't even like root beer even though it's not a beer."

"Just an expression."

Tonya slipped beside James and whispered into his ear. "Thanks, Dougie just told me and it's not a problem for me."

James nodded his acknowledgment. He had become interested in the Chinese acrobats. They seemed to be a little upset about something. The translator crossed the room and approached Mabel.

"Miss Mabel, sorry to bother you at this tragic time, but we are missing Quon."

"Is that a festival?"

"No, Mother, the young acrobat who found Ryan's body."

"Oops, sorry, I will never get used to their names."

The door opened and Quon entered. He looked a little red faced, as though he had been running.

The translator said something in Chinese to him and they joined the other acrobats in the corner.

The police arrived and positioned themselves by each door. The Inspector, whom James had not met, entered. He was about forty years old, his hair already going grey, and had started to put on the extra weight. Men tend to do, as they get older. He consulted the other officers before clapping his hands to get the attention of those in the room.

"Ladies and gentlemen, if I may have your attention, please. I am Chief Inspector Bryce; I am the senior officer investigating the murder of Ryan Cleeves. We now believe we have identified the person who committed this crime and we are here now to arrest that person."

Those in the room looked at each other. For some unknown reason James began to watch Quon. He seemed very nervous and had slipped to the back of the Chinese acrobats. James had to move his position to see him more clearly.

"I cannot go into detail as to why we think the person committed the crime, and at this time I would like Bryan DeWitt to step forward."

"He is not here," said Fiddles.

"He's not? Then where is he?"

"We don't know. We haven't seen him for about three hours."

"Everyone must stay in this room! Sergeant, get your men to search the grounds and check with the front gate that no one has left."

James was still staring at Quon who had been looking at the floor while the Chief Inspector was making the announcement. When Quon looked up he made eye contact with James. Fear was in the young man's face. He knew something and was scared.

Quon quickly looked back at the floor and didn't raise his head again. James would try and talk to him. The language barrier may be a problem but that had never stopped him before trying to get to the truth.

"James you were right," said Dougie.

"Right about what?" asked Mabel.

"James said he thought the police would accuse Bryan."

"He's not guilty. Someone has set him up and I'm not sure why," said James.

"Of course he is not guilty! The man wouldn't hurt a fly. The police are just being ridiculous."

"I'm sure James will find out the truth for us," said Tonya and for the first time in several hours she gave a warm smile.

"James, please do what you can. I know Bryan didn't do it."

"Mabel, I'll do my best."

"Ladies and gentlemen, the Inspector has asked you stay here for a little longer while we investigate the disappearance of Mister DeWitt." The young officer that spoke turned and shrugged his shoulders at the two remaining officers in the room.

James was still watching Quon, who had not looked up from the floor since making eye contact. His attention was distracted as he saw Bublay and then Cooper slip out of the room while the two police officers were talking.

CHAPTER FIVE

Death of a Clown

The Chief Inspector returned. He was very annoyed and spoke to the two officers in the room. He stood in the middle of the room and clapped his hands again to get everyone attention. The man obvious unable to control his annoyance and became very snappy. The Spanish balancing act thought he was clapping to start every one dancing and took up the clapping. They started to clap and stamp their feet as though they were doing a Flamenco dance. The clowns joined in and soon half the room was dancing and clapping. The Chief Inspector went bright red with anger. James could see the funny side and began to laugh. One of the police officers took out a whistle and blew it. The dancing and clapping stopped.

"Ladies and Gentlemen you may return to your living quarters please do not leave the compound."

Several of the clowns started to goose step out until Tonya gave them a disapproving look.

"James would you like to come through for something to eat."

"Before you go, Madam, may I have a word with you." said the Chief Inspector.

"Certainly but whatever you have to say can be said in front of my family and friends."

The room had emptied and Tonya, Dougie, and James stood by Mabel. The Chief Inspector wasn't too happy to have them stay but he really couldn't stop them.

"We have searched the area for Bryan Dewitt and haven't yet detained him. If you or any member of your company know where he is they should give him up or better still get him to give himself up."

"Inspector, I think you are making a big mistake Bryan wouldn't kill anyone."

"We believe otherwise, Madam."

"What evidence do you have?"

"At this stage, I'm sorry, I can't divulge that."

"Well, I think you're wrong."

The Chief Inspector ignored her comment and left the room. They all slowly went to the kitchen. The group was silent as they sat at the table drinking tea and consuming the chocolate biscuits. James knew they expected him to solve this case and he had several leads but it was going to take time. He wanted to speak to Quon but he would have to find the right time.

Cooper appeared and spoke to Dougie. The boy seemed very agitated about something.

"Cooper just told me Bryan received a call here in the office and then left the compound afterward."

"I remember that I was crossing the hall when I heard him on the phone. I couldn't hear what he was saying but from the tone, he seemed very upset." Said Tonya.

"Cooper do you know what time it was."

The boy spoke but so quietly no one could hear what he was saying.

"Hey sweetie, you need to speak up some of us old ones are getting a little deaf," said Mabel.

Cooper spoke again and this time most of them heard him give the time.

"Yes, that was about the time I heard him on the phone, I didn't look at my watch but I was sure it must be around that time."

"Okay, we have established a time when Bryan was last seen or at least heard. I wonder who the call was from."

"I can check caller ID if you like," said Dougie.

"Oh yes, I forgot we had that installed. Well, it may have paid to have the service."

Dougie returned. "It's the pay phone across the street. I just called the number and one of the reporters answered. They've been told by the police Bryan has been arrested for the murder of Ryan."

"They must have found him. Do you think I should call old Harris the solicitor?"

Tonya nodded her head and then rested it on Dougie's shoulder. She seemed very despondent.

"It's killed our news."

"What news love?"

"Mom, Dougie asked me to marry him and I've said yes."

"Finally, it took you long enough Dougie I have been waiting for you to ask her for several months. Congratulations."

Cooper looked worried and then ran from the room. Dougie stood to go after him but Tonya stopped him.

"Let me go he may need an outsider to explain what it will mean," said James.

"Good idea he likes you, says you're a cool man.
James tells him nothing changes except now he got a
sister in law to look after him as well."

James left and ran out into the compound. He saw
Cooper run around the Big Top. James followed; a
policeman on duty outside the entrance to the big top
looked at him as he half walked and half ran to catch
up the youngster. The door to the workshop closed as
he came around the end of the Big Top. The workshop
was in darkness and James automatically switched on
the light. The boy wasn't visible and so he pulled the
old office swivel chair over to the door and sat down
on it. He wasn't going to let this young man escape
without talking to him first.

"Cooper, its James can we talk? I need your help."
There was no answer and James peered into the dark
shadows from where he was sitting in the workshop.
There were so many places a boy Cooper's size could
hide.

"Cooper, about your brother and Tonya, nothing
changes. Well, that's not completely true. I should
know. When my older brother Peter married... I was so
cut up about it. I hated him for weeks when he
announced he and Rose were to marry. He was my
best friend, the only one that didn't make fun of me."
James heard a noise some were deep inside the
workshop. He continued his story.

"I didn't want to go to the wedding, then my oldest
brother, Donald, told me I was being selfish and if the
I thought it through I wasn't losing Peter I was gaining
Rose as my friend. At first, I didn't believe him. Then,
when the wedding came, and Peter and Rose got
married, I found I saw more of them than I did before."

Cooper slowly appeared from behind the oil drums and stood looking at James. He had tears running down his face.

"Besides, you will be living with Dougie and Tonya. Peter and Rose moved a few streets away. Don't you like Tonya?"

The boy walked up to James and sat on his knee. He put his head on his shoulder and sobbed.

"It's okay I understand."

In a whisper only just audible Cooper spoke. "How many brothers and sisters do you have?"

"Four brothers and five sisters."

"Wow, your dad was busy."

"It's nice having a big family."

"Do you think they will want me?"

"Who Tonya and Dougie?"

Cooper nodded his head.

"They need you. Without you, Dougie would be lost and you know that."

Cooper sat and thought about it. He sat up and then shuddered.

"I have a secret."

"Me too. What's yours?"

"It's a secret. I can't tell you."

"Okay."

"I saw something."

"What was it to do with Ryan's murder?"

"No, Bryan and one of the Chinese acrobats were friends."

"Do you know which one?"

"Yes."

"Quon."

"Yes."

"How do you know?"

"I saw them in here when you and Dougie were talking I was hiding up there."
 He pointed to the rafters. Several planks of wood had been placed across the metal beams.
"Is that your tree house?"
"You know?"
"When I was your age I had a tree house in the basement."
"In the basement?"
"Yes, you see we didn't have a tree and the attic was a bedroom."
"Funny."
"So what else did you see?"
Cooper sat silently thinking. James could see the boy was working out if he should say something.
"After you and Dougie left Bryan gave Quon something, I couldn't see what it was."
"Did they speak to each other?"
"They were whispering, but Bryan was giving the acrobat some instructions."
"In English or Chinese?"
"English. The Chinese make out they don't speak English but they all do. I know. I have heard them imitating Tonya."
"Cooper, if you hear anything else tell me."
"I know Bryan didn't kill Ryan. He was always good to me."
"How do you get up to your tree house?"
Cooper pointed to the oil drums and a flat roof of the office. He then used a drainpipe to climb the last little bit. The boy was obviously a good acrobat himself.
"Let's go before they send out the search parties looking for us."

James closed the light and shut the door. He waited a few minutes then opened the door again and switched on the light. There was no one inside.

Cooper laughed he realized what James was doing; it was then the boy slip a little piece of wood at the bottom of the door. It was James turn to smile if the wood was moved he knew someone had either been into the workshop or was still inside.

James stood by the window in his caravan, he wasn't sure what he should do. The police had made it clear they wanted everyone to go back to their caravans and wait. He had left his mobile phone in the caravan when he went to the meeting, it buzzed he had several missed calls and one message. His mother was watching the news on television and had seen about the murder she wanted to know if James was okay.

He sat looking out of the window, this had become his new pastime and it was beginning to wear thin on him. He needs action, to do something, ask questions not to sit and wait.

If they had knocked on the door he didn't hear it, the clowns trouped inside and stood bunched together looking at him.

"What's this a clown attack?"

"James we need to talk to someone and we thought as you are not part of the circus you'd listen." Said Fiddles who had been pushed to the front by the other clowns.

"And we heard you were investigating Ryan death for Mabel," said Antonioni.

"Please find a seat and tell me what's the problem."

"Bryan didn't murder Ryan."

"I know that but why do you say that?

"Because he couldn't hurt anyone."

"The police think he did it."

"We know but we don't know where he is and wondered if you were hiding him."

"Me? Why would I hide him?"

Professor Brick leaned forward in his seat. He was not used to talking in public. Even in this small gathering he found it difficult to make a comment, but he knew he must. It had been his idea to come and see James. "Bryan told us how kind you had been to him, lending him money even though you didn't know him."

"Bryan, or Brinarno as I knew him, had given millions of children and adults laughter. It's a small price to pay to help him out when someone has cruelly tried to destroy him."

Peering around Professor Brick, a small man whose face looked as though he had never taken his make-up off spoke. "He has gone missing and we are worried. Bryan always tells us where he is going," said Bolt.

"Does he have any friends other than you clowns?"

Fiddles looked at the others who all shook their heads.

"Did he befriend any of the other performers?" asked James.

"He spoke to them. We all do, except the Chinese. They don't speak any English."

"They do. I've heard them. Bryan joked they were spies and could speak English very well. But I never heard them, " replied Antonioni.

"Me, neither." said Cuckoo.

"Did he have any visitors other than circus people?" This sent the clowns into a frenzy of looking at each other. From the way they behaved James understood they were trying to work out who should speak. It was Fiddles, who coughed before speaking.

"Several people came to see him in the last few weeks including some old girlfriend from his college days. You know he went to college here in Malvern for the government?"

"Any idea of the names of these people?"

"No, his past was off limits. He said it was to do with Official Secrets Act but I think it was more to do with the fact he didn't have a good experience in those days and didn't want to be reminded of it."

"James, can you help?"

"I'll do my best. First we need to find him."

It was as though he had said good-bye. They stood up and left. He felt their behavior was a little strange. Then again if they only really had each other they would become like a family and behave in that way. He suddenly felt like sneezing and searched his pocket for a handkerchief. He pulled the crumpled paper Dougie had thrown away and then found a paper tissue. He opened the paper. It was for a meeting, 'to discuss how they, the rightful people of Britain, could remove the unwanted scum — the gypsies and new age travelers. The 1994 Criminal Justice Act no longer seemed to be working and the people of Britain needed to fight, to cleanse the country of vermin'.

James had seen this kind of hate literature many times before. It never failed to amaze him how some people could not live and let live. If what Nobby had said was true, then Martin Dougdale was recruiting from the lost youth of Malvern to join up and cause trouble. He wondered if his superiors knew of Martin's involvement in the Far Right. He folded the paper and placed it in a drawer. He would call a few of the so-called New Age travelers and let them know of the upcoming meeting.

Silence descended on the compound and James nodded off on the sofa. He woke with a start. Something had jolted him awake. He looked outside. It was still dark, and his watch read 3:30. He undressed and climbed into the bed. The sheets were cold and it took several minutes for his body to warm up. His mind was awake. Something someone had said, or he had seen was playing on his mind. He began to replay the events of the day. Martin and Nobby kept reappearing in his mind. There was something they had said, or done, which seemed important but he couldn't remember. Finally, he slipped into a deep sleep.

It was 9:35 when he opened his eyes and looked around. The caravan's door was open. A wind blew gently, making the curtains move. He had locked the door! He had been careful to make sure it was locked. He checked to see if anything was missing. Several of the drawers had been opened and not closed properly. The drawer with the Anti-Traveler leaflet was open by an inch or so. He was surprised to see the leaflet still in the drawer. Whoever had searched the caravan had not found what they were looking for. He would change the lock on the door today and set up some sort of device, which would make a sound if someone entered while he was sleeping.
He showered and ate breakfast. He must have been very tired to sleep so long. The noise of the building site grew louder. He must check to see if there were any problems. Hopefully, the police would allow him to leave the compound.

He stood on the inside of the compound gate and looked out at the Media camped on the roadside. Maybe the Criminal Justice Act should have included a part about Media intrusion into people's lives.
He returned to the caravans and found the place Cooper had first appeared from. Looking out, he could see several of the journalists talking to Arthur. If James stepped through they would know he wasn't another worker. He needed to change his clothes. Next to the workshop was another building with 'Costumes and Props' was written on the door. He tried the door and found it unlocked. Inside, two old ladies sat at sewing machines. They looked up at him. He asked if they had any old workman's clothing. They both shook their heads. Then, a lady who reminded him of his mother, appeared from behind a rack of costumes. She said he should look in the workshop as they always had old overalls for the tentmen in there.
He quickly found a very dirty pair of overalls and some Wellington boots. He raced back to his caravan and changed into them. Stepping onto the building site, he was surprised that no one questioned him. Arthur was in the site office, which had been moved off the common, close to the hole in the fence he had just climbed through.
"I was wondering if I was going to see you today. The journalists say the police have locked down the circus compound."
"They have, but I needed to check you had no problems."
"No, touch wood. All is going to plan."
"Good. If you have a problem, call me on my mobile."
"So, what happenings in there?"

"They are looking for one of the clowns. They think he murdered Mabel's boyfriend."

"Did he?"

"Don't know, but he didn't seem the type."

"Oh, by the way, your skinhead friend, Nobby, came by. Told me to tell him if anyone gives us aggro. Looks like you've got a protector."

"I did him a little favor. He is just paying me back."

"Always best to have the local thugs on your side."

"You sound like my dad, Arthur."

"Good bloke your dad. Looks like we have a delivery. See you later, James."

A large flatbed lorry had arrived with a load of London Red bricks. Several of the men started to unload them. James stood and watched the men work. He had always been fascinated by how they seemed to know what to do without being told.

He climbed back into the compound and checked that no one had followed him. The worst thing that could happen was a journalist finding there was way into the compound. He crossed the compound and behind the Big Top. He wanted to peek inside but he knew the police would still be there. In the area in front of the workshop and costume store, the Chinese acrobats were practicing a tumbling routine. He watched, and realized that Quon wasn't with them.

He spoke to the acrobat nearest to him, who pointed to the man who was their official translator.

"Good morning, is Quon around?"

"No, he is not well today. Is resting, sorry."

James stood watching them for a short time. The circus had several cats, which roamed around the compound. He knew that Fiddles fed them, but they seemed to avoid human contact. At least he hadn't seen any mice or rats around. A silver-colored fat long-furred cat ran in front of the workshop and costume store, disappearing down a small alleyway between the two buildings. James suspiciously peered down the alleyway. It was narrow and would be a tight fit to go down it but he slipped into the alleyway and followed the cat. Alice in Wonderland came into his mind. Was the cat his White Rabbit? He didn't know why he followed it. Something just compelled him to.

At the other end of the building was an area, which opened out and was just a storage space for old equipment. A tangle of metal, which was some sort of climbing apparatus, was rusting away behind what would be the mechanic's workshop. The cat had stopped and was about to pounce on something. James couldn't see what but began to climb through the maze of twisted metal. As he grew closer, he saw the foot then the leg. Someone was lying down. The cat pounced and a very large rat raced past James followed by the cat. He knew before he arrived at the body he had found Bryan. His left hand had several bites taken out of it presumably by the rat but that was the only sign of trauma. He checked to see if the body was cold and if rigor mortis had set in. It had, so the body had been there at least ten hours. More likely longer. He knew this because of his sister's boyfriend Trevor, an amateur filmmaker who'd studied the effects of dead bodies for his horror films.

He looked around. This was going to be his only chance before the police taped off the area. On the floor, the other side from the way he had entered, there were heel marks — as though Bryan had been dragged into this place. At the far end was a large metal solid gate. It looked like it hadn't been opened for some time. There was a rolling steel door on the back of the mechanic's workshop. It had been opened recently from the way the debris had been left. Whoever had opened it would have had a struggle. The door couldn't have been opened for a very long time indeed. Several weeds, which had grown in the concrete, had been disturbed. He wondered if he should check his pockets but decided not to. He needed to get back and tell the police as quickly as possible. He stopped at the end of the alleyway and checked to see who was in the area beside the Chinese acrobats. He slid back into the area and stood for a few moments looking at the people who had gathered. Several of the clowns had arrived along with the trapeze act. He crossed to the Big Top and pushed open the flap. An arm stopped him from going any further.

"I need to see the Chief Inspector."

"Why?"

"Because I have found a body." He said it in a rhythmical way out of annoyance to the way the policeman had asked him why.

The policeman spoke into his communicator and another officer appeared from the circus ring area. James was taken into the ring. Several tables had been erected around the ring but where Ryan's body had been was still taped off.

The Chief Inspector didn't look up at him but spoke in a tired 'what's this now?' tone.

"So, you found a body."

"Yes."

"Whose and where?"

"Bryan DeWitt and it's behind the mechanic workshop in an old metal equipment storage area."

"Okay, thank you. We'll take a look."

James was surprised at the lack of interest the Inspector had shown. He stood outside by the alleyway and watched as the police, after another two hours, finally sent someone down the alley to check out his claim. The young policeman flew out of the alleyway and ran at full speed into the Big Top, missing several of the Chinese acrobats who were still rehearsing a routine. The Chief Inspector came through the flap first and had difficulty squeezing down the narrow alleyway. If they had asked James, he would have suggested they use the workshop access. But they had ignored him, so he ignored them.

According to James's watch, it took seven minutes for a contingency of police officers to arrive and order everyone back to their caravans. James slipped into the house and found Mabel, Tonya and Dougie in the living room. Mabel was the first to see he had bad news. Her reaction was a groan of despair, which made the others looked at James.

"I've just found Bryan. Sorry, but he is dead."

"Oh God, no! Poor Bryan."

"Murdered?" asked Dougie.

"To me, it looks like it, but I couldn't see any signs of violence."

"We better tell the clowns before those fools the police do."

"I'll go Mom, you stay here."

"I'll come with you," said Dougie.

"James, what's going on?"

"Not sure."

"Where was the body?"

"Behind the mechanic's workshop."

"We haven't used that area for years! Full of old equipment we used to perform with, all metal and twisted in a funny way. It was a good act though."
They sat in silence, Mabel looked tired. James thought she was obviously worried about what this would do for the next season's bookings.
Dougie returned. He had Cooper with him. The boy smiled at James then stood next to Dougie head bowed.
"Tonya is with the clowns. She is staying with them. I think they had prepared themselves for the worst. The police have said they would like to see everyone in the Big Top at five today. In the meantime, we are supposed to stay in our caravans."
"James, please find out what the hell is going on."
"Mabel, I can tell you this. Both these murders had nothing to do with the circus. Despite what the police say."
James left and returned to his caravan. Something about the door being open that morning was bothering him. Maybe who had entered wasn't looking for something, but was planting something instead.
After checking the obvious places, he slowly checked each cupboard and places someone could plant something. He was about to give up when he opened a very small cupboard above the sink in the kitchen. Behind the bottles of sauces his mother had left, was a small wooden box. He grabbed the tea towel and took it out. Inside were a syringe and a little vial of liquid. The tip of the needle still had blood on it. James wrapped the box and, opening the door, was surprised to see Peter Kipler about to knock. James grabbed his bag of rubbish and, going down the steps, said, "Peter go inside. I'm just throwing out the rubbish."

He walked quickly across the compound to the garbage bins and dropped the rubbish into one, which was empty. He leaned over into the bin and placed the wooden box inside a paper rubbish bag. He pushed this bin to the back behind the others and hoped that no one found the box before he had a chance to recover it later.

Peter sat on the sofa when he returned and had obviously been watching him.

"We should really recycle more in this country. All the bins are clearly marked and people still put the wrong rubbish in the wrong bin."

"I just thought I would come and see how you're coping with all these problems here."

"If I'd known I would be involved in a murder case I would have stayed on the common and put up with the locals complaining."

"Pretty bad luck that, but the house building seems to be going on okay."

"Oh good, I can't get out to check."

"It won't be forever."

"The other officers say you found the body?"

"I was following one of the cats. It looked like it was injured.-Found the body and left the area as soon as I saw it was Bryan."

"Well, the Chief Inspector thinks it a closed case now, Bryan killed Ryan and then took his own life."

"Why would he think that?"

"Martin Dougdale heard Bryan and you talking. Bryan confessing to murdering him."

"He didn't confess he said he hated the man but would never kill him."

"That's not what Martin told the Chief Inspector."

"Then maybe I should correct the Chief Inspector's thinking."

"Good luck. The man is known as 'The Steelhead', not because he is from Sheffield but because he never changes his opinion when he has decided on something. Even when he is in the wrong and it's proven he is wrong. Totally stubborn."

"Thanks for letting me know. I shall have to correct him before it's set in stone."

"Good luck."

"Any more problems with those skinheads/"

"No, they are all mouth, except maybe one group who have formed a right wing hate group."

"Ah, the Malvern Nazis. Several years ago we had a problem with them but they seemed to have disappeared. I didn't know they were back."

"Officer Dougdale seems to know all about them."

"You noticed he's a little to the right in his politics?"

"I wouldn't say 'a little' I'd say bang in the middle of them."

"He is a good officer. Maybe a little misguided but honest."

"I can't say. Only he wants to bring back the Death Heads."

The communicator on his shoulder squawked. Peter spoke into it and then stood up.

"Got to go. We are going to do a search of the place and everyone must go to the big tent."

"Top. 'Big Top' not a tent."

"Right. I keep forgetting that."

"Is that an order?"

"Sorry, James, yes. So, if you'd go over I'll close your door until the search team arrives."

James left and watched as Peter went to the other
caravans and told the occupants to go over to the Big
Top.

As he passed the garbage bins he looked to see if the
rubbish bin he had pushed to the back had been
moved. It seemed to still be in the same place. He
hoped he could rescue the box before anyone found it.
The rest of the circus people had arrived and were
sitting in the seats around the side of the ring. He
looked over to the Chinese acrobats. He couldn't see
Quon. He tried to count them but they were standing
up and then sitting down and moving around.

The clowns had gathered together at the top of the
stand and sat looking down on everyone else. They
had a look of being sad and broken. James wondered if
he should go and speak to them but changed his mind
this wasn't the right time. They would need friends
later once the Chief Inspector proclaimed his verdict.

The side flap opened and an officer escorted Quon into
the ring. The man who acted as an interpreter rushed
forward and took Quon over to the other Chinese
acrobats.

James watched, contemplating whether he should say
something when the announcement was made, or solve
the murder and show the Chief Inspector for the fool
he was.

Quon caught James eye by standing up and down and
moving his head from side to side. He wanted to speak
to James, but the other acrobats seemed to be stopping
him. Using sign gestures, James tried to indicate they
should meet later. Quon at first didn't respond because
the interpreter was looking at Quon. Once the man's
attention was distracted he gave a nod of his head to
James.

Mabel arrived. She had changed into a black dress and had been crying. To lose two people in one week must hit someone hard, even if she was going to dump one of them.

The remaining performers arrived with Dougie and Cooper. They sat with Mabel until Cooper saw James. He moved up to join James and just sat down next to him. Dougie turned and looked where Cooper had gone. He smiled when he saw him sitting next to James and then waved to them both. The ring curtain opened and several police officers entered and stood in a line as though they were expecting trouble.

Chief Inspector Bryce entered. He didn't look at the gathered crowd. He stood with his back to them talking to one of the other officers.

He turned and looked at them, his face was set and James wondered if his jaw would break if he spoke.

"I hope you can all hear me. At this moment I have obtained a search warrant for each of your residences and a group of police officer are searching the caravans. As I am sure you already know, Bryan DeWitt was found dead earlier. We now believe he murdered Ryan Cleeves and then took his own life out of guilt."

"Rubbish!" shouted the clowns in unison.

"I know you may be upset, but that is what we think happened."

Mabel stood and asked, "What brought you to that conclusion."

"One of the officers heard him confess to it."

"Never!" shouted the clowns.

"Sorry, but he was talking to someone here when he confessed."

James stood up the Inspector looking at him his eyes narrowed.

"He was talking to me. He didn't, and I mean *didn't* confess to murdering Ryan. He said he hated the man but would never kill anyone. I suggest you check out Officer Dougdale's motive for saying he confessed to the murder."

"His motive, what do you mean?"

"I thought the police had removed Right-Wing thugs out of the force," said Tonya.

James was surprised at her comment but she was right. The Chief Inspector looked uncomfortable and quickly said, "That is the thinking of the police and is what the press will be told in a moment. Bryan DeWitt murdered Ryan Cleeves, then took his own life."

"Lies, lies and more lies!" shouted the clowns who had now stood up and looked as though they were going to charge at the Chief Inspector.

The Chief Inspector left and the officers who had entered the Big Top stood firm. They stopped one of the Chinese acrobats from leaving. He reluctantly returned to the other acrobats.

The Circus performers sat for over an hour before they were allowed to leave. James checked to see if the garbage bin had been moved as he made his way back to his caravan. The bins had been turned over and the garbage lay on the floor. He went back to his caravan every cupboard and drawer was open most of the contents pulled out. He sat on the sofa he hated being searched by anyone. This was a violation and he felt dirty. He would have to clean everything.

The paper Martin Dougdale had given Dougie had been removed.

James collected his clothing and went over to the costume store, Tonya had told him, when he moved into the compound, to use the company laundry facilities. He loaded the machines and started to wash his clothes.

He returned to his caravan and began to replace the items into the cupboards and drawers. It was then he saw the wooden box sitting on the sofa. It wasn't there when he'd left for the laundry. A small piece of paper had been placed under the box.

It read 'Keep safe.'

CHAPTER SIX

Cooper's Surprise

Cooper watched as James left the caravan and returned to the laundry. He slipped into the caravan unnoticed and looked for a place to hide the picture he had taken from Ryan's pocket. He opened and closed several drawers, looking for the right one, determined to find a hiding place that only James, and not someone else, would discover. In the bedroom he opened the underwear drawer. It was almost empty and was one of the most obvious places someone would look. Maybe he could hide it inside the bed; then again what if someone searching took the bed apart, they would see it.

It was then he realized the best place to hide something to be found only by the person it was intended for it was in that person's pillow. He picked up the white pillow off the bed and looked inside the cover. If he placed it inside, it could just fall out. The main pillow was encased in an anti-sweat cover, which had a zip running along one end. He opened the zip and slid the picture inside. He zipped it up and replaced it on the bed as it was before. Looking out of the small window he could see James talking to Tonya. The noise of someone opening the door and entering the caravan made him stop. He opened the window on the other side and climbed out, catching the window before it banged shut. He crept along the fence and in between the caravans. He crouched down looking at the door to James caravan.

The man left James's caravan after about five minutes. Cooper didn't really know how long it had been. He had lost his watch earlier that month and hadn't been able to tell Dougie about it. He had never seen the man before and was surprised when he darted between the caravans and climbed through the hole in the fence. The man was dressed in black and wore a ski mask over his face. Only his eyes were visible. Cooper thought he had seen those eyes before. Cooper followed and watched as the man crossed the building site and then drove off in a dull gold colored BMV.

CHAPTER SEVEN

Quon

James had asked Tonya if she had seen Quon. To
her, they all looked alike and she wasn't sure which
one he was and therefore couldn't say if she had seen
him. He had knocked on Quon's caravan door but no
one answered. He wandered around looking to see if
they were rehearsing but the place seems deserted. The
police had released the Big Top after completing their
investigation. He entered the Big Top. This too was
empty. James couldn't believe that the Chief Inspector
was so blind. Then he remembered the police
Inspector he had dealt with in Birmingham a year
earlier who had turned out to be stubborn and
prejudiced.

Sitting on a ringside seat he lowered his head and
rested it on his hands. He didn't hear the soft footfalls
of Doctor Liko Song, the Chinese interpreter, as he
approached.

"Why you look for Quon?"

James looked up startled and took a few seconds to get
his thoughts together.

"Sorry, I just wanted to speak to him."

"Why you know him?"

"We spoke a little by signing to each other."

"No, understand."

"Your English isn't very good for an interpreter, is it?"

"I speak good English! I learned in Japan."

"You learned to speak English in Japan? Why?"

"Good English schools in Japan."

"If you say so. Where do I find Quon?"

"He is sleeping. Not well since finding the body."

"In his caravan?"

"No, he with other boys, no disturb. Soon he rehearses. No time to see you, or speak to you."

"Are you his guard?"

"No guard. We do not watch Chinese citizens all the time in foreign countries."

One of the acrobats entered the tent and spoke to the interpreter. Whatever the young man said, Doctor Song was very upset.

"You no see Quon now he has gone for a walkabout."

"Why are you hiding him from me?"

"We no hide him, he went walking."

"You've lost him."

"Maybe, he not with other boys when he should be."

"I want to help, Doctor Song. That boy saw a dead man. It must have upset him. He needs to talk about it, so it doesn't haunt his dreams."

"Is that why you want to see him?"

James noted the phony Chinese accent had gone and Doctor Song spoke with a solid English tongue.

"Not a very good act, Doctor. I take it you are a doctor?"

"Yes, I am. The boys need to be protected from being exploited I play games with those who try to mess with the boys."

"Especially Quon — because of the murder?"

"We were going to hide him from everyone so he didn't get involved. We don't want him to have problems with the murderer."

"That I understand, but you know I have been asked to find out who really murdered Ryan and maybe Bryan."

"Yes, but we trust no one until we find out more about them and you are new here."

"Can I see Quon?"

"Maybe. If we can find him. He seems to have gone for a walk by himself which, as you can gather, we try to discourage."

"Please, if you see him let him know I am only trying to help."

"Mister James, if you only want to help then I will see what I can do."

"Thank you."

Doctor Song left and James sat pondering the doctor's performance. It was like listening to a very bad nineteen-fifties 'B' movie where the white actor was trying to be Chinese.

If they wanted to hide Quon maybe he had said something about what he saw when he entered the tent and found the body. He could have seen the murderer, which would put the boy in danger. And why was he talking to Bryan if what Cooper has said is true?

The tent flap opened, and Peter Kipler entered. He was carrying a large envelope. He seemed to be searching for something when he spotted James sitting in the front row.

"Not sure when the next show starts."

"I was just relaxing. This business has been stressful and now I have to get back to building those houses next door."

"Well I hope it's over, the Chief Inspector's convinced that Bryan did it then committed suicide."

"The man's a fool," said James under his breath. He wasn't sure if Peter heard him.

"Some of us think it may not have been suicide."

"Why what have you found out?"

"It not what we found out, it's what we didn't find."

"No suicide note?"

"For one, when Ryan was murdered Bryan DeWitt was at the bank. It seems he spent a lot of time there this last week."

"His identity was stolen and his money taken."

Peter Kipler sat down next to James and placed the envelope on the seat next to him.

"In this town, circus folk are regarded as travelers, and you know how they are treated."

"What are you getting at?"

"I think Bryan may have upset some people here. I heard he had been seeing a girlfriend from the past who hated him so much she threatened to kill him once."

"I met her. She certainly isn't the nicest person in the world."

A policeman peered into the tent and saw Peter. He motioned for him to leave.

"I think I have to go, see you later, James."

"Later Peter, and if you can tell me more I would be interested."

Peter Kipler left the tent. James had never trusted the police and he wasn't going to start now. Peter was up to something and James was going to be on his guard. Why would the police tell him anything? He wasn't even part of the circus.

He stood to leave and saw the envelope still on the seat. He picked up and instinctively opened it. Inside were the preliminary post-mortem results and a typed report on the death of Bryan DeWitt. It was a note at the bottom of the report, which caught James attention. A copy of the report was being sent to the Ministry of Defense. Why would the police send a copy of this report to the government? He sat down and read the papers; Bryan had died of a severe blow to the back of the head. No other signs of cause of death could be found. The report said he either fell and hit the metal equipment he was found under, or something hit him on the head. The way the words were used had been very carefully selected so it could be reported as accidental death rather than murder. One comment in the report was the mention of the drag marks, which James had seen when he found the body. They were waiting on a toxicology report. For James, it was conclusive Bryan had been murdered and for some reason, the police were trying to cover it up.

The tent flap opened and he quickly put the papers back into the envelope. Dougie, accompanied by Cooper, entered. They seemed very serious and crossed the ring to James.

"We were looking for you."

"Problem?"

"Not sure. Cooper had just told me he saw a man entered your caravan and then leave via the hole in the fence and get into a gold-colored BMW."

"What did he look like Cooper?" asked James.

In his soft whispered voice Cooper described the man he had seen. Neither James nor Dougie had seen the man before.

"Thanks, Cooper for keeping a watch. Someone broke
in earlier, but nothing seemed to be taken."
"The woman who hit you on the head got out of a
gold-colored BMW."
"True. I wonder who they are?"
"I saw one of the policemen enter your caravan, this
was long after the search had been done."
"Which one?"
"Sorry didn't see his face and in uniform, one copper
looks like and another."
"Thanks, now all I have to do is find Quon."
"The Chinese acrobat?"
"The very same."
"I'll find him," said Cooper, in a volume, which
surprised both James and Dougie.
Dougie and Cooper left, and James strolled back to his
caravan. He knew for certain that Bryan had been
murdered. By whom and why he would find out.

Ever since he was a little boy and his brother had
played jokes on him, James had regarded his bed as a
sanctuary and if anything was touched, he would know
instantly. It had saved him from many a trick, which
always made his brother annoyed that they couldn't get
him. This was why they always said he had a sixth
sense.
He looked at his bed. Something wasn't right.
Someone had touched it since he had made the bed.
He checked under the sheets and under the bed in the
drawers built into the base. He remade the bed and
placed the pillows back as he liked them. He sat on
the edge of the bed holding a pillow in his arms and
squeezed it. He thought about Bryan and how as a
child the man had made him laugh so much. The first

time he went to the circus he didn't want any ice cream in the interval just in case he missed something. Why would someone kill him? And then, there was the thing with his credit. Were they connected? He fluffed the pillow and felt something inside. He carefully felt the item. It was flat as a piece of paper. He opened the pillow but couldn't see anything. He felt again, and realized it was inside the pillows protective cover.

He took out the picture and was surprised when he looked at it. It was a picture of twelve men. Six in the front row sitting and then six men standing behind. On the back in two lines was a list of names. Bryan Dewitt was in the back row second from the left. Some of the faces on the front of the picture had been crossed out. James put a little tiny cross on the back above the names of those who had crosses on the faces. He cleared off the marks so he could see the faces.

He left the caravan and climbed through the hole in the fence. He made several photocopies the site office and then locked the picture inside the safe. He returned to the caravan and sat in the window seat looking out onto the compound. He needed to talk to Quon. He was sure the acrobat knew something or at least had an insight into what Bryan was all about.

Fiddle and Tonya crossed the compound and approached his caravan. They looked depressed and dejected.

James opened the door and let them enter. The smell of Tonya's perfume was light but refreshing. Fiddles was depressed, and looked at the floor.

"Problem?"

"Not really. We would like to ask you for a favor."

"Sure, if I can help."

"The police have released Bryan's caravan, and the other clowns don't feel comfortable going through his things. We were wondering if you would."

"If that's what you would like I would be pleased to oblige."

"It's not that we don't want to, but Brinarno was such a special clown. If there is anything which would shatter our opinion of him it would be better we didn't know," said Fiddles.

"I understand."

"I'll go and tell the boys," said Fiddles leaving before he had actually finished speaking.

"Thanks, James. They are all very upset and asked if I would ask you. Bryan had told them you were someone they could trust."

"He didn't commit suicide, although the police will record it as that. He was murdered."

"Are you sure?"

"Positive, and I intend to find out who did it and why."

"Thanks. Here are the keys to his caravan. There is a special lock that was put on by the clowns and they told me they are watching to make sure no one breaks in until you have gone through his things."

"What do you want me to do with his belongings?"

"After you have searched to see if there is anything which should be removed, we can box up the stuff."

"Did he have any relatives?"

"Don't know. He never talked about his family. I don't know if he had a brother or sister even. Look for his will. He was supposed to have made a new one."

"I might as well get started."

"Whatever you find, if you think it will hurt the man's image please destroy it, unless it has something to do with how he died."

Tonya walked with James over to Bryan's caravan. Several of the clowns stood looking at them. They came to shake James's hand and thanked him. His own emotions began to rise. He remembered as a little boy his own father having to clean out his parents' house after they had died. He found out family secrets, which made his father go into a depression for several months. Opening the door to Bryan's caravan he entered, closing it behind him. If he did find something, which would destroy the man's reputation he was going to keep it a secret. Last time he had seen inside was when Bryan had been beaten. The place had been a mess from someone ransacking it. Today it was very neat and clean. He started in the bedroom area and went through all the drawers and cupboards. He found nothing and, as an expert in having hiding places, he checked every possible place he could. In the living part, he found several boxes full of photographs. James took them out. He would take them to his caravan and go through them. Maybe it would shed some light on this dark time. Bryan had been a methodical man everything had a place and everything was in its place. After an hour of searching and finding nothing, James was convinced he had missed something. Bryan had hidden something somewhere and it wasn't in the usual hiding places most people pick. He placed the boxes with the pictures by the door and sat at the table. Bryan was a man who would make his hiding place in front of you, and you would never in a thousand years think of it. If he was going to hide something and have it staring you in the eye without you seeing it, he would pick an everyday object. Nothing seemed to fit what he was looking for. He rested his elbows on the table and held

his head in his hands. His eyes focused on the table, it
was beautifully made of inlaid wood. It was then he
realized he had seen this table before. His Uncle Cyril
had one and it was a trick table. When his uncle had
his card school, and the police raided the place, at a
press of a button the table opened, and you could hide
things inside. James knew you had to find two places
to press at the same time to open the drawer. The
maker was clever he always gave a clue what to look
for. He scanned the top until he found one then the
other little dot in the pattern. He pressed and nothing
happened. He laughed it was good no one was
watching or he would be seen as a fool. He tried again
and still, nothing happened. Checking the pattern
again he suddenly saw that the little dots were
everywhere. He checked again and found a little
triangle shape and then another. He pressed and the
drawer opened. He smiled he wondered how many
people would have known about the table. Not many,
he guessed. His uncle said the man who had made
them had only made ten tables and most of them had
gone to America. The drawer contained two folders
and a notebook. The first folder contained information
about his will and who kept it. Next was a list of
people who should be informed of his death. This list
had recently been updated, as James was one of the
people on the list. The notebook had tiny writing
inside with a number of drawings. To James, it looked
very old and seemed to be some sort of electronic
device. He placed them in a box of pictures and was
just going to close the drawer when he stuck his hand
inside and felt on the roof of the drawer. He pulled the
envelope out and was surprised to see his name and
that of Tonya's written in pencil. Opening it, he read

the letter. It explained that if they read this then he had
been murdered. He had come to realize that the events
of the last few weeks were not coincidental. Someone
had gone to great lengths to destroy him, and others.
He couldn't really understand why someone hated him
so much that they wanted to destroy him. It could only
be his past catching up with him. If that was so, then
Big Brother was to blame.

James opened the door and exited the caravan carrying
the boxes of photos.
"I have found who has his will and who we should
contact regarding his death. I found nothing which
would destroy the man's good name."
A smile spread from Fiddles to the other clowns
waiting outside.
"Mr. James, thank you," said Fiddles.
"I have a few photos to check through but everything
else is good. He was a very neat clown and his table is
beautiful."
"Oh, he loved his table. Said it was made for him."
"I couldn't find the computer he told me he had."
"You remember when he was beaten up? Well, he told
me his computer had been stolen," said Fiddles.
Cooper appeared and offered to carry one of the boxes.
He seemed very excited as though he was bursting
with news but wasn't going to say anything in public.
Tonya followed them and after placing the boxes on
the table Cooper made a quick exit. James knew the
boy would be back once Tonya had left. He handed
her the folders but kept the notebook.
"I can make the funeral arrangements now, James.
Thanks for helping."
"Quid quo pro."

"I suppose, but you have been a brick since you arrived. I'll tell mother that Bryan was murdered, but I think for the time being we should keep it quiet from the other performers."

"There is a letter in that folder. It was addressed to you and me. Bryan said if we read this then he would have been murdered. Please keep that for the time being to yourself."

"Okay. Is it an upsetting letter?"

"No."

"I just want the Chief Inspector to know he is wrong."

"You will but not until I have found out why and who did it."

"Dougie asked, when you do, could he be the one to tell the Chief Inspector?"

"Sure, as long as I can be there to watch the man squirm."

Tonya left and a few seconds later Cooper arrived he was very agitated this time.

"Hi, Cooper what's up?"

"I found Quon, but he is scared, he thinks whoever killed Bryan will kill him."

"Can you get him here without anyone seeing you?"

Cooper nodded and then the corners of his mouth turned up into a smile.

"Then bring him here I will hopefully hide him and he can then talk."

Cooper nodded but didn't leave.

"Something else?"

Cooper nodded and then closed the door. He stood by the bedroom door and pointed to the bed.

James wasn't his usual quick self and took a few minutes to realize what Cooper was trying to say.

"Yes, I found the photo. You put it there?"

Cooper nodded.

"Where did you find it?"

" In Ryan's pocket."

"After he was dead?"

Cooper nodded.

"Why did you hide it for me?"

"Because it is important, I took it before the police found it and destroyed it."

"Why would they destroy it?"

Cooper shrugged his shoulders and then stuck his hand out for it to be shaken. James shook the boy's hand. For someone so young the hand was hard, as though the owner worked on a building site.

Cooper left and James hoped Quon would arrive shortly as he wanted to get this over with. He was slightly scared of what he might uncover.

Going through the photo in the box was an easy and quick task. Most were of the circus. It wasn't until he arrived at the last few pictures in the third box that James found pictures from Bryan's college days. Most of the people in the pictures were the same as those in the one Cooper had left in the pillow. There was one picture he decided to keep; it was of a group of friends. Bryan was in the middle with a girl grabbing at his left arm. She was holding him such a way it was as if she was scared he would run away. James didn't want to speculate but he wondered if this was Alison Noble. The shock of finding Quon standing in the bedroom doorway took a little time to recover from. He hadn't heard either Quon or Cooper enter via the window in the bedroom. Cooper was smiling he had achieved his mission and even James hadn't detected his plan. James sudden felt an affinity for Cooper; he acted just as James had when he was the boy's age.

Cooper saluted James and disappeared back into the bedroom. Quon stood looking scared and at the same time very sad.

James locked the door and closed the blinds on the window a little. He pointed for Quon to sit in a seat, which couldn't be seen from the outside.

"Tea?" asked James, holding up his teapot.

"Yes, please, Mr. James."

"You speak English?"

"Yes, we all do, but we don't let on as then we get asked too many questions."

"How did you learn?"

"English school in Nanjing."

"Really?"

"It is important if you are going to travel the world to speak English as in most countries someone will speak it."

"Well, that's going to help us talk anyway."

"I am scared."

"I understand, so let me tell you what I know. Bryan DeWitt, also known as Brinarno the Clown, was murdered by someone because of something that happened many years ago."

"He told me he was scared someone would kill him."

"Was that when you saw Dougie and I talking in the workshop?"

"Yes."

"What else did he tell you?"

"He and my father were friends back when my father was here on a diplomatic passport working at a house here in Malvern."

"Spying?"

"He said it was gathering information."

"So was Bryan a spy for China?"

"No, my father said even though Bryan had access to a great many secrets he never told him anything. Bryan even knew my father was gathering information."

"Why were you and Bryan talking?"

"My father wanted to send his greetings and tell Bryan who the British traitors were."

"So, you gave Bryan a list?"

"No, we never got that far, I'm not sure Bryan wanted to know. Also, the list was very old. My father sent it to me ten years ago. He said if I ever came to England I was to find Bryan and give him the list."

"He didn't want to know. He really didn't care enough about who has the knowledge only what they were doing with it from what I have learned about the man."

"Bryan was a very clever man, my father told me he invented some sort of device that detected pain."

"Did he say anything else?"

"Only that the British and American government would do anything to get their hands on it."

"When I asked Bryan he said the device didn't work. He and others had destroyed it."

"I wonder who else knew what his device did."

"My father left just after Bryan's friend Kipper died. Some believed my father was involved. I asked Bryan and he said it wasn't my father but someone else who was implicated."

"I wonder who?"

"Mr. James, Bryan was worried that someone was going to kill him. He said others had already died and he was next. He also told me they had been after him for a very long time only didn't realize he was Brinarno the Clown."

"Why did he tell you this?"

"He asked me to ask my father a question."

"Did you?"

"No, my father has disappeared so I wrote to him not knowing if he would get my letter. I received a typed letter supposedly from my father. He was reluctant at first to answer but had I explained that Bryan was worried for his life and he told me the answer."

"Which was?"

"The question was puzzling; who was left after Kipper left? In the letter it said on that night only John Bunty, Ken Williams, Derek Plum and Stephen 'Beam me up' Kirk."

"Doesn't mean much to me either, but I know someone who could make sense of it if she willing."

"What should I do?"

"You can hide here for as long as you want. Obviously you and Cooper know how to enter and exit without being seen."

"Cooper is good, he has been very nice to us acrobats. We are teaching him how to do things."

"Good, that's what he needs."

"He is like a brother to us."

"Why don't you want to be with the other acrobats?"

"My father told me not to trust Doctor Song. They worked together gathering information."

"Did they? Thanks, I may need that information."

"Sorry, you need the information Doctor Song is gathering?"

"No, just the fact he is spying will help all of us somehow."

"I see. I am tired. May I sleep?"

"Sure, use the bed."

"Don't need to. Cooper has made me a tree house. He takes me there now."

"Okay."

"I come back later when not too many people are
around, and hide here if that is okay."
"It's okay, but please be careful."
Quon went into the bedroom while James cleared
away the teacups. He was becoming too domesticated
for his own good. He checks the bedroom. Quon had
gone and when James tried the window it was locked,
he didn't know how they got in and out but at some
point, he would ask Cooper.
He sat at his table and took a writing pad and pen out
of a drawer and the photocopy from his back pocket.
It was time to start to put together what he had,
especially if he was going to meet Alison Noble. He
wrote down the names of the twelve and then against
those who had crosses on their faces in the picture he
put an X. Then against the names Quon's father had
mentioned he put a Y. He needed to find out how
many were dead and where the rest lived.

After he had returned from the building site office,
where he had placed the notebook and pictures in the
safe, he went in search of Tonya.
Quon had helped now he needed to help the acrobats.
Who employed the interrupter Doctor Song was what
the needed to find out. Was it just a coincidence that
Quon would join that circus with Bryan in it? The
lights in the main house were out and the door, which
was normally left unlocked, had been locked. James
heard applause and went into the Big Top. Most of the
circus people were sitting around the ring. The clowns
were performing a large picture of Brinarno hung
above the ring. James slid next to Cooper who was so
concentrated on the clowns he didn't notice. At first,
James's reaction was surprising as they were laughing,

then he realized he had seen this performance before.
It was the one Brinarno was famous performing. They
were in their own way paying tribute to the great
clown. He watched and felt himself shrink to the size
of a small boy watching the clowns in the circus ring.
He laughed and clapped at the antics. It was a very
clever way to remember someone. He found himself
crying, and, at the same time, laughing. In the routine,
a large wooden plank had been used. Brinarno would
be almost hit in the face but then fell onto his back.
James remembered trying it at home and ending up in
bed for a week with a sprained back. It was at that
point he realized that clowning was a very serious
business and if you're not careful you can get hurt.
At the end of the routine, everyone stood and
applauded. Fiddles and Antonioni carried the plank
and laid it on two boxes. Then, a black cloth was
draped over it. The clowns stood on either side and
bowed their heads. Slowly, the other circus people
filed out in silence. The laughter had stopped, and now
it was a time to mourn the great performer. James
joined the procession. Outside, they stood talking in
small groups. The Chinese acrobats, minus Doctor
Song, seemed lost. One of the acrobats approached
James. He seemed very nervous.
"Mr. James, may I have a word, please, sir?"
"Sure, what can I do for you?"
"One of the acrobats is missing and I heard Doctor
Song say you wanted to see him. Have you seen
Quon?"
"Briefly, earlier today. He is okay and said he will be
with you all very soon."

"Thank you. Please don't tell Doctor Song I asked. He doesn't like us to mingle too much with the other performers."

"Where is he?"

"We think he may have gone to the Embassy because Quon is missing."

"Quon will turn up. He is just scared after finding the body."

"Thank you, Mr. James, for understanding."

James didn't ask his name. He didn't want the acrobat to think he was going to tell on him. Tonya was talking to her mother when James approached. Mabel stepped forward and gave James a hug and kiss.

"Thank you for coming. I didn't know if anyone had told you it's a tradition of ours to show respect. The clowns will stand guard on the plank until Bryan can have a proper funeral."

"It was strange. I was crying for him and laughing at his memory at the same time."

"Are you sure you weren't born in a circus, I have never heard or seen a non-circus person feel that before."

"Living with my family was like a circus."

"Tonya just told me so you think it was…" She didn't finish her sentence but mouthed the word 'murder'.

"Yes, and the more I find out the more I am convinced there is a cover-up by the police."

"It would be so easy for them to say Bryan killed Ryan and that's the end of it." said Tonya.

"So what happens now, James?"

"I need to go to a pub, and meet a girl."

"Didn't think you were the type."

"Strictly business. She may, I hope, open up and tell me all about Bryan back in his college days."

"Oh, you mean that dreadful Alison. Nothing but a country bumpkin."

"She's not that bad. Just has a few chips on her shoulders, which need taking off."

Dougie and Cooper appeared out of the Big Top. They seemed deep in conversation and Cooper looked a little worried as they approached Mabel and Tonya. James wondered if he should excuse himself but Dougie came up beside him and, touching his elbow to get his attention, whispered 'thank you'.

Cooper stood back from the adults and watched closely as they talked. James noticed how the boy listened but gave the impression of not being interested. After a few minutes, he was aware that James was looking at him. He placed his index fingers on the corners of his eyes and pulled them back. Then clasping both hands flat together and lay them on one side of his face indicating to James that Quon was sleeping. Dougie changed the position of his stance and automatically Cooper followed. James watched as the boy imitated what his older brother did.

The boy was oblivious to what he was doing. He had been doing it for so long he didn't realize. Watching them he suddenly felt homesick and wanted to call his parents and then his brother Peter. The urge faded. He was just reacting to these outpouring of brotherly love. Mabel had been speaking to him when Dougie touched his arm again.

"Sorry, I was daydreaming."

"Do you want to come in for a meal before you go to the pub."

"I don't want to put you to any trouble."

"No trouble I want to hear all about this family of yours."

After they had eaten, and James was preparing to leave, doorbell rang. Tonya went to see who was there. She returned with the Chinese acrobat who had approached James earlier.

"It's Huang Fu, he is worried Doctor Song hasn't returned from the Chinese Embassy and wondered if we could call and see if there was a problem."

"Would you do it, Tonya? You have much more patience than I do," said Mabel.

James nodded to Huang Fu before saying good night. Mabel walked to the door with him.

"Let me know if they find Doctor Song, I want a word with him about Bryan."

"And you let me know how you get on with Alison. She's a dark horse if there ever was one."

"You know her?"

"Oh yes, she came here once and told me about her and Bryan. How she had faked a pregnancy to get him to marry her. I think she was really in love with him."

"What did Bryan say?"

"I never told him she had been here. She still loved him. He once told me he had only loved one girl, a girl called 'Alison'."

James left Mabel and checked his caravan before he went to the Nag's Head public-house. He thought he saw Cooper hiding behind some wooden crates, but he didn't stop to investigate. He needed a drink. Hopefully, he would get to speak to Alison.

CHAPTER EIGHT

Girl Talk

The Nag's head was crowded with drinkers; the smoke from cigarettes filled the air. It was a smell James hated but he knew it would be a long time before British public houses followed the smoking ban of other first world countries. The big powerful tobacco companies would fight very hard to retain the status quo as drinking and smoking. It seemed to go hand in hand in the minds of the British working class.

Alison Noble and Pauline King sat on their usual bar stools. They had taken claim to these seats so many years earlier that no one could remember anyone else ever sitting on them. Standing at the bar James ordered his drink and then gave the ladies a courtesy nod. He was playing for time. They needed to have consumed a little more alcohol for him to start asking them questions. Alison seemed the sort of woman who would be very tight-lipped about things until she got drunk. The bar filled with people who belonged to the local football team and had just finished an evening's practice. From what he could hear they had a big match on Saturday and needed to win if they were going to move onto the next round of the competition. It had been a long time since the team had been in the final and they were determined to be there this year. Alison and Pauline acted like groupie cheerleaders for the team. James was a football fan and had spent countless Saturday's at a game alone. While the rest of his family supported Birmingham City he was a loyal supporter of Aston Villa. For a long time, he was the brunt of the family jokes on a Saturday night. Now that Aston Villa was in the premier league and doing very well, his brothers and sisters hated his Saturday evening text messages. He could understand why this local team was so enthusiastic.

Alison and Pauline were the center of attention and knew each of the men some; it seemed, a little too intimately. The beer flowed like Malvern water in at St. Ann's Well and by nine o'clock most of the football players had left to return to their wives and girlfriends. Pauline made the first move toward James. She seemed drunker than Alison.

"Not good enough to talk to us tonight, are we?"

"You seemed to have your friends around you, Pauline. I didn't want to interrupt."

"Oh, such a gentleman, isn't you?"

"I try to be. Can I get you and Alison another drink?"

"Now you're talking my language. Come join us and tell us the latest gossip. If you have any."

He ordered more drinks and moved to the seat next to Alison. She seemed a little reticent at first but after a drink of her beer she relaxed and even gave him a smile. This un-nerved him at first, but then he regained his composure and decided now was the time to ask them about Bryan.

"You both knew Bryan when he was at college?"

"You want to talk about that loser?" said Alison.

"I'm trying to understand why you hated him so much."

"Dumped me, and in my book, I'm the one who does the dumping."

"Why did he dump you?"

"Well, it wasn't for another woman, I know that much."

They sat and drank their beer, placing the empty glasses in front of James. He knew what was expected. These ladies rarely brought their own drinks. He ordered more drinks, asking for tonic water for himself.

"You said hated, that's past ten... or something, I think," said Alison.

"Past tense," said the barman delivering the drinks.

"Yeah, that's it, which means someone dead."

"The circus owner boyfriend's dead."

"I know that, Pauline, but he was talking about Bryan."

"Bryan was found dead today at the circus winter quarters."

"Oh no, poor sod," said Pauline.

"It true? You're not bullshitting us?" asked Alison, her speech gaining normality.

"It's true, I think he was murdered."

"The police?"

"Not sure what they think."

"They don't think, the bastards," said Pauline.

They sat in silence while the music jukebox played and old song from the 60s. '*Silence is Golden.*' The tears began to run from Alison eyes. James took her in his arms, and comforted her. He was the only man around who wouldn't misunderstand why she was crying. Her whole body sobbed and it took about ten minutes for her to calm down and sit back in her seat.

"Sorry to break the news to you like that."

"It's okay I didn't think I loved the little shit anymore."

"But you did."

"He was my first real love and I never understood why it stopped. He could or wouldn't say why he dumped me."

"I think it was something to do with what was happening to him then. Not you, because he told me you were his only true love."

"Truth?"

"Yes. Now, I need to understand more about him."

"If he was murdered and you want to find out who did it you can count on me and my family to help. Nobby is a useless git, but he does as he is told."

"Thanks, I need to find all those who worked on some project he was working on."

"The Little Black Box," said Pauline.

"The Little Black Box?" asked James

"It was his life for so long and suddenly it all stopped."

"I have a picture of those I think worked with him. Can you tell me who they are?"

"If I can remember. It's a long time ago and these days I don't remember what I did yesterday let alone what happened forty years ago. I think I need to stop drinking so much. I can't think straight these days."

James took the folded photocopy out of his pocket and placed it on the bar counter. Pauline picked it up, Alison took it from her and looked at the picture wiping her eyes on a tissue as she did.

"Oh my gaud, I remember the day this was taken."

"Me too, it was just before Kipper died," said Pauline.

"Do you want me to write their names under them on the picture?"

"Sure, and if you know where I can find them would be helpful."

"Well, this one on the left is John Bunty he died of a heart attack at forty-eight. Next to him is Derek Plum. He still lives here in Malvern."

"That's right. Down by the station. I think he married that bitch, Carol Drake."

"That's right. 'Duck Face'. Her real name wasn't Drake. She changed it just after she left school."

"That's right, she claimed Mr. Drake, the geography teacher, had married her."

"Oh, yeah. He had to leave the school. He committed suicide because he couldn't get another job."

"Didn't she go into Powick Mental Hospital for psychiatric treatment?"

"If she did I don't think it worked."

They took another drink of beer, and returned to looking at the photocopy.

"Ken Williams. We all joked about him being like the actor in the '*Carry On*' films. He was a great laugh though. Dead. Not sure how, but he lived in Kent and had a wife.

"And some kids," added Pauline.

"It was because he always looked down his nose at you as though he had a funny smell under his big nose. This is why we called him '*Carry On*' Kenneth."

"The next one is Stephen, what was his last name?"

"Kirk like in the '*Star Trek*'. They all called him 'Beam me up'". He's dead too. Not sure how."

Alison wrote the information under each person. She named the next person she came to without saying his name out-loud, and James leaned across to see what she wrote. 'Kipper. Dead.' Under Bryan, she just wrote his name and drew a small heart shape.

"Not sure where Peter Devan lives, but Chris Parrott lives over in Colwell on the other side of the hills."

"Is that Phil next to Chris?" asked Pauline, trying to look over Alison's shoulder.

"Philip Langley was Bryan's best friend at college. If anyone knew what was going on it would be Phil. For a long time, we all thought he was in love with Bryan. He never left his side. Now I think it was because he knew something, and he was keeping it a secret because of Bryan."

"What happened to him?"

"Left college early and then just disappeared."

"Roy Churchill and Tom Saunders are both dead. Don't know how, just know they died suddenly and rumors are it was mysteriously."

"And lastly, standing right at the back not really part of the picture, is Tosser. Robert Cross. Pauline here still has how can I put this delicately? She still has a relationship with him. "

"He is my boyfriend."

"Only he is not a boy anymore. A complete loser as far as I am concerned."

"Alison don't be bitchy, not in front of James."

"Pauline, you know how I feel about him."

"Whatever. Come to think of it he would know where Chris Parrott lives. They were in the Territorial Army together."

"Would you ask him, and call me on my mobile?"

"I would, if I had your mobile number."

James took a business card out of his pocket and gave it to Pauline. Seeing the expression on Alison's face he gave her a card too.

"Where will I find Derek?"

"Derek the charmer. Do you remember that TV program called 'The Charmer' some years back? Well, that could have been about Derek."

He had every girl in Malvern by his second year at college."

"Didn't have me."

"Liar."

"Well, not until his fourth year and only because I got drunk."

"Married. Lives down by the station on Clarence Road."

"You can't miss the house, it's like the Chelsea flower show only smaller. With a red front door," said Pauline.

"It's not red anymore, he painted it a shocking pink."

"You've got to be kidding!"

"No. Saw it last Sunday when I took Nobby for a driving lesson. We almost crashed because of his stupid front door. Nobby fell out of the car laughing."

They grew silent and drank the remains of the beer in their glasses.

"Would you like another drink, ladies?"

"No thanks, I think I want some tea."

"Me too, James come along to Pauline's and we'll tell you about the good old days when love meant something and men just didn't want to get their legs over."

"Oh, Alison, don't push it. They want to get some, just like us. Only in those days they were a little more gentlemanly about it."

"James, could you hang on a minute. I need to go to the little ladies room."

"Sure."

Alison left the bar quickly followed by Pauline. After five minutes James wondered if they had escaped by a back door.

When they returned Alison had retouched her make and brushed her hair. James also noticed her skirt had been pulled down several inches.

The walk from the pub to Pauline's terrace house, it took five minutes. The smell of boiled cabbage hit then as Pauline opened the front door. She showed them into the room at the front of the house and switched on a two-bar electric fire. Alison took off her coat and slumped into a chair.

"The news of Bryan's death has just hit me. He was my first and only love. I wanted to marry him. When he broke off the relationship, I was in a daze for weeks. I couldn't eat or do anything. It just didn't make sense. Now I will never know why. I'd seen him on several occasions and wanted to ask 'why', but he seemed not to notice me, so I just let it go".

She caught James looking at her. The tears had collected again in her eyes and were about to run down her face.

"Alison, it's okay to grieve. We never forget our first love. Some of us never find a replacement."

"You too? You're still such a kid. You'll find someone."

"I doubt it. Tell me about you and Bryan."

"That's the problem. We were the perfect couple, I thought we would marry, and I would have a great life. He was the gentleman, always opened the door for me and pulled out the chair in a restaurant. And could he dance? When we took to the floor at the weekly dance at the Winter Gardens, people gave us space so they could watch."

She took a paper handkerchief from her sweater sleeve and wiped her eyes.

"I heard you had said you were pregnant by him."

"I was a stupid girl then. Made a fool of myself. It was something I have regretted all my life. For a long time, I wondered if that was why he dumped me."

They sat looking at the electric fire bars change from red to orange. James looked around the room. Like his parent's house the front room was rarely used except for visitors. The furniture was a few years old but had been kept in good condition. A few pictures and ornaments were on the table and sideboard. Above the fireplace was a 1950s mirror. The thick chrome chain starting to rust as the plated chrome wore off. The corners had lost the metallic shine and were now just a black color.

The lamp hanging in the center of the room was a 60s chandelier. With five arms sprouting from a central gold-colored bow and the arms, also gold-colored, formed into a trumpet cup with a tulip light bulb.

Pauline arrived back, carrying a very large wooden tray, which she placed it on the coffee table. She'd brought in three china cups with matching sugar bowl and milk jug and the teapot hidden under a bright red tea cozy.

"Sorry to take so long, but I don't let the family use my best. And, as my old mother would say, a watched kettle never boils."

"You shouldn't have gone to so much trouble."

"I'm not having you thinking we are common. Even if we are."

Alison continued to look at the electric fire. Both James and Pauline were very aware she was in some sort of shock.

"You okay, Ali?"

"I was just thinking, whatever happened that night when Kipper died was the reason why Bryan dumped me."

"You think so? Here, take your tea."

"Tell me about Bryan. What kind of person was he back then?"

"Kind. Understanding. Never got angry. Always tried to listen to your point of view."

"What I remember how fixated he was about the Black Box."

"I need to find more about this Black Box."

"Good luck."

"That was later, Pauline. He would sit and listen to me going on about my mom and what a cow she was to me. He would try and make me see it from her point of view, but he never made any criticism."

"That's true. Do you remember when you cooked that meal when your parents were at Blackpool and it tasted awful."

"Oh yeah, and he tried to eat it and said it was okay. I knew he was lying but he didn't want to upset me."

"See, that's how he was. So, what changed to make him dump Alison?" said Pauline.

"He wasn't very kind to me when I arrived the other day. Then, after the graffiti problem, it was Bryan who asked Mabel to let me move inside the winter quarters."

"I met him a few months back in the High Street. We had a coffee together. He was just like he used to be. So nice. He listened to me going on about our Nobby and the problems he was getting into. He just said, remember what I was like at that age."

"Couple of wild tarts that was what we were."

"Talk for yourself, we were young ladies looking for a gentleman to sweep us off our feet and take us to Paradise. Just like the girls in that film, '*Officer and a Gentleman*'."

"Oh, that Richard Gere he could have me anytime."

They sat and drank the tea, Pauline had used loose tea and although the teapot had a built-in strainer some of the fine tea leaves had filtered through and floated on top of the rich brown tea.

"You see in those days the town was divided between the Royal Radar Establishment college kids and the townies. The private school kids didn't get involved because they were always locked away in the schools. Even though Pauline and I grew up here we knew if we wanted a better life we needed to meet a college boy and marry him."

"So how did you meet Bryan?"

"I was a very shy girl."

"That's true. I would drag her out to go to meet boys."

"You were going out with Chris Parrott at the time, Pauline, and asked me to go to this party."

"Oh, yeah and I lost my knickers that night."

"That's not the only thing you lost."

"Shoosh, Ali! James doesn't need to know the sordid details."

"Bryan was at this party and seemed bored by what was going on. I sat by the door with a Babycham and watched the others. Pauline had disappeared with Chris so I decided just to leave."

"Wasn't 'alf mad when I found you'd just left me on my own."

"As I put the glass on the dining room table, Bryan asked if I was leaving. I said, 'Yes'. My friend had gone off with someone, and I felt awkward. He said he would escort me home."

"I didn't know that."

Alison ignored her, and continued. "He was so different from the other men. Such a gentleman. At our front door, he asked me if I would like to go to see a film with him the next Friday night. I couldn't speak for a few minutes. There was this nice intelligent man, asking me on a date."

"It must have been the first man who did."

"The other men just assumed they pick you up by telling you a time and day and expect you to be ready."

"Like fools we were."

"Anyway, we started seeing each other and the rest was history."

"How did his other friends react?"

"To me?"

"No, to him. How did they treat him?"

"He was a leader. They just did as he said. He made you trust him. You'd tell him your most inner secrets."

"So, when did this Black Box come into it?"

"I'm not sure, but it took over his, and their, lives."

"What was the Black Box anyway?" asked Pauline pouring more tea into the teacups, then leaving the room to add water to the teapot before Alison answered.

"Don't know. It was the one thing he and the others wouldn't talk about. As they worked for the government, we just didn't ask."

Pauline re-entered, the teapot in one hand, and a plate of broken biscuits in the other.

"Hey, Ali, do you remember the night Tom Saunders got drunk and started to tell everyone about the Black Box. It was the Friday night of Rag Week."

"Rag Week?"

"That's when the students collect money for Charity by doing stupid things."

"It was the only time I'd known Bryan to get angry. He punched Tom. Knocked him out cold. Scared the other men."

"So, who should I talk to first?"

"Derek, he is the nearest as he still lives here in Malvern."

"Ladies, thank you for the tea and for talking to me."

"You're a proper gentleman."

"Pauline behave, James if you need any other information or help please remember we will do whatever we can to do to help find out who did this."

"And if it has anything to do with sexy young men I want to be first."

"Shut up Pauline, don't embarrass yourself."

James ignored Pauline's comment. He could see the embarrassment on Alison's face.

"If I need help Alison, I'll get in touch."

The living room door opened and a shirtless man in his late forties entered. He was either drunk or high on drugs but looked at them and just giggled. Pauline grabbed his leather belt and pulled him forward. Then let him go. He fell backward into the wall and slid down onto the floor.

"This is my brother. A complete loser."

He just giggled some more.

CHAPTER NINE

Tamworth Connection

S tanding by his car, he looked at the house. Pauline
had indicated that this was where Derek Plum
lived. Built in the 1920s, the house was at the end of a
terrace. White and black paintwork gave uniformity to
the row of three-story houses. Only the front door
gave each house its individuality. Each door had been
painted a different color from blue to gold. He
climbed the seven steps, knocking on the neon pink
door with the large brass knocker. Although the door
looked solid only the right half opened. A small,
muscular woman peered out at him not showing any
expression on her face. She wore a cleaner's white
cotton coat and a headscarf. Her white trainers were
covered by cling film.
"Is it possible to see Derek Plum?"
She didn't answer but stepped aside holding the door
open for him to pass. The hallway smelt of polish
even though the floor was carpeted. Two doors were
closed on the left side. In front of him was a red-
carpeted staircase leading up to the second floor. She
passed him and knocked on a door. A man, who
looked older than fifty, opened the door. His portly

figure was dressed in drab grey clothes. The clothes matched his grey hair brushed forward to hide the bald patch on top. James could see into the room. A table was visible, full of pictures in various frames. The man followed James' eyes, and realized what James could see. He stepped into the hallway closing the door behind him.

"Sorry to bother you, Derek. My name is James and I was a friend of Bryan DeWitt."

"Oh yes, I was expecting someone to come and see me."

Derek opened the other door and indicated for James to enter the room. It was a well-furnished sitting room. There were no pictures or ornaments anywhere. The bookshelves on either side of the fireplace were also bare. A large mirror hung over the fireplace and seemed to dominate the room. A brown imitation leather sofa and chairs were positioned to face the dead fire grate.

Derek and the woman sat on the sofa; James sat in one of the chairs and had to twist his body to face them.

"We, that is Carol my wife and I, were very saddened to hear of Bryan's death. I knew him at college, although that was a very long time ago."

James's instinct suddenly warned himself to be cautious of what he said. He didn't feel he could trust Derek.

"I was trying to find all his friends from those days, so I could tell them when the funeral would be."

"Oh yes, we would like to go to that. Wouldn't we, Carol dear?"

She gave no facial expression but her upper arm muscles flexed a kind of acknowledgment.

"I was wondering if you had any idea where I might find any of the other people he was at college with."

"I only know that Chris Parrott lives somewhere in Colwell, other than him I really don't know what happened to the rest."

"Do you have his address?"

"No sorry, we only heard he was living over there. We don't see him."

"Well, I will be on my way then and I will let you know when the funeral will take place."

"Please do."

In the hallway, Derek returned to the other room while Carol opened the front door. James turned to say 'good-bye' but she had closed the door as soon as he had stepped outside.

He sat in his car and replayed the voice message Pauline had left him. He wrote down the instruction she had been given by Robert 'Tosser' Cross as to which house was Chris Parrott's. As James drove away from the Plums' he saw the upstairs curtain move, and then swing back into place.

Finding the house, which Tosser had indicated wasn't as easy as James thought it would be. He knocked on the front door for a few minutes but there was no answer. Sitting in his car he looked at the red brick bungalow. He was convinced someone was inside looking at him. The discolored cream curtains had moved.

A man walking his dog passed, then suddenly stopped and turned around. James had been concentrating on the house and jumped when the man knocked on his driver side window. He rolled down the window. The man poked his head inside the car before James could roll the window back up.

"You looking for someone?"

"Yes, a man called Chris Parrott."

"Why?"

The question made James stop for a moment. It seemed so unexpected.

"We had a mutual friend who died and I want to talk to Chris about him."

"You were a friend of Bryan's?"

Again the direct question made James pause before continuing.

"Yes."

"You're not from the police, or anything?"

"No, I was a friend. We lived next to each other in the circus winter quarters."

"Right the circus. Chris says you can't talk to him here. Meet him up at the British Camp parking lot."

The man then walked swiftly away and disappeared behind some trees. The dog sat looking at James in the car.

James had heard of the British Camp, but in all his visits to Malvern had never been there. The two-thousand-year-old ramparts of the Iron Age hill fort were still visible. James drove into the parking lot. He was going to have a look at this famous hill. From his viewpoint, it looked like a giant layered wedding cake covered with green icing.

James had parked on the far side of the car park away from the entrance. A small German car entered, crossed the parking lot and parked twenty feet from James. The windows were slightly tinted so it was difficult to see inside. A man climbed out of the car, keeping his back to James. He wore a raincoat with the collar turned up, trilby hat pulled down over his face, and sunglasses. Approaching James, he stopped a few feet away from him. The man lifted his head and James saw it was the man with the dog who had spoken to him earlier.

"Chris Parrott?"

"Sorry, but I need to be very careful."

"Why?"

"People maybe after me."

"Chris, what do you know about Bryan DeWitt's death?"

"Nothing, I didn't do it."

"Then why are you so scared?"

"Because..."

Chris walked over a concrete bench, which in the summer was used by picnickers. He sat down and pointed for James to sit opposite. The wind began to stir and gather momentum. They sat in silence listening to the wind as it rushed between and around them. Dark rain clouds assembled above, forcing the daylight to an early bed.

"Bryan was murdered because of something which happened years ago. The police don't seem to care. I want to find out what happened so others don't die."

"I was one of Bryan's friends at college, but I wasn't really very close to him. You asked me why was I scared. It was nothing to do with Bryan or the others. I started taking drugs back then and have never stopped. I owed a great deal of money to some Birmingham dealers. That's why I'm scared."

"So, tell me what you know about Bryan and why someone might kill him."

"Not much. He invented something, can't remember what. Then he destroyed it. We left college and I never saw him again."

"Never?"

"Well, we occasionally met in Malvern, but we didn't speak."

The clouds waited no longer, and opened up over them and the rain fell. Chris ran towards his car, stopped and waved James to join him. The car smelt of something James wasn't sure what. He had never smelt the smell before, but he wondered if it was a smell of drugs. The leatherwork on the seats was torn. Foam rubber oozed out.

"What else can you tell me?"

"Nothing."

"You were part of the team which created the black box."

"The what?"

"Bryan's invention."

"I was there, but I don't know what I did. I can't remember. The drugs, you know."

James could see Chris' reticence wasn't because he didn't want to say anything. It was because the man had taken so many drugs he couldn't remember anything.

"What do you remember about Bryan?"

"The most popular guy at college. A great leader. He was always in the thick of anything happening. Organizing the Christmas decorations, on the Rag Week Committee, working at the local theatre at night. He even organized the best riverboat shuffle we ever had. Then this kid fell overboard and drowned. Bryan said it was his fault because he had organized the event."

"What was the real verdict?"

"No idea; just remember Bryan telling me it was his fault the kid drowned."

They didn't hear the car approach until it rammed into them. James felt himself fall forward and then whip back. He grabbed his neck to protect it while trying to turn around and see who or what had hit them. The car bumped again and this time tried to push Chris' car forward towards the edge of the steep bank and into the dense woods below. Chris turned on the ignition and spun the front wheels to the right and drove out of the way of the car behind. For someone who was so heavily into drugs, his reaction was a little too quick for James to believe the man was drugged out. More lies. The glove compartment of the car sprang open. Little plastic bags of white powder tumbled out. "Fuck, shit, bollocks!" Chris stopped the car and leaned over trying to pick the bags up and stuff them back into the glove compartment. The other car rammed Chris's car again sending more of the bags onto the floor. In the side mirror, James could see a very large wrestler type man get out of the car and run towards Chris's car.

"I think you should do that when we have lost the men in the other car."

Chris looked in the rear-view mirror and drove out of the car park miss hitting a truck by inches.

James turned to see if the other car was following but it had stopped. They drove down into Malvern and parked in the Abbey Hotel parking lot.

"Who was that?"

"I don't know but I think it was the dealers from Birmingham. They have cut my brake fluid pipes, tried to set my house on fire and poisoned my pint of milk. If the dog hadn't peed on the doormat so many times the fire would have spread and yours truly would be ashes."

"You must owe them a lot."

"A packet."

Chris started to pick up the little plastic bags with the white powder. He careful stacked them back into the glove compartment.

"What are you going to do?"

"Me? Hide. Until I've sold this lot, so I can pay them back or they give up."

"How much is this white powder worth?"

"On the street? About a hundred and fifty thousand pounds. I will sell it in about a week. What other job can you earn that sort of money in such a short time?"

"It does have its dangers though," said James rubbing the back of his neck.

"So, what can I do for you now since you have seen through my charade."

"Who was Bryan really close to?"

"Phillip Langley. We called them the bum boys on account they were never apart. We knew they weren't gay or anything. It was our bit of fun. Bryan wasn't gay, but I sometimes wonder if Phillip was. He never married and left college to return to live with his parents. I think we were all jealous of Phillip."

"Why?"

"Because he was really close to Bryan and, deep down, we all wanted to be."

"Do you know where Phillip is now?"

"No idea."

"Pity."

"Look I've got to pack and then make the great escape. I'll drop you off at the parking lot to get your car."

They drove to the British Camp in silence. After James had climbed out of the car Chris drove away without saying another word. His car was the only car left. The rain had stopped but the wind continued to rush back and forth. He wasn't sure if it was the drug men from Birmingham who had bumped the car. In his limited experience with drug dealers, they just didn't give up. There was always too much at stake and if you owed them money what good would you be if you were dead? What if they had gone over the edge after the second time the car was rammed? There was the possibility that they would both have been killed.

He was still thinking about this when he sat down at the computer in his caravan. The winter quarters had been quiet when he returned. Not even the dogs or cats had been running around. The dark, rain-filled clouds hovered over the town and hills. The light from the computer screen illuminated the caravan, but only added to the gloom.

He typed Phillip Langley's name into a search engine and pressed 'enter'. He wasn't expecting to see anything that would help him track down Phillip. There were several Langley's but only one, which included the name Phillip. He read the item. It was on an online chat room thread from a girl called Ashley Langley in Norfolk. She was telling whoever was asking the question that the only Phillip she had found was on Schoolmate.

James had joined Schoolmate many years earlier when he was trying to find a girl he had been to junior school with. He opened the site and was surprised to see how it had changed. How much more information could be found out about a person. He logged in and typed Phillips' name in the search box.

There were six people with that name who had joined Schoolmates. He found only one, which mentioned Malvern and clicked to open up the information. The page had been updated two years earlier. This Phillip was working for an engineering firm in the Tamworth area. He was not married and had been to the Royal Radar Establishment in the 1960s. James wondered what the likelihood was of Phillip still working for the engineering firm in Tamworth.

The only other information on the page was a note that if anyone knew Phillip, and would like to email him, they could do so via the Schoolmates mail service. He checked to see if Phillip was in the phone book online and knew that it was unlikely he would find a phone number. He wasn't disappointed; there were several Langley's but none living in the Tamworth area.

James was second-generation house-dwelling Romani and didn't have the knowledge his father had about the small towns in the Midlands. He had heard of Tamworth but couldn't fix in his mind where it was. He returned to the search engine and typed in Tamworth. The town was northeast of Birmingham and was mentioned in the Domesday Book. Although most of the town's history has been buried along with the ancestors, the Norman Motte and Bailey castle still remained. It wasn't this history, which intrigued James. The infamous three-wheeled Robin Reliant car had been built in the town. For a long time, James had been musing over the idea that people moved to a new place because they had some strange connection to the place they already lived in. Malvern had the beautiful Morgan sports car and an ancient history. Tamworth was in some ways very similar, even if the Robin Reliant had been the butt of many a comedian's jokes. The day had been long and after working out his route to Tamworth, James fell asleep. To those outside, in the winter quarters, all they could see was the glow of the computer screen through the pastel blue net curtains. This suddenly disappeared as the computer changed to sleep mode and the screen went black.

The drive to Tamworth via the motorways took a lot less time than James had imagined. Turning off the M42 and cruising into the town center James realized that it was just like so many of the other towns he had seen on his travels. The engineering factory Phillip had said he worked for was on a small industrial estate. The factory was large but from the roadside looked as though there was no activity. He drove around the side and saw the buildings burnt-out shell, which had once seen employment for two hundred people. Except for a stray dog that was searching for food in the street was empty. James drove back into the town.

After asking in several shops about Philip, James bought a sandwich and crossed the street to the Churchyard. Sitting on a wrought iron bench dedicated to someone's husband and father, he ate his sandwich. A woman walked briskly past and began to clear away dead flowers from a grave. She was in her early sixties, her hair no longer dyed to make her look younger. She was thin and seemed to have trouble bending for any length of time.

She became aware of him staring at her. He wasn't sure if she was frightened or angry.

"You should show some respect for the dead, this isn't a café you know."

"Sorry. I thought this would be the perfect place to reflect and pray."

She stood erect and looked at him, contempt on her face.

"My late husband's ashes are here."

"Sorry."

"Sorry! So you should you be. You city folk think you can just come into the countryside and do whatever you please."

"Actually, I was looking for someone who lives in this area Mrs…"

"Barb, everyone calls me Barb. Who are you looking for maybe I will know them?"

"Philip Langley."

"Charlie Langley's son?"

"You know him?"

"My late husband Jonathan worked with Charlie. They weren't friends or anything. Charlie didn't mix if you know what I mean. I'm not sure if it was because of his religion. I heard he was a Plymouth Brethren. Very strange and secretive they are. My late husband wouldn't go near them."

"Do you know where he lived?"

"Charlie? No. As I just said, he didn't mix so we never really knew much about him."

"What about where they worked?"

"Gone like all the small industries in this area. I don't know what the young kids of today are going to do for a job. There's none around here now."

James sat and took a bite of his sandwich. He didn't know what else to say. Barb returned to the site of her husband's ashes. She may act as though she is angry,

James thought, and to those who meet her for the first time this was probably the impression they would take away. James had watched enough people in his life to know she was hurting and alone, not angry. She didn't want people to get too close in case they too died and left her alone again. He finished his sandwich and looked around for a waste bin. Barb rose from her bent over position and approached him. He expected another tirade of verbal chastisement.

"Sorry, we don't have a waste bin anymore. Someone took it. Heaven knows why."

"I'll find one in the street."

"Sorry, I could help you find Philip. You could always try the county records office. They know where everyone lives. Like the KBG they are."

"Right, that's a good idea, thank you."

"It's in Birmingham, I told it's a nice place now, but when I grew up there it was a dump."

"Parts of the city are very European, but there are still the bad bits."

"Take care, young man, and good luck." She went back to her husband grave.

He drove out of Tamworth, missed the A5 road and headed south on the A51. The sign said the motorway was ahead, but he took a left because the sign seemed to indicate he should. The sign for Wood End just after he had crossed over the motorway made him realize he had gone wrong. He pulled into the side of the road behind a blue van. The owner of the van wandered around the back, expecting to see the police. James climbed out of his car. Something about the man instinctively told him he was Romani.

"Car trouble?" asked the man.

"No, lost my way."

"Where are you heading?"

"Birmingham, although I'm really looking for someone who lives in this area."

A woman in her late sixties joined the man and stared at James. She then whispered something in the man's ear, which made him smile.

"You be a Pidgley kid right?"

"James. How do you know?"

"My mother here recognized you, she knows your family."

"And you are?"

"Bob Willett and this is Ma Willett."

"I know your father. He is a very handsome man married the Welch girl," said the woman, her Midland accent heavy.

"You have a brother? Charlie? Met him in Worcester several months ago," said James.

"We don't talk about him anymore. Does he come and see his old ma? What sort of son is that?"

Bob ignored his mother and stepped closer to James.

"Who you looking for in them here parts?"

"Philip Langley is his name."

"Lives in his parents' house over in Nether Whitacre." said Ma Willett.

"That's right, Ma. On Station Road, just down from The Railway pub and next to the little shop."

"White house with a telephone box outside, one of those old red phone boxes."

"Thanks, you need any help?"

"No, waiting for a bloke to do some business."

James knew not to ask any questions when a Romani was doing business. Unless he wanted to tell you about it, it was none of your business.

"If you keep going straight on this road to Over Whitacre and then turn right you will soon find yourself in Nether Whitacre."

"Great, thanks."

"Say 'hello' to your father for me. I had the passions for him when I was a girl."

"Ma!"

"I will," smiled James.

James drove down the road and found himself very quickly in Nether Whitacre. It was a small village with two public houses. He found the Railway Public House, a building painted black and white. The public house sign hung from a wrought iron bracket. The sign had a stream train painted in bright fresh colors. Three easel boards, ten feet apart, advertised a variety of food served all day. James decided he would go there for something to eat once he had spoken to Philip. The small shop, which seemed to sell almost everything, was packed with pensioners.

The house they had indicated being the Langley residence was tall and thin. The small black-painted gate opened easily and he walked up to the front door. After knocking several times he wandered around the side of the house to the back door. A garage was set away from the house in the back garden. James knocked on the back door and still no one answered. He tried to peer inside through a heavily curtained window. He didn't hear any footsteps and was only aware someone was behind him when he felt the muzzle of a shotgun in his back.

CHAPTER TEN

Dying like Flies

James slowly turned to face a thin, haggard-looking man in his fifties holding a shotgun. The lines of his face were so deeply drawn the man seemed more of a caricature than a real person. Brown eyes sunk into their sockets peered suspiciously at him. For a few seconds, neither man moved nor made any gestures. The two-barrel shotgun was new and had a 'for sale' sticker still stuck to the barrel.

James sensed the intense tension in the man, whose whole body seemed taut.

"Hi, I'm looking for Philip Langley and I was told he lived here."

The man didn't react. He continued to stare at James.

"Sorry, I must have the wrong address," said James, beginning to edge around the man as though he was going to leave. The man pushed the gun forward to stop him from moving. The stand-off continued until the man indicated for James to move towards the large self-standing wooden garage built to the left of the house. James opened the door and had to hold it up, because the hinges were so rusted from age and weather they could barely support the weight. The man

pushed James from behind with the muzzle of the gun.
The garage was empty except for a wooden kitchen
chair. This had been placed in the center of the garage
facing the door.

James turned to face the man again, Using eye
movement the man indicated that James should sit on
the chair. Once seated, the man stood behind James,
the gun muzzle touching the nape of his neck. The
man then took James' left hand and handcuffed it to the
rear left leg of the chair. He did the same with the
right. It was then James realized the man was using
both hands yet the gun muzzle was still pointing into
the nape of his neck. The man secured his legs to the
chair with washing line rope. The noose placed around
his neck was pulled tight and for a moment James
thought this was the end of his very short life. Once
again he had found himself in a dangerous situation.
He needed to find a way out of this predicament. Why
didn't he see this type of situation arise? His
preparation for such encounters would have to be
overhauled if he survived. The man produced a rag
and wrapped it around James's face covering his mouth
but not gagging him. The man stood looking at him
then left the garage. James tried to move the chair but
it had somehow been fixed to the floor. The rope
around his neck tightened. James relaxed. He was at
the mercy of this man who may, or may not, be Philip
Langley. If the man had used ropes on his hands to tie
him to the chair James could have escaped. Several
years ago his uncle Tommy had shown him a trick to
get out of being tied by rope. Unfortunately, the man
had used handcuffs and although Uncle Tommy had
mentioned there was a way to get out of them he hadn't
shown James how. One day he would sit down with

Uncle Tommy and make him tell his entire collection
of tricks for survival.
He knew if he didn't relax his body would swell up
from the fear and panic. His younger brother Paul had
once become stuck under the floorboards of their
parent's house. Why he was there was still a mystery
to the rest of the family. The fire brigade said that
because of the fear of being trapped, and then the
panic of suffocation, the boy's body had swelled up.
This made it impossible for him to escape without
help. James took long deep breaths and relaxed.
Starting with his legs then his arms and finally his
torso. He felt the ropes loosen and the mouth gag
slipped down but didn't quite fall off his face.
He sat relaxed for several hours without the man
returning. He watched through small gaps in the
wooden slated door as the daylight faded. The noise
of a motor starting woke him out of a semi-doze.
Behind him, a petrol-driven motor spluttered into life
and droned noisily as it gathered speed. The rope
around his neck began to pull then release. Each time
it pulled it seemed to pull a little harder. James tried to
turn and see what was happening but, as he turned, the
rope became very tight. He tried again. Turning his
head, he saw that the rope had been tied to the motor
casing and each time a wheel turned it would catch the
rope. This time it had caught the rope and, pulling
hard, it began to choke him. He quickly put his head
back and pushed against the rope with the left side of
his head. The rope tightened, lifting him up off the
seat. He pushed hard against the rope. Suddenly, it
gave and became unstuck from the motor wheel.
James sprang forward with the release. He began to
cough from the choking, his eyes filling with tears.

The tension on the rope had caused the chair to become loose on its floor fixings. He rocked the chair until it fell backward and then sideways. He hit the floor with some force. His left hand was trapped under the chair side. The rope around his neck had caught on the wheel again and was being wound around the spindle. Although he had fallen closer to the motor it wouldn't be long before the rope was pulling on his neck again. He tried to roll the chair over but his efforts kept failing. The rope was quickly disappearing on to the spindle. James began to feel it tighten and using his feet, pushed himself closer to the motor. He couldn't get a grip on the floor. His feet kept slipping. The rope tightened and he was dragged towards the motor. A loud screeching sound, which to him was more like a slipping fan belt, wailed. Then the motor started to splutter and finally, it stopped. The rope pulled tight and James's head was now resting against the motor mounting.

The man entered the garage carrying a heavy-duty rubber flashlight in his left hand. Seeing James on the floor next to the motor, and the rope wrapped around the spindle of the motor, he rushed forward.

"Shit, oh man, shit."

He ran and felt for a pulse on James' neck. He untied the ropes then searched his pocket for the keys to the handcuffs.

"Sorry, shit, I'm sorry."

James lay still. He needed to get his strength back before making a move. The man turned to the motor and unwound the rope from the spindle and removed the handcuffs.

James moved and the man stopped. Placing the chair upright he helped James to sit down.

"Look, man, I'm sorry. This wasn't supposed to happen."

James sat rubbing his wrist and then his neck.

The motor started and the man threw the rope into a garbage bin. James took this moment to stand. The speed of the man surprised him because the man suddenly had James in an arm lock and then had a pair of the handcuffs on his wrist again.

"Sorry, I have to make sure. Let's go into the house." He took James' arm and helped him out of the garage and up the two steps into the house. The kitchen was as clean as the garage. The man sat James on a wooden chair similar to the one in the garage. Filling a Union Jack painted mug with tea, he placed it to James's lips. James sipped at the tea, his throat sore from the rope. The man placed another chair in front of James and straddled it, facing James

"Why do you want to see Philip Langley?"

"I need to ask him some questions," said James, his voice sounding like a person who had a severe sore throat.

"About what?"

"What happened in Malvern?"

"Who are you?"

"A friend."

"They all say that."

"My friend died and I think it was murder and had something to do with what happened when he was at college in the 1960s."

"Who was your friend?"

"If you're Philip, you knew him as Bryan DeWitt."

"Shit, another one? Why are you saying its murder?"

"Because Bryan was scared of something."

"Philip's dead."

"Really when?"

"Years ago."

"How did he die?"

"Cancer."

The man grew more and more tense as he sat looking
at James. He took a mug of tea and began to sip it.
His hands shaking until he was forced to place it on
the kitchen table.

"Philip. What are you scared of?"

"I told you. Philip's dead."

"You were Bryan best friend. Don't you want to know
why he died and who did it."

"I know why he died."

"The Black Box?"

"The Death Box I call it. Because of that, they have all
died. I told Bryan we would have trouble if we didn't
hand it over. Now most of them are dead. He was
always so stubborn. Brilliant, but so pig-headed.
When he told us we had to destroy it I knew at that
point I would always be looking over my shoulder
waiting for someone to come."

"Could I have some more tea please, Philip?"

Philip ignored James request and continued, "My
parents didn't understand. They thought I was just
paranoid. They had forced me to go to the Royal
Radar Establishment straight from school. I didn't
want to go. I told them I could get a job around here
but they wouldn't listen. I met Bryan on the first day.
We all had our pictures taken. He and I stood next to
each other and we became friends. After I came back I
told them I was in danger but they didn't listen. Then
they started to die. First was John Bunty, I told Mom
soon they would get me. I played a game of cat and

mouse until it seemed to stop. Now it's started all over again."

"Philip, I'm here to find out who killed Bryan and maybe the others."

Philip sat staring at James. His eyes didn't blink, they just seemed out of focus. He picked up his mug of tea without looking at it and began to sip. He was in deep thought. James had never seen anyone hold a stare without blinking for so long before. The lights flickered and brought Philip back from the dark place he had retreated too.

"Sorry, you've got to understand I'm scared."

"I understand. I just need to know a few things to help me solve Bryan's murder."

"Bryan was a beautiful man. Like a brother to me. Always around to help when I made mistakes or got depressed. I miss him."

"Did you keep in touch after leaving Malvern?"

"Sure. We wrote to each other regularly. His last letter came a few days ago. I still haven't read it."

He stood and walked over to the mass-produced Welsh dresser, the plates and cups neatly displayed. He took an envelope off the third shelf, tore it open, and read it.

"What's your name?"

"James Pidgley."

"Bryan says you're a Gypsy. Is that true?"

"Yes, what else does he say?"

"Here, read it for yourself."

James showed the handcuffs to Philip, who gave a smirk before removing them. Rubbing his wrist, James took a gulp of tea. The letter was affectionate. In it Bryan spoke of Philip as though he was a brother. He told him he had met this gypsy who was not only

kind, but also an honest man. It was this paragraph
James lingered on and read again;

*'I think you're being paranoid again, Philip. The Black
Box has gone. No one knows how it worked except me
and I'm not telling. As for the other things they never
existed. Right? Lucky for me, I'm not a great painter so
my artwork will not be hanging in the National
Gallery. In fact, it is not even hanging in its old place
any more. Destroyed for good, I hope. So, Philip, stop
worrying! I will come and see you when we play
Tamworth this summer.'*

James folded the letter and handed it back to Philip.
"More tea?"
"Please, and will you help me?"
Philip stared at him before rising from the chair. He
didn't speak until he had organized the tea. The kettle
stood on the gas stove, the blue flames turning red and
orange. A drop of water on the outside of the kettle
rolled down the side. The flames of the gas stove
evaporating the droplet only to be followed by another
and another.
"Tell me how Bryan died and what makes you think
it's murder and the police don't."
James explained what happened and why he believed
Bryan was murdered. He told Philip of his meeting
with Derek Plum and Chris Parrot.
"I never liked Derek. Too slimy for me, one of those
people who would tell you what you wanted to hear. I
don't think he has ever told the truth in his life."
"He seemed very uncomfortable when I met him."
"Where is he living now?"
"Still in Malvern."

"Silly sod. Never was much of an adventurer."

"What was it like in those days?"

"We were taught not to trust anyone. According to the Establishment, the government that is, there were spies everywhere. Some of it was true. I mean, the Russian and the Chinese had their Consular Houses right opposite the main entrance to the Establishment. And then there were the girls."

Philip became lost in thought, trying to remember the girls. James spoke to break him out of the daydream.

"What about the girls?"

"Sorry. They would invite us to these parties and we would be introduced to Vladimir or Chung. They would try to become our friends. I know some fell for it. Bryan always warned me to be careful. When the Black Box became known, some of these girls offered us whatever we wanted. I could have had anyone of them and all the drugs in the world. Thanks to Bryan I didn't fall. Not like Kipper. He fell in love with this girl then got a warning from the Establishment and sulked for weeks after breaking up with her."

"Do you think he saw her later when it calmed down?"

"No, he died not long after. It was the night we destroyed the Black Box. Bryan had told us the military wanted the box and he convinced us if they got it they would use it for torture. Then we found out the Russians and the Chinese had somehow found out about it and had offered millions of pounds to get it. I think Kipper was going to sell it to them and that why he was killed."

"Kipper was murdered?"

Philip ignored the question.

"I think the Box still exists and that's the reason why we are all in danger. Hence, the reason why I pulled the gun on you."

James wondered if he should ask the question again about Kipper's death. The expression on Philips' face told him now was not the time.

"What did the box do?"

"Bryan was a genius. He invented all sorts of devices. He had been working with some doctor at the hospital in Worcester on a stomach pump for people who tried to commit suicide by taking pills. Anyway, he found out that a lot of people are injured when the ambulance men try to move them without checking their hidden injuries. If they were unconscious they couldn't tell where the pain was. So, Bryan invented this box, which read brain patterns, and before long he could tell where the pain was. At first, we tested it on ourselves sticking pins all over the body and the machine told us where we had stuck them. Bryan wasn't convinced. He said it would be possible to work out where the pins had been stuck by watching the test victim. So, he set up this test where we were in one room with the machine and someone put pins in the person in another room. It was incredible. It really worked. Next, we tested it with the doctor on several road crashes and each time the results were correct. We were just about to go public when the government suddenly showed interest. Bryan realized they had an ulterior motive."

"What was it?"

"Bryan and John set up an experiment in which Bryan was at first tested for pain, then John did something to the box. Bryan was given pain through his brain, a lot of pain. They had reversed the effect and suddenly they had a torture machine. There would be no

physical marks. At first, Kipper didn't believe, until
Bryan told him to try the equipment. Kipper freaked
out after that and some said it was that reason he died."
"You mean that is how Kipper died?"
"No, he committed suicide by jumping off the roof of
Park View Hostel. Only he didn't jump."
"Someone pushed him?"
"Yes."
"For what reason."
"He was going to sell the black box secrets and one of
the group had to stop him. The police ruled it suicide."
"What did Bryan think?"
"As always he couldn't see the bad side of anyone and
said Kipper wasn't going to sell the box. He agreed it
wasn't suicide. Also Bryan had seen Kipper earlier that
evening after we had all agreed to destroy the box. He
never told us why, only he said he knew it wasn't
Kipper who was trying to sell the box."
"Maybe he knew something you didn't."
"Never. We were best friends. He told me everything."
"Best friends don't tell each other everything."
"Anyway, Kipper was supposed to be in Priory Park
for the initiation of the first year's students in the pond.
It was a tradition each year the first years were
gathered at midnight and thrown them one by one into
the water."
"After we had done the deed and returned to the hostel
we found the police everywhere and then found out
Kipper was dead."
"Must have been a nasty shock."
"At first everyone except Bryan said it was because he
had tried to sell the secrets, only Bryan kept saying it
wasn't him."

Philip poured the tea and handed a mug to James.
They sat drinking it both in deep thought. James was
thinking of the questions he should ask Philip.
"You said you knew how the others died?" asked
James.
"Each time someone died I would write to Bryan and
each time he said it wasn't connected."
"Bryan was scared he told me so."
"We both were. Only he always tried to see the
positive side to everything. The first to die was John
Bunty, he drove his car into a wall at the end of his
road after telling his wife he would see her that
evening for a romantic dinner. Ken Williams was
either pushed or jumped under a London underground
train. He had just been promoted and his wife was
expecting their fourth child. He had everything to live
for and his work colleagues all said he was the
happiest man alive. Stephen Kirk was killed in a
shooting accident; his army buddies said a sniper in
the woods shot him. That was neither proved nor
disproved except they say they found shell casings,
which were not theirs in the woods. Roy Churchill
just dropped down dead while servicing his sexual
desires with a prostitute in Wolverhampton. The
inquest found no reason for him to have died. His heart
was good. The prostitute said she had left him several
hours earlier. She said that he was asleep in the hotel
room. His wife said he had complained of a pain in
his left knee and the coroner found a little puncture
mark. But nothing was inside. I read not long ago
about someone using an ice pellet to kill someone by
putting the poison inside the ice and when it melted
inside the person it slowly killed them."

"I remember reading about that. Didn't it happen in New York?"

"Somewhere like that."

"So, is that all of them?"

"No .Tom Saunders. He was supposed to have died at the hands of some gay hustler in Rome. Only the kid has always maintained he didn't do it and after the retrial, the kid was found not guilty."

"Bryan and I looked into this one and we both agree the kid didn't do it, and the Rome police were hiding something. I mean why did MI6 interview the kid before the Italian police did?"

"Do you know what the kid's side of it was?"

"Bryan had a friend who somehow got an English translation of the statements the kid made."

"Can you remember what it said?"

"The kid said he and Tom had been together and had sex at Tom's hotel. But the kid left when this English man arrived. He thought it was Tom's boyfriend by the way they greeted each other."

"Didn't the kid describe the man?"

"No, and here is the curious thing. The kid said the other man asked 'where is the Black Box'? He left before Tom gave the man an answer, but was told to come back later."

"Hence, why they thought the kid was involved."

"The kid died several months later. The kid 's boyfriend said it was an Englishman who killed him."

"So, Tom Saunders was gay?"

"That's the funny thing. Neither Bryan nor I thought he was. Bryan's friend in Rome said a woman prostitute had come forward saying she had been having sex with Tom."

"Meaning the kid was paid to lie and then killed so he couldn't tell anyone."

James pulled the picture of the group out of his pocket and handed to Philip.

"Where did you get this from? Look at me! So young and thin."

"There two others in the picture. Who are they and, Philip, do you know where they may be?"

"Peter Devan. God knows where he really is. He didn't have much to do with the Box. He was more a friend than part of the group. The other one is Robert Cross. We called him 'Tosser" for obvious reasons. Last I heard he was in jail for stealing car tires. Not a set of four. He stole thousands of them and sold them through a retail stores. He was a very clever man when it came to business and cards. Best poker player I ever knew."

"I didn't think he was part of the group."

"He wasn't. Just a hanger-on."

"So, why is he in the picture?"

"He wasn't really. See how he is at the back almost out of the frame? Tosser wanted to be part of the group but no one liked him. So, he was always on the side. We would be in the pub and he would sit at the next table trying to get into the conversation. It was really very sad and I think we treated him appallingly."

They fell into silence both drinking the tea.

"I wonder sometimes how it would have all worked out if the government hadn't interfered."

"What do you mean?"

"Bryan told me he had worked out the progression of the black box. One day he quoted this Latin phrase 'Omne vivum ex vivo'.

"Sorry, my Latin not that good."

"It means 'all life is from life'. A German professor called Schumann had proved that man's body frequency was the same as the earth's, seven point eight three hertz. Bryan realized that if we could read the body frequency of each part of the body we would be able to see the pain, or even, if there was no pain, the problem someone might have, like cancer."
"Seriously?"
"As I said, Bryan was a genius. If only he could have continued without Big Brother stepping in."
James looked at his watch. It was 1:35 in the morning. "Philip, I'd better be going. Thank you for your help."
"Don't go. Stay until the morning, please."
"What haven't you told me?"
Philip produced a small piece of paper out of his back pocket and handed it to James. Two words had been scrawled in pencil; 'Your next'.
"Grammatically incorrect. How did you come by this?"
Philip handed him the envelope the note had been in.
"Postmarked Worcester and it came this morning."
"And that is why you pulled the gun on me."
"Yes, I thought you had come to get me. Then I almost killed you."
"History. Do you have any idea who might be behind this? It has to be one of those left."
"If I knew I would tell you."
"Some believe the Box, or the plans for it, still exist. And I think the Chinese may be behind the new interest."
"Is that what Bryan thought?"
"Yes, well I think so, Philip. It's been a long day for me and I need to get a little sleep."

"Sorry, you can sleep in the spare room, it's at the front and you won't hear the generator going all night."

"You make your own electricity?"

"Only for the security system, at first my neighbors complained until I fixed the system up to the shop and it stopped someone breaking in one night."

Ten minutes later James lay between the soft white sheets of the spare room bed. He laid for an hour before falling asleep his mind going over and over what had been said. It was something he had been told and seen. Something he knew that was the clue he needed. He heard Philip pacing before going to his bedroom. James rubbed his neck he could still feel the rope tight around it.

He woke when his mobile rang. He had forgotten he had set himself a daily alarm so he didn't sleep in. Downstairs he could hear Philip moving about. He quickly washed in the bathroom and went to the kitchen.

"Good morning. Full breakfast?"

"That would be very nice, Philip, thank you."

"Least I could do after what I did to you yesterday."

"You didn't sleep very well? I heard you pacing about."

"I had the best night's sleep I had for years, and I realize I need to find someone to live with me. I think my problem is I'm lonely since my parents died."

"I know what you mean. Sometimes being on your own can get to you."

"James, how did you find me?"

"It was a Rom connection.'

"Sorry, I don't understand?"

"We Romanies, Gypsies, know who lives near them. I met a couple in Wood End who knew who you were."

"They won't tell anyone else, will they?"

"Not if they are not Rom. We are very good at keeping secrets to ourselves."

"So, what's your next move?"

"I need to go back to Malvern and to think, I think I have been told the answer but just can't see it."

"Don't you hate that?"

"I also have to get back to work I have some houses to build and if my brothers find out I'm not around they will tell my mother who will nag me."

"Lucky you, to have a mother to nag you."

"She doesn't really nag. That's it! Someone was nagging someone when I arrived to see them, and I heard the name Kipper. But who was it?"

"Who have you visited recently?"

"Besides Derek and Chris? Let me see... Alison Nobel and Pauline King."

"Are those two slag' still around?"

"Alive and well and they have been very useful in helping me."

"If anyone knew what's happening today to the gang, they would. Pauline is still having an affair with Tosser until he ends up in jail again. Well, she was according to Bryan."

"Really? I must check that out. Alison told me they were back together."

After the breakfast, he left but promised he would return if he found out anything. He drove to Wood End and found Bob Willett. He asked him to keep an eye on Philip. Bob said he had a cousin who was camping in a field behind Philips' house and would get him to make sure Philip's was safe. James took the motorway, and drove back to Malvern.

As he drove along Malvern Link road the rain forced him to drive at five miles an hour. It had started just as he entered the motorway near Tamworth. A light drizzle that soon became a monsoon. He parked the car in the winter quarters yard before running to the caravan. Not surprisingly, the place was deserted and only Mabel's dog, Walter, ran about enjoying the rain. James changed out of his clothes into his jeans and a dirty tee shirt. He sat on the bed and pulled on his olive green thick rubber Wellington boots tucking his jeans inside. The yellow sailor's storm coat was being christened. It still smelt new and unused. The bright yellow sou'wester hat swallowed his head until only his chin was visible.

The building site was flooded and the trenches were full of water. He carefully inspected the site and wondered if they needed to install more drainage. He stood by the workman's port-a-loo toilet looking for signs of the toilet's blue liquid. He said a silent prayer, hoping the sewage hadn't escaped. The noise of something moving inside startled him. Expecting to find some wild creature hiding inside from the rain, he opened the door.

Nobby stood crouched on the toilet seat. His expression was of a frightened child caught stealing the candy from grandma's jar. His aggressive attitude had gone, and a little frightened boy had taken its place. Neither James nor Nobby spoke. It seemed as though some hidden ancient language passed between them. Each one knowing what needed to be done and acting accordingly.

James took him by the hand and carefully led him to the caravan. Nobby was wet through. James told him to go into the bathroom and strip off his clothes. James

founds a pair of jeans he never wore and didn't
particularly like. The tee shirt was one Tonya had
given him. He knocked on the beige plastic concertina
door. It opened slightly and a hand shot out. James
handed the clothes over and closed the door. His
search for footwear had resulted in finding his
mother's orange fluffy bunny slippers.

He made a cup of tea and sat down at the table waiting
for Nobby.

The boy entered. His normal attitude had begun to
emerge. James looked at him and Nobby shrank back
to the lost soul looking for a home.

"Sorry, the only footwear I have are my mother's
slippers." He pointed the orange fluffy bunnies.

Nobby smiled and slipped his feet into them.

"Reminds me of my mother's slippers when I was a
small boy. They were the warmest shoes I ever wore.
Sorry, too."

"What happened?"

"I was coming to see you when the rain started. I
couldn't think of anywhere else to keep dry. Only the
water just kept rising and I can't swim."

"You didn't read '*Boot of the Amazon*' when you were
a kid?"

"I did. I loved those books."

"What were you coming to see me about?" James
pushed the mug of tea to him.

"Me Mum," said Nobby taking a large gulp of tea.
"She's upset about the clown's death."

"A lot of people are."

"With mum it like she lost a lover, if you know what I
mean."

"I do, I think you mother still loved Bryan even after
all this time."

"Maybe, she was okay until the copper came round."
"The police?"
"Yeah, the one who was always hanging around here."
"Peter Kipler?"
"Yeah him. At first, he asked about the Clown. Said he knew she was once his girlfriend and he had dumped her. Then he started to ask about you and if you had said anything to her about how the clown died."
"What did Alison say?"
"Said she hadn't spoken to you about the clown's death and it was none of his business what relationship she once had with the clown."
"Go Alison."
"He called her a liar; said he knew she and Auntie Pauline had been seen talking to you. He used some big fancy word like frater or something."
"Fraternizing."
"Yeah, that's it."
The knock at the door was very light and had there not been a lull in the conversation neither of them would have heard it. James opened the door. Cooper stood covered in a large plastic sheet. The rain was hitting it making the sound of water dripping onto a taut drum skin.
For a brief second, James wondered if he should let him in. Without waiting for an invitation Cooper ran up the steps and into the caravan. He saw Nobby and then looked at James. His expression was as though he had been betrayed. He took off the plastic sheet and placed it in the well of the stairs. Pushing past Nobby he entered the bedroom. Standing in the doorway he looked at James then at Nobby. Indicating with his index finger he summoned James to follow.
"What is he doing here?"

"Came with a message from his mother."

"The copper left this for you." Cooper handed a brown envelope to James.

Cooper watched as James opened it and studied him as he read the contents. Before James could say anything, his mobile phone rang. Cooper returned to the living area.

"Hello."

"James, Bob Willett here. Just wanted you to know that some official-looking people have been inquiring about Philip. Ma told them he had moved to Blackpool."

"Good. Look out though, they may not have believed your mother."

"I will."

"Thanks, Bob. I will be in touch."

James entered the living area to find Cooper and Nobby laughing. Cooper had put the slippers on his feet and was walking up and down in them. He did it as though he was a model on a catwalk.

Seeing James, Cooper sat down, slipping the slippers off and pushing them towards Nobby. He looked embarrassed and, after a quick look at James, lowered his head and looked at the floor.

"It's okay, Coop. James is cool."

Cooper didn't change his position, but from the relaxation, in his shoulders, he had understood.

"Cooper and I have been friends for a long time, only his brother thinks I'm no good. When I brought messages from mom to the clown I would see him."

"And at school, if I went."

"You brought messages from your mother to Bryan?"

"Yeah, she would tell him if Tosser had told auntie Pauline anything about the guys they knew."

"How often?"

"Once or twice a month, please don't tell mom I told you."

"She doesn't want his Dad to know," said Cooper looking up and giving his little boy lost smile.

They sat in silence neither of them knowing what to say. Nobby kept looking at Cooper and nodding his head as though he was prompting Cooper to speak. Finally, the tension broke and Nobby said, "You going tell him, or what?"

Cooper looked at James. The color had drained from his complexion.

"Go on tell him." said Nobby. "It's okay. I told you this guy is cool."

Cooper sat back in the seat placing his hands in his lap and looked straight at James.

"That copper who left the envelope for you. Well, when the police were here after Bryan's death. Well, he searched your caravan several times and took a computer disc from your briefcase."

James rose and picked his briefcase up from beside the table. Opening he inspected the contents.

"Shit, it had all the information about the site and some very confidential stuff too."

"I thought it might," said Cooper, a big grin appearing on his face. He took out of the back pocket of his jeans a medium sized wallet. Opening it a picture fell to the floor. James scooped it up and looked at it. A very beautiful young woman was posing for the camera.

Cooper stood in front of James and handed him a computer disc. James handed him the picture.

"Your mother?"

"Yeah," said Cooper looking at it before returning it to the wallet. "I saw him take it and place in his jacket pocket. When his jacket was placed inside a cop car I snook in and took the disc."

"Cooper, I owe you."

"That copper is a friend of Dave Matchen, the builder," said Nobby.

"Really? He was the guy who tried to get the work of building the houses for us."

"Mom knows him and says he's a dodgy-do."

"With this information, he could have caused us some real problems."

"The copper came to our house and said I had stolen some computer disc out of his car. Mom said if he wanted to search the house, he would have to get a search warrant. He said he didn't have a warrant but the disc was to do the clowns death, and so he was at liberty to search. He took my bedroom apart but didn't find anything."

Cooper gave a little shiver as though he was cold.

"Can I make some tea?" asked Nobby.

"Sure. I think Cooper could do with something to warm him up.

James took the papers out of the envelope and read it again. He was puzzled by the report. First, it said nothing was found which would indicate no one else was involved. Bryan DeWitt had committed suicide after ingesting a large amount of cocaine. He had over two ounces in his right hand when he was found.

James turned the paper over and made some notes. At the inquest, there had been no mention of drugs in Bryan's system found during the post-mortem. James had found Bryan and both his hands were open. Nothing was in them. His other observation from the report was a typing error. At the end of the sentence about the cocaine in Bryans' hand, the last word was cocaine. This was followed by a full stop and then the word cocaine and another full stop. Obvious someone had changed the report and made a mistake.

Cooper handed him a mug of tea then retreated to the sofa next to Nobby. The two boys become engrossed in conversation. James read the report again he found two more typing errors someone had left by mistake. Or had they? James couldn't believe that the report had been changed and then not checked for mistakes. He was intended to find them, but why and who had done the changes?

He looked at the two boys. He had never seen Cooper so relaxed and happy. He needed to talk to Dougie at some time about Nobby.

"What's next, Sherlock?" asked Nobby making Cooper laugh.

"I think I need to talk to our friendly copper, my irregulars."

"We're not irregular!"

"Then you don't know your Sherlock Holmes. They were the street kids who helped Sherlock solve the crimes."

"Oh yes, I remember that now. We're the Malvern Irregulars." This sent them into fits of laughter.

"I wonder where Officer Kipler is right now."

"Watch him. He's a sly dog. He once tried to get me brother Tyler for stealing some lead off Malvern Priory church. Our Tyler swore blind he hadn't taken it. My dad beat the shit out of him and still Tyler said he hadn't taken it."

"Had he?" asked Cooper.

"No. One of his mates had. Still, they got him for robbing that factory in Worcester. "Twenty-five years he got and him only nineteen."

"Wow, he'll be old when he comes out."

"My mom was so mad she almost hit that copper."

"He did the robbery?"

"Oh yeah, they caught them all coming out with the cash. One of his old girlfriends had heard about what he was going to do and told the police. Not sure what happened to her only she hasn't been around much lately. Tyler's barrister appealed and his sentence was reduced to eight years"

The knock on the door made them all jump. James opened it and saw a very wet looking Dougie standing in the rain.

"Dougie, come on in."

Dougie stepped inside the caravan and stopped on the top step. When James turned the two boys had vanished, tea mugs with them.

"Sorry to bother you, James, but have you seen Cooper?"

"Not today. Why? What happened?"

"Doctor Song dead."

"What, when, how?"

"The police said he died this morning at about eleven. The copper Kipler said he was stabbed in the neck. I never really liked the man but no one should die like that."

"Do they have any suspects?"

"No, but they said it may be something to do with the fact he was part of the Chinese secret police."

"Well, that's what they told the acrobats."

"Where did he die?"

"In his caravan, which means the police are running all over this place again. That's the reason why I need to find Cooper. I don't want him to get into any trouble."
"If I see him I will tell him you're looking for him. He is probably keeping out of the rain somewhere."
Dougie left. James closed the door behind him. He saw two faces appear around the opening to the bedroom. Both had large grins on their faces.

CHAPTER ELEVEN

Family Secrets

James towered above the Chinese acrobats as he stood among them in the circus ring. Everyone in the winter quarters had been told to report to the Big Top again. Cooper had finally confronted Dougie. The tension between them was obvious, only Cooper had a smirking expression on his face. James looked around for Quon. Only when two of the acrobats parted did he become visible. He looked dejected and afraid, his pent-up emotion ready to flow. A flood of tears being held back. One wrong word from someone and the dam would burst. Quon lifted his head, saw James, and quickly looked back at the floor. Sitting down next to the acrobat, James felt huge and overbearing. Quon's dark-blue eyes made contact with James. The boy needed a friend and the other acrobats didn't seem to notice his pain.

James put his hand on the young man's shoulder. "Slowly. Tell me what's happened."

Quon looked at his acrobat friends, their backs turned. "Doctor Song is dead and most of my friends think I did it."

"Why do they think you did it?"

205

"Because Doctor Song was trying to stop me."

"From doing what?"

"Finding my father, well, the truth about him."

"I'm sorry, I don't understand."

"My father was a friend of Bryan's. I told you. Something happened and he was sent back to China. He escaped via Hong Kong and returned to the United Kingdom."

"He defected?"

"Yes, the family were told he had died, had an accident just after he arrived here. Two years later my mother received a letter from him explaining why he had run. In the letter, he mentioned Bryan and how he had helped him set up a new life here in England."

James took out a little notebook and made a few notes, then turned to Quon. "Do you know when and where he died."

"Murdered. And Doctor Song knew the truth. He told me if I tried to find out what happened I would be sent back. It was here in Malvern in June 1998."

"And that's why the others think you killed him?"

"Yes."

"Well, I know you didn't. I'll make sure the others know the truth."

"Promise?"

"Yes. As for the police, tell them all you know."

Police officers entered the Big Top, followed by several detectives. An Asian officer approached the acrobats and, in Cantonese, asked them to follow him to the other side of the Big Top. James felt awkward and searched for someone to talk to. Peter Kipler swept back the tent flap and strolled into the Big Top as though he was in charge of the investigation. Seeing James, he tried to avoid him by talking to a

group of policemen. James waited for him to finish
and then approached.

"Peter, I think we need to talk."

"What about? I don't think we have anything to talk
about."

"You can talk to me or I will go to your superiors and
ask why you gave me a report which had been
doctored."

James knew Peter wouldn't really care if he did that,
but to use the word 'superiors' would make the
policeman angry.

"Over here!" said Peter pointing to a seating area away
from everyone.

"I was trying to help."

"Who? Me, or the killer?"

"You."

"By misleading me?"

Peter looked at the floor like a little boy who had just
been caught stealing from the corner shop.

"Want to tell me the truth?"

"It's not what you think. If my mother finds out she
will go berserk. Kipper was my cousin; his real name
was Ian Kipler. No one from the day he was born ever
called him Ian. My mother said if the press started to
dig up his death again it would kill her. "

"Why?"

"Kipper's family always acted as though they were
above everyone else in the family. My mother hated it
that they were in the spotlight when he died."

"So, you decided to mislead me in the hope I would
not dig too deep into how Kipper died."

"Yes, sorry. Look, I don't see how it's connected to the
murders going on here."

"I think it has everything to do with what's happening here."

Peter dropped his head again, obviously under some spell conjured up by his mother.

"Where can I find his family?"

"His parents are dead. His twin sister could be anywhere. After Kipper died our families never talked. His parents said there was more to his death and they wanted to keep it quiet."

"Kippers parents you mean?"

"Yes. We weren't invited to his sister's wedding or the parent's funeral. My mother was so upset, she found out three weeks after the funeral. We went to the old house only to find it sold and no forwarding address."

"Do you know the sister's married name?"

"No. My mother met an old school friend. Someone from Malvern Girls School where they both attended. She knew Kipper's mother and told my mother about the funeral and the sister's wedding."

"Did the woman go to both?"

"No, her husband owns a chain of florist shops and told his wife of the events."

"What do you think about Kipper's death?"

"I spent an hour thinking about it, I'm not sure what would be worse for my mother. Suicide or murder."

"Pride has killed too many people."

They sat in silence on the tiered public seating in the Big Top. The detectives were still talking to the acrobats. The other circus people had gathered together near the circus ring entrance. The flap to the outside world was pulled back. Two men entered, both dressed in Marks and Spencer suits. Peter straightened his back. The sight of the men visibly upset him.

"Who are they?"

"You really don't want to know. They are from MI5."

"Really? Now that is interesting."

"If you speak to them you won't find it so interesting, they are nothing but a couple of thugs."

"Well, coming from you they must be bad."

They sat and watched the MI5 men order the police around. James now understood why Peter was so apprehensive.

"Why are they here?"

"I don't know, but they have been on the case from the day Bryan died."

"I wondered if they would be."

"Why?"

James didn't want to mention what he knew about Bryan's past.

"Because of the Chinese connection."

"Right."

One of the detectives talking to the acrobats signaled for Peter to join them. James watched as he walked across the circus ring. He didn't trust Peter. For a start he hadn't explained why he had given him the doctored report. He didn't buy into the mother and her pride excuse.

CHAPTER TWELVE

Shouting to the Wind

Tom Potts was in his early forties and was married to his only girlfriend. He had worked for the British government since leaving Oxford University. He had obtained a first degree in medieval English so was surprised when a woman from Military Intelligence had offered him a job. Like so many graduates he really didn't know what he wanted to do so he accepted and slowly rose in the ranks. Most of his colleagues regarded him as arrogant with a bitter sarcastic   approach to dealing with the general public. He himself saw it as being efficient. Time was always important and wasting it on small talk was useless. Walking around the circus ring he gave the impression of a Sunday stroll around the Serpentine in St James. He came level with James for a moment, but soon passed him. James was surprised when he suddenly stopped and, turning, faced him.

"Can I have a word with you, Mr. Pidgley?"

James quickly composed himself. "Which word would you like?"

Tom looked at the young man and smiled to himself because that was exactly the answer he would have given. He knew that from now on he mustn't treat James Pidgley as just another public run-of-the mill moron.

"Very droll, Mr. Pidgley. I think we should move away from any listening ears. My car is outside. Why don't we sit in that for a short while?"

The Java Black V8 Supercharged Vogue SE Range Rover was, for James, a dream he had not yet realized. The soft leather interior seemed to swallow him.

"I won't waste your time with small talk. Could you tell me why you are investigating the death of Bryan DeWitt?"

The directness of the man shook James a little. He was proficient in dealing with police officers that for one reason or another tried to belittle him. This man was direct and concise. He wondered for a few seconds if he should bluff.

"I could say I wasn't, but I know, with you that would be foolish."

Tom didn't reply. Years of training himself to listen to what others said had always yielded more.

James continued. "I'm not really investigating in a police sense. I met Bryan briefly and he was scared. I'm not sure, but someone was causing him a great deal of anxiety."

"What about his death didn't you think was right?"

"He didn't die from drugs."

"Why do you say that?"

"He wasn't the type to take them. Even though the police report says he was."

"You mean from the phony report Peter Kipler has been circulating."

James showed surprise on his face and knew it. He needed to take some lessons on being a better poker player.

"We know what Mr. Kipler has been up to and why."

"I don't think he was trying to impede the investigation. His family is very sensitive about a relative's death and obviously, don't want it raked over in the press again.

"I don't think that will happen. The Home Secretary is about to put a blackout on this case. Kipler is full of bullshit.

"Oh!"

"I think you know a lot more than you're telling me. With your past experience with the Birmingham Police, it doesn't surprise me."

He handed James a business card. "When you're ready to share call me."

"I'm just a humble property owner."

"After what you did last year in the Crowhurst Road murders?"

"I merely showed how careless the local police were in their investigations."

"Sure and the rest. You have an incredible ability to find out things."

James looked out of the window; he didn't want to be reminded of what happened in Longbridge. It had torn his family apart and was the reason why he had agreed to oversee the house building in Malvern.

"Obviously I can't tell you everything, but Bryan was murdered and it wasn't anything to do with drugs."

"Are all these murders connected?"

Tom hesitated before answering. He wanted to tell James everything, but his training stopped him. It was people like James Pidgley the secret service should be recruiting. Not the privileged rich from Oxford or Cambridge universities.

"There is a possibility that they are connected. What I do know is that someone in this place knows a lot more than they are letting on. Too many people with criminal records hide in traveling fairs and circuses."

"Or the police force."

Tom gave him a look; he knew that ten percent of the police force had something criminal to hide.

"What do you know about Bryan's background?"

"A little," lied James. "It's hard to find anyone who knows the whole story."

"If you ever find an official file on him, please don't share it with anyone."

Tom Potts opened his door and climbed out of the car. James sat for a few moments. Had he just been given permission to continue investigating? Even though to everyone else the case was closed? What did Potts mean when he said 'if I ever find a file'?

When James alighted from the car, Tom Potts had disappeared. He entered the Big Top. The clowns were huddled in one corner and, seeing him, motioned for him to join them.

"What's happening?" he asked.

"The police have gone for now, so Tonya wants a dress rehearsal," said Antonioni.

"I think she's crazy, how can we concentrate if there is a murderer on the loose?" said Bublay

"It's not one of us!" retorted Cuckoo

"How do you know?" responded Bublay.

"Stop bickering and let's get ready," said Professor Brick. "James, join us, but please don't talk about murder."

James stood in the middle of clown alley. Costumes
hanging on costume rails and props lined the outside
wall of the area. A strange looking box stood in the
middle of the area. It had pigeon holes like the one
used in a mailroom for sorting the mail. Each slot
contained a pair of shoes. Some looked like ordinary
ones that had been painted bright colors. Two pairs
were very long and stuck out of their slots. One very
large black pair, if given a size, would be at least a '60'.
It sat on top of the box. The black polish shine was so
deep it was like looking into the paintwork of a brand-
new new Rolls Royce. Each clown had his own
makeup table and mirror. The mirrors had little tiny
lights around them only one was dark. James had
never seen backstage just before a show. He stood
amazed how each clown transformed themselves into
their unique character. The makeup tables contained
sticks of greasepaint and white socks filled with baby
talcum powder. After applying the make-up, the
clowns took the sock and slapped the area of the
greasepaint. The powder dried the grease paint, then
gave it a dull solid look.
Bolt, who was the quietest of all the clowns, suddenly
spoke, after watching James looking at the other clown
apply their makeup. "It's to stop the makeup from
running."
James moved towards his table. Several photos had
been pushed under the edge of the inside of the mirror.
One picture was of a beautiful dark-haired girl. It was
her smile, which caught James's eye. Fiddle had
finished applying his make-up and made several very
strange facial expressions before speaking into the
mirror.
"Good afternoon Mr. Fiddles, and how are we today?"

The other clowns, in unison with him, replied.

"Very well, thank you — now let's make 'em laugh."

"Does that every time we all have our little idiosyncrasies. Brinarno would finish his make up and do a silly little dance," said, Antonioni.

"Oh yes, he used to say he was calling up the clown spirit so he could take the day off," said Cuckoo.

"Crazy, the lot of us. I wouldn't stay with us too long James, or we might turn you into a clown," said Professor Brick getting up and entering the circus ring.

"James who did it?" asked Bublay once the Professor was out of sight.

"It has nothing to do with the circus."

"Honestly?" asked Bublay.

"Honestly, whatever caused Bryan's murder…"

Cuckoo interrupted, "Brinarno, in clown alley we only go by our clown names."

"Sorry, whatever caused Brinarno death was something from his past."

"Are all the deaths connected?" asked Bublay.

James replied guardedly, "Maybe."

"How far in Brinarno's past are you talking about?"

"I think it may have been something to do with his college days."

"He was always talking about the death of a friend which wasn't right," said Bublay.

"Did he say which death?"

All the clowns began to talk at once.

"Stop please only one of you speak."

A little head and face gesturing took place and Bublay was picked to speak. James was amazed at how they communicated without speaking. At the same time, they all understood each other. He surmised that it must be from working together so closely and in the circus ring it would be hard to say something without shouting.

"Brinarno said the death of his friend Kipper was not suicide but murder. He said the last person to see Kipper alive was someone he called 'The Slime.'"

"Sounds like some character out of a comic book," said Antonioni.

"He never said who 'The Slime' was?"

"Not by name. It was someone else at the college."

"You don't think it was the acrobat, Quon, then?" asked Professor Brick returning from the circus ring.

"No."

"Quon and Brinarno talked a lot."

"Brinarno knew Quon's father."

"What's going to happen to his paintings?" asked Cuckoo.

"Paintings?"

"Brinarno was a great artist, not just in the circus ring but his painting and sculptures were beautiful," said Cuckoo.

"Oh yes, he would take you to an art gallery and show you things in painting you would never have seen," said Bublay.

"True, he told me he had once had an exhibition, in his college days at the local theatre."

"His greatest work, that's what he said. 'One of my pictures is the greatest work I have ever done and they would never know, the fools'," said Professor Brick.

"What did he mean?"

"We never found out."

"I think I must…" James stopped talking and looked at the table Brinarno had used.

The clowns followed his gaze and watched as Cooper appeared from under the table dressed as a clown.

"Hiding from his brother," said Professor Brick in a whisper. He took James elbow and guided him away from the others.

"The Slime, as Brinarno called him, was someone at the college. Someone Brinarno had trusted."

"How do you know?"

"He told me. He never told me who it was or what had caused him to change towards him."

"Brinarno said Kipper wasn't a traitor and the Slime knew that."

"Did he ever talk about Kipper's twin sister?"

"No."

Music had started to play in the circus ring. The clowns hurried out of clown alley and James stood looking for a few seconds at Cooper. The boy suddenly ran after the clowns.

He needed to think, get away from everyone and go over what he knew. As a teenager, James had visited Malvern and had sat on the hills looking out over the Severn valley. He had made several major life decisions on those hills.

The climb was slow as he was very out of shape, having missed several weeks away from the gym. On the way to the foot of the hill path, he had stopped at St Ann's Well café to purchase a sandwich and fill his thermos with hot tea. If he was going to think, he couldn't do it on an empty stomach. Before continuing up the hill path he visited the actual well. The ornamental arch above the entrance was painted white and wrought iron gates were open. He walked up to the marble basin; water ran into from the dolphin head spout. Someone had removed the plug that allowed

the water to flow over the basin and on to the floor. He
replaced the plug and watched as the basin filled and
overflowed. The healing powers of the water had been
known for a very long time. Even mentioned in 1622
in *Bannister's Breviary of the Eyes*. James wondered
if it was still safe to drink. He left the well after two
teenagers entered, dressed in private school uniforms.
The girl's long blonde hair floated on the light breeze.
They obviously were looking for somewhere to get
intimate. The boy seemed younger than the girl. She
controlled what they were doing. Standing in one of
the corners she pulled the boy to her, forcing her
mouth onto his. Then she grabbed his buttocks and
pulled him in closer while massaging them. James
left, remembering those were the happy days as a
teenager.

He laid the olive-green plastic ground sheet over a
grassy patch. He wasn't sure if the ground underneath
was dry from the recent rain. The freshness after the
rain was always the best time to appreciate the
countryside. The Severn Valley arranged itself in an
orderly fashion below. The fields neatly farmed and
the small villages fighting for the position of being the
best. He put his headphones on and pressed 'play'.
Elgar's *Severn Suite* played. James listened and drank
in the view. The slight wind swayed the trees in time
with the music. He knew he would have to
concentrate if he wanted to get anywhere. The music
and the scenery were hypnotizing him. His thoughts
about the murders sucked out of him and slipped into
the moist earth beneath. He found himself dragged
backward to a time when his Uncle Albert had
accompanied him on a visit to the hills. They had sat

eating sandwiches and talked of his Romani inheritance. The wind had become fierce and his uncle had told it to go lie down and rest. Suddenly the hillside had become calm.

A large black crow squawked and James came out of his daydream. The wind had picked up, and he remembers the other thing his uncle had told him ten years earlier.

'If you have a problem, my boy, tell it to the wind. Better still, shout it at the wind. It will be carried away and then return from unknown places with the answers.'

He smiled at the time, thinking his uncle mad or at least a little crazy. Only when he had tried it several years later did he realize how true it was. He closed his CD Player and stood up, then sat again quickly. He hadn't worked out what his problems were, all he knew was someone had lied to him.

If Bryan was murdered because of his invention what as the connection to Ryan's murder. Then there was Kipper's death, which Bryan thought was murder. Ryan died not because he worked in the circus but because of something to do with Bryan's invention. Kipper had died because he was selling the secrets. But a fact he had either heard or read was that Bryan believed Kipper was trying to stop whoever was selling it. That's it! Kipper was murdered and it was made to look like a suicide because he had found out who was selling the secret of the invention. Only, Bryan had destroyed it and although Kipper knew his murderer did not. Okay, he could connect Bryan and Kipper's murders. Ryan? What was his connection? Had he seen who had killed Bryan and therefore had to die? Not possible. He was with Mabel, according to

Tonya, and she had no reason to lie for him. Quite the reverse actually, she would have wanted him out of the way because he was trying to get her mother to sell the circus. That couldn't be it. Ryan died first. Before Bryan. Didn't he? That was his question. He stood looking around to see if anyone was nearby. The hills seemed deserted, only the black crow sat on the topography that pointed to places far and wide. He took several long deep breaths to fill his lungs before shouting into the wind.

"Why was Ryan killed?"

The crow squawked back at him and James laughed. The crow flew off and circled around swooping low several times towards James. He watched the beauty and majesty of the creature as it performed it aeronautical display. At first, he didn't feel the wind rise. A gust swept over him and an image of a picture came into his mind. He had seen a picture somewhere that would make the connection. He tried hard to remember but his mind drew a blank. Okay, if he couldn't remember where he had seen the picture maybe Ryan had a copy of it.

He gathered his things together and ran down the hill passing several day hikers on their way up to the top of the Worcestershire Beacon. Several times he almost collided into different groups of hikers.

The winter quarters seemed calm except for a police car outside the main entrance to keep reporters from disturbing the residents. Mabel wasn't in her house and Dougie said he didn't know where she had gone. As James was leaving the office he heard a noise from upstairs. Mabel was in her bedroom. She was sitting on the bed looking at several pictures in silver frames of her late husband.

"I'm sorry to bother you, but are Ryan's belongings still here?"

"James! I was thinking about my late husband. He would be horrified if he knew what Ryan had asked me to do."

"What was that?"

"Sell up and move to Spain to open a bar."

"Would you have done?"

"At first maybe, but I suddenly saw through him. He was just a lousy gold digger."

"Sorry."

"Don't be. Every woman meets one in her life. He was just so good in bed."

James gives an embarrassed cough.

"Sorry, love, I didn't mean to embarrass you. When you get to my age, young people think we are past sex. Well, let me tell you... I still hope to be doing it at ninety."

James laughed, "I expect you will too, with some handsome young stud."

"Oh God, let's hope so." She looked back at the picture she was holding and replaced it on a bedside table.

"How can I help you? Oh yes, Ryan stuff. Still, in his room, I expect."

The puzzled look on James face made Mabel blush a little. "He didn't sleep with me, no one shares my bed. That was my late husband's and mine. Let me show you his room."

At the far end of the corridor, they came to a flight of steps.

"Top of the stairs, first door on the left. What are you looking for?"

"A picture, which connects Bryan and Ryan."

"I'm not sure he had many pictures but go and have a look."

As James mounted the stairs, the hollowness of the wooden steps echoed as he climbed.

Ryan's bedroom was an attic room long and narrow it ran the length of the house. Most of the cupboards and drawers were empty. Either Ryan didn't own much, or he had another place where he stored his possessions. James was about to leave, feeling very disappointed. Only three books stood on the bookshelf and nothing else except clothing in the drawers and cupboards. He returned to look at the books; two of the books on financial accounting for small business. The third was a very thick copy of the Holy Bible. He flicked through the accounting books. Maybe a picture or letter was inside. Neither yielded a promised secret. He picked up the book titled Holy Bible. Inside it was not the sacred word but a scrapbook. The first page was a picture of Ryan followed by the picture James had been looking for. He knew he had seen this family photograph, but he wasn't sure where. Turning the page he found a press cutting dated 1968 from the Malvern Gazette. Freelance journalist Gerald Maurice was writing about an exhibition of student art. The Malvern Festival Theatre, James read, was proud to host an exhibition by two mechanical engineering students from the Royal Radar Establishment. *The Paintings of Ian Kipler and Painting and Sculptures by Bryan DeWitt* would be on show for three weeks.

James found Mabel in the office. She was looking through the account books.

"Did you find what you were looking for love?"

"Just this." He showed her the Holy Bible cover.

"Oh, you can have that if you want, it won't be much use here in this unholy place."

"I'll return it when I have finished with it."

"You don't have to, no one has come forward to claim his belongings."

"I found one picture of his family." James took the picture out carefully. He didn't want her to see the press cutting.

Mabel looked at the picture and then smiled, "Oh yes, I remember this. That's his cousin. Well, one of the people in the picture is, but I'm not sure which one."

"I've seen this picture before but I'm not sure where."

"My mother would say stop thinking about something and then it will come to you."

"My grandmother would always say that."

"Funny really but those old folk did seem to be very wise."

"I think it because their lives were so much less complicated."

It was late afternoon when James arrived at the Malvern Festival Theatre. He had placed the scrapbook in the building site safe and checked with the foreman to make sure everything was going according to plan. He was surprised to find they were several days ahead of schedule. The foreman, on the other hand, was pleased to have an employer who didn't stand over him. Knowing the reputation of the Pidgley family he also knew not to cut corners and get caught.

The Festival Theatre and the Winter Gardens Conference center was surrounded by armed security

personnel. James approached and was told in a
brusque authoritative voice "It's closed."
"I need to see someone in the theatre."
"What part of 'It's closed' don't you understand?" said
a tall, testosterone-fuelled ape-man.
James wandered away from the entrance and sat on the
wall opposite looking at the modern-day stormtrooper.
Most people would be intimidated by their look and
attitude. It was the effect they wanted to give to scare
the people off.
The Reverend Gilbert Tosh had been an anti-war
campaigner since the days of Aldermaston. He had
heard that a conference of top-level US and UK
officials were meeting in the Winter Gardens
Conference Centre and he wanted to protest their
presence. The black tail part of his dog collar was
stained from his cereal breakfast. His wife had given
up years earlier from trying to get her beloved husband
to look smart. In those days she had ambitions for him
to become a Bishop. He just wanted to be a country
parson. He saw James sitting on the wall and observed
the young man watching the Para-military security
force guard the people inside.
James had lost himself in thought although he was
staring at the black-clad officer. He was thinking
about the picture of Ian Kipler's relatives.
The Reverend Tosh slid up to him and stood for a few
moments before speaking.
"You're too young to remember, but this must be how
Berlin looked just before the war."
"What scares me is that they are supposed to be on our
side."
"After Margaret Thatcher, you never know who's on
which side."

"You sound like my father, I've never known him to get involved in politics until she became Prime Minister."

"I hope he was against her."

"Vehemently."

"So, you're here to protest."

"Not really I came to solve a murder."

"Is that a new play the theatre is putting on?"

"No, I'm looking for a picture which once hung in the bar of the theatre."

"That's the trouble these days. The young just don't want to get involved. Take away their computers and iPods or worse, their mobile phones, and you could have a real revolution. But anything to do with war and how the Americans seems to bully everyone and they just don't want to know."

"Sorry, I am interested but at this present time three murders need solving."

"Are you a policeman?"

"No, they haven't a clue to what is really happening."

"Lemmings the lot of them."

"Sorry I can't help today, but I need to get access to the theatre."

"I understand, try the stage door."

"Right, of course." James gave a slight bow of the head and walked across the road to the stage door. He didn't know if he should knock or just walk in. He tried the handle and the door opened. Once inside he found himself in a long corridor with steps on the left going up. Several doors stood open; each room was a dressing room. The ones nearest the stage seemed more luxurious. At the end of the corridor, he found an old man sleeping, his head resting on a fire hose affixed to the wall. James lightly touched the man's shoulders.

"I wasn't asleep just resting my eyes. As you get older they seem to hurt more."

"I'm sorry to hear that."

"How can I help you? The theatre's closed today due to some bloody government conference."

"I'm looking for a picture. Well, more a picture of a sculpture that hangs in the bar."

"Not anymore. We took the pictures down five years ago. Sad really because some of them were really nice."

"What happened to them?"

"Not sure. Dumped I suppose."

"Pity."

"You could ask Ray, the stage manager. He might know what happened to them."

"Where will I find him?"

"In the scene dock, I should think."

"Which way is that?"

"I'll take you, so which picture was you looking for?"

"One by Bryan DeWitt."

"The clown? He was a really nice man. Always came to see me when he was up in town."

" He was only here a few days ago looking for a picture."

"When was that?"

"Must have been Thursday as Ray, the stage manager, was off that day. He is always sick on Thursdays when the racing is at Worcester. Did you know Bryan worked in this theatre? A long time ago, of course."

"I didn't. Did Bryan find the picture he was looking for?"

"No."

They entered the large scene dock to the left of the theatre. A man in his late fifties was sitting reading a newspaper.

"Hey, Ray what happened to those pictures which hung in the bar?"

"Who wants to know?" Without looking up.

"This young man."

Ray closed his paper, folding it carefully before putting it on a chair.

"Sorry, sir I thought Wally was just having me on."

"It's okay, I just wondered what happened to the pictures which use to hang in the bar."

"Dumped I think."

"Pity. I wanted to buy one of them."

Ray suddenly changed his attitude. It's okay, Wally. I'll look after the gentleman now."

They both watched as Wally left the scene dock.

"Now I come to think of it, we may have stored them pictures under the stage. I believe one should never throw things away. You never know when you might need it."

"Or sell it."

"Right."

James stood at the entrance to under the stage. The door was only four feet high and he expected he would have to stoop while in there. When Ray switched on the lights he was relieved to see several steps down.

"I think we stored them over in this corner."

A stack of pictures stood against the wall. James looks through them and found the one by Ian Kipler. There was nothing by Bryan DeWitt.

"Is this all of them?"

"Yes, except for that piece of junk."

James turned and knew immediately it was the picture.
He didn't want to arouse Ray's suspicions, so he
calmly replied. "I see what you mean, although it's
interesting."

"Do you want any of them."

"I quite like this one." James pulled Ian's picture out.

"Fifty quid."

"Thirty pounds."

Ray thought for a moment. "Forty pounds and you can
have that piece of junk too."

James hesitated before answering. "Okay but I want
them wrapped in something."

"I can do better than that." Ray produced a canvas bag
and placed the pictures inside. "Someone left this
about twenty years ago, I don't think they will want it
now."

James paid him and returned to where Wally was
sitting.

"Did he rip you off?"

"No, he thinks he has but I have the Bryan DeWitt
picture and now he is dead it will be worth
something."

"Good for you. Ray thinks he's clever but most of the
time he's just a fool."

"Thanks, Wally for your help." James pushed a five-
pound note into Wally's hand.

"Very kind of you, sir."

James left the theatre. Outside in the street, several
women and young men dressed in rainbow-colored
clothing had joined the Reverend Tosh. They had
formed a line and were sitting across the road, arms
linked. The Reverend Tosh seemed to glow with
pride. He saw James and waved then gave him the

thumbs up sign. The traffic was stopped but no one seemed to be upset by this delay.

He arrived back at the Winter Quarters and unpacked the pictures in his caravan. He placed Ian's on a chair; the subject was a landscape from the Worcestershire Beacon. James liked it even though as a painting it was very naive.

He took Bryan's picture out of the bag. The small title card was still fixed to the bottom right-hand corner. The picture had been titled 'Schematic' and was a mixture of paint and objects stuck to the canvas. In the center of the three-foot by two-foot picture was a black box with a single screw in the middle.

James tapped the box and was surprised to find it was made of cardboard. He stood back from the picture and realized he liked it because it reminded him of a Piet Mondrian Painting. The lines and shapes were very similar to the Dutch master's work. He turned the picture over. Something had been written in pencil on the back. It was just readable after James had turned on a light.

'Never judge a book by its cover. How you see a picture is very different from how I see it. Not everything is art so look beyond. It's my vision. Bryan DeWitt June 10, 1968'

The hammering on his door made him put the picture under his bed sheets. He would find a better place for it later.

Cooper stood on the lower step crying. James could see that the boy was very upset and indicated for him to enter the caravan. James tried several times to get Cooper to tell him what has happened. The boy made no sense through the crying and sobbing. James gave

him a tissue, then a glass of water. His mother had
said if someone is so upset they can't speak, give them
some water and it calms them down. After a few sips
of water Cooper was able to speak.

"The coppers have arrested Dougie for the murders."

"Why?" was all James could think to say.

"James, you've got to help, please."

"Cooper, Dougie didn't do it and as usual the police are
just taking the easy road instead of finding the truth."

"Please help."

"I will, I know why they were murdered, but not who
did it."

CHAPTER THIRTEEN

The Wages Snatch

Mabel handed James the glass of whiskey. She had always admired a man who could take Malt whiskey without anything in it. Although she liked Dougie, James was the sort of man she had hoped her Tonya would marry. There was something positive about the way James conducted himself.

Cooper sat silently on the couch making sniffing sounds at an irregular pattern. James felt for the young man. It was less than a year since his own father had been wrongfully accused of murder. He sipped at his drink, his passion for neat malt whiskey had started when he was fourteen and his father had allowed him to have a drink at Christmas. He became aware that both Tonya and Mabel were staring at him.

"James, do you think Dougie did the murders?" asked Tonya.

Before he could answer Mabel spoke, "I just can't believe he did it."

"He didn't," said James looking directly at Cooper. The boy stood and without saying a word left the room.

"Poor boy it's really cut him up."

"I tried to comfort him but he just doesn't want to know," said Tonya.

"I think he is still trying to take it all in," said James putting the glass down on a coaster in front of him.

"Why James, haven't you solved it yet?"

"Tonya, I can say without contradiction that Dougie didn't murder anyone."

"How can you be so sure?"

James thought before he spoke. He didn't want to give too much away. "The murders had something to do with Bryan's past."

"Then Ryan doesn't fit into it he met Bryan four years ago when he started dating mom."

"I am convinced they either knew each other before or Ryan knew someone who was a friend of Bryan's years ago."

"What about the Chinese doctor's death?" said Mabel refilling James glass.

"At first, I thought it was connected, but now I'm not so sure."

"I was positive you would have solved it by now."

"Sorry, but I had a few misleading clues and a very difficult problem of finding out who is telling the truth."

"I understand that we circus folk tend to keep things to ourselves. If I can help in any way just ask."

"Thanks, Mabel. I need to go and see a lying policeman."

"Don't all policemen lie?" said Tonya.

"I look at it this way they are all economical with the truth."

"I thought that was politicians."

"Them too and to think we pay their salaries."

James took on a gulp of his drink and left the house.
He found Peter Kipler in the Big Top talking to one of
the circus hands. The man nodded to James and left.
"Tight-lipped this lot. It as if they didn't want us to
find out who did it."

"Peter, you have to understand, they are a very secret
group of people. Having police all over them asking
questions they panic."

"Why?"

"Everyone has something to hide."

Silence enveloped them and the two men stood staring
at each other. James made the first move and sat on
one of the seats nearby.

"Dougie's innocent."

"I know. So do the detectives. The press is hounding
us for an arrest. The Chief decided he would give them
one."

"Even though they are wrong."

"It's a game. We know we have the wrong man. So do
the press really. James, I know you don't think much of
the force but sometimes we do have a strategy to flush
out the real criminals."

"Meaning?"

"First, by arresting Dougie we can completely
eliminate him. Secondly, it gives the press a story so
they will leave us alone for at least forty-eight hours.
And thirdly, the real murderer may do something
thinking he has got away with it."

"You're not as dumb as television portrays you."

"Thanks. Oh, I can tell you Doctor Song died of a
heart attack. He wasn't murdered."

"So, the news about him being stabbed in the neck
wasn't true."

"Started by the press."

" I was told you were the one who started the rumor."

"Well, I can tell you he died of a heart attack."

"The press hasn't said anything about that."

"Not yet. The Chief is telling them tomorrow."

"Another diversion?"

"Something like that."

"I thought there was a news blackout on his death."

"There is... but what do you think leaks are for?"

"When will Dougie be free?"

"Next twenty-four hours."

"You never told me why you gave me the wrong information."

"To protect my mother, she has a thing about the family name being in the press."

"Status symbol."

"Something like that. Her neighbors would talk. She would feel they would think less of her."

"Never had that problem with my mother."

"Lucky you."

"Thanks for the information about Dr. Song, Peter."

"No problem. If I hear anything, I'll let you know. I think I may owe you after the way I treated you."

"'Bye," said James, not wanting to respond to the statement. It was obvious now that Peter Kipler was, in fact, working for someone who wanted to give out disinformation. He would make a note of all the information given to him by Peter and see how much of it was true and how much was pure propaganda.

He went in search of Cooper. The boy would want to know his brother was going to be released.

Cooper was standing near the main gate looking out at the people who had arrived to gawk at the murder scene. From the back, James saw how vulnerable he looked. His small frame was accentuated by his tight clothes. The shoulders stooped forward, and he stood on one leg. The other leg was bent at the knee and stuck out backward.

He didn't look at James as he stood next to him.

"Funny how people come to see a murder scene. Hoping to see something, hear something," said, James.

"Dougie told me it was why traveling fairs were so popular. Not just the thrill of the rides, but the idea you could see something different in the freak shows."

"My father told me, as a child, that the house they lived in had graffiti written all over it. People from all over Birmingham came to see what had been written."

"What was written?"

"'Go Home Gypos'. At least a hundred times"

"Bastards."

"That was life then, as it still is today. Prejudice hasn't changed towards the Romanies."

"Or the fair and circus people."

"Cooper, I have good news. Dougie will be home in the next twenty-four hours. The police have said he didn't commit the murders and just wanted to eliminate him from their inquiries."

"No bull?"

"No bull.

"The bastards. I could have told them he didn't do it."

"It's politics, Cooper."

"I'll believe it when I see him," said Cooper walking back into the circus tent.

The boy has become a man. The cynicism of adult life was drifting into boyhood.

James sat looking into his teacup. His mother had always said 'make a cup of tea and all your problems will go away'. After hearing it so many times as he grew up, he automatically did it. He stared at the photocopy of the picture he had taken from Ryan's possessions. He had seen this before or one very much like it, but couldn't remember where.

He began to go over in his mind all the places he had visited recently. A tinkling noise to his right kept distracting him from visualizing the places he had been to. He looked at the ceramic mobile hanging above the dining table. The upturned cups and figure eights that were part of the sculpture moved and clinked together. He stared for a few seconds before the thought 'why is the mobile moving?' came into his head. He looked around to see if a window or door was open. He couldn't feel a draft and he wasn't moving to make the hanging piece move. In the silence, he heard the click as though a cupboard was being opened.

He carefully stood up and moved to the door. Someone was searching the storage space beneath the caravan. He reached the back of the caravans just as the robber ran down between the next caravan. James gave chase, but the person was fast and nimble. It was hard to work out if it was a male or female. The head, covered by the hood of the baggy sweater, and the loose-fitting jeans, didn't indicate the sex of the thief. James saw the figure climbing through the hole in the fence and into the building site. James followed and searched between skeletons of the houses for the person; they had disappeared. He ran towards the road and looked up and down. It was empty. He turned and looked back at the building site. The place was deserted. He carefully picked his way to the hole and noticed the site office door open. Grabbing a piece of wood, he stepped warily into the office. The site foreman was lying on the floor, a cut on his head. The office safe was open and papers were scattered around the room. James called the emergency services and then checked on the foreman. The man was breathing but seemed to be unconscious.

Quickly, James checked to see if the inner safe drawer had been opened. He could hear police and ambulance sirens getting closer. The drawer had not been opened. The seal was still in place.

The paramedics were the first into the office and began to tend to the injured man. James left and stood outside watching through the open door. A very tall policeman carefully picked his way across the muddy building site. He nodded at James, then entered the office. His retreat from the office was less dignified as he fell on the last step and sat down in a water-filled mud hole. James turned away to hide his laughter.

"Fitzgerald, don't just sit around you need to get statements," said Inspector Bryce.

The police officer tried to stand but, whether it was the water or the mud, he was stuck. James held out a hand and tried to pull the officer out of the hole. The Inspector gave a laugh and told two other officers to help pull officer Fitzgerald out of the hole.

They were interrupted as the paramedics brought the site foreman on a stretcher. The man was still unconscious. His sunburnt weather-beaten face was a very pale brown.

The officers continued their struggle to rescue their colleague while Inspector Bryce approached James.

"Anything taken?"

"Just money from the safe, the week's wages for the builders."

"Not connected to my murders then?"

"No, unless the murderer wanted the money to flee the country."

"Do you think?"

"Inspector, according to the press you already have your murderer."

"It's in the papers already?"

"No, I don't think so, but the reporters on the winter quarters gate said you had arrested the murderer."

"Reporters! They will make up anything to get the front page. We took in one of the circus employees to help us with our inquiries."

"Oh, so the rumors that you were going to plant evidence on him weren't true then?"

"Mr. Pidgley we are not like the Birmingham police you dealt with before."

"You know about that?"

"Oh, I think everyone knows about your exploits."

"So, Inspector, in your view who committed the two murders?"

"If I knew that I would be home with the wife. I still think it was someone in the circus."

"Why?"

"Opportunity and motive. Bryan was a very difficult man to deal with, one of those perfectionists who was never satisfied. From talking to the other clowns he upset a lot of people. Ryan, on the other hand, wanted to take over and, in some of the circus folks eyes, wanted to destroy the place for easy money."

"Makes sense."

"And you, Mr. Pidgley, what do you make of all this? It's not that you haven't had experience in such matters."

James didn't answer but stood looking at the ground as though he was thinking about the question. "Inspector you have a lot more information than I do, so it seems you have got a lot farther than me."

"So, you think it's someone inside then?"

"Looks that way, from what you have said."

"Right. If there's nothing for me here I might as well get on." The Inspector turned and walked back to the road.

The two policemen had helped Fitzgerald to his feet. The back of his uniform was covered in cold wet mud. In helping himself, he had covered his hands with mud and, in turn, had plastered mud on his face. The two officers began to laugh. At first Fitzgerald was very annoyed but, as laughter can be infectious, he too began to laugh. They walked past James, still laughing. Fitzgerald turned as he reached the pavement.

"Mr. Pidgley, could you lock the place up and someone will be around later. Fingerprints and photos unit, I expect. Looks like druggies or kids."

James stood for a moment unable to believe the actions of the police. He locked the office and climbed through the hole in the wall. Nobby was standing inside at the back of his caravan looking scared.

"The fuzz gone?"

"Yes, but they will be coming back."

"What happened?"

"Someone broke into the office to steal money, I think."

"I have a message from my mum, she said..." A noise, as though an army was running towards them, made Nobby bolt through the hole. He turned back and said, "See you later."

James came around the caravan to see the Chinese acrobats running back and forth. Quon was there and seeing James gave a nod of his head.

A hand suddenly placed itself on James' shoulder. The shock made him jump. He turned and saw Peter Kipler smiling at him.

"Hi, just heard. Anything taken?"

"Just money."

"A lot?"

"Wages for the site."

"Sorry. What about the foreman?"

"Big John is in hospital, I was going down to see him now."

"I'll give you a lift if you like."

"Fine, I need to call the builder and tell him what's happened."

Peter dropped James off at the hospital and drove away. James was sure he was still hiding something. Big John, as everyone knew him, was really John Carson and lay in bed, his wife beside him.

James didn't have a chance to say anything before Mrs. Carson attacked.

"What do you want? I hope you have insurance because my husband is going to sue!"

"I came to see how he was."

"Well, he is very ill because of you, and once our solicitor gets through with you we will own those houses!"

"Let's see what the police come up with first, shall we?"

"The police? They are useless…"

"It's okay, love. Don't upset yourself, it wasn't Mr. Pidgley's fault."

"It's his building site and therefore he is responsible"

"It's okay."

"It's not! What if you're off work for weeks!"

"I'll be back at work on Monday, sweetheart."

"Like hell, you will."

"Enough," said Big John, the tone of his voice firm.

"As I said, I will be back on Monday Mr. Pidgley, no worries about that."

"Not if your solicitor says 'no'!"

"Shut up. Sorry, Mr. Pidgley. Thank you for coming."

James left as husband and wife began to argue. Something Big John had said made him suspicious. Why would a man who had been injured want to go back to work so soon?

Officer Fitzgerald, in a clean uniform, walked down the corridor. Seeing James, he smiled.

"Mr. Pidgley, look I'm sorry if I said anything earlier but, as you know, I was not in the best of spirits."

"It's okay, sorry for what happened to you."

"Been to see Big John?"

"Yes... strange... he says he'll be back at work on Monday."

"Doctor said he had a little bump on his head. Unlikely to cause him to go into a coma. Also, the paramedics said they thought he was faking it."

"Interesting."

"I've come to interview him."

"Good luck. With his wife, you'll need it."

James left the hospital and took a taxi back to the building site.

The rain drizzled as the night closed in. He stood outside the site office. Why did the foreman fake being in a coma? What was he doing in the office at that time anyway? The questions flooded James mind. He opened the door and stood in the doorway looking around the room. The only thing that had been disturbed in the room was the safe. He checked the lock to see if it had been forced. It hadn't. Whoever had opened the safe had used a key and he thought he was the only one with the key.

If they had a key then they must have known about the compartment at the back of the safe. Nothing had been touched inside the compartment. It was just the money they were after.

He sat on the edge of the desk and looked around the room. Except for a piece of plastic at the foot of a metal locker nothing had been moved. He bent down to pick up the piece of plastic. It was stuck under the end locker in a line of six. He pulled hard but it didn't budge. Several of the other lockers were open and full of workmen's clothing. He opened the locker expecting to find it full of tools or clothing. The locker was empty; he lifted the locker up and moved it to the side. The piece of plastic was part of a bag pushed quickly under the locker. Opening the bag, he found the money from the safe still in its bank wrappers. Something made a metal sound from the bottom of the bag and James produced a set of keys. The safe key stood out, as it was big and long. The Yale lock for the door and several keys were on the key ring. The plastic nametag had in red marker pen the name; 'Big John'.

He took a small box and emptied the contents into a drawer in one of the desks. He placed the money and the keys in the box. Taking the waste paper from the trash bin he stuffed it into the bag. He wrote a note on a piece of plain white paper; *'Big John, see me I have your keys, James.'*

He replaced the bag and the locker, in the same way he had found it only, this time, he didn't leave a piece of the bag sticking out. He was sure that it had been a mistake that the plastic bag had been sticking out beneath the locker. He didn't want anyone else finding the bag. He removed the safe key off the ring and placed it on his own key ring.

Back inside his caravan, he placed the box under the sink in the kitchen area. He filled the kettle with water and placed it on the stove. He needed a cup of tea while he thought through what his next move was. A giggle aroused him from his thoughts and he carefully walked up to the shower room. Opening the door wide he found Nobby and Cooper trying not to laugh. James looked at the two skinheads, whose bodies shook from internal laughing. He left them and went back to the table.

Cooper approached him. The giggling fit had almost subsided as he now wondered if James would be angry.

"Sorry James, we came to see you and when you put the key in the lock we panicked and hid."

"Yeah sorry, but I have some things to tell you from my mom and also what we saw."

James didn't answer but looked at the two boys. Several years earlier, when he was going through his rebellious stage as a teenager, he had contemplated being a skinhead. He knew this would have irritated his father a little but would have made his older brothers Donald and Brian very angry. He still wished he had done it, but he lacked the courage. He also knew his brothers would have given him so many problems if he had. From that moment on he had never gone back on a decision.

"No problem. Can someone make the tea?"

"We are not that useless," said Cooper.

James sat staring at the floor as the two boys made a pot of tea. As Nobby placed a tray on the table with three cups James smiled, relaxing the atmosphere.

"We are sorry," said Nobby.

"It's okay, I just have things on my mind."

"Well, my Mom said I have to find you and tell you of something she found in her diary."

"Your mother keeps a diary?"

"Since she was a little girl, she says, but I think it's only written when she feels in the mood."

"I kept one once, until Dougie found it."

"Why? What did it say?" asked Nobby.

"I was keen on this girl at school and every time I had a wank, I wrote about it and told the diary what I would like to do to her. Only, Dougie thought I was doing it for real but I was only ten."

Both James and Nobby looked at him.

"What! You have never wanked over a girl?"

"Yeah, many times, but I've never written about it," said Nobby.

James looked at them and gave a huge laugh. They too started to laugh, slipping into a giggling fit again.

"Nobby, what did your mother remember?"

"She said it was a quote from the clown guy."

"Brinarno," said Cooper.

"Yeah, him. Well, it seems they were up the hills, the night after some guy had fallen off the roof. She said the Clown Brinarno said..." He took out a small piece of paper and after turning it right side up continued.

'*It's right in front of them and they'll never see it. Not after what they did. Art is art after all.*'"

"What's it mean?"

"Not sure Cooper, but I think it may be very important."

Nobby folded the paper and carefully placed it in his pocket.

"I think I should have that just in case something happens to you."

Nobby handed the paper over. Cooper poured the tea and handed a mug to James.

"You said you had seen something?"

"Oh yeah, the guy who was taken to the hospital."

"Big John."

"Yeah, hi. Well, just before he was attacked he spoke to the guy who attacked him."

"Not just before," added Cooper. "He was arguing with Big John, who stormed off to the office. The man followed after fifteen minutes and hit him, then ran off."

"Was he carrying anything?" asked James.

"No, that's what I don't understand. They said it was a robbery and money was taken," replied Nobby.

"Inside job," said Cooper.

James and Nobby looked at him as he sank back in the chair.

"What d'ya mean?"

"Nobby, if the guy slugged Big John and took nothing, but the police say something was taken, then whoever is left took it."

"So, you're saying Big John took the money."

"Yeah, plain as anything. Right, James?"

James smiled and nodded his head.

"Hang on. James came just after the guy had bolted then called the police and medics. So how could Big John get the money."

"Why did the man have to wait fifteen minutes?"

"So Big John could hide the money? Right! So let's go looking for it."

"Done and found. Keep it to yourselves though. I need to confront Big John on Monday. I think he will be working for me without pay."

"Dougie said you were no fool, and now I know what he meant."

"If you were watching, did you see someone come through the hole just before me?"

"The hooded guy?"

"If it was a guy."

"It was a man, but I'm not sure who he was. He almost ran into the man who hit the foreman."

"Where did he go?"

"Not sure. He hid somewhere on your building site after you arrived."

"Then he slipped away while the police were mud wrestling."

"That was the best, I couldn't stop laughing."

James didn't reply, sipping his tea and looking at the floor.

"I got a theory," said Cooper.

"About what?" asked Nobby

"The murders. I think it all has to do with Ryan trying to sell the circus. See, he murdered Brinarno because he found out what he was trying to do. Brinarno was close to Dr. Song and told him what Ryan was doing. So Ryan killed him too."

"So, who killed Ryan?"

"Suicide," said Cooper.

"Never, people don't commit suicide that way.
Somebody murdered him." said, James.
"Okay, it was one of the Chinese acrobats because
they had lost their translator."
"You told me they could all speak English and he did
too," James said. "They just pretended not to be able
to."
"I told you that in confidence."
 Nobby looked at Cooper. His head dropped and he
said in a slow quiet voice, "Sorry, I forgot."
"It's okay. James is one of us anyway."
"A skinhead inside." Said, James.
Sensing the tension build between them James smiled
and handed his empty mug to Cooper for some more
tea.
"Good theory, Cooper. But I think you're a little off
track. Ryan was killed first because he saw who
murdered Brinarno. The doctor wasn't murdered but
died because he ate too much rice."
"Really?" said Nobby.
"Maybe. But he wasn't murdered."
"Okay, Brinarno was killed first. So, who killed him?"
asked Nobby.
"I think I know but it is going to be impossible to
prove."
"Anyone in the circus?"
"No, and I know that for sure. This has to do with what
happened many years ago." James suddenly stopped
speaking. He was having a moment of 'déjà vu'.
"What's wrong?" asked Nobby and Cooper
simultaneously.
"Sorry. Not long ago, when I lived in Birmingham,
something happened which had to with the past and it
seems to be repeating itself again"

"Like my Mom's Shepherd's Pie," said Nobby, laughing so much he fell off his chair.

James and Cooper laughed not at his joke, but at him falling off the chair and onto the floor.

"I wish I had a photo of that," screamed Cooper.

It made Nobby laugh even more and Cooper slid to the floor as they both fell into fits of uncontrollable giggling. They both looked at James who had gone into a trance-like state. This sent them into even more fits of giggling.

James continued to look into the distance, which made Nobby and Cooper calm down.

After a few minutes, Cooper became concerned at James' manner and asked, "What's wrong James?"

"Nothing, it just what you said."

"Sorry I didn't mean to…"

"You didn't say anything wrong, it's just I remembered where I had seen the photo before."

"Is that good?"

"I need to go and see someone."

"Can we stay here?"

James hesitated.

Nobby reacted quickly and, raising his voice said, "Come on, Cooper. He doesn't trust us."

"I trust Cooper."

"Meaning you don't trust me."

"Correct, I don't trust you yet."

"Nobby, that's fair after the way you have behaved."

"You can stay because I know Cooper wouldn't allow you to do anything."

"Forget Cooper. If I did anything against you my Mom would kill me."

Cooper laughed and Nobby punched him on the arm.
"Nobby thinks his Mom may be in love with you or at
least lusts after you."
This sends both the boys into another fit of giggling.
James blushed and left the caravan quickly without
saying another word.

James arrived at the Plums' home to find the place
empty. The front door was open as he approached the
house. He rang the doorbell. From behind the four-
foot high fence, a man suddenly stood up.
"Left! Done a runner sometime in the night. Wife
heard them go but I was dead to the world."
"Do you know where they went?"
"No."
"Is there someone inside?" The man shook his head.
"So why do you think the door is open?"
"No idea, why don't you have a look around? I mean,
if you're looking for them, they may have left a clue."
James entered the house, later he would wonder why
he had placed being cautious to the wind. The Plums
had left in a hurry. A few scraps of paper and the odd
book were scattered around the living room floor.
Stepping on the bottom step of the stairs he froze as he
heard a noise from above. It was as if someone was
running. The man came down the stairs two or three at
a time and it wasn't until he was level did James
recognized him. Chris Parrott stood in front of James
with his whole body shaking.
"Where are they?"
"Who?"
"The Plums I want to see them. They killed him."
"They're not here. According to the neighbor they left
sometime in the night."

"Shit."

"Who did they kill?"

"Kipper, Ian Kipler."

"You have proof?"

"No, not really, it's just I know something was wrong that night."

"Chris, calm down and explain from the beginning." Chris looked around and, taking James by the elbow, guided him into the kitchen.

The kitchen was spotless. The white tiled wall above the sink and counter was sparkling. Carol Plum had been a house-proud woman. She must have spent her day cleaning the house. The stove looked new and unused. James opened the refrigerator, expecting to find it empty and clean. The food inside looked fresh and several bottles of milk were unopened.

"They left in a hurry, and I mean in a hurry."

"The murdering bastards would."

"Chris, please explain what you mean. You said you knew they murdered Ian Kipler. Was it Derek or Carol who committed the murder?"

"I'd left my girlfriend. We had just broken up for the sixth time, so I wasn't in a good mood. Derek was walking down the stairs from the top floor. He had a grin on his face. Even though he looked like he had just lost a fight."

"Did you speak to him?"

"Yes, but he didn't look at me and continued down the stairs and out into the street."

The door from the hall opened and a large tall woman filled the kitchen doorframe. The man James had spoken to outside peered around her.

"Who are you?" she asked, in a loud authoritative voice.

"Chris Bird, Estate Agent and Renter's Friend." He pushed his right hand forward to shake hers. She looked at his hand but didn't move hers.

"Don't shake hands with men, you never know what it might lead to. I am a respectable married woman."

"Really?" was the only reply James could think to say. She turned and looked at him, "Who are you?"

"My client," responded Chris."

"My husband said you were asking after Derek and sweet Carol."

"Err yes…"

"They had told this gentleman the property was available."

"I see. I thought you might have been some drug sex ring. Read in my paper how older men lure young pretty boys into an empty house and do things with them after they've drugged them."

"Nothing happening like that here, now if you had said a mature beautiful lady like yourself I might have been interested."

James was astonished how this huge woman suddenly turned into a fidgeting schoolgirl after Chris had made his comment. The silence between them grew and became a little uncomfortable for James.

The woman sensed it too.

"Well, if there is anything I can do for you, I live next door. My name is Marsha."

"Thank you, Marsha, do you know when Derek and Carol moved out?"

"Yesterday. They didn't say anything to us, but they wouldn't. We really didn't talk that much on account of her being so jealous."

"Of what?" exclaimed James.

"Well, Derek liked to chat with me and then, last Christmas, we caught Carol and Peter that's my husband naked in the spa pool. We have one in the new extension at the back of the house. If you ever want to try it, please just let me know. I'll show you how it works."

"What I can't understand is Derek not telling the allotment association he was leaving." The voice of Marsha's husband echoed in the empty hallway.

"Oh, I'm sure he would have," said Marsha.

"An allotment?" asked James.

Peter pushed past his wife and into the kitchen. He seemed a lot small than James had first thought.

"Derek has an allotment near mine up the road. He would never have just gone and left it. He worked on it almost every day."

Chris looked at James who gave him a slight nod of the head.

"Well, Marsha I hope to see you again soon, maybe in the hot tub. I have other properties I must show James."

"Anytime. Just come round. I'm always free."

Chris and James walked to the allotment, following the detailed directions Peter had given them. The chain link gate was open, and several men were bent over attending to their gardens. The wooden shed, Peter had described as Derek's, proudly bore the name 'Plum' above the door.

The vegetables and flowers in the garden had been pulled up and thrown to the side. The squeak of a wheelbarrow made both Chris and James turn around. The man who stopped and looked at them was very old, and had a slight stoop.

"Vandals again," said the old man. "Kids or market thieves."

Chris looked at him, blankly. The old man realized he didn't understand. "The Farmer's Market by the library. They steal our fruit and vegetables to sell as organic. It's becoming a big problem here now."

"When did it happen?"

"All the time. We think the council should hire a security guard to protect the place."

"Sorry, I meant when did this happen to Derek's plot?"

"-Last night. Must have been, because when I left at four the place was as beautiful as it always is. Derek was over here, cleaning out his shed."

"You saw him?"

"Well, I think it was Derek, my eyesight is not as good as it was, but I think it was him."

"But you're not sure?"

"Well, to be honest, it might not have been him, because whomever it was didn't say 'hello' when I shouted over. And Derek was always ready for a chat when he came by."

The old man picked up his wheelbarrow and continued along the path.

Chris opened the unlocked shed door. The inside of the shed, like the garden, was a mess of papers and gardening tools.

"Done a runner," said Chris, "he knew I was close on his tail."

"How did he know?"

"I saw him and his dreadful wife last week. They were shopping. He said he had retired and was spending time on his garden."

"A cover."

"I don't think so. You see, James, Derek was always so hyper and this time he was calm. She, on the other hand, was as she always is. Loud and obnoxious."
"Where to next?"
"I need to keep on looking for the murdering bastard."
"You don't know he did it."
"I do," said Chris looking James in the face.

CHAPTER FOURTEEN

ELF

At the height of the water cure period in Malvern, the Victorians had placed cast iron benches around the hillside. Very few had survived, either from the weather or vandals. James and Chris sat looking out over the Severn Vale on one of the few left undamaged.

James knew he needed to find out more about Bryan and the college days. How could he ask Chris without him either racing off, or clamming up? That was the question on his mind.

Chris turned to look at him, "Why are you doing this?"

"Doing what?"

"Trying to find the Plums?"

"I met Bryan DeWitt and he asked me for help. Then he died along with others. I was asked to find out why, but as I started to unravel his life I realized that he was an important man. And the world was about to forget him."

"He wasn't just important, he was also a good friend who, even though most didn't see it... he was always there for us."

"I understand about the Black Box, well, that it was an incredible invention, but that's all I know."

"So, you're asking me to fill you in?"

"Please, if only to understand what's really going on."

"The box was only the start, it's what came after that caused the others to be murdered."

"You mean John Bunty, Ken Williams, Roy Churchill, and Tom Saunders?"

"Don't forget Ian Kipler. Bryan invented this box, which could detect pain in a person's body. Even if they were unconscious or asleep. The tests were unbelievable. He then took it another step and started using extremely low-frequency waves. At first, he was trying to give warmth to the pain areas in the hope it would help. Then one day he realized it could change the mood of a person. A person could be happy and elated, then in a deep suicidal depression within seconds. At that point, he destroyed the equipment and we all took an oath to never tell anyone about it."

This was new information to James. Philip Langley hadn't told him everything.

"You all knew how it worked though?"

"No, that was where Bryan was very clever. He had read an article or something about how the IRA used cells, so it was harder for them to be detected. He made it so only he and one other knew the whole thing. It was brilliant because none of us knew who the other person was."

"Do you know?"

"Yes, Ian Kipper. And that's why he was killed, because he wouldn't tell. He loved Bryan like a brother, I think we all did."

"And his secret was kept?"

"Sort of. Today it's known that the British and Americans use ELF to control their populations."

"ELF?"

"Extremely-Low-Frequency waves. Ask yourself. Do we really need all those mobile phone towers?"

"For better service?"

"Not if we are supposed to be satellite-linked. There are those out there who say this is all conspiracy theory or, as the mental health people say, dangerous fixation time."

"The only real conspiracy, I think, is the government itself."

"James, that's funny."

"Wasn't meant to be."

"And here's me thinking you're a member of the Young Conservatives."

"Don't own a tie." They both laughed. "So, they know now what Bryan invented?"

"They have a version of sorts; Bryan invented something which I think will take a thousand years to recreate. Because it did more good than bad. Once he had read about the German Professor, Schumann, his ideas just exploded. Who knows what he would have come up with if they had left him alone? "

"Why did Derek kill Kipper?"

"At first, when I began to think about it, the murder that is, I thought it was to do with Derek not being told the secret. Then I realized that Derek didn't know the other person was Kipper. So now I think Kipper found out something about Derek and threatened him with it. So, Derek pushed him off the hostel."

"What now?"

Chris didn't answer, but looked out across the vale as the sun began to set. James remembered from his teenager years views like this and how happy it had made him.

"I need to go home. Derek will turn up sometime soon he can't hide. What about you, James?"

"I'm trying to find out who killed Bryan. Don't think it was Derek, so the search goes on."

"Sorry. I don't want to talk anymore I keep thinking there are microphones everywhere. That plant isn't really a flower, it's a microphone and the government is listening to what we are saying. The Prime Minister is in 10 Downing Street listening to you and me."

"I understand. The whole government thing since the 60's does make you think like that. Chris, I think you may be a little too paranoid."

"Maybe you're right. I have seen too much and know too much to feel really safe. I need to go home and hide for a while. I need to get my mental balance back to normal."

They began to walk down the hill, Chris looking behind him every few steps.

"If you remember anything please call me on my mobile. Here's the number." James handed Chris a business card. He took it and placed it carefully in his wallet.

They returned to their cars and James watched as Chris drove off, wondering if he was safe from danger.

The assumption that the Plums had fled would become written into local street lore. The truth of what really happened was destroyed the night they disappeared never to be known. The dark clouds once again gathered. James found comfort in his caravan bed.

CHAPTER FIFTEEN

The Plums

There was nothing really strange about Pauline, on an early morning visit to Worcester, stopping at the outdoor antique market. Searching through a box at one stall she found a picture frame she liked. After haggling with the stall owner, she bought the frame for five pounds. The picture was still in the frame and, as she made her way back to the car, she tried to remove it. The clasps on the back of the frame had been bent and made it difficult for her to open the back.

Coffee mornings with Alison had become a daily event so, instead of driving home, Pauline arrived at Alison's and met Nobby on the doorstep.

"What you got there?"

"Just bought it in Worcester."

"Let's have a look then?"

Pauline gave Nobby the picture frame. He looked at it and then smiled.

"Nice. Is it really silver? You know James has this picture too, but it is not in a frame."

Alison had arrived at the door and took the frame from Nobby. She looked at the picture.

"I recognize these people. We'd better show this to James."

They arrived at the Winter Quarters just as James was getting up. He opened the door reluctantly and waited for the comments about his pajamas. They had been a present from his sister Ann when she was in one of her silly moods. The soft beige color background was covered with ten different teddy bears. No one made a comment. Once inside his caravan, Nobby began to make some tea while his mother and Pauline watched as James looked at the picture.

"The Plums had this picture on their mantlepiece. Where did you get it?"

"Worcester market this morning."

"Can you remember who you bought it off?"

"Of course, why?"

"The Plums have gone missing and if their belongings are making their way to a market stall then something is definitely wrong."

"We need to go and find out where this antique stall holder got this."

"We'd better hurry, the market closes very early."

James changed from his pajamas and washed his face. There was no time to take a shower. He would have to do that when he got back, even though he hated leaving the house as he put it; 'unwashed'.

"Oh, you've changed," said Pauline, "We thought it was a new London style."

"I liked them," said Nobby.

"You would. You may dress and look like a hard man but underneath you're still my little sweet boy."

"Mom!"

"Nobby, you stay around here and keep your eyes out. You have our mobile numbers so just call if anything happens," said Alison.

"I want to come too."

"It's more important you stay here and that's final." Nobby's shoulder sank, but he knew better than to argue with his mother.

They arrived in Worcester just as the market was closing. Several stalls had already packed up and left. Boxes and plastic crates were open and spread all around the place as the stallholders packed away their antiques. Pauline walked quickly through the market to where she had purchased the picture frame. Several boxes stood open as a woman in her late 40s packed away cups and plates.

Pauline seemed stunned. For a few seconds she stared at the stallholder and then at the boxes full of crockery.

"This is not her. She must have gone."

James smiled at the stallholder, "Sorry to bother you, but do you know where we can find the lady who had this stall earlier this morning?"

"Gone."

"I can see that," said Pauline coming out of her trance. James continued to smile, ignoring Pauline's outburst. "Do you know where we could find her?"

"No."

"Do you know when she will be back?"

"No."

"You don't speak much do you?"

"No."

James guided Pauline and Alison away from the stallholder. He knew she wasn't going to say much to them. His own family had taught him to be very cautious when speaking with strangers. Alison started to look at another stallholder's items as antiques had always fascinated her.

Margaret Livesay had, for as long as she could remember, hated the weekly antique market. It stopped her being able to get off her bus and cross the market square quickly to get to Keymart for her cashier's job. This morning the market stallholder seemed to make it almost impossible for her to weave between the stalls. She knew most of the ladies that worked the stalls as they came into the supermarket deli to get coffee and sandwiches. She passed James, Pauline, and Alison and stood for a few moments talking to the monosyllabic stallholder.

Alison heard her speak and quickly turned. She knew Margaret. They had worked together at Fritz's Mini Market in Malvern.

She waited for Margaret to finish speaking and as she began to walk away she raced after her.

"Margaret!"

"Pauline King, you look younger every time I see you. How are you."

"Oh, I can't complain and yourself?"

"The usual work and then more work. Husband did a runner and now the creep wants to come back. Like hell, I said."

"Men!"

"What you doing here?"

"Looking for a stallholder. She had this beautiful picture frame and now she has gone."

"Which stall?"

"You know the lady you just spoke to?"

"Darlene, right bitch she can be, but has a heart of gold if she knows you."

"The woman had a stall next to hers."

"Wendy Jarvis. Lives in Colwell. Husband works on the oil rigs, so she says."

"Do you know the address?"

"No, but I can tell you which house it is. Go through Malvern, over the hill and on to Walwyn Road. At The Crescent turn right, then on the corner of Crescent Road and The Crescent there's a little white house."

"Thanks, Margaret you're an angel."

"Tell that to my boss. Got to go, or I'll be late."

The journey back to Malvern for James was hard. Trying to concentrate while listening to Pauline and Alison talking in the back of his car. As they drove down Walwyn Road, Pauline leaned forward and began to give him instructions. The little white house was set on the corner.

The garden was overgrown with weeds and a rusting van stood on the driveway. James knocked on the front door, while Alison pushed a button in the wall. They stood for several minutes and no one came. Alison pushed the button again several times. James knocked, and then Pauline thumped on the door.

The door opened a little and a woman peered out at them.

"Hi, you sold me a picture frame this morning."

"Maybe."

"We need to know where you got it."

"Who are you?"

"Wendy, we just need to know how you obtained the picture frame."

"Sorry, I don't remember." She began to close the door.

Pauline put her foot in the crack stopping her. "Look talk to us or we go to the police and tell them you're selling stolen goods."

"Wait a moment."

The door closed and they wondered if she had just gone back inside and ignored them. Then the door opened, and Wendy stepped to the side, "Please go into the sitting room on the left."

"When did I sell you the picture frame?" said Wendy, once they had all assembled in the sitting room.

"This morning. Look, let me show it to you." Pauline produced the frame and handed it to Wendy.

"Wait here." Wendy left the room, returning a few minutes later carrying three boxes.

"Last night I found these on my doorstep. People do that sometimes. They think I want their junk."

"You don't know who?"

"No, and if it's stolen, I don't want it. You can have it back if you want."

"Thanks," said James, before either Pauline or Alison could reply.

"How much did you pay for the frame?"

"Ten pounds."

Wendy took out her purse from her apron pocket and gave Pauline a ten-pound note.

"If there is nothing else, I want you to go."

Once they were back in the car and driving back to Malvern, Alison who had been very quiet since leaving Wendy's said, "I thought you said you paid five pounds for the picture frame."

"I did."

"But you told her ten."

"I know. We need to give the five to James for petrol
and I also wanted to know if the woman remembered.
She either didn't or she wanted to just get rid of us —
but she didn't want us to see what was in the other
room."

"Two young men dressed in army fatigues," said,
James.

"How do you know?"

"I saw them reflected in the hall mirror when we
entered the house."

"You're sharp."

"My mother taught me two things, always have on
clean underwear and watch when you cross the road."

"James, what has that got to do with seeing those
guys?"

"Everything. Wearing clean underwear means being
prepared for the unexpected. Watch when you cross
the road means to know where you are and who's with
you."

"I see how come you're so smart."

"His mother, it figures. Is that why you're not
married?"

"He is waiting for me to get my divorce, aren't you?"
said Pauline.

James just smiled and drove back to the building site.
The three of them carried the boxes into the site office.
The site foreman was just leaving as they arrived.
Pauline and Alison entered, and James stood talking to
the foreman.

"Isn't he the one who stole the money?" asked Alison
as he entered the site office.

"Yes, and now he is so scared he is working for
nothing."

"What did you say to him?"

"Nothing. He knows I found what he was up to and is too scared to say anything. Fear is always a great manipulator."

They each perused into a box, pulling out items, examining them, and then returning them. After several minutes, Pauline gave up and sat on a wooden kitchen chair. Alison had found a Japanese-patterned silk scarf, which she'd wrapped around her neck. Taking it off she found several holes and tears in the fabric.

"It's a load of junk." said Pauline looking at her co-conspirators.

"Looks that way. What do you think, James?"

James continued to go through his box, examining each item carefully. Alison leaned against the office wall and watched him. She caught Pauline looking at her and they both smiled before returning their stare to James.

"Okay, Sherlock who stole the Irish Crown Jewels?"

"Possibly the Pope or the Arch Bish of Canterbury." said Alison.

"Really, I didn't know that."

"I'm just kidding."

Pauline blushed at her gullibility.

"Junk. Thrown away and not stolen"

"No, Alison, these items were stolen or at least deliberately got rid of."

"Who would steal junk?"

"It's not junk to the person who owned it."

He took a silver-plated beer tankard out of the box and placed in on the table. A small bedside carriage clock and two small metal boxes followed.

"These items were collected or given to someone as presents. You don't give away items you like or treasure. Nor were they dumped while running away."

"Maybe the Plums gave them away because they were running away."

"No, whatever happened to the Plums these items were taken and then thrown away."

"Sorry, you have lost me."

"The Plums have gone, I think. Not voluntarily, but taken by force and their house emptied to make it look like they had done a runner."

"The allotment shed, you said, was empty. So who did that?"

"Some old man told you he had seen Plum cleaning it out the day before," interrupted Pauline.

"It wasn't Plum, the old man couldn't recognize his own wife if she stood five feet in front of him."

"You're saying they were kidnapped or at least abducted?"

"I'm not sure, I know they were planning to disappear, but someone changed their plans."

"So, what makes you so certain?"

"I don't think Carol Plum would leave behind her wedding and engagement rings." He produced two rings out of the box and held them up. Pauline and Alison moved forward to get a better look at them.

"How do you know they were hers?"

James produced a picture of Carol from the box. Her left hand was gently resting on her cheek and the rings very clearly visible.

"Okay they are her rings and we all know a woman wouldn't leave her rings behind unless she was dumping the man."

"Even then, Pauline, she'd take them to sell."

"You're so cynical, Alison. James, where do you think they went?"

"I think they were going to leave the country, but I'm not sure if they made it."

Alison and Pauline looked at each other, both trying to see if what James had just said meant the same to the other. Alison looked down into her box and produced an ashtray from the Savoy Hotel in London. She showed it to the others and replaced it in the box. James took out a small very worn teddy bear, the sort a child of the 1950s would have owned. Alison took it off him and looked at it carefully before showing it to Pauline. The reaction from her surprised James. He watched as Alison held the teddy bear close to her breasts. Pauline had turned away and stepped away from the table and the boxes.

"Ali, please put it back in the box. If what James has said is true, I don't want to touch any of this junk."

"Sorry, I had one like this once. Lost it a long time ago. What are you going to do with this stuff?"

"Well, if you and Pauline would like a ring each…"

"No thanks, I don't want a dead woman's ring."

"Me neither."

"I'm not sure they are dead, but I think it likely. Is it okay to give these boxes to Nobby? I thought maybe he and Cooper could sell them to make some money for themselves?"

"What if they get caught?"

"They can say I gave it to them. We will depersonalize the things first "

"Oh, shit look at the time, I've got to get going," said Pauline, looking at her watch.

They watched as Pauline grabbed her handbag and left the site office. An awkward silence enveloped them, and they both stood looking into the boxes. James began to take pictures from picture frames and check to see if other items had any personal markings tracing them back to the Plums.

Alison looked at him. She studied his actions to see if she could read his mood. Unable to, she spoke very softly.

"You know what's really going on, don't you?"

"I have a good idea, but I can't say just now."

"Why? Don't you trust me?"

"It's not that. I learned a long time ago to be cautious in what I say. If I'm wrong I could hurt a great many people and I don't want that."

"I'm not sure what you mean."

"If someone calls you a troublemaker and several people overhear them then those people may think you are a troublemaker. Even though you're not."

"That happened to me once. Took me months before people started to believe I wasn't a troublemaker. Even today there are those who hear my name and say 'what she has done now'."

"Precisely my point."

"Be careful James, we don't want anything to happen to you." She placed her hand over his and gave a squeeze. "Thanks for thinking of our Nobby. Not many people understand."

"He needs to trust a little, and more people would trust him."

"I'm not sure skinheads will ever be trusted or, for that matter, liked."

"Like so many at his age he's just making a statement." James collected the boxes together and placed them in the empty file cabinet. Locking it he gave a little laugh.

"Not the safest place in the world."

He locked the office door and suddenly they could hear laughing and clapping from inside the circus winter quarters. James, leading the way, climbed through the hole in the fence. He helped Alison climb through. The clapping was coming from the other side of the Big Top. As they approached, they saw a small crowd gathered around Dougie. Cooper saw them and ran up shouting, "Dougie's home!"

Seeing James, Dougie came over and shook his hand, but turned it into a hug. The smile on his face ran from one ear to the other. The other performers had moved over with Dougie. James watched as one of the Chinese acrobats turned and ran off towards their caravans.

"Thanks for keeping Cooper straight."

"Didn't need to. Your brother is an honest, truthful kid."

"Thanks anyway."

A silence fell over the small crowd as Peter Kipler walked across the yard. The clowns and acrobats parted as he walked up to James. Dougie and Alison in unison said, "I've got to go and ..." Dougie led Alison towards the main gate.

"You know how to clear a room, as they say."

"I wanted to come and see you before you hear it from anyone else. Derek and Carol Plum are dead. They were found out at Hanley Castle in their car. A hosepipe connected to the exhaust."

"Suicide?"

"That's the official verdict."

"You don't think so?"

"They left a taped message. It just said they were sorry for all they had done over the years and hoped the

people they knew, and the country, would forgive
them."

"Interesting."

"There will be a press statement later saying that the
police believe the Plums murdered Bryan and Ryan
and the case is closed."

"Is that what Inspector Bryce thinks?"

"You know him, but he has to go along with the MI5
version of things."

"Why did they do it?"

"Official Secrets Act. We will never know."

"Bullshit. Just another cover-up."

"Maybe, James, if I hear anything else I'll let you
know."

James nodded and Peter walked towards the main gate,
passing the clowns and Mabel who were heading
toward James.

Mabel smiled as she approached, but the tone in her
voice indicated she wasn't a happy person.

"What did he want?"

"Derek and Carol Plum have been found dead and they
are being blamed for the murders of Bryan and Ryan."

"No way," said Antonioni, the remnants of clown
make-up still around his mouth.

"Why do you say that?" asked James.

"I don't believe Brinarno was killed by them, whoever
they were,"

"I agree," said, James.

"You know who did it, don't you?" said Antonioni.
The clowns suddenly surrounded James. They pushed
and shoved each other to get closer to him. He had
this vision as if he was in the Italian film director
Federico Fellini's film 'I Clowns'. He had seen it at

the art house cinema in Birmingham when he was
supposed to be at school.

Mabel, thinking James was getting hassled, shouted,
"Move back and let him have some space."

The clowns did as they were told and moved away
from James forming into a circle around him. Mabel
pushed through and moved closer to him.

"Sorry about that. They just want some answers.

"I understand. I don't know who did it, but I know who
didn't and it wasn't Carol and Derek Plum."

"Why do you say that?" asked Cuckcoo, who had
stepped forward and stood next to Mabel.

"It all too convenient, if I was the sort of person who
believed in conspiracies, I would say this smelt of the
biggest conspiracy around."

"James, if you find anything out, would you let us
know?"

"Please." The 'please' came from Bolt, his eyes filling
with tears.

"I promise. As soon as I know I will tell you guys."
The clowns each shook his hand and left. Mabel gave
him a kiss on the cheek then went into the Big Top.
Cooper appeared from behind a caravan and shouted,
"A promise is a promise." then ran off.

After checking his caravan and the site office, James
walked along the road towards the Unicorn public
house. He needed a change of venue. A car flashed by
and suddenly stopped, before reversing towards him.
Pauline stuck her head out of the driver's window. He
looked inside the car to see Alison in the passenger
seat, her eyes shut tight and both hands gripping the
seat.

"Hey sailor, want a lift, or would you prefer a drink?"

"I think Alison needs one. I didn't know you could drive."

"I haven't passed my test. I borrowed my little brother's car so I can get in some practice in before my test."

"I was going to the Unicorn for a quiet drink."

"Band night. Let's go over to the New Inn in Storridge, you'll like the place. It's a real country pub."

"Do you want me to drive?"

"No, I told you! I need the practice, hop in the back." James climbed into the back seat and, after moving a bag full of clothes and several pairs of men's briefs off the seat, tried to relax. Pauline turned the car around and accelerated down the street. Alison still had her eyes shut and was gripping the seat even harder. He had lived through his brother Paul's driving lessons to know not to show panic. As Pauline ran through her third red light, he too began to grip the seat tightly. He noticed the black Range Rover because it too ran the same red lights they had. As they entered Storridge the vehicle overtook them and turned down a side lane. The windows were tinted and seeing who was driving was impossible.

They arrived at the New Inn parking lot. Pauline had problems trying to park at the side of the public house. She gave up and drove to the back of the parking lot, behind the public house. She climbed out, looking at James and Alison who were still seated gripping their seat. She gave a laugh and slammed her car door. Alison jumped and, realizing they had stopped, leapt out of the car. James slowly opened the door and climbed out. He had only been this scared once before. When he was six, his older brothers, Donald and Peter, had taken him to the fair and forced him onto the whiplash ride.

"What's wrong with you two? I think I drove well tonight. I think I am ready for my test."

"Going through three red lights wasn't what I was expecting."

"What red lights?"

"James, where did you come from?" asked Alison.

"I picked him up going to the Unicorn."

"Really, I didn't notice?"

"Hey, James do you think that black car was following us?"

"You noticed it... but not the red lights. I did at first, but now I'm not sure."

"I think we have all become a little paranoid. I know I have."

"Why what's happened, Alison?"

"You'll think me mad, but I am sure someone has been going through my drawers in my bedroom."

"Nobby maybe."

"No, he wouldn't dare. Anyway if it were him or his father the place would have been a mess."

"So, what makes you think it was someone else?"

"Well, I have this blouse which is pure silk and I always keep it wrapped in tissue in my drawer. For a start, the tissue wasn't folded the way I fold it. Then I have this drawer, which I keep my lady things in, if you know what I mean. I also placed some pictures in the same drawer. Stop the old man and Nobby looking at them. "

"What sort of pictures?"

"Nothing dirty, just me as a young girl and a few of the gang. Well, I had this great picture of Bryan and the others and now I can't find it."

"What do you think, James?"

"We are not paranoid. Something is going on, but who and why I just don't know."

They opened the door to the public-house. The smell of beer mixed with a roast meat hit them as they walked in. The bar was full of women, all standing around the dartboard.

"About bloody time! We had almost given up on you ladies coming," said a very large, masculine woman.

"Sorry."

"Don't be sorry, we need to get this competition going so let's go."

"What competition?" asked James.

"Are you the Upton ladies dart team?"

"No, we came for a quiet pint."

"You'll be lucky once this lot get started," said the barman.

The masculine lady turned her back on them and went over to the dartboard. James approached the bar and ordered the drinks while Alison and Pauline looked for a table far from the dartboard as they could.

The window seat on the other side of the bar was empty. Even so, it was becoming hard to hear each other as the Upton ladies dart team arrived.

Pauline asked James, "What's new?"

"What did you say?" James shouted back.

Pauline shouted back "What's new with the murders?"

Silence spread over the bar and everyone suddenly turned and looked at Pauline. The masculine woman shouted from the other side of the bar. "Could you keep it quiet over there, we are trying to have a competition and it's a league match."

Pauline looked at James and Alison then busted out laughing.

"At least we can talk for a while until they get noisy again... and they will. I remember them coming over to Malvern and causing a riot."

James leaned into the others and in a low voice said, "The police have closed the case. They say Derek and Carol committed the murders."

"That's not right."

The door opened and two men walked into the bar, they looked out of place for a country public house. Dressed in suits and gabardine raincoats, they looked more like secret service police or the American CIA than ordinary people. James, Pauline, and Alison watched as they ordered a beer at the bar and found a table about ten feet from them.

"So, Pauline, when you see a red light it means to stop and green means go," said James, a grin on his face. Pauline and Alison immediate realized he was changing the subject because of the two men.

"Really, I didn't know that. I like the orange one in the middle such a nice color."

The door opened again and a woman wearing a Salvation Army uniform entered, putting a leaflet on each table. Alison watched her and couldn't understand why the woman took a piece of paper from the bottom of the pile when she placed it on their table. James took some change out of his pocket and placed it in the tin the woman was shaking as she passed each table. As she left the bar the two men also left.

"I really think I am becoming paranoid," said Alison.

"Why?"

"Well, those two men and a Sally Army girl. Don't you think that a little strange?"

"The men yes, but not her. They are always coming around the bars giving out leaflets and asking for money," said Pauline.

James picked up the leaflet, read it, then folded it and placed it in his inside jacket pocket.

"Pity they can't spell. There are six spelling mistakes and four improper grammar errors in their leaflet."

"Let's have one more drink and go, I don't think the ladies dart team likes us being here."

James got up but was pulled back as Pauline rose and went to the bar to order the drinks. She returned carrying two beers and one glass of soda water. James and Alison looked at her.

"What? I'm driving remember."

"Oh, we remember alright."

They sat in silence and watched the ladies throw their darts. Once both James and Alison finished their beers Pauline stood up and said, "Let's go." She had left the bar before James had placed his glass back on the table.

Once outside the cold night air seemed to soak them. Alison gave a shiver and wrapped her coat tightly around herself. They walked around the public-house to find Pauline standing at the back looking as though she was lost.

"What's wrong?"

"Car's gone."

"What! I told you to lock it."

"No, you didn't but I did."

Pauline searched her handbag as her mobile phone screamed out an insipid tune.

"Hello... I know the car has gone... The bitch I'll kill her when I see her... No. "

"What happened?"

"My brother's girlfriend thought he was in the bar with some girl, so she took the car."

"Okay, so how do we get home?"

"We could take a taxi."

"That will take forever, it did the last time and we were left standing here."

"Tosser, I suppose."

"Right. Went off with his mates and left me behind.

"So, how do we get home?"

"Walk I suppose. Across the fields. It's not far if we keep a good pace going."

As they exited the car park three motorcycles swerved and just missed hitting them. One of the bikers stopped and turned to shout at them. "Hey man, what are you doing with those old bags?"

Pauline stopped and was about to turn to answer him back when Alison grabbed her arm and dragged her across the road.

They walked out of Storridge towards the fields they knew they would have to cross.

"Why did you stop me?"

"Because you're with a gentleman and I think it's time we acted like ladies."

"What!"

"You heard me. All my life I have acted like a slapper an old slag. Well, it's over. The one thing I found out being around James is you can get by without reacting every time someone has a go at you."

Pauline stopped and stood looking first at her friend, then at James who had walked a little ahead of them.

"Pauline, look at him. He opens doors. Helps us with our chairs when we sit down. That kid was brought up properly and I am not going to let him think I'm as common as muck even if I am. I'm also going to take some lessons on makeup and hair. Maybe a lesson on how to dress correctly "

"You in love with him?"

"No, I am not but it is the first time since Bryan DeWitt that anyone has treated me like a lady. I think it is the reason why I was in love with Bryan."

"Sorry, I just took it... his manners I mean."

"Me too at first. Then our Nobby suddenly said he wasn't going to do something because James wouldn't like it. I almost choked on my fish and chips."

They walked a little faster, trying to catch up with James.

"Ali, if I step out of line again slap me on the head, will you?"

"Good heavens, no. That wouldn't be ladylike. I'll kick you on the ankle. Pity your skirt isn't longer, then he wouldn't see me doing it."

They looked at each other and laughed, James turned to look at them.

"I'm sorry you had to hear that biker."

"James, it wasn't your fault. So where do we go from here?"

James stood by a gate. On the other side of it ran a path between two fields.

"According to the sign Cowleigh Bank is that way and that is where we need to go."

"Not too fast, and let's keep together. I've never been very good in the woods at night."

Pauline went to speak but was kicked on the ankle by Alison. James looked at them both and busted out laughing.

"Keep it clean, James," said Alison, trying not to laugh.

They walked along the path. The moon flitted between the clouds and gave them light. The path between the fields stopped, and they found themselves facing a dense wood.

"Looks like we have to go into the woods after all," said James, laughing.

"If we keep to the path, we should be okay. Let's keep together."

"Do you want me in front or behind?" asked James.

"James, I told you to keep it clean."

They all began to laugh.

CHAPTER SIXTEEN

Wood Shenanigans

The wood was a lot darker than they had realized, and Pauline kept giving little squeals as branches or plants brushed against her. At first, the path hugged closely to the edge of the wood but then sharply turned into the darkness of the trees. James took Alison's hand. Pauline took her other. They walked slowly, James trying to keep to a path that now was covered thickly with leaves and vegetation. He stopped and peered into the darkness ahead of them. The moon moved from behind a cloud and he could see the way to go if only for a few seconds. Alison clasped his hand so tightly he stopped several times to get her to relax, so the blood could flow back into his hand. They had walked some way into the wood when Alison tripped on something and fell, pulling Pauline on top of her. Both ladies screamed. James quickly helped Pauline up. Alison stood but then, as she took a step forward, she screamed out in pain.

"What's wrong?"

"My ankle! I think I have twisted it."

"Okay, let's find something for you to sit down on."

The moon slid from behind a cloud again and they could see a tree trunk ahead lying on its side. With Pauline on one side and James on the other they helped Alison to the trunk. She sat down on it, but not before feeling it first to see if it was dry.

"Sorry, I didn't mean to."

"Don't be stupid, Ali. We know that."

"What should we do, James?"

"I need to find the path out of here. Do you think you ladies would be okay while I go ahead and find the way out?"

"You're not going to leave us on our own?"

"Not for long. And it will give Alison time to rest that ankle."

"Ali, remind me when we get home to put a flashlight in my handbag."

"Along with the kitchen sink."

"Stay together, and don't talk to any strangers."

"Oh, thanks. I was okay until you said that."

James left them and continued along the path. It twisted and turned. He began to wonder if he would ever find his way back to them. At first, the noise sounded like someone running then he heard the whisper.

"Alison? Pauline? Is that you?"

No one replied. He continued along the path, going deeper into the wood. The sound of someone close by became louder. From somewhere behind him he heard a whisper of his name 'James'. He was sure it was his name but then trees and wind could make strange sounds. He turned, wondering if the ladies were calling him. In front of him, he heard his name again — then from the left. He walked quickly, the darkness wrapping itself around him like a velvet cloak.

He became scared. Stopping, he found himself surrounded by trees and bushes. They had not been around him a moment ago. Trees and bushes don't move, do they? The voice started again. 'James, James, James.'

"Who's there?"

"James, stop what you're doing."

"Who said that?"

He turned to where he thought the voices had come from. Each time he turned the bushes seemed to block him in. The moon had gone behind a cloud and he couldn't see anything. Only hear the rustle of feet on the leaves and the breaking of twigs.

James became aware that he was being manipulated. Someone was trying to make him scared, and therefore he wasn't alone in this wood.

"Okay, what do you want?"

For a few moments, there was no sound. Then the voices started again, saying his name.

He felt like his head was spinning. The voices seemed all around him. They stopped, and one deep slow voice spoke.

"James, James, stop what you're doing. Leave well alone. Let the past lie and the spy die." Laughter sudden swirled about him.

"James, go home. Give up playing the detective before it's too late. You could be next if you don't. The police verdict is the right one"

"Who are you? Did you kill them?"

"I killed him said the crow." Laughter from all around him was making James angry. Did they, whoever they were, know he didn't like being laughed at?

A jolt of nausea and a strange vibration washed over him. His head began to spin, and he swayed before falling to the ground. The sound of feet stopped and he lay in silence. Standing, he pushed through the bushes moving back towards where he thought the ladies were. He wasn't sure if he was going the right way, and as he came to a group of trees a skeleton suddenly rose from the ground then disappeared. James screamed out from the shock.

"James, is that you?"

He heard Pauline's voice not far from where he was, and so he ran towards the voice. He hit a tree with his left shoulder and fell to the ground. It didn't hurt at first and he stood up and hurried towards where he thought he'd heard Pauline's voice. The ladies were sitting huddled together. Both had sticks in their hands.

"James, what happened? Why did you scream?"

"I think it was a fox or something gave me a fright."

"Did you find a way out?"

"Yes," James lied.

The moon emerged from behind a cloud. He could see the path leading out of the woods.

"We go that way. Do you think you can walk?"

"I think so, as long as we go slowly."

Pauline and James helped Alison to stand. One on each side of her, they exited the wood. They made slow progress across the field stopping for Alison to rest. James and Pauline changed sides before continuing. The night air was cold and damp. The pains of being in her 50s nagged at Pauline's joints. James could feel the pain from hitting the tree intensifies. He began to feel depressed. The mood deepened, and he wanted to lay on the ground and just die.

They reached the gate on to a lane and leaned on it.

Pauline gave the first scream, followed by Alison, as Dougie, Cooper, and Nobby suddenly appeared. The three boys laughed at the shock on the others faces until Dougie realized that things were not okay. The pain on Alison's face made Nobby rush to his mother's side.

Dougie was looking at James, his ashen face and shaking body wasn't only from the scare they had just been given.

"Cooper and Nobby stay here, I'll run and get the car. We need to get them back to the winter quarters." James turned away from the others and vomited in the hedge. He wasn't sure what had made him do this, but something was definitely wrong. The depression deepened. He hated his life. Dougie returned and helped Alison and Pauline into the car, Cooper was going to sit in the front but a nod of Dougie's head stopped him. He opened the door for James, who sank into the seat as a wave of dizziness washing over him. Cooper touch James forehead. He was so hot that Cooper removed his hand quickly. Dougie started to drive. Cooper and Nobby only just managed to climb in.

They arrived at the winter quarters and were taken to Dougie's caravan. Dougie felt James forehead again. It was still very hot. He took an ice pack out of the refrigerator and wrapped it in a towel before putting on James' head.

"Put your head back. You're burning up but his should help."

Nobby gave a spontaneous laugh. They all looked at him, he lowered his head but gave another snorting laugh.

"What?" asked Alison.

"Sorry, I just thought you had been you know 'playing in the woods'."

"With James!"

The explosion of laughter from Alison soon grabbed the others.

"So, what really happened then?" asked Nobby.

Pauline told them the story of going to the pub, having the car taken, and walking back through the woods. She explained how Alison hurt her foot and then how James had been spooked by something.

"Must be the badger."

"The badger?"

"Yeah, that is why we were on our way to the woods. Nobby said there was a badger living in the woods and I've never seen one," said Cooper.

Nobby was staring out of the window. The dark night was illuminated by a red flicker from behind a caravan. Dougie followed his gaze and saw the red glow.

"Fire!" he shouted then, "Blue!" as he raced from the caravan with Cooper behind him. Nobby and James slowly left the caravan. Several of the clowns ran past them. When they came around the side of a caravan they saw it was James' caravan on fire. The clowns and skinheads worked together to put the flames out. Mabel arrived and stood next to James. She put her arm around his shoulder. He flinched. He had really hurt his shoulder when he hit the tree. Mabel removed his shirt. Graze marks and a large bruise were showing.

"That needs seeing to."

James said nothing. He was still feeling very strange.

"They thought someone had a bonfire going until Dougie shouted it was a 'blue'."

Seeing the puzzled look on James's face, Mabel continued, "We don't shout 'fire' as it can cause a panic, especially with an audience. So, we use the word 'blue' to tell everyone there is a fire."

The speed the clowns and Dougie's skinhead crew worked to put the fire out amazed James.

Dougie came over to Mabel and James. His face was streaked with black dirt marks.

"Someone had pushed one of the garbage bins up against James' caravan. There wasn't any damage to caravan except from the smoke, and it may have seeped inside."

"Any idea who?" asked Mabel.

"No, but I'll ask the boys to snoop."

James opened the door of his caravan. Smoke billowed out. One of the clowns, still holding a fire hose, rushed forward thinking the fire wasn't out.

"We need to open all the windows to get the smoke out."

Dougie entered the caravan a handkerchief over his mouth and nose. The smoke gushed out of the windows.

"I think you will need to wash everything inside," said Mabel

Alison and Pauline had moved closer to James. "We can help do that."

"Me too," said Nobby.

James sank to the floor. The blood had drained from his face and he felt weak. He was carried back to Dougie's caravan and placed on the sofa. Pauline sat next to him. She stroked his forehead.

"I'll make a cup of tea, that should revive you."

Alison climbed the steps and stood on one leg, keeping the weight off her twisted ankle.

"You know Pauline, something happened in the wood.
Did you see his face when he came back to us?"
"Seen a ghost is what I thought."
Cooper and Nobby pushed past Alison, sitting down
next to James.
"Everything is okay except for some smoke damage.
We can clean that off tomorrow."
"Your picture has been covered in a film of black dust,
but I think we can clean it. Dougie has gone to the site
office to check if that's okay."
"Oh, Antonioni said that he had seen someone
climbing through the hole and back to the building
site."
"He didn't say who it was or if he had seen them
before. We are going to interrogate him later," said
Nobby.
"Hey, Alison listen to these two Inspector Morse's."

After a cup of tea Alison, Pauline and Nobby left.
Dougie arrived. He seemed to be in charge, giving an
order to Cooper, who obeyed without question.
"We set up a guard for the night. This happened
several years ago so it may be nothing to do with you.
Nobby's mother and her friend said they would be
back tomorrow to help clean up so you just rest. You
can sleep on the couch tonight."
"Thanks, I'm not sure what happened."
"Shock. And I don't think you ate anything today."
"Can't remember."
"Big day tomorrow. Tonya has arranged for a press
conference. Cashing in on Brinarno's death. The show
must go on that sort of thing."
As Dougie talked, James drifted off to sleep. He felt
warm and secure, like he had when he was a little boy

and his father had just tucked him in bed for the night. As he slept, he dreamt of the wood and the strange voices. He was being warned off, at first. Then he wondered if it had been Dougie and the boys. But he would have recognized their voices. He was stuck in a bush and Bryan was half dressed in a clown costume and in his clown makeup when he ran up to James. He asked him to help free him from the slave masters. James woke in a cold sweat, not remembering where he was. He left the caravan and walked his own. The damage was, as Dougie had said, superficial. A good wash down and the place would be back to normal except for the smell of smoke. He would call his mother later and ask her how to get rid of the smell He would make up some story about a bonfire making his caravan smell smoky. He wasn't sure if he had been the intended target, but had he been asleep inside the caravan he would have been dead. There were two smoke detectors inside so why hadn't they gone off? Entering the caravan, he opened up the first smoke detector in the living area. The battery had been removed. He checked one in the bedroom and found that it too had its battery removed. When he'd moved in, his father had placed new batteries in each smoke detector. Someone had removed them. He was the intended target.

Cooper arrived and stood next to him, looking at the black grime from the smoke.

"Dougie's making breakfast. He is a good cook."

"Thanks."

"When we saw you and Nobby's mother and her friend come out of the woods we thought you had been, you know, messing around."

"Nobby said that last night."

"You have to admit it did look funny."
"What's he cooking for breakfast?"
"Bacon and eggs, I think."

Everyone from the circus was in the Big Top preparing for the press conference. The clowns were cleaning all the bench seats. The arrival of the police surprised everyone. They spoke to Mabel who pointed out Bolt. He had been one of the clowns James had not really spoken too. The police placed handcuffs on him and left as quickly as they had arrived. Mabel came and sat down next to James.
"I don't know what's going on anymore. Why do you think they arrested Bolt?"
Before James could answer two of the other clowns began to argue and push each other. Although he couldn't hear what they were saying the fight was obviously about Bolt's arrest. He hadn't realized that the clowns weren't a happy-go-lucky, friendly group. Underneath, a vicious dislike for each other had been brewing. Maybe it had been kept in control when Bryan was alive. They were lost without their leader. Mabel was looking at the melee. James could see she didn't know what to do. He placed his hand on top hers and gave it a squeeze.
"If it rains it pours. I am not sure what's going on anymore."
"What do you know about Bolt?"
"Not a lot. A friend of Ryan asked me to give him a job. He worked for the government and they wanted to keep an eye on the Chinese acrobats. Well, that's what Ryan said."
"And now you don't believe it."

"He never went near them. I watched him one day and all he seemed interested in was what Bryan was doing. The other clowns would complain he was always missing when he was needed for rehearsal or to help set up."

"What did Bryan say about it?"

"Nothing, but I wondered if that was why he was going to talk to the BBC reporter."

"What BBC Reporter and when was he going to talk to him?"

"Don't know which reporter, only he had made arrangements for the day after he was…"

"I wonder what he was going to say?"

"He told one of the clowns he had some really hot scandal to report."

"Not about the circus?"

"No, he would never betray our secrets."

Tonya arrived and calmed down the clowns, mostly because Dougie stood by her side. Either out of respect or fear for him, the clowns sat down quietly. The press started to arrive, and Mabel joined Tonya in the circus ring.

James sat back and watched the reporters vying for the best positions. The word of Bolt's arrest had already reached them, so they were expecting something juicy to be said at the press conference.

The camera crew from the BBC had set up in the front row. A tall thin man with a mop-like hairstyle looked around the circus tent. He approached James and sat down next to him.

"Are you James Pidgley?"

"Who wants to know?"

"I'm Vincent Dase from the BBC, Brinarno, I mean Bryan, was going to see me."

"What was he going to see you about?"

"I don't know, but the funny thing is our news desk got a press release of his death the day before he died."

"Do you have proof of that?"

"I have a copy of the memo/police press report."

"With you?"

"Of course. I think there must have been a mistake, I checked it out and it was dated the day before he died." He handed James a large manila envelope. James took out the single piece of paper and read a report of Bryan's death. The date on the press release from the police was dated the day before Bryan died.

"Is this real or fake?"

"It's real. If you want a copy of the whole press release call the BBC and ask for Archives. Quote the number at the bottom of the page. They will ask you for a password. It's Henry Hall."

"Who's behind it?"

"I wish I knew. I checked a few things out about Bryan and I think it had something to do with the college he went to in the 1960s. It seems a lot of the people he was at college are dead or missing. Which in my book is very strange and needs someone to investigate."

"You're going to make a program about it?"

"I was thinking of doing something, but I need a really good angle to get the boys above interested. If you're interested in following it up, you need to talk to a guy called Michael Oberhauser. Don't be put off by his name or how pompous he is."

"Never heard of him."

"He has some very interesting things to say about Bryan. He had been helping me with a piece about

Radar for Panorama, but I got called away on another story, so we never finished it."

"How do I find this Michael?"

"I'll give you his number."

The press conference started. James wasn't interested and wandered outside. He needed time to think about what had been said to him. At the site office, he re-read the press release. He called the BBC and provided all the information officious woman asked of him. He sat by the fax machine and waited for a promised fax to arrive.

After ten minutes he began to laugh he could hear his mother saying, 'a watched kettle never boils'. Maybe she was right.

John Carson, the site foreman, opened the door and asked James to look at something. James returned to the site office twenty minutes later and had forgotten about the fax. He was going to leave and return to the circus Big Top when he looked at the fax machine. Vincent had given him a cut and paste version of the police press release. The original was three pages long and went into detail about how Bryan had died. A note on the cover page from the woman at the BBC was a reply to a question he had asked. She had written *'yes, the date of the police press release is the day it was received by the BBC, as all press releases are logged in'*.

He placed the press release in his notebook. He wasn't sure whom he was going to share this information with. As he was leaving, the fax machine started to print again. He picked up the one page and read it. Vincent had sent him the phone number of Michael Oberhauser. Vincent also mentioned that he had

contacted Michael, and that Michael was now
expecting a call from James.

James sat looking at the fax. How had Vincent
obtained James' fax number? He hadn't given it to him.
James called and arranged to meet Michael at his
home at 2:30 that day. That gave James three hours to
eat lunch and make his way to the small Cotswold
village of Morton in the Marsh.

Alison, Pauline, and Nobby arrived as he was leaving.
They were armed with buckets, rubber gloves and an
arm full of dishcloths. He told them he would rush
back to help, but he was following a clue.

Viewed from the front, Michael's house was more like
a cottage. But it opened up at the back and became a
six-bedroom house. The neat well-kept garden would
have featured on any mother's day chocolate box had
the main door into the house not been painted a dirty
purple color. It was an odd contrast to the rest of the
house, and its Cotswold stone exterior. James looked
at the other houses in the street with their plain
wooden doors. Someone was making a statement and
not very well. James pushed the doorbell button and
listened to the Westminster chimes. A woman opened
the door and then just walked away. James waited for
a few seconds before stepping inside. The hallway
was lined with bookcases and, from what he could see,
so was every room he passed. A tall, thin man in his
70s appeared out of one of the rooms and smiled when
he saw James.

"You must be James Pidgley, please come this way."
The man had small, wire-framed glass perched on the
bridge of his nose. His brown corduroy trouser had
started to lose their cords. His shirt was also very old,

and faded from years of use. If he was an actor in a film, the costume department had picked the right clothes for the character.

Michael indicated for James to sit down in a brown leather chair. As he sank into the softness the leather oozed around him, almost swallowing him. James tried to pull himself up and it took a few minutes before he felt comfortable. The woman who had opened the door entered the room, carrying a tray with a pot of tea and cups. She left without looking at Michael or James.

Michael sat looking at James as if he was trying to read his body language. The woman suddenly returned and placed another tray on the small table. It contained a milk jug, a sugar bowl and a large plate of homemade fairy cakes.

"Thank you, my dear."

The woman gave Michael a look of contempt. As she turned, she had a wicked smile for James. Michael leaned forward, poured the tea, and offered James a bone china cup.

"So, James how can I help you? Vincent, the dear chap, didn't say very much."

"A new friend died recently, and I would like to know more about him. Vincent said you had researched him."

"What was his name?"

"Bryan DeWitt, but he worked in the circus as the clown Brinarno."

"Ah, Bryan. The Malvern Genius as he was called."

Michael sat back in his chair and drank his tea without continuing. James drank his tea. He had never been a fan of Earl Grey tea. For him, it tasted like dishwater, with a touch of sugar added. He had often wondered if it was a perfect place to hide a poison, because of the smell and taste being so strong. Michael sat looking at the ceiling, then spoke his head still tilted and not taking his gaze away from it.

"My brother went to college with him in Malvern. The Royal Radar Establishment's College of Electronics. We all thought it was very prestigious."

"It's not there anymore."

"So, I have heard. I must visit the site some time. Alan, my brother, was older than Bryan."

"Did your brother talk about Bryan much?"

"Oh yes. For weeks he bore us with stories of this young guy at the college who was a genius inventor. It wasn't until our father lost his temper that Alan told us about this invention of Bryan's. It was a black box device that could detect pain in unconscious people who had been injured. Of course, we were duly impressed."

"You heard that Bryan was murdered recently?"

"Yes, Vincent told me. I was shocked to hear that. My brother said Bryan was a very charismatic person whom no one would ever want to hurt."

"Someone did, and I was wondering if he died because of the black box invention."

"Because he destroyed it, you mean? Well, that could be a possibility. Rumors have been around for years that he kept a plan of it. Alan said he thought that, if he did, Bryan would have hidden it in such a place as to be so obvious no one would ever see it. You never found anything did you?"

"No, but I wasn't looking for it. I just wanted to know more about the man."

"He was a very secretive person. According to Alan, in his last letter to me, he said Bryan and his friends had suddenly stopped meeting."

Michael saw James 'cup was empty and offered to pour him more tea. James shook his head and placed the cup back on the tray.

"Where is your brother now?"

"Dead."

"I'm sorry. When did your brother die?"

"1984.

"How did he die?"

"Committed suicide, bloody fool."

"Why? Sorry, that may be too personal."

"My brother was a very unhappy man. He left Malvern and took a job working in research for a company with government contracts. I think underwater warfare. He just didn't like it, so he left and became a farmer, only he didn't know a thing about farming. Soon he was bankrupt and going from one job after another until he couldn't take it anymore."

James looked at Michael who seemed to be forcing an emotion rather than letting it just happen.

"My father blamed Bryan. He said if he hadn't given Alan such grandiose ideas, Alan would still be alive. "

"This must have been a long time after Bryan and Alan had been at college, did they keep in touch?"

"No, I don't think so. I think it was because when Dad went through Alan's belongings after his death, he found a letter. Alan had written to tell us he had been on a riverboat shuffle social event at college and met this guy called Bryan who was a genius and had told him a big secret. Dad said it gave Alan ideas."

"What big secret do you think Alan was told?"

"He never said, but did say he put notes about it in his books."

"These books?" James said, pointing the hundreds of books lining the walls.

"Yes, but I have been through every one of them."

"You said his books. Did your brother make notes?"

"Yes, in school exercise books. Do you think he meant those?"

He didn't wait for James to answer but left the room, returning with a old brown leather suitcase. He undid the straps, pressed a large brass button and the case opened. He took out a few exercise books and handed James one. The book was full of mathematical equations and drawings. As James handed it back, he saw three initials inside the suitcase. Michael quickly, closed the case and placed the books in his hand on top.

James felt the atmosphere had changed, Michael sat staring at him, his eyes narrowing.

"Michael, I think I have taken enough of your time. Thank you for the tea, and the information."

"Are you sure you don't want to stay?"

"No, I need to get back."

"Here's my card. If I can help in any way please contact me."

James extracted himself from the leather armchair and stood. Michael didn't move or put a hand out for James to shake. James just left the house in silence, as though he had been dismissed as a naughty boy.

When he reached his car, he looked back at the house. The woman was standing at the door watching him. He started to lift his hand to wave 'goodbye' but changed his mind and climbed into the driving seat.

Several things had unnerved him. First was the way Michael had changed when James saw the initials inside the suitcase. Then the woman at the door. Was he becoming paranoid?

He drove out of Morton in the Marsh and in the rear-view mirror to see if he was being followed. After several miles, a red car seemed to be going in the same direction as James. The tinted windows made it difficult to see who was driving and if there were passengers.

James decided to make a detour and took a left turn. The red car followed. Paranoia was beginning to wash over James. He took a right, then another, before returning back to his intended route. The red car kept following. The road narrowed and James slowed down as he came up behind a tractor with a trailer behind. He wondered if he should overtake, and several times pulled to the right to see if the road was clear ahead. The red car suddenly, in a bust of acceleration, overtook James and the tractor-trailer. The tractor driver slammed on his brakes and James only just missed hitting the back of the trailer.

James rushed to see what had happened. The driver of the tractor climbed down and was running up the road. James saw bales of hay thrown across the road and a flatbed lorry sticking out of a field. James ran after the tractor driver who had stopped at the fence.

The red car was floating on a pond. The driver's door was open and a young teenager was stepping out and into the water. He disappeared below the surface of the water, then popped up, sputtering and coughing. His car began to sink into the water.

"Stupid bugger," said the tractor driver.

The young man pulled himself to the side of the pond and the tractor driver helped him out of the water. The driver of the tractor looked at James, a sickening grin spread across the man's face. The red car driver scowled at James.

James, realizing he could do nothing to help, returned to his car. Carefully going around the tractor-trailer and the bales of hay, he passed the accident and continued on his way.

He started to drive a little slower than he normally did. His mind was racing, which finally made him pull over to the side of the road and stop.

The three initials he had seen in the suitcase lid were 'B J D'. Could the suitcase have really belonged to Bryan? James didn't know his middle name and whom he could ask. Mabel would know. When he arrived back at the circus, he would go and ask her. If it was his suitcase, why was Michael pretending it belonged to his brother? No, James was becoming too conspiratorial and paranoid. The writing in the notebooks didn't look like Bryan's. Then again, he had only seen one letter supposedly written by Bryan. Why did the driver of the red car scowl at him and the tractor driver have the scary grin on his face? Was it James's fault the young man had raced ahead and had an accident? Or was it a setup, and was James really the one who was to have had the accident?

James' head began to spin with all these thoughts. He felt dizzy and hungry. He had not had food since that morning. He started the car and drove to the first small roadside café he could find.

After an all-day breakfast, he felt positive and back to his normal self. The rest of the journey back to Malvern went smoothly. As he parked the car inside the winter quarters a feeling of relief flowed through him.

Instead of going to the caravan, he walked to the building site. He had been neglecting it and felt guilt pricking him. He stood looking at the progress from the road. Even though he hadn't been around much, a great deal had changed since he last looked. Several of the buildings were beginning to look like houses. The site office door was locked, and he was fumbling in his pockets for the keys when a hand appeared around the corner of the site office. The long fingers of the thin hand beckoned him to approach. It was not a woman's hand, nor could it be said to be a masculine hand. The person who it belonged to had not performed manual labor in their life.

James cautiously reached the edge of the site office and standing a little back from the corner stepped forward a little so he could see whose hand it was. Philip Langley, dressed in black clothes, put a finger to his lips to silence James. In Philip's left hand was a small electronic device. He ran it over James' body, before stopping on left side of his jacket. He placed a hand inside, and withdrew a piece of paper. James recognized it as the Salvation Army leaflet. Philip struck a match and the paper burst into flames. James was surprised as it burnt with a soft green glow.

They stood and watched as it blackened, and Philip let it fall to the floor. As the last part of the paper burnt Philip stamped on it and then picked up a very thin piece of thread. He pulled it apart and then threw it down into a ditch.

He ran the detecting device over James one more time before whispering in his ear.

"We need to talk."

"Let's go to the caravan."

"No! It and your office here are both bugged."

"Bugged by who, and why?"

"Later, We need a safe place."

"My car?"

"No that's bugged too. Let's go to my car and I'll take you to a place I know that is not bugged."

Philip started to leave and walked towards the road. He turned and looked back at James who was hesitant to follow.

Philip returned and whispered, "If you want to know the truth then follow me."

James followed. Something about Philip's attitude didn't feel bad. They sat in silence as Philip drove towards Malvern Link. Philip parked in Archer Close and quickly walked towards Sayers Avenue. James had to almost run to keep up with him. They crossed the road and climbed a fence into a field. Philip pointed to the building to their right.

"That is the old Ministry of Defense Royal Radar Establishment's North site. It is where Bryan and I started our training."

The site had been converted into an industrial park. They crossed into another field before making a ninety-degree turn. Philip stopped, looked around, and disappeared into the hedge. James stood looking to where Philip had disappeared. He expected a hand to poke back and beckon him to follow. It didn't, so he stepped forward and found he could pass through the hedge at this point.

On the other side, they were in the grounds of a building that had once belonged to the Ministry of Defense. It had been abandoned and the windows were boarded up. Philip ran across the open space and stood against the building. He indicated for James to do the same. It was moments like this that James always dreaded. What would happen if he fell, or the ground opened up and he was swallowed? James ran as though he was still at school and it was sports day. They crept around the side of the building. James wasn't sure why. If anyone wanted to see them, they could. Nothing hid them from view.

A small door with a heavy padlock was the only visible entrance in this part of the building. Philip unlocked the padlock carefully putting the lock just inside the door. Standing to one side he indicated for James to enter. James gave a little nervous laugh before saying. "No, after you."

Philip smiled and entered.

CHAPTER SEVENTEEN

The Invention

James followed Philip into the building and almost fell down a steep flight of stairs. Philip had stopped two steps down. In the light from the open door, James saw him swipe his hand over a brick in the wall. The stairways and the room below flooded with light. "Close the door and push the lock across."
James pulled the heavy wooden door closed and pushed the cast iron bolts into place. As he passed the place Philip had turned the light on, he looked at the wall. There was no sign of light switch. He descended to the room below and was surprised how big the cellar was. A table and two chairs were the only things visible in the room. The room had been painted completely white. After his eyes had adjusted to the room's blinding glare, he began to see the other furniture. This too had been painted white and blended into the walls, rendering it impossible to distinguish at first.
"This place is safe. I know because I have checked it several times for bugs. I'm sorry I can't offer you

anything to drink. I expect you wouldn't take it anyway."

"Why did you burn the Salvation Army leaflet?"

"I'll explain later. Why don't you sit down?"

James sat on a wooden chair and positioned himself so if he needed to run, he could reach the stairs before Philip.

"Sorry, I am not very good at the small talk stuff. I have a lot to tell you. I think we may have very little time to talk. Michael Oberhauser's brother didn't go to Malvern."

"Okay."

"Michael has been planted to give you disinformation."

"He had this old leather brown suitcase with initials BJD on the inside. Was the suitcase Bryan's?"

"Did it contain notebooks full of calculations and drawings?"

"Yes."

"Then it was Bryan's, I wondered what happened to his notebooks."

James didn't respond. He nodded his head, encouraging Philip to continue.

"You were getting too close and they wanted to frighten you off. Hence, last night in the woods."

"You know about that?"

"I think I may be the only person who knows everything that is happening. When we last met, I told you I was scared. I am scared but it was really a front. I needed to know who you were. I've been listening and watching you and them.

"Were you there last night?"

"Not in the wood. I was in my car listening to what was going on. I had to check you out; at first, I wasn't sure which side you were on. Especially as you're so friendly with the Chinese acrobats and those circus clowns. I don't trust them, and I was proved right. They arrested the one called Bolt. What a stupid name for a clown. So, what are you really up to?"

"I wanted to find out who had murdered Bryan."

"I have decided I can trust you. Well, at least you're open to understanding what's really going on."

"What changed your mind?"

"I spoke to a guy and his mother near Tamworth."

"Bob and Ma Willett?"

"Yes, they are now living in my driveway. Ma told me all about you and how you saved your Dad from going to jail."

James moved into his seat; he didn't want to talk about it. He still had nightmares and was trying to push the memories away. He ignored the comment.

"Why don't you begin at the beginning…"

"… '*and go on until you come to the end and stop.*' Alice in Wonderland one of my favorite books."

"I drive people crazy with my quotes from books or poems."

"That's nothing, James. I have the habit of quoting old radio programs from my childhood. You won't remember this one; '*Are you sitting comfortably? Then I'll begin'.*"

"No, I don't."

"Mother's Hour on the BBC radio."

"Before my time."

"I was at college with Bryan; we were, I suppose, what you would call a gang. There was the core group of five of us. The others were on the edge, and only told what they needed to know.

"Who were the core group?"

"Bryan, obviously, and me. Chris Parrott until he started selling drugs, then we dropped him."

"He was selling back then?"

"He started selling when he was thirteen years old at school. His whole family is into dealing."

"Who else was in the core group?"

"Kipper, Roy Churchill... we replaced Chris with 'Beam Me Up' Kirk."

"You're the only one left alive of the core group?"

"Yes, which is why I act as I do."

James shifted in his chair. He had forgotten how hard wooden chairs could be.

"Michael Oberhauser told you about the Black Box but you already knew about that. Bryan invented a microphone; he was so scared that people were talking he wanted to bug them."

"Did the others know he was bugging them?"

"No. He told me after he had bugged me and found I was very loyal to him and his inventions. The reason why no one knew was that the microphone was hidden inside a piece of paper."

"Is that why you burnt the Salvation Army leaflet?"

"Of course, it had a transmittal range of a mile. I sat outside and listened to you. I wanted to tell you not to pick up the paper, but you did. It gave them extra help."

"So, the Salvation Army lady worked for them?"

"And the two men who came in first, they were the distraction force and the lady the delivery force."

"So, who are they?"

Philip didn't answer, but looked at the floor in front of his chair. James could see that he didn't want to answer the question.

"You don't have to answer, but I think I will need to know eventually if I am to solve Bryan's death."

"Bryan invented the paper microphone, but it wasn't until after he left the Royal Radar Establishment that he perfected it. Then one night someone broke into his flat and took the information about it. He spent weeks working out how to tune into what they were listening too. Of course, it wasn't long before he found out we were all being bugged."

"I created the scanner which detects if there is a microphone near you. Now I constantly scan everywhere I go."

"The little device you used on me very clever. Have they known what I have been up to from the start?"

"They, and me. It doesn't stop there, because that is not what this is all about."

"It's about the Black Box?"

"No, Brian invented something which will, if it ever gets unearthed, change the world. It was his unbelievable visions of the past device. It is based on the idea of images being recorded in the atmosphere. You then tap into those images and see things it would normally be impossible to see. Remember he invented this in the 1960s."

"I don't understand."

"He invented a way of recording sorry, *reading,* past events. A device like that could tell you who killed Kennedy. Who committed which murder? Even tell you if Richard the Third murdered the Princes in the Tower."

"Or who Jack the Ripper really was?"

"And then there are political secrets. He told me in a letter in 1981 he had been able to record color pictures.

Then only last year, when we met, he told me he had a full recording device of moving pictures and sound."
They both sat in silence. The dramatic way of what Philip had told James took some getting used to. James mind started to race at all the thing he would want to know. Philip stood and began to pace the room.

"I remember years ago reading or seeing something about stone tapes. Stonewalls recording events then replaying them. I think someone said it was how ghosts manifested when people saw them."

"I think that may have been the seed of the idea Bryan took and developed."

"Philip, did you ever see any of these pictures?"

"Yes, I saw the first black and white picture. Of course, I also saw the equipment and how it showed the images."

A loud thump from the ceiling made James jump out of his seat. Philip laughed and opened a cupboard James had not noticed before. He took out a small radio. He placed it on the table and punched a few buttons. The sound was of young men running and bouncing a ball. Their language was crude, and an imitation of a modern-day American gangster film.

"The local kids use the upstairs room to play basketball. They make me laugh because they try to be American and fail."

"Scared the hell out of me."

"Sorry, I should have warned you."

"Okay, tell me more."

Philip turned off the radio and pulled his chair up to the table. James felt obliged to join him.

"Bryan was a genius and he knew whatever happened no government should get their hands on his inventions."

"They did. The microphone."

"True, hence the reason why I destroyed the Salvation Army leaflet."

"You picked up the wire part and ripped it apart. It was so thin and almost invisible."

"The papers from the council giving you your permit, a pamphlet about safety on building site in your caravan. In the back of your car seat is a piece of paper. James from the start they have been listening to what you said and too whom."

"I'm sorry, but who are they?"

"I have no proof, but Bryan thought it was a very secret group. He said it was a British government department not even MI5 or MI6 knew about. In 1967 the government found out about the black box and began to bug him. Not with his microphone paper in those days they used very crude methods. They also followed him. He became very good at spotting them and would make the hike up to the top of the hills. Derek and Carol were working for them. Derek was the spy within. Bryan found out, after Kipper died, that he was bugging everyone and soon realized which side they were on. He used them to give false information, which their masters thought was the real thing."

"Ryan Cleeves. Where did he fit in and why was he killed?"

"Derek hated him... no... hate is the wrong word. He wanted him dead from the start. He was related to Carol not sure how but he was the worst kind of conman. So, when he tried to do a deal behind Derek's back with the Chinese doctor, Derek stopped him."

"He killed him."

"Yes, I heard the whole thing. I was outside hiding on your building site, listening."

"You heard the murder?"

"Not the actual murder. I couldn't listen to that, but the argument just before. "

"So, who killed Bryan?"

"I was hoping you knew that."

"You mean you don't know?"

"No, but James... I think you do."

"I might, but I can't put all the pieces together. What happened to the vision invention?"

"Bryan hid it somewhere. I know everyone is looking for it. Even though most of them don't know what it was. They think it was the black box."

"The black box. What about that?"

"I have a copy of it. We agreed, Bryan and I, that if we needed to give up something, we would give up that. The vision project was too dangerous. No one would be safe ever again."

"Could they alter the pictures so they could change history."

"Bryan said 'no'. He tried it and found the original image kept reappearing."

"The picture Bryan made the first time. Do you have a copy of it?"

"Not the original. It faded with time. Then a few years ago Bryan gave me a color version of it. From what I remember it was the same as the original, only it was a color version. Told me he had upgraded his invention; he had moving pictures and sound."

"Do you still have a copy?"

"Yes, would you like to see it?" Philip gave a laugh,
"Stupid question, of course, you want to see it."
James nodded. Philip opened a drawer in the side of
the table and took out a picture. He looked at it before
handing it to James. It was a strange picture of
children falling on top of each other at the foot of a
staircase.

"Victoria Hall Stampede."

"I don't understand."

"June 1883 three at the Victoria Concert Hall
Sunderland. One hundred and eighty-three children
died in a stampede for free gifts after a children's
variety show."

"This is impossible! How can someone get a picture of
a dreadful thing like this as it happened?"

"The genius of Bryan invention."

"Could this be a fake? You know. Computer
generated?"

"I wondered about that. A friend told me her sister
worked at the BBC in computer animation. I called her
and asked her to see if she could recreate it. She did
but it looked like a fake. She said it's impossible to
really get the color synchronization and the lighting
correct. As far as she was concerned it was a genuine
picture."

"Didn't she ask where you got it from?"

"That's the strange thing. No one did."

"Why did he pick the stampede?"

"He said it was one of those places it would have been
impossible to get a color photograph. I did some
research in Sunderland. There is no known picture of
the event at the time and if there was it would have
been black and white."

James looked at the picture and his eyes began to fill with tears. Philip rested his head on his hands and closed his eyes. They sat for several minutes in silence the thumping of the basketball above them the only noise they could hear.

"This is a lot bigger than I realized."

"The big secret, and only a few know about it. There must be a stack of pictures showing other events."

"How do you know?"

"Bryan disappeared for about a month just after he showed me the original. When he came back he said he had recorded so many events from the past. Some, he said, dated back to the thirteenth century."

"Do you know where they are?"

"I know that everywhere was searched several times and they found nothing."

"What would this vision equipment look like?"

"A flat plate was the main piece; Bryan destroyed it a long time ago. Only the schematic plans exist. I have no idea where they are either."

"And you want me to find them?"

"No way I want nothing to do with them. Everyone who has is now dead."

"Except you."

"That's because they think I'm an idiot."

The thumping of the ball stopped, and silence engulfed the place. James remembered Bryan's painting. It had been entitled 'Schematic'. He would have to take another look at that picture.

" You don't appear to be an idiot. Not to me. What did you do so they do not come after you?"

"This girl said I got her pregnant, so I dropped out of college and got a real job to look after her and the baby. Only there wasn't a baby and the girl left and married someone else."

"Why didn't you go back?"

"I hated college and it gave me an excuse to leave. Bryan said it may be a good idea too, as things were beginning to get hot. I kept in the background and we met in secret."

"Who knew?"

"No one. That was how I could find out what Derek was up to."

"Did he kill Ian Kipler?"

"Yes, but I don't think Carol knew, even though they were twins. Derek and Kipper never really spoke to each other. Kipper was gay, well, more effeminate than anything else. I was never sure if he was a practicing homosexual. Derek was worried that if the Chinese or Russians found out they wouldn't do a deal."

"What difference would that make?"

"In those days you could still go to prison for being homosexual. Imagine if that law was still in place. Half the government, and most of the entertainment industry, would be behind bars."

"You think Carol didn't know?"

" To be honest, I think Carol pushed Derek to do something. They created paranoia; you saw how they were when you went to see them. She didn't realize he had killed her brother, but she was very glad when he was dead. I caught her dancing on his grave one night with a group of women. The next day she said she had done it because she was drunk. I knew different."

"Doesn't sound like a very good family."

The thumping started up again, and they both looked at the ceiling.

"James, I want to know who killed Bryan. You know what he was like. Full of life and always thinking up new ideas. He said he was working on a new kind of energy source. He must have had notes somewhere. "
"I promise I will solve this, but it is getting hard to trust anyone."
"You may not believe everything I have told you. After all, it's human nature not to. All I want is to know who did it."
"Me too, and you have answered a few of the questions I had. If you were watching and listening to me, who can I trust?"
"Good question. Let's go through the list. You might not like what I tell you."
"First. Alison and Pauline."
"Be careful. It's not they will give you away, but they do like to talk."
"The circus people?"
"Mabel and Tonya? Don't trust them. They didn't tell you the truth about the clown 'Bolt'. His real name is Andrew Fleet and he was an MI5 plant. Dougie and his brother Cooper are okay and so is Alison's son Mike"
"You mean Nobby?"
"Him. Strange kid, but really honest."
"Why do you say that?"
"I was listening one day when they were in your caravan. It was obvious that Mike, I mean 'Nobby', respects you. When Cooper wanted to eat some biscuits, Nobby stopped him. Nobby said 'you don't steal from your own'."
"Not really stealing, if you're hungry."
"Maybe, but to him it was."

"The police press release about Bryan's death, it was dated the day before he died. Why?"

"They could say it was typing error, but I think he was going to be murdered the day before only Ryan Cleeves was. This messed up their plans and someone forgot they had already sent the press release."

"ELF."

"Ah, Chris was never very good at keeping his mouth shut."

"When we met you didn't mention it."

"I still wasn't sure who you were. In the wood, you felt nauseous and dizzy. That was the effect of Extremely Low Frequency and they gave you a heavy blast. Much more and they could have damaged you for life."

"I became very depressed, almost suicidal."

"It's been known to have made people commit suicide. I think it may have been used on some of the other guys."

"So, the government are really using it against the people."

"Go to Iraq or Afghanistan and ask the citizens there. The American are trying to perfect the use of it. And we British use it every Saturday at football matches and protests."

"Can nothing be done about it?"

"Bryan said we should invent something to send the frequency back to its source and destroy it. I have developed an electronic pulse I use on telemarketers. My phone is programmed. If they call, I push a button, and it sends a program back to the equipment. It doesn't destroy their equipment it only sends it into electronic chaos. They don't call me anymore. Next question."

"Do you know what happened to Quon's father?"
He is living in Edinburgh; I have already told him
about Quon. He said when the circus goes there, he
will make contact. The man is really scared. The
Chinese police don't give up the chase. They are still
looking for him. They intend to take him back to
China and try him as a traitor."

"You really do know what's going on. Who put the
box with the syringe in my caravan?

"First time it was Martin Dougdale. Not sure why he
did it. I think he was hoping for a job with Tom Potts
in MI5. The second time... it was me. I think they
injected Bryan."

"So, the post-mortem was a sham, is that what Peter
Kipler was trying to tell me with the misleading
report."

"He may be a stupid copper, but he was trying to do
the right thing. Only he couldn't just come out with it.
I think he found out you were bugged."

"This may sound trivial, but who cut the water pipe
when I was on the common?"

" That should have been a red flag for you. It wasn't
Nobby or any of the skinheads. Not even Martin. One
of Tom Potts men did it. They wanted you inside the
circus winter quarters."

"Why, what good would that do them?"

"Keep everyone together makes it easier to control.
They knew all about you before you even arrived.
Why did you think you had problems with your
planning permissions? Yes, Tonya did her bit, but the
council had so much pressure put on them to reject
your plans. If Peter Goode wasn't such a left-wing
councilman and hated any interference from the
government, you would have lost."

"I think I need a handful of those paper microphones.
"I send you some and a listening device. Just
remember you may not always like what you hear."
"What happens now?"
"I disappear again. I only came out into the open to
help you. If you find out something put an advert in
the Malvern Gazette classified '*Frost the dog has been
found*.' I'll find a way to contact you."
"I may have moved by then. You will just have to
listen for me. I suppose now I have to find out where
those bugs of yours are!"
"Easy. What's your mobile number?"
James gave it to him and watched as Philip played
with a pen. Philip handed James a simple-looking
ballpoint pen.
"When a microphone is within forty feet of you this
will send a text message to your mobile phone saying
'*Silence, boy!*'"
"Really? You invented this?"
"When the need is necessary it is surprising what you
can invent."
"Thanks"
"Let's go. If I am to disappear, the sooner the better."
James was the first up the stairs and opened the door at
the top. Daylight was beginning to fade, and heavy
rain clouds were gathering over the hills again.
 The walk back to the car took a few minutes. Philip
drove James back to the building site and stopped at
the corner of the street by the Common. James turned
to say good-bye, but Philip accelerated, leaving him
standing with his arm in the air.
He walked to the building site and entered one of the
almost-completed houses. The wooden staircase
echoed with his footsteps. His mind was running

ahead of his body. He needed to think. The houses
would be finished in a few weeks and he would be
moving on. His time in Malvern would soon be over
and he still hadn't solved Bryan's murder.

For a time, he had wondered if the government were
behind it, using Derek and Carol to commit the
murders. Now he wasn't so sure. He had been misled
so many times it was hard to know what was true and
what wasn't.

One thing he had concluded was this; the murder of
Bryan had nothing to do with his college days or the
Black Box. For a start, the Black Box wasn't the main
invention and secondly, not many people knew about
the vision project.

He looked out of the window and watched as a couple
of old men met. They seemed so polite to each other.
The one man had the same round-shouldered bent
body as Bryan had. James remembered the first time
he had seen Bryan. It was in the bank. Bryan had just
learned that, according to the bank, he was dead. A
man behind James made a comment *'after all these
years you're still as obnoxious as you always were'*.
What did the man mean? Did he know Bryan? If so,
how? It was at moments like this he wished he had
Bryan's vision invention. When he left the bank, the
man was waiting for Bryan and they argued. The man
became very demonstrative and pushed Bryan.

He was assuming that this man had something to do
with the past forty years earlier. They looked the same
age and Bryan had said he was from the past. There
was no proof he was from the college days. It could
have been twenty or ten years earlier. Maybe Alison
or Pauline could tell me him who the man might have
been. Was he clutching at straws; trying to invent

reasons, situations and suspects who could have murdered Bryan?

It was something about the man's manner, which had bothered James. Bryan knew him, and the dislike they had for each other was evident. Could he describe the man? He had only seen him very briefly. Just saying the man was tall with grey hair wasn't enough. Watching from the window, he saw Nobby and Cooper talking. They were very excited about something, and watching the two skinheads do a little dance out of happiness lifted James' spirit. He was being too hard on himself. He waited for them to leave before going downstairs. He stopped to inspect the plasterwork in the hall. He needed to talk to the site foreman about the quality of the work. Were they taking   liberties because he wasn't around? Tomorrow he would inspect all the work being done. He left the half-built house and walked to Alison's. He searched his memory, hoping to remember something particular about the man. He was just an ordinary, thin, tall, grey-haired old man.

The front garden of Alison's house had been cleaned up and a few new plants graced the otherwise dry soil. He knocked on the door and waited, then tried again. The woman from the house next door opened her window, a cigarette hanging out of the corner of her mouth. "She's out, luv. Gone to see that friend of hers, Pauline."

"Thanks"

The woman hung out of the window, and watched him walk down the street. His mother would have hated this neighborhood. She liked her neighbors to be friendly, but being that nosy would have driven her insane.

He couldn't remember which street Pauline lived on; he knew it was very close.

He crossed the road and began to walk back to the main road. A police car pulled up beside him and a young police constable stuck his head out of the window.

"Mr. Pidgley, Inspector Bryce would like a word with you, sir."

James wanted to be flippant and ask which word the Inspector would like, and could he pick the word this time. He had used this response before, and he needed to find something else to reply. Instead, he said, "When would the Inspector like this word?"

"Now sir, please. Could you get into the car?"

Several young men, and a few women, had gathered to see what was going on. The police constable was obviously nervous about the situation. James opened the car door and sat next to the young officer.

"I think you should get going Officer, before this mob of riotous young people decides to turn your vehicle over."

The police officer accelerated, and the tires squealed on the road. Alison and Pauline stood at the end of the road.

"I wonder where they are taking him?"

"Don't know Pauline, I hope he's not in trouble."

The police station was one of those Victorian edifices with a modern extension added. James was shown into interview room number four. There was a table fixed to the floor with four chairs, two on each side. On the table, next to the wall, sat a dual tape recorder. Two tapes, in their original wrappers, sat on top of the machine.

James sat down in one of the chairs facing the door. A policeman stood just inside, trying not to look at James. It became a game between them, James trying to catch the officer's attention, while the officer looked everywhere but at James. Finally, their eyes met, and both began to laugh.

James had been in a police interview room before and wondered if a committee had decided on the color scheme. It was a grayish dull color, inspiring only a cold, unresponsive feeling in him.

The officer shifted his weight from one leg to another. He had been standing for over an hour. James was aware of this waiting tactic. According to the experts, it weakened the resolve of the person being interviewed. Maybe the guilty would have time to reflect. For him, it was a nice rest and a time to think through what he knew.

The more he thought about it, the more he was convinced the man at the bank was important. Bryan had said, *'He was a diseased mind from the past.'* Meaning he knew who the man was. When people talk about someone from the past, they usually mean thirty years or more ago. Before he could continue this thought, the door opened. Inspector Bryce and another plain-clothes officer entered the room. The Inspector put a manila folder on the table and sat down. The other officer undid the wrappings on the tapes and placed them into the machine. As he turned on the machine, James' mobile phone rang once. He took it out of his pocket and looked at the text message that had arrived. It read *'Silence, boy!'*. James gave a laugh

"Something amusing you, Mr. Pidgley?"

"No, Inspector. Only a friend sending me a funny message."

326 | EDWARD ARNO

"Because this is no laughing matter."

"Sorry, what isn't?"

"Murder."

"Well, not for the victim."

The other officer gave a snort, stifling a laugh.

"Last time we met you said you would inform me if you found out anything regarding the murders at the circus."

"Correct."

"Well, you have not been in touch with us, Mr. Pidgley."

"Because I haven't found anything out that is relevant to your inquiry."

"I think I am the best judge of that."

"What would you like to know, Inspector?"

"We have concluded that Derek and Carol Plum murdered Bryan DeWitt and Ryan Cleeves"

"They then committed suicide?"

"Correct."

"If that is your conclusion then there is nothing I can add."

"Do you agree with it?"

"I am a member of the public, Inspector. I don't have all the facts, unlike you gentlemen."

"Well, yes. I see. It would be difficult for us to share our information with just you."

"Then you can't expect me to have a conclusion, can you?"

"Put like that, no. You must have heard other things from the circus people."

"Only that one of the clowns was working for MI5."

"Really? Which one?" The Inspector leaned forward in his chair, as though he was about to hear some very juicy gossip.

"Inspector, you didn't know?"

"I think we may have been told."

"If you're bugging me and following me, then you must know."

"We are not bugging you and I don't have the men to follow you."

"Someone is."

"Who?"

"I was hoping you would tell me."

"I'm sorry, I have don't know. Maybe MI5 are checking everyone out because of the Chinese acrobats.

The other officer was beginning to show irritation with the way the Inspector was conducting the interview. He started to play with a pen he had taken from his pocket. James watched him. He knew that if he really understood body language, he would be able to read what the officer was thinking. The Inspector had opened the manila folder and was reading a report.

"Inspector, can I ask you something?"

"What is it?" Irritation in his voice.

"The note Derek and Carol left..."

"It was a tape recording, what about it?"

"The tone of their voices. Did it sound as though they were reading a statement?"

"I don't know."

The other officer whispered something into the Inspector's ear.

"Right. Mr. Pidgley, this is Sergeant Baxter. He may be able to help you."

"I listened to the tape several times and it did sound as though they were reading from a script. I asked a policewoman to read the transcript with me and we recorded it. Like Derek and Carol, we are amateurs. My conclusion was they were reading a script."

"Why do you ask?"

"Inspector, it seemed strange to me. It was obvious they were going to run away. I don't think they intended to commit suicide."

The Sergeant looked at the Inspector, waiting for a signal before he spoke.

"Are you saying they didn't commit suicide?" asked Sergeant Baxter.

"I think there is some doubt they did. They had been spies for forty years."

"For the Russians?"

"No, for MI5 and maybe MI6. But they could have been double agents. British traitors."

"Double agents? Who told you this?"

"Tom Potts."

"Who's he?"

"MI5"

"You spoke to MI5?"

"No, they spoke to me."

"I wish they would tell us when they are in our area."

The Sergeant waited again for the Inspector to nod his head before he spoke.

"Do you think they are the ones bugging you and following you?"

"Maybe. I am sure they are listening now. It is possible they could have wired the microphone in such a way they are listening to our every word. "

"James Bond rubbish," said the Inspector.

The Inspector returned to reading the report in his folder.

"Can I get something for you to drink, Mr. Pidgley?"

"Good idea, Sergeant, why don't we get some tea. I need the toilet."

The Sergeant turned off the tape machine. The Inspector pushed the manila folder towards James. It was such a deliberate move. They left the interview room taking the police officer that had been standing inside the door with them. Why would the inspector push the folder towards James unless he wanted him to read it? And taking the police officer with them also indicated they didn't want any witness to see James read it.

He opened the folder and began to read the report. In 1968 Bryan was involved in a car crash. His girlfriend was killed. Although Bryan was driving, he wasn't at fault. A drunk driver crossed on to the wrong side of the road and hit Bryan's car on the passenger side. The girl was killed instantly. The former boyfriend of the girl had been chasing them. Bryan insisted at the time that had the ex-boyfriend not been chasing them, the accident could have been avoided. At the inquest, the former boyfriend said he would kill Bryan for taking his girlfriend away from him. The boyfriend had attacked Bryan outside the courthouse. There were several reports of the two of them getting into fights over the years. Although no actual police report was ever filed. The boyfriend ended up in prison for stealing car tires. That was twenty-five years ago, and he had not been in any trouble since. He still lived in Malvern and had been seen recently loitering around the circus winter quarters.

James finished reading the report. Why had the Inspector allowed him to read it? Did the Inspector, like James, think that the Plums had not murdered

Bryan? James sat looking at the report. Could the ex-boyfriend be the man at the bank?

James scanned the report for the ex-boyfriend's name; 'Robert Cross'. The door opened. The Inspector and Sergeant returned carrying mugs of tea. James closed the report and pushed the manila folder back to the Inspector's side of the table.

"Sorry we took so long; the kettle wouldn't boil."

"It won't, Inspector, if you watch it."

"While we were waiting, the Sergeant here was wondering out loud if you had any doubts if the Plums had murdered Bryan DeWitt."

"Inspector Bryce, I am of the same opinion as you are."

"I see. The trouble is there is very little evidence."

"I'm sure it would be possible to get it if someone dug deep enough."

"Sometimes our shovels are too short."

James took a sip of tea, hoping they hadn't put sugar in it. They hadn't, and he enjoyed the refreshing drink.

"On another subject, have you heard of a man called Philip Langley?"

"He was at college with Bryan, but I have not met him."

"It's only, we have been asked by the Home Office to see if he is still in the district."

"He was one of the people I wanted to meet, but I was told he'd left Malvern, and no one knew where he had moved to."

They all drank the tea, while the Inspector sat opening and closing the manila folder.

"So, how's the house building going"

"Almost completed. I'll be moving along very shortly."

The Sergeant coughed then said, "According to my wife, you have already sold them."

"Your wife is correct. I sold the lot in two days."

"Very nice."

The door opened, and a young policewoman indicated to the Sergeant she needed to speak to him. James watched as they spoke. The Sergeant became stiff then returned to the table.

"We may have a problem, Inspector."

"Do we need to step outside, Sergeant?"

"I think Mr. Pidgley should hear what I've just been told, as it affects him. We have just received a report that someone has planted pipe bombs at Mr. Pidgley's building site. A quick inspection by a uniformed officer has unearthed several possible pipe bombs on the site. The bomb squad from Worcester has been called."

"Are you joking, Sergeant?"

"No sir, I think we should make our way to the site."

"Mr. Pidgley, I would be pleased to give you a ride back to the site."

They stood and drank the last of the tea before heading out. The Inspector said he needed to stop at his office first. James and the Sergeant stood waiting for him, just inside the police station. Several officers passed and spoke to the Sergeant. From the way he was approached James could see that he was a popular man. James' mobile phone rang once, and he looked at the text message. '*Silence, boy!*'

James looked about him and wondered where the microphone could be. There were notices pinned to the notice board and several piles of leaflets stood on the station counter.

The Inspector arrived back, carrying a small black bag. James wondered if the policeman was a freemason and if this was his regalia.

An overweight older policeman opened the door and the Inspector and Sergeant stepped outside. James stood behind them.

The car carrying the bomb had been parked by the police station main door and exploded. The Sergeant and Inspector took the main blast, and fell back on to James. The glass doors shattered.

A car alarm screamed and the police station's own fire alarms went off. Several officers came running out from the back offices. James lay below the Inspector and Sergeant, who lay motionless. The breath had been knocked out of James, as the two police officers had fallen on him, and his left wrist was hurting. He wasn't sure if the Inspector and Sergeant were still alive.

He could feel the blood trickling down his face from the glass of the doors, which had blown onto his face. The Inspector began to moan, and several officers came forward and began to move him off James. They very carefully moved the Sergeant, who was covered in blood. James could tell the Sergeant was in a worse condition than the Inspector.

James' right arm was suddenly pulled, and he found himself being dragged across the floor, and into the police station. The Inspector and Sergeant were then dragged backward. As the Sergeant was laid carefully on the floor James lifted his head and saw the blood trail from where he had been dragged.

Someone shouted, "Paramedics on the way!"

A policewoman knelt beside him and began to pick the glass off his face. Several others were tending to the Sergeant and the Inspector. The Sergeant began to shake, and James knew from experience that he was going into shock. A very dangerous situation for anyone as the heart could stop.

"Get some blankets and cover him so he is warm. It will help with the shock," said James.

The policewoman looked at him with surprise, then relayed his message to others who ran about looking for blankets.

The Inspector began to wake up and was a little belligerent until an officer told him to lie still and wait for the medics. The officer turned toward the policewoman and said in a whisper, which James only just heard. "I've always wanted to shout at him."

The second explosion shook the building. The windows that had remained intact shattered and glass flew in all directions. The officer fell on top of James, a large piece of glass embedded in his head and blood squirting out of the wound.

CHAPTER EIGHTEEN

Terror Attack

A fter the second explosion, everyone was dragged or carried to the back of the police station. The paramedic's triage area was set up in the car park and the ambulances lined the alleyway adjacent to the station. He had never seen such devastation in his life before. His grandfather had talked about the bombing of Coventry during the Second World War. How people would be found on the streets after an air raid, their arms or legs blown away. Lying on the yellow tarpaulin sheet waiting for someone to examine him, he looked around and saw police officers and civilians in a worse state than he was.

Ambulance after ambulance was loaded. The injured were rushed to area hospitals. The Inspector and the Sergeant had been the first to be taken from the scene. A hand touched James and a blond-haired man in a fireman's uniform said, "We are going to take you to the hospital now. Sorry to have kept you waiting." James went to speak, but the man had gone. He didn't remember the ride to the hospital, and awoke being carried out of the ambulance.

James lay on a gurney looking at the ceiling as he was wheeled down a corridor. Looking at the fluorescent strip lights as they flashed past above him. He realized he'd seen this point of view in countless films. He'd always found phony, seeing it if for real, however, was scary.

James knew he wasn't badly hurt, maybe a broken wrist and a few cuts from the flying glass. If the two officers had not been in front of him, he would have been one of the first taken to the hospital or possibly dead.

The most difficult thing he had endured so far was when they'd cut off his clothes. He tried to protest several times. Each time he'd sat up, the nurse had gently pushed him back down. They'd left him covered with a single sheet, which didn't help generate any warmth. He could hear someone having a painful time in the next curtained area. The second blast seemed to have caused more injury than the first. The problem was it came too quickly after the first for anyone to realize the possibility of a second bomb.

He closed his eyes, trying to blank out the cries of pain from others in the emergency room. He wasn't really a religious man, but he began to pray that those injured would be okay.

The curtain around his bed was pulled back and the policewoman who had picked the glass off him entered and stood by the side of his bed. He could tell she had been crying and sadness had consumed her body.

He took her hand and held it.

"How are the Inspector and the Sergeant?"

"The Sergeant is still in the operating room. The Inspector will be okay. There are two policemen dead,

and over twenty people were injured. Some very
seriously."

"Who did this?"

"Not sure, but they think it may be connected to the
pipe bombs at your building site."

"Anyone hurt there?"

"No, thank God. They cleared the area, then removed
the bombs and exploded them elsewhere."

"I didn't think I had any real enemies."

"Your brother has arrived and ordered security. He
thinks it could be one of those groups who target
people buying second homes in beautiful places."

"Possible. I know the Welsh had a dreadful problem
with that."

"Not just the Welsh, it's everywhere these days."

"If it was aimed at my building site why was the police
station targeted?"

 She shrugged her shoulders. "I must go and see if the
others need any help."

"Please, let me know how the Inspector and Sergeant
are doing."

"He said you knew who did it."

"Who said?"

"The Inspector said you knew who did the bombing."

"I don't, but I think it had to do the Bryan DeWitt's
murder."

"Funny, the Inspector said that."

"Don't forget to let me know."

"Sure, I'm glad you weren't too badly hurt."

James lay for another hour listening to the noises of
pain before someone came to see him. He was poked
and prodded, then x-rayed. He had a small fracture on
his left wrist and would need it set. He expected a
Plaster of Paris cast but was surprised when they

tightly bandaged his arm and said he could go. James protested, but the nurse explained Plaster of Paris hadn't been used for years; it was too messy and cumbersome.

He waited while they found some clothes for him to wear before he could leave the hospital. He planned to take a taxi back to the circus winter quarters and looked around to find a public telephone.

To his surprise and delight, Dougie and Cooper were pacing up and down outside the hospital entrance. Dougie shook his hand. Cooper went to shake his hand but instead gave him a hug.

"We thought you had been blown up."

"Not this time. I was lucky. If the two policemen had not been in front of me I would not be standing here now."

"So, the police can be useful," said Cooper then realized that may not have been the best thing to say. Dougie looked at James to see how he would react. James's laugh was delayed, but broke the tension.

"We wanted to come in and see you, but the police are keeping everyone away."

"Do the police know who did it?"

"They think it could be a terrorist group."

"We came to take you back to the circus, except the police are all over the place. There were bombs on your building site."

"So, I have heard."

"Your brother is here with Mabel and Tonya."

"Which brother?"

"He said his name was Donald. How many brothers do you have?"

"Four brothers and five sisters."

"Wow, a big family."

Cooper sniggered, remembering his joke about James's father.

James sat in the back of the car and didn't speak on the way back to the circus.

He wanted to go to his caravan, so he could change his clothes. He stopped and looked at Cooper.

"I've got a job for you. Would you find Nobby and tell him I need to see his mother, Alison, as soon as she can."

"Sure, no problem. Did you know that Nobby is joining the circus with Dougie and me?"

James suddenly understood the little dance he had seen Nobby perform out in the street. He smiled and nodded his head as though he was approving the move.

His brother Donald, a partner in the Pidgley property company, sat nervously on the sofa. When he saw James, worry washed off his face. He gave James a 'family' hug, which seemed to go on for a very long time. Cooper and Dougie closed the caravan door and retreated.

"James, what the hell has been going on?"

"Oh, the usual. You know me. A few murders and a couple of bombings. Nothing new."

"Mom's been going out of her mind with worry."

"Donald, I'm fine. According to the police this has to do with an Anti-Second Home terrorist group from Birmingham."

"I hope they are right and it's not personal to the family."

"Brian had a problem with vandals at the car showroom. Police think it's a rival seller but I'm not so sure. It's not anti-Romani, and it's not personal."

"I hope you're right. Do you need me to stay for a few days?"

"No, I can manage, I need to crack the whip on the site foreman a little but that's nothing new."

"Dad's found a hotel in Brighton we could convert to flats. That could be your next project if you want."

"As long as the work keeps coming, I don't mind."

"May's pregnant."

"So, you are going to be a father! Congratulations!"

"Mom's over the moon, of course, a new baby to fuss over."

"Donald, I don't want to throw you out, but I need to change out of these clothes and sleep a little. I feel very tired."

"I understand. I should get back and report to Mom and Dad. I could phone, but you know what they will be like. They want every detail about how you look."

"Tell Mom I'll be home next week at least for one day."

"If you need anything James, call us."

They hugged, and Donald left the caravan. James was relieved. He loved his family but, for now, he needed to be by himself. The realization of what had happened was beginning to sink in.

He locked the caravan door before stripping off the hospital clothes. He stood under the shower letting the water run over him. He had placed his bandaged wrist in a plastic bag. He hoped it didn't leak. He didn't want to go back to the hospital.

He closed his eyes and let the warm water splash on his face. The image of the first explosion came into his mind. He shook it away but knew he would have the nightmare of that moment for the rest of his life.

He dried himself and lay in his underwear on the bed. He had to conquer the images before they began to consume him with fear. At least he was alive. Two police officers had died and many more had been injured.

A girlfriend he had dated several years earlier had been taking psychology at university. She had told him if you had something causing you nightmares, the best way to free yourself of the images was to confront them.

He closed his eyes and replayed the bomb explosion. At first, he had to stop it because he saw the destruction, not the explosion itself. He tried again and found he could look at it and what was around. It was then he remembered seeing a man standing at the end of the road. He tried again to see if he could get his mind to zoom in on the man. He hadn't seen him clearly, so he couldn't. The man could have been innocent, but the police had said someone had triggered the bombs. They had cameras all around the police station. He was sure they would soon see who had done committed this atrocity.

He dressed in jeans and a tee shirt and made a cup of tea. He needed something stronger, but if he had an alcoholic drink he would not be able to think clearly. The knock on his door made him jump and he knew for the next few weeks any loud noise would make him react negatively.

He opened the caravan door and looked down to see Alison and Nobby.

"Come in. You got my message from Cooper?"

Alison didn't say a word but hugged him; he could feel her body shaking.

"I'm okay."

"I thought we had lost you."

"Sorry, not yet."

Nobby, like Cooper, hugged him. Tears had formed in his eyes. James suddenly understood that he had bonded with Cooper and Nobby just as his older brothers had with him.

He picked up the pen Philip had given him and held it. His mobile beeped and he received a text message '*Silence, boy!*'

He motioned them to follow him into the bedroom. The pen still in his hand, he waited for his mobile to beep it didn't. Philip had said he didn't need to do that. If he moved from one area to another, and there were a bug, then the phone would tell him.

"Okay, we can talk now."

"Sorry, James, I don't understand."

"We are bugged. Someone is listening to everything and telling others what we have been up to."

"You mean, it wasn't Mom's big mouth?"

"No, not this time."

"The cheek. I'll give you both a good slapping."

"Wow, how nice."

"James! Remember I'm still a kid."

"So, what really happened?"

"Someone tried to blow up the police station."

"Why were you there?"

"They wanted to ask me some more questions they mentioned a man called 'Robert Cross'."

"Tosser Cross. That's Pauline boyfriend. He was the guy who told you where Chris Parrott lived. I can't stand Tosser he is a complete idiot."

"So, he didn't know Bryan?"

"They went to the same college, but I don't think they were ever friends."

"He has known Bryan and Pauline since his college days."

"He is a Malvern lad. Grew up here. We all went to the same secondary modern school. What a dump, most of us played truant."

"You played truant?"

Alison ignored Nobby's interruption. "He had this girlfriend at school, everyone thought they would marry. They were so much in love he kept telling everyone."

"I take it they didn't."

"No, she died in a car crash."

"Funny thing is, she had dumped him two months earlier."

"Why was that funny?"

"Because she died in a car driven by Bryan. He had been dating her for those two months. Tosser knew about it. He was following them when the crash happened."

"How did they crash?"

"A drunk driver slammed into the side of the car. Tosser raced away from the scene not wanting to help."

"More like not wanting to be seen. Coward," said Nobby, as he made a pot of tea.

"Next day, Tosser went ballistic at Bryan, blaming him for the death and said he would kill Bryan one day."

"We all say things we don't mean when we are faced with a loss."

"Bryan went into a depressed mood, I'm not sure he ever got over the death."

James hadn't interrupted Alison even though he knew about the crash. He wanted to hear her side of it; this was what had been said on the street after the crash. Nobby gave each of them a mug of tea and sat down next to his mother. James remembered how he would sit next to his mother; just being near her was enough to make him feel secure.

Alison continued, "Tosser wasn't very good with rejection. Pauline tried to end their relationship several times and each time he said he'd commit suicide. Anyway, these days he walks around as though he is on drugs. A real dopehead, he is."

"That's just an act," said Nobby, before taking a sip of tea.

"What do you mean?"

"Two weeks ago, me and Cooper saw him in town. He looked real drugged out of his head. Then an hour later he was over by the old railway line near the golf course. Using a catapult to shoot at crows. He was so quick I thought it was a different man."

"Are you sure it was him?"

"Mom, it was Tosser. I'm sure of that. We watched for over an hour until these guys arrived and he went back into the dopy druggy routine."

"Are you sure you're not just making this up?"

"No, Mom. Even when the men pushed him around, he didn't drop the druggy act."

"Where does he live?"

"Wych Cutting on the way to Colwell. He has a great workshop at the back of his house."

"How do you know that? Been snooping and robbing again?"

"No, Dad took me."

"When? I didn't know anything about this."

"You remember when Dad and Tosser were in the Territorial Army together? Dad had to drop off some gear at Tosser's and we found him in his workshop at the back. He was really annoyed we had gone round the back and into the workshop."

"Well, you're not to go there again."

"Alison's it's okay. Nobby, did you go there again?"

"Six months ago. Nic Colson and me were up on the hill above Tosser's house. We sneaked down and had a look inside his workshop. Through the window like, not actually inside."

"So, what did you see?" asked Alison, suddenly becoming intrigued by the story.

"It looked just the same, only this time it had a lot more equipment in it."

"Then what did you do?"

"We didn't break in Mom, if that is what you think." Alison sipped at her tea, not wanting to look at James after her son had admonished her.

"Nobby, what type of equipment did you see?"

"Not sure what you would call it. Once on the telly, this man was showing how he made his own bullets and the machine Tosser had looked like the one the man had on the television."

The three of them sat in silence. Nobby poured more milk and tea into the mugs. Alison stared into her mug, watching the brown liquid swirl around after she had stirred in a teaspoon of sugar. Nobby looked at his Doc Martin boots. James wondered if he had told his mother about joining the circus.

Only James seemed focused on the situation, he knew whoever it was had to be close to them. He or she was always just one step ahead. As though someone had told them, or they had heard from the listening bugs what they, or he, were going to do.

He broke the peace. "Were Bryan and Tosser friends?"

"I don't think real friends, but something had a happened between them. Once in a pub, the Unicorn I think, me, Pauline and Tosser were having a drink waiting as usual for his Dad, when Bryan came in. He stood at the bar and drank by himself. Tosser kept making remarks, hoping to get Bryan to react. Tosser was really looking for a fight. Bryan didn't and after a while, I went and suggested he should leave. He did and took me along for a Chinese meal."

"Did Dad know?"

"It was before your Dad and I got married. I could go out with whomever I liked. Anyway, Tosser hasn't spoken to me since. Then Pauline started acting really strange and finally told me Tosser had told her she couldn't be friends with me anymore."

"That's not right," said Nobby.

"So, we stopped seeing each other until he dumped her again for some stupid little piece of skirt in Worcester. Once he was bored with her, he returned, and stupid Pauline took him back."

"Mom, is that why they call the 1960s the age of free love?"

"You're going to stop watching BBC Two."

"Channel Four, a program about Woodstock and how the Glastonbury festival was created. I want to go to Glastonbury one day before it gets closed."

"James, do you think Tosser was involved in Bryan's death?"

"Not sure, really. Just trying to find out who Bryan's enemies were."

The conversation dried up and they drank their tea. James' eyelids began to close. He was very tired. Alison, seeing him almost fall forward asleep, gathered her things together.

"I think I should be going, but I don't think you should be on your own. Nobby can stay tonight."

"It's okay, I can manage."

"It's not about managing. I think, for safety, he should stay."

Alison left, and Nobby washed the mugs and teapot. James had gone back to the bedroom, stripped down to his underwear, and climbed into the bed. He was asleep before Nobby could say 'good night'.

Being so tired he didn't have the sleepless night he had expected. Only as he woke did the day before flash across his mind. Later he would phone to see how the Inspector and Sergeant were. He lay warm and secure in his bed. Even as a child he had believed bed was the one place you could be safe. Since then violence had crept into the world, and his life nowhere was safe now. His arm hurt from lying on it during the night. He climbed out of bed and went to the toilet. He was relieving himself when he realized someone was asleep on the sofa.

Nobby's rhythmic breathing was like that of a contented baby. James returned to the bedroom, gathered some clothes, and took a shower.

The noise from making tea and cooking breakfast woke Nobby. The smile on the skinhead's face surprised James. Without speaking Nobby went to shower returning a little later a clean glow to his face and the smile wider than ever.

"Why are you grinning like the Cheshire cat from Alice in Wonderland?"

"I have always seen myself as the Mad Hatter. We watched the play in junior school and I just wanted to be the Mad Hatter."

"I wanted to be the White Rabbit only my older brothers always told me it was played by a girl."

"Was it?"

"I don't know. Breakfast?"

After they had eaten, Nobby began to wash the dishes. "James, you should make your bed, I'll clean up here." The smile had returned to Nobby's face. He was enjoying being in a caravan, experiencing what it was going to be like when he was working in the circus. He had spent most of his life with his mother doing everything for him and now, with an insight into the freedom to come, he was very excited.

James stood in the doorway to the bedroom looking at his phone. He beckoned Nobby to the bedroom and closed the sliding door. He checked the phone once again before speaking.

"Nobby, can you show me Tosser's workshop?"

"Sure, we need to drive up the Wyche road and park in the hillside parking lot.

"Don't speak in the car."

"Why?"

"I think it may be bugged."

As they drove up the hill James remembered this was the route he had taken to Colwell to see Chris Parrott. Nobby pointed to the entrance to a large parking lot on the right side of the road. Several cars were already parked. A woman and a man dressed in what would be regarded a stereotypical country outfits were leaving their car. The woman's hat had several long feathers sticking out of at the back. Each time she turned her head her husband was tickled in the face. They headed for the entrance to a hill walk trail and disappeared into the trees. Looking at the other vehicles, James noticed a black van with tinted windows. It was impossible to see inside. If anyone was in the black van neither James nor Nobby could see them. Nobby stared hard at the van until he felt the van itself was watching them. He turned to look where they would be walking, then swiftly turned his head back. Something, or someone, in the van had moved. He was sure of it. He stared a little longer but as nothing moved, he motioned for James to follow him.

James checked twice to see if the car was locked. They crossed the road and began to walk down the hill. Nobby stopped and sat on a low stone wall on the other side was a small wood. He looked up and down the road before swinging his legs over and running for the cover of the first few trees. James followed, suddenly realizing how much he used his hands and arms. Now he was restricted to only one arm, as the one in the stiff bandage was almost useless. The plastic bag had leaked that morning, and the edge of the bandage was still a little soggy.

They marched single file in a straight line deeper into the wood. Through the old trees beneath a canopy of thick green leaves, ferns had grown. As they walked James expected to hear Richard Attenborough or Steve Irwin explain about the environment, the plants and the animal life living in the woods. He thought how much television clouded the imagination with its brand of perception and expectation.

Someone had used the path they were taking, as it was clearly cut into the undergrowth of vegetation.

The path veered sharply to the right and began to climb upwards. James slowed his pace watching Nobby race ahead. He lost of the boy and quickened his pace until he became breathless. The path became narrower and a smaller spur broke off to the left. James stood wondering, which way he should go when he heard the '*pss*' sound from his right side. He looked, but saw nothing. Then Nobby stood up and gave his infectious smile.

James joined him and they crouched down together. From this vantage point, James was surprised how much of the houses on Old Wyche Road could be seen. Nobby pointed. James took a small pair of binoculars out of his pocket.

"Which house?"

"The one on the right with the washing on the line." Using his binoculars, James found the house Nobby was indicating. Several bed sheets hung from a white plastic washing line. Old wooden dolly clothes pegs held them in place. The two-story red brick house looked like one of those that had been built just after the Second World War. The back door was open, and a young girl stood on the top step, smoking a cigarette. Someone was talking to her from inside the house and she kept shaking her head. James panned the binoculars down and studied a small single-story building about twenty feet from the back door. Its windows were heavily barred.

"Who's the girl?" James asked, handing Nobby the binoculars.

"Karen Biddle. She's a real slut. Still goes to my old school. She only fourteen years old. She'll sleep with anyone."

A man appeared from inside the house. He was dressed only in a pair of yellow briefs. A small triangular tear in the left buttock cheek of the material exposed a tattoo. His extended stomach, the result of fast food and beer drinking, hung over the brief's waistband. He leaned forward and kissed Karen on the neck. She responded by pushing him away.

"That's why she is there." Nobby handed James the binoculars.

The man was obviously getting aroused, but the girl didn't seem interested. From his body language, it seemed he was pleading with her to go back inside. "That's Tosser's half-brother. Tosser must be out because he would never allow Kirk to bring a girl into the house for sex."

James continued to watch as the man began to make thrusting movements with his hips. Finally, Karen gave in and they went back inside, closing the door behind them.

"Mom once caught Dad in a pub with Karen; it must have been about three months ago. He said he was just talking to her, but I think I know what was really going on."

"Maybe he was."

"Yeah, and pigs have wings. Karen's Mom is a daytime-at-home prosie, and I think Karen is doing the same."

"What's a daytime-at-home prosie?"

"The husband goes to work, and the woman has paying men around to break the boredom and make some extra cash. Most of the time the husband doesn't know about it."

"They must know!"

"My Mom may flirt but she would never cheat on Dad. He would... and has. Several times I've seen him do it. When I was nine, I'd pour cold water over him and this woman. He was so mad until I told him I would tell Mom."

"What happened?"

"He just started to treat me like a Dad should and we became pals. I don't understand why he does it but at least he has become much more discreet."

James put his hand over Nobby's mouth. His reaction was to pull it away until he also heard the soft footsteps approaching. Sitting as still as they could, they waited for whoever was approaching. James had become alert to someone when he heard a very faint tuneless whistle. It had stopped, and he wondered if the person had heard them, because the sound of his footsteps became much louder.

A tall, thin figure appeared wearing black jeans and heavy army type boots. The man wore a navy-blue top with a hood, which he'd pulled over his head to cover his face. t He stopped just beside them. Nobby desperately wanted to sneeze and fought the desire. The man didn't notice them and stood looking around, before taking the spur path down to the houses below. They watched as the unknown person entered Tosser's garden by a small gate. Unless you knew the gate was there, you would not have seen how to enter the garden.

Nobby looked at James before speaking. "Who is that?"

"I was hoping you were going to tell me. I couldn't see their face."

"Me neither, but from the walk, it could have been Tosser not pretending to be a druggy."

"It was a man though. Well, it smelt like one."

"What do you mean it smelt like one? Do men smell differently from women if they are not wearing perfume?"

"Oh yes, very differently."

The man entered the house by the back door then returned to the backyard. He entered the small workshop after unlocking several padlocks. James watched as the man reappeared carrying a two-barrel shotgun and entered the house.

"What was he carrying?"

"A shotgun."

The scream was the first thing they heard followed by a naked Karen running out into the yard. She was holding her left arm across her breasts and trying to cover her pubic hair with her right hand. Kirk, also naked, followed. He had his hands in the air and seemed proud to show his naked body. James wondered if he would have been so blatant if he had a small penis when it was erect. Kirk was pleading with the man who ignored him and just kept pointing the gun at them. Something Kirk said made the man very angry and he pointed the gun at Kirk's semi-erect penis. It quickly lost its rigidity and shrank. The condom he wore hung loosely on the head.

"What's happened?" asked Nobby excitedly. James gave the binoculars to Nobby.

He scanned the scene and gave a low whistle, "She's naked and so is he. Do you think the man caught them doing it? She has nice tits. Small but very nice."

James looked at Nobby, realizing he was still very naïve when it came to sex. He nodded and took the binoculars back.

Karen had gone behind Kirk and, as he moved, she tried to keep him in front of her. The gunman began to circle around them and herded the pair out of the yard onto the street. Karen started to scream as she half ran onto the road. Several neighbors had appeared and stood watching. A man started to take pictures of the naked couple. James was surprised the neighbors showed no fear of the loaded gun. Kirk backed into a car, fell over the trunk and slid onto the ground. From the expression on his face, he had hit the road with some force. Standing up he opened the trunk of the car and took out a blanket. He handed it to Karen, who was now hiding behind the car trying to open a rear door. Taking out another blanket, he wrapped it around himself before trying to open the driver's door. The gunman threw something at Kirk which landed a few feet behind him. Kirk turned and bent down to pick it up. The blanket fell and the naked backside of Kirk shone like the moon. The neighbor with the camera took several pictures while the others applauded this spectacle. Kirk grabbed the blanket and quickly opened the car door. He started the car and began to drive away leaving Karen standing in the street. She started to scream. Stopping the car, Kirk reversed back and let her get in. The car's wheels screeched and they drove off at high speed.

The gunman walked to the back of the house and into the workshop. When he re-appeared the hood had fallen off his head and he didn't have the gun. James stared. He had seen this man before. Well, someone like him. It was the man who had been arguing with Bryan outside the bank. Only, he'd had grey hair and this man had black hair. The man entered the house. "Does Tosser dye his hair?"

"If he remembers to. Auntie Pauline dyes it for him. Very vain is Tosser. Still thinks he's seventeen."

James looked at the house. Tosser opened the back door and crossed the yard to the workshop. He re-emerged carrying the shotgun and laid it down on the

ground while he locked the padlocks. James handed
Nobby the binoculars.

"That's Tosser. What an idiot showing your shotgun
off. Someone must have called the cops."

"We won't have long to wait if they did."

"Why are you interested in stupid Tosser?"

"His name came up at the police station. He didn't act
as though he was a druggy when he chased Kirk and
Karen out of the house?"

"No, he looked normal. Do you think he murdered the
clown?"

"Possibly. He does have a violent streak from what we
have just seen."

"From what *you* saw, you mean. I didn't see much
unless you count seeing Karen Biddle's tits."

"Better not let your mother know."

"Tosser once told my Dad he could make a bomb."

"Truth, Nobby?"

"Truth honest. They were drunk at our house and I was
listening behind the sofa. Tosser never lets anyone into
his house. That's why he was so angry at Kirk just
now."

"But doesn't Kirk live with him?"

"No, he lives with a forty-year-old woman in a flat in
Malvern Link."

"Not for much longer, if she finds out about this."

The noise of the police sirens grew louder and soon the
front of Tosser's house was barricaded with police
cars. James had only seen the tactical method of
entering a house on the American TV show *Cops*.
Now he watched it 'live', as they formed a tight group,
guns out and ready to fire. Tosser came out and was
quickly thrown to the ground. After several police
officers had jumped on his spine, he was handcuffed.

A policewoman searched him and lingered, James thought, a little too long in one of his pockets. A police officer emerged from the back door carrying the bent shotgun wrapped in a plastic bag. Nobby had become restless, "What's happening now?"

"They have handcuffed Tosser and it looks like they are taking him away. Once they have all gone, we will go down to the house and see if we can get in."

"Great. A spot of 'B' an' E"

"'B' and 'E'?"

"Breaking and Entering."

Kirk's car arrived. He and Karen were escorted into the house. They emerged a little later, dressed. Then, they too were taken away in a police car.

James watched to see if all the police cars had left before he and Nobby stood up. They took the small spur path down to the gate Tosser had gone through. At the gate, James told Nobby to stay there until he had checked to see if the coast was clear. James entered the back garden. It was a lot bigger than it had seemed from up the hill. He checked around the side to see if anyone was at the front. All was clear, and he called Nobby to join him. Nobby tried the back door and almost fell in as it opened. The kitchen was spotlessly clean, as though it was never used. The cupboards were full of tinned food. Enough to feed an army for at least three weeks. The hall to the front door had two doors off it. One room was a dining room, decorated plain and simple. The other was the living room and, from the look of it, this was never used.

James climbed the stairs two at a time. He wasn't sure why he was so eager, but he felt he was at last on to something. The front bedroom was obviously the master bedroom. It was a mausoleum dedicated to a dead woman. The room had many pictures of this woman, depicting her from youthful beauty to her final days as an old lady in a wheelchair. The rest of the room was as if the woman had just left it. All her personal belongings, her hairbrush, and makeup were on the top of a dresser.

"His mother's room. He must have idolized her."

"James, would you do this for your mother?"

"I love my mother very much, but this is going over the top."

"I have a picture of my mom hidden in my sock and briefs drawer. That's my tribute to my mom."

"Does she know?"

"I think so. Only now she doesn't put my socks and undies away. She puts them on the bed."

The bathroom and toilet were combined and, like the kitchen, was so clean it looked like it was never used. The back bedroom was where Tosser slept. It was where Kirk and Karen had been having sex. It still smelt of sex and the bedclothes had been thrown all over the floor. A chair had been turned over. A used condom had been hastily thrown, missing the waste bin, and was stuck to the wall. Several others were unopened on the bedside table. It looked like Kirk had been planning to make an afternoon of it. James stepped carefully into the room and opened several of the drawers in a large chest. Tosser's clothes were very neatly arranged inside each drawer.

"Doesn't look like there is anything here."

James stood in the doorway and nodded to Nobby to follow. Something stopped Nobby from moving and he half shut the door, discovering another door behind a door that would remain unseen if the main door was left open. Thinking it was a cupboard, Nobby opened it.

James came back into the room. He and Nobby entered a small room. The walls were lined with old pictures of a half-naked girl. A dartboard with a picture of Brinarno the clown taped to it and three darts sticking out of the clown's red nose. Bookshelves were lined with books about bomb-making and guns. Someone had placed a wooden child's desk by the window looking out on to the street. James noticed a leather-bound book on the desk and picked it up. It was a diary. On the front page Tosser had written '*The Words and Thoughts of Robert Cross, Mastermind*'. He tapped Nobby on the shoulder, his index finger to his lips. He motioned that they needed to leave. Nobby nodded.

James took one of the pictures, which only showed the girl's face and the diary. Nobby had found a collection of hard-core girl magazines and stuffed them into the back of his jeans.

They left the house, closing the door as they did, and exited the garden by the small gate. Once on the hill, they stopped in the same spot they had been watching from. A car pulled up on the street and Kirk climbed out. He ran around the back of the house and entered.

"Just in time."

"Time, James? What time is it?"

"Ten minutes to five."

"I've got to get going. I don't want to miss the party."

"What party?"

"The circus party! You know, the one they have before they hit the road. We start packing up tomorrow."

"Where is it? In the Big Top?"

"No, they have booked the Abbey Hotel. It's a real dress-up affair."

"You're going like that?"

"No, I have a suit."

"A suit"

"Yep, a real Ben Sherman suit. Remember last week when Dougie, Cooper and me went up to London? Well, we went to the Ben Sherman shop in Carnaby Street and I got a new suit."

"Does your mother know you're joining the circus?"

"Not yet. I was wondering if you would tell her for me."

"No way, Nobby. I don't want to die young."

"So, you think she will be mad at me."

They crossed the road and into the car park. The only other vehicle was the black van with the tinted windows. Nobby walked up to it and peered inside. It was empty.

As they drove back into Malvern Nobby seem distant.

"Nobby, your mother is going to be little upset, remember she is losing her little boy."

"It's a real job with a contract. Tonya made me sign it and agree to the terms of employment."

"Make sure you tell your mother about the contract."

"The best bit is Dougie said I could bunk down with him and Cooper."

"Nobby, mate, I think it's great news."

They arrived at Nobby's house.

"Thanks, James see you at the party."

James drove slowly back to the winter quarters. He wanted to read the diary.

CHAPTER NINETEEN

The Murderer Revealed

The keyhole opening on the caravan's door was blocked. A large envelope covered it.
Inside, was an invitation from Tonya to the circus' Season Opening party. Tonya had written that she was sorry it had taken so long to give him an invitation, but with everything going on it had slipped her mind. The picture on the invitation was of Brinarno in his clown costume. On the back, it read; '*In loving memory of Brinarno, the World's Greatest Clown*'. James felt sad. He had only known Bryan briefly, somehow Brinarno's personality had touched something deep in James. It was as though they had been friends for a long time.

James stripped off his clothes and took a shower. He felt drained and really wanted to go to bed and sleep. Guilt had been one of the things he had grown up with. His siblings used guilt to get him to do things for them and now it was deeply imprinted in his mind. At some point, he would have to confront the Tosser situation but, as he was probably still in the police cell, it could wait until tomorrow.

Laying on the bed the bath towel wrapped around him, James fell asleep. A knock on the caravan door woke him with a start. His mind replayed the explosion of the first bomb, and he sat up in bed unable to focus or think clearly. He panicked, then calmed himself down when he realized it was only someone at the door.
He shouted, "Come in!"
Dougie opened the door and looked inside. "You in there James?"
"Yes, come in."
Dougie was dressed in a new dark blue suit and a white shirt with a pastel yellow and blue tie. James could hear his mother saying, 'He cleaned up well in the end'.
"Not ready yet? You are coming, aren't you?"
"Yes, just fell asleep. I'll meet you there."
"You know where to go? It's at the Abbey Hotel. You know where that is, I hope?"
"Abbey Road?"
"Great. Then I'll see you there. Don't be too late or you will miss all the fun."
"I'll leave in about ten minutes."
James took a clean light pale pink shirt and a red and gold tie from his drawer. His best suit, black silk and Italian-made, was still in its dry-cleaner's plastic bag. He was tying the laces of his Ferragamo dress shoes when someone knocked on the door again. He didn't look up, just called out, "Come on in, it's not locked."
James stood up to find the twin barrels of a shotgun a few inches from his face. He looked at the person holding the weapon and saw a plastic clown mask covering the face. The motion of the gun indicated for him to sit down. James obliged and sat at the small table, nervously straightening the papers and the

invitation lying there. The gunman stood looking at him, neither moving nor showing signs of sitting down. James picked up the pen Philip had given him and placed it by the papers. His mobile beeped. He picked it up and was about to open it when the gunman, in a muffled voice said, "Close it."
James flipped the phone open, read the message *'Silence, boy!'* and shut the phone down.
The gunman kept looking at his watch, his restlessness increasing the tension. James could see the finger on the trigger of the gun and, with the gunman becoming so nervous, he was beginning to worry.
The gunman peered out of the window, then glanced at his watch. The sound of a car driving away seemed to relax him. He looked out of the window again. In his muffled voice James could just hear him say, "Stand."
James went to pick up the mobile, but the gunman shouted, "Leave it!"
So, James scooped up the papers and carried those with him. The gunman opened the caravan door and walked backwards down the steps. He held the door open while James came out. He pointed to the Big Top with the gun, and James began to walk. He glanced from side to side between the caravans, hoping to see someone, but the place was empty.
As they approached the Big Top James wondered if he could pull the flap back and let it go, hitting the gunman. This idea backfired because the flap of the Big Top was already open. The gunman indicated for James to enter. Stepping inside he stopped and felt the gun in the small of his back pushing him towards the circus ring. The sound of the tent flap falling and the light going dimmer meant the gunman had closed the flap.

In the center of the circus ring, two chairs had been placed facing each other. James sat down on one, assuming the gunman would take the other. He didn't but stood to the side of the ring. Stepping into the ring the gunman shouted through the mask.

"What's that in your hand?"

James looked at the papers then at the gunman before replying, "An invitation to a party."

"Throw it down!" shouted the gunman, although to James it sounded like he had said 'Joe quit clown'. James placed the paper carefully on the floor. The gunman ran and kicked them. They slid towards the other chair.

The gunman walked over and straddled the other chair, using the back to rest the gun, with the barrels pointed at James. Studying how the gunman was dressed. James realized he recognized the boots the gunman was wearing. The clown mask had, at first, looked like a replica of Brinarno's face. But on closer examination, James could see it was a novelty shop plastic mask. The gunman was obviously very nervous. While his finger wasn't on the trigger, James knew he would be safe. The muffled voice from behind the mask spoke again. "What the fuck are you looking at?"

James quickly bit his lip. He knew if he came out with one of those quick-witted sarcastic comments, he would find himself shot. This was a time for tact. A time to take the situation very seriously

"I was wondering Robert… or can I call you Tosser? I was wondering what you want from me?"

The gunman stiffened in the chair. His legs stretched apart, then released tension. His finger gripped the trigger, then released.

"It's okay," James continued, "I know who you are, and why you're doing this."

"You can't know," was the almost inaudible reply.

"Sorry, I didn't understand what you said. Could you repeat that?"

The clown-masked gunman replied, shouting even louder but the muffled words failed to make sense to James.

"Tosser, just take off the mask and we can talk."

The gunman sat upright, his straight back so tense it must have hurt.

"It is comical. You wearing a clown mask in a circus ring, and wanting to talk about the world's greatest circus clown."

The gunman stretched his legs apart again, and this time the stitching on the inside leg of the camouflage pants split. It made James stare harder. He hadn't realized he was so focused on one spot. James had read somewhere a story that after the Iran embassy siege in London, one of the hostages had said that he had watched a male terrorist so closely that the terrorist had tensed while straddling a chair and so much that the seams of his jeans had come apart. Things had only got worse. As tension increased, the stitching gave way further, until there was a large hole. In the article James had read, the author, a psychology professor, had said watching for those kinds of signs was a good way of monitoring the state of mind of a hostage-taker.

"Tosser, take off the mask so we can talk man to man. Looking at your clown mask doesn't help; it's making me want to laugh. I don't want you to shoot me because you think I am laughing at you. The gunman released the tension in his legs and removed his finger from the trigger. The front of the gunman's shirt was beginning to get wet. Large drops of sweat dripped from under the clown mask.

As the gunman went tense again the hole on the inside of his pants became a little larger. James mused how in times of stress your mind focused on very unimportant things.

The gunman stood up, swinging his leg over the back of the chair. The gun was still pointing at James, even though the gunman was facing the other way. Taking off the mask, the gunman shook his head. Sweat sprayed like a dog getting out of a river and shaking itself dry.

He turned and looked at James, sweat still running down his face. This was the man Nobby had pointed out as Tosser. He lifted his tee shirt and wiped the sweat off his face. His six-pack tight stomach surprised James. Most men who were over sixty didn't have such an athletic body. James could understand why Pauline was attracted to him. He had the body of a forty-year-old. Tosser turned the chair around and sat facing James.

"So, you think you know why I have you here in this tent with a gun pointing at your balls."

"Not only do I know why I am here, but why you murdered Bryan DeWitt."

"Ha! Well, that's one thing you got wrong. I didn't murder Bryan."

"You murdered the others."

"Let's not use the word 'murder'. It's so negative. Let's say, I eliminated the distractions to my cause."

"Your cause?"

"How do you know I knew Bryan?"

"Outside the bank, before he died. You and Bryan had an argument. I saw you. Then, of course, Pauline told me a little about your college days."

"She's got such a big mouth."

"You told the bank and credit card companies he was dead, sent them a phony death certificate."

"Didn't that make him mad! Not that you or anyone could prove I did it."

"I don't have to. The police told me the bank had handed over a video showing whoever had given in the death certificate." James hoped his lie would be believed by Tosser.

"How do you know that?"

"I've seen it. The police showed it to me and asked if I recognized you."

"What did you say?"

"At that point, I didn't know who you were."

The conversation wasn't going the way Tosser wanted it to, and he became very agitated. He stretched his legs apart and more stitching unraveled. He suddenly shouted, "Shut the fuck up!"

They sat in silence and James refocused on the stitching. He wasn't sure why, but when Tosser relaxed so did he.

"Stop staring at me!" shouted Tosser, the finger on the trigger tightening.

James looked down at the floor and the papers. He hoped the microphone was working and someone, somewhere was listening. It would just be his luck whoever listened in on his life had taken the night off, or gone to the pub. Bored listening to his mundane activities.

"Do you think I didn't see you and Nobhead spying on my house? You wouldn't stand a chance in a real warfare situation. People like you think playing at war is what we Territorial Army blokes do. Well, let me tell you. We are trained soldiers, ready to go into battle."

"So, the gun show with your brother was for us?"

"My brother is a prick, fucking an underage teenager in my house on my bed. I should have blown his balls off. I still might when I get hold of him."

"So, the police let you go?"

"No, they are morons. Left me sitting in a car having taken off my handcuffs because I said they were hurting me. They didn't even close the door properly, so I just got out and walked up the street. When they found out the girl Kirk was bonking was under-age they lost interest in me."

"They let him go?"

"Sure, he talked his way out of by saying they hadn't had sex. "

"I spoke to him when he came back after you and Nobhead had left my house."

"You saw him?"

"Yep, he is tied up in my house until I can deal with him. Why did you go into my house?"

"I wanted to know why you murdered Bryan."

"You have no proof I murdered him."

"You wanted to and many years ago, when Marilyn died, you said you would kill him."

"He murdered her."

"How Tosser? He wasn't the drunk driver that night and you knew that because you were there following them."

"If he hadn't stolen her from me, she would never have died."

"She wasn't a piece of property! She dumped you before they went out."

"She was my girlfriend, I wanted to marry her."

"If you hadn't been following them the crash wouldn't have happened. That's why you ran and told the police you weren't there."

"I couldn't stand him touching her, kissing her. It made me sick. He had everything. Always got what he wanted."

"It's not really about her, is it? You wanted in on Bryan's inventions."

"You know nothing."

"If I know nothing then how do I know that he wouldn't let you in on the inventions? He wouldn't even let you be part of the gang. You had to sit on the outside looking in. Bryan told me about how you tried to say they were yours."

"They were!" shouted Tosser.

"If they were your inventions, then why aren't you famous?"

"I just told you! Bryan cut me out, because of Marilyn."

"It wasn't because of Marilyn, he stopped you because you were nothing but a bully who wanted to be the boss man."

"I was until he took over."

"I spoke to Philip Langley and he told me the truth. Derek Plum also told me. Then you murdered him and his wife."

"That bitch deserved to die."

"Why?"

"She taunted me about Marilyn! Told me I would never get her back. When she died, Carol told me Marilyn was pregnant with Bryan's baby. They were going to marry if she hadn't died. Carol wanted it all and was trying to steal it from Bryan's invention so they could sell it to the Chinese. In our younger days, it was the Russians. Now everyone is selling secrets to the Chinese or Iran."

"Nothing wrong with the Chinese, Tosser, unless you're taking their imitation medicine or playing with some kid's toy with lead paint on it."

"The Chinese of all people! Then you come along. A fucking Pidgley digging up all the dirt. Why couldn't you just leave it as the police said? It was Derek and Carol who murdered Bryan, then committed suicide."

"But that's not what happened, Tosser."

"You don't know that!" he shouted.

Tosser sat tensely. The stitching ripped some more. James decide not to focus on it anymore. He watched as the finger gripped the trigger then released it. Years earlier, when James was at school and being bullied by a tall, fat kid, his father had told him to always try and defuse an explosive situation. James had shouted at his father at the time. How, he'd asked, do you react when the other kid has you by the throat wanting to wring your neck? His father had calmly replied that he should make a joke or talk about something, which would distract the other person.

"You're going to marry Pauline?"

"Maybe." There was caution in Tosser's tone.

"Was it Pauline telling you about me?"

"She's a loyal woman and does as she is told."

"Scared more like."

"Of me? Never. She knows I love her."

"Then you should marry her, after all, she let you come back after your fling with the woman in Worcester."

"She has other men."

"I don't think so. She may flirt a lot, but I think Pauline only loves you."

"Whatever."

"So, what happens now?"

"What do you think is going to happen now? We have a tea party? Are you stupid or something? What kind of idiot are you?"

"Didn't know I had a choice."

"Very funny, ha ha."

"You're going to kill me and afterwards you'll find you have nothing. I died knowing, and you don't."

"What do you mean, I have nothing? What do you know?"

"What Bryan told me and showed me."

"Did he show his big secret invention?"

"Which one? What are you looking for Robert?"

"He told you, and he showed you? Bullshit, he would never show someone like you."

"Of course, he did. We were friends."

"No fucking way. Bryan trusted no one. Let alone someone new."

"Who said I was new? Why do you think I moved into the circus winter quarters?"

"Right, so you know. No fucking way."

"So, why did you kill him?"

"There you go again. I didn't kill him! I needed him alive until he gave me the secret of the big invention which would change the world."

"Now you won't get it, will you? Bryan's gone and you're going to kill me."

"You're going to tell me!" The words spat out of Tosser's mouth, his anger growing.

"No, Robert, because there was no big secret. Bryan made it up. He conned everyone."

"Why would he do that?"

"He wanted everyone to think he had invented some really important thing. Then everyone would give him food and presents, hoping he would share with them his big secret. He never did."

"Okay, but why did he do it?"

"I don't really know what Bryan got out of it. No one really knows why a conman con others. Yes, there are those that do it for the money, but some do it for the pleasure of deceiving the people they despise."

"You're lying."

"Okay, Robert. If I'm lying, where is the big secret? Bryan's dead. So is John Bunty, Ken Williams, Stephen Kirk, Roy Churchill, Tom Saunders, Ian Kipler and Derek Plum. All dead, Robert, and no big secret."

"I know they are all dead! They had to die! They wouldn't give me the secret! They kept saying there wasn't one!"

"And you wouldn't believe them. You murdered them all for nothing."

"I didn't murder Bryan."

"What a 'tosser'. Now I know why you got that nickname."

"Wrong again, Pidgley. I got the name because I couldn't stop wanking off at school."

"You kept masturbating?"

"Yeah. All the time in the classroom, until the teachers found out and I got expelled,"

"Still do it?"

Tosser thought for a moment then shouted at James.

"Stop distracting me! I was there the night Bryan told

the others about the Black Box! The Big Secret that no one must know about, especially the establishment."

"I was told you weren't part of Bryan's group."

"I wasn't invited that night, so I hid under the old hostel ballroom. The ruins of an old Victorian water spa are underneath the ballroom. If you stand in the ruins, you can hear everything said in the ballroom."

"That was Bryan conning the others, and you fell for it too."

"There is a Black Box! The Big Secret, and I want it!"

"If there was, don't you think the government would have found it by now? They have been searching for years, like you, and found nothing."

"That still doesn't mean it doesn't exist. The government are a load of wankers. They keep leaving secret papers on trains, or have computers with top secret stuff stolen from their own offices."

"Did you blow up the police station?"

"Fucking brilliant! I got the idea out of a book. When I saw you coming out of the police station, I thought it was my lucky day."

"Did you plant the pipe bombs on my building site?"

"Well, who do you think did it? Martin Dougdale and his Malvern Aryans? Of course, it was me. I'm the genius, not fucking Bryan DeWitt, the shit!"

Tosser had become agitated. Standing up, he threw the chair out of the circus ring. His anger exploded, and he started to walk around James pointing the gun at him. James saw the quick glint of light, as though the tent flap had been opened a little and someone had entered. He couldn't see anyone but hoped it was the police come to rescue him. From the way Tosser was building up his anger, James wouldn't have very long before he was killed.

Tosser increased his pace and was now walking faster and faster. He was shouting, "You know nothing! It is not going to stop me from getting what I want, so stop bullshitting me and tell me where I can find it!"

James didn't answer, trying to keep in sight where Tosser was. If James moved now, then Tosser would explode completely, and the gun would go off.

Tosser started to slow down and stopped in front of James. The gun was bouncing around in his hand. James needed a new tactic so, keeping very calm, he spoke in a very low volume.

"Speak up," shouted Tosser.

"I said you win, Tosser. Bryan told me never to tell anyone. But I think you and I should work on it together. I had to test you to see if you knew what the Big Secret was before I told you."

"I knew you were lying, you fucking bastard! You wanted to keep it for yourself, just like the others!"

Tosser moved closer to James, the gun pointing directly at James' chest. For the first time, James began to shake. His left leg at first, them the right. It was obvious Tosser had gone over the edge and would be totally unpredictable. James closed his eyes. When nothing happened, he opened them. Tosser was now standing a few feet from him, the gun pointing to the floor.

"You really know the secret?"

James nodded his head.

The feet were the first thing to appear, as the person swung from the side of the ring. Tosser didn't see what hit him. The gun fired into the air, making a hole in the tent roof, and then seemed to catapult across the ring. As Tosser picked himself up, the swinging person swung back and landed on top of him forcing

Tosser back down. James quickly joined Quon, who was now sitting on Tosser head with his feet on the prostrate man's hands.

Tosser was screaming something but Quon's body muffled the sound.

James realized he didn't have his mobile. Quon produced one and handed it to him. James dialed the police but stopped the call when a group of police officers ran into the ring. They pounced on Tosser and handcuffed him to a police officer on each side. They weren't going to let him get away this time.

The police ordered James and Quon to sit at the side of the ring. The police searched Tosser, producing from one pocket a remote-control device. One of the policemen removed the batteries from the device. The gun was picked up from the floor by a gloved police officer. He unloaded the second cartridge and placed the gun in a plastic bag and sealed it. Several cartridges for the shotgun were taken out of another of Tosser's pockets.

Several more police officers arrived, including a plain-clothes man in his fifties. He walked up to Tosser and spoke with the officer's hold him. One of the officers pointed to James and Quon. The plain-clothes man turned and looked at them before continuing his conversation with the officers. He stood to the side and let the officers march Tosser out of the tent. It was strange because Tosser had gone very quiet until he saw James and then had exploded into a torrent of abuse. He had rushed towards James shouting, "I'll kill you! I'll kill you!" The two officers had difficulty keeping him from reaching James. It took several other officers to stop him. They then carried Tosser out of the Big Top. His legs had been manacled.

James noticed the tear on the inside seam of the camouflage trousers was now a gaping hole. James smiled. Tosser's Union Jack underwear was waving in the breeze.

The plain-clothes officer approached James and Quon. "Mr. Pidgley and Mr. Cho, sorry for keeping you waiting. I am Chief Inspector Dodding. We will need to get a statement from you. I have been told you have a very important party to go to, so it can wait until tomorrow."

"If you're sure it can wait."

"Positive, I think you may have been through enough for today."

James was about to ask another question when Tom Potts from MI5 entered the Big Top and walked into the ring. He collected the papers James had brought into the ring with him. Sorting through the papers he walked over to James handing him all but one piece of paper.

He nodded at Chief inspector Dodding and left the Big Top.

"What a strange man our Mr. Potts is," said James, the note of sarcasm in his voice.

"He is, I must be going. I need to interview Robert Cross about some murders."

The Chief Inspector left the ring followed by the other police officers. James and Quon watched them go.

"Quon, thank you. I don't think I could ever repay you for saving my life."

" Mister James, it was my pleasure. Do you know who murdered Brinarno?"

"Well, the police think it was Robert Cross, but I don't think I will be completely convinced."

"Sad he has gone. Brinarno was a very funny man.
Would you like a ride to the party? I have a taxi
outside waiting for me."
"Yes please, Quon. How did you know I was in
danger?"
"I saw clown mask man with a gun enter your caravan.
So I hid and watched what happened. Then I climbed
up the tent pole and swung down."
"You were very brave, thank you."
"I was scared. I thought clown mask man was
Brinarno come back."

James and Quon entered the Elgar Room at the Abbey
Hotel. The room seemed full of people James didn't
recognize.
"Quon, your father isn't dead."
"Really? You tell me the truth?"
"Yes, he is in hiding because of the Chinese secret
police. At some time during this season, while you are
on the road, he will find you."
"Thank you, Mr. James."
Quon saw his friends and started down the steps into
the room.
He turned and said to James, "I leave you now."
"Quon, if you ever need my help, get in touch with
me."
"I know, Mr. James and I will. After the season is
over, I will find you and you help me deflect." Quon
gave James a very big wink with his left eye and then
ran down the stairs to join the other Chinese acrobats.
James smiled to himself. Quon had learned the art of
deception.
Tonya and Mabel saw him enter and waved to him.
He wasn't sure if he would stay very long as most of

the people he just didn't recognize. He hated meeting new people and having to answer all those banal questions such as, 'Where are you from? What school did you go to? What do you do for a living? He had always wanted to answer 'Hell, Borstal, and a male gigolo'. But he knew he never would have the courage to be so outrageous.

An arm slipped into his and the strong smell of Gardenia's hit his nose.

"You okay, James? You look a little ruffled?"

He didn't turn and look at the women. He knew the voice. "I'm fine, Alison. So, Nobby told you about joining the circus?"

"Didn't need to. Tonya came round and saw me. She didn't want any trouble and asked me if it was okay. I wasn't sure until she told me he would have to sign a contract. Well, I said if he has a contract then it must be good. Of course, I didn't let him know I knew."

"Does he know you're coming tonight?"

"He sneaked out earlier and went to the circus. Haven't seen him yet. I wonder what suit he has on?"

"I think he said a Ben Sherman."

"So, that is what he wanted his Christmas money for."

James was staring at Alison.

"What's wrong?"

"Nothing, you look beautiful tonight."

"You noticed. I got this lady to do my hair and makeup."

"It makes you look younger."

"You're just saying that."

"Alison you're going to need all your strength for the next few days. Maybe weeks."

"Why what's happened?"

Alison's mobile rang. She took it out of her bag and
answered without looking at who was ringing.

The person on the other end spoke and Alison replied.
"Pauline, what's up?"

James watched as Alison listened, then moved to the
side of the staircase. The news shocked Alison who
became very animated in her replies.

A waiter walked by carrying a tray of Champagne in
tall, elegant, fluted glasses. James stopped the waiter
and took two glasses.

Alison had finished her call and joined him.

"James, is it true?"

"Sadly, yes. And you will need to help Pauline."

"I will. Oh, my God, when did you find out?"

"About three days ago, but it wasn't until Nobby took
me to see Tosser's house I really knew. I found several
pictures of Marilyn and Bryan there. They had been
defaced. Tosser had gone mad over the years and
plotted to kill everyone in Bryan's circle from his days
at the Royal Radar Establishment."

"Do you think I was in danger?"

"No, you didn't have any real knowledge of Bryan's
big secret invention."

"That was a hoax."

"I know."

"Well, that's what I tell everyone, but I think Bryan did
invent something."

"Because you told everyone it was a hoax is why
Tosser didn't hurt you. I'm sure, after that time when
you and Bryan went for dinner, Tosser wondered if he
told you about his big secret invention."

"Me and my big mouth."

They stood at the top of the stairs and drank the
champagne. Dougie, Cooper, and Nobby approached.

The three were dressed in Ben Sherman suits and Alison, seeing Nobby, burst into tears. Nobby ran up the stairs and hugged his mother.

"Sorry, it's just that you look so handsome. Reminded me of how your father looked when I first met him."

"Well, you look very sexy tonight, Mom."

"See, Alison. I'm not the only one who noticed."

"Mom, I have something to tell you."

"Not bad news, I hope."

"Well, not for me, but I'm not sure how you're going to feel about it."

Alison took Nobby's arm and led him to the side of the stairs.

"Just heard there was a bit of bother in the Big Top after I left," Dougie said.

"Oh, nothing I couldn't handle with the help of a Chinese acrobat," James replied, with a smile.

"You can tell me all about it tomorrow."

"Aren't you packing up tomorrow?"

"Starting to. It takes us a week. We take down the Big Top and then put it up again several times, so the crew gets to know what they need to do."

"I think it might need some repairs, there's a big hole in the roof."

"James, I found my watch. Actually, I hadn't lost it. Dougie had taken it to jewelers to be cleaned," said Cooper, proudly showing his watch to James.

Nobby and his mother returned. He was smiling.

"Look, I think I need to be with Pauline tonight. Will you explain to Tonya for me, James? "

"Sure, and I will see you and Pauline tomorrow. Alison, I didn't thank you, Pauline and Nobby for cleaning my caravan after the smoke damage."

"Take us for a meal. I know Pauline would like that."

James watched as she left. He walked down into the main area and found a table. After eating, the dancing and fun began. By now everyone had heard about the incident in the Big Top and was coming over to James. Dougie told Nobby and Cooper to act as his bodyguards and keep everyone away from him. For Cooper and Nobby it was a dream come true. They were there to protect someone and felt very important. They even tried to stop Mabel from speaking to James. She clipped them on the ear, gave James a hug and a sat down next to him. She opened her handbag and took out two envelopes and gave them to James. He placed them in his inside jacket pocket.

"Where ever we are, James, if you see Morris Brother's Circus, come and see us. You are part of this family now."

"Thanks, Mabel."

She left him and started to dance with Dougie.

The music stopped and people began to leave. James finished another drink followed by several cups of coffee. His bodyguards had fallen asleep, leaning against each other. Dougie came over shook them awake and they left.

James walked out of the Abbey Hotel. The night was over. Dusk was only an hour away. He walked across the street, and up Church Street. The walk up the hill passed Saint Ann's Well and gave him time to reflect. He reached the top and sat on the grass. The morning dew had made it a little damp, but James didn't care. He was alive and had solved the murders. Or had he? He still wasn't sure if Tosser had murdered Bryan. The first rays of sun broke through the morning clouds. It was going to be a beautiful day.

The man appeared from nowhere. He was dressed in hiking gear and was as surprised as James to see another person. He had on a headset and was intently listening to the music. James remembered the days when he would come here as a teenager with his cassette player and listen to Edward Elgar. The man stood behind James. He was now conducting an imaginary orchestra. The man then began to walk away. He stopped at a stone plinth and took something out of his backpack. The smell of spray paint drifted on the cool breeze. James watched as the man walked down the hill. After the man had disappeared from sight, he stood up and ran to the plinth. The man had spray-painted in bright pink paint. 'Sir Edward Elgar Rocks'. James smiled. A mature tagger.

He returned to the grass and took the letters Mabel had given him out of his pocket. He opened the first letter. It was from a solicitor. He was the executor of Bryan's Last Will and Testament. Bryan had left his forty percent of the circus to James, because he was Bryan, The Good Samaritan. He also knew James would make sure the circus continued and so millions more children could enjoy the clowns and laugh. Could James make an appointment to see the solicitor some time to finalize the terms of the Will?

The second letter was from Bryan himself;

'James, if you are reading this letter then I have died, possibly murdered. Who did it? For me, there is only one murderer and that would be Big Brother, if you get my meaning. Under the front left wheel arch of my caravan, you will find a small package taped to the roof of the arch. It's the key and password to my safe

*deposit box. My solicitor has instructions to give you a
letter for Coutts Bank in London. To think my secrets
are possibly next to Her Majesty, the Queen's! Please
keep the contents secret and safe. There may be a time
in the future when the world will be ready. I know you
will understand. If you haven't found Philip Langley
he will find you, and explain more. Philip was the
only person I trusted.*
I know you will understand.
*Now tear this letter into little pieces and let the
Malvern winds take it to the four corners of the world.
Make them so small it will be impossible to put them
back together again.*
God bless you, and may the show go on. Brinarno.'

James read the letter again. He would have loved to
keep the letter. The dangers of doing so would have
been too great. He tore the letter into tiny pieces. He
stood on the Toposcope and let the tiny pieces of the
paper fly on the wind. The wind swirled and took the
paper in different directions. Bryan had been right.
They floated to the four corners of the world.

His mobile made its customary ding-dong when a text
message arrived. He took the phone out of his pocket
and looked at the message.
'*DeWitt's Murderer wasn't Tosser.*'
James texted back; '*How do u know?*'
He waited for a reply, but nothing came. He tried to
see who had texted him, but the number was blocked.
He began to walk down the hill. He felt sad, as though
he was leaving the place and wouldn't be back for a
very long time. He reached the town and stood by the
monument to Elgar. The town was waking up and

soon everyone would know what had happened in the Big Top. He must find out how the Inspector and the Sergeant were. He would visit them later in the day, after he had spoken with the site foreman. The project wasn't over.

His mobile made its familiar 'ding-dong' sound. The text message read;

'*Big Brother told me.*'

MUSIC THAT INSPIRED THE WRITING

Forty: Forty - The Dr. Marten's boxset

Edward Elgar - Severn Suite

Les Yeut Noirs – tchorba

Beautiful South – Carry on up the Charts

Brumbeat – the Story of the 60's Midland Sound

Adam Faith – A's B's & Ep's

Small Face – from the beginning

Edward Elgar – Enigma Variations

n'klabe – I Love Salsa

Edward Elgar – The Dream of Gerontius

ABOUT THE AUTHOR

Edward Arno was born in a field in Frankley Beech, Birmingham, England. His father was a milkman and his mother was a house parlor maid. They met during a bombing raid at the end of the Second World War. Growing up on a council estate, he attended the local public schools. The Issigonis Mini auto plant at Longbridge was the symphonic sound of his childhood. He moved to America to pursue a screenwriting and directing career.

He resides in Burbank, California and is also an active member of the Mystery Writers of America.

www.edwardarno.com

387

BRIGHTON HO

Pidgley Properties is expanding its empire and its next project will convert a Victorian hotel into luxury apartments. James Pidgley has been sent to the seaside town of Brighton to oversee the project. The building had been abandoned for several years. An unscrupulous security firm is hired to vacate the premises. They send their employees, operatives recently returned from a tour in Iraq, to remove squatters from the hotel. Drugs, sex and smuggling had been the recent business of the dark damp corridors.

A high-profile supermarket tycoon's son is murdered in the old hotel's once prestigious blue room. James and his new girlfriend are drawn into the investigation and face a stone wall of silence from the local criminals. James reveals the secrets of the hotel and its hub of activity for the English south coast underworld

AUTHOR LINKS

It's my heartfelt hope that you've enjoyed Three Ring Circus. If you have a question you'd like to ask, or an opinion to express, I'd be delighted to hear it and respond. And don't forget — the first book in the Pidgley series Coronation Souvenir is available from Amazon.

Your reviews, comments, questions and opinions are invaluable and appreciated. There's a variety of ways to engage;

Face Book
> https://www.facebook.com/edwardarnoauthor

Reach out to Victory Rose Press directly at;
> victoryrosepress@gmail.com

My web site has latest news and links to my titles;
> www.edwardarno.com

Twitter
https://twitter.com/EddieArno

Printed in Great
Britain
by Amazon